Literary Criticism and Cultural Theory

Edited by

William E. Cain
Professor of English
Wellesley College

T0347248

A Routledge Series

Literary Criticism and Cultural Theory

William E. Cain, *General Editor*

THE SUBJECT OF RACE IN AMERICAN SCIENCE FICTION

Sharon DeGraw

Routledge
New York & London

Routledge
Taylor & Francis Group
270 Madison Avenue
New York, NY 10016

Routledge
Taylor & Francis Group
2 Park Square
Milton Park, Abingdon
Oxon OX14 4RN

© 2007 by Taylor & Francis Group, LLC

Routledge is an imprint of Taylor & Francis Group, an Informa business

Transferred to Digital Printing 2009

International Standard Book Number-10: 0-415-97901-3 (Hardcover)
International Standard Book Number-13: 978-0-415-97901-6 (Hardcover)

Library of Congress Cataloging-in-Publication Data

DeGraw, Sharon, Ph.D.
The subject of race in American science fiction / Sharon DeGraw.
p. cm.
Includes bibliographical references and index.
ISBN-13: 978-0-415-97901-6 (alk. paper)
1. Science fiction, American--History and criticism. 2. Race in literature. 3. Subjectivity in literature. 4. Burroughs, Edgar Rice, 1875-1950--Criticism and interpretation. 5. Schuyler, George Samuel, 1895---Criticism and interpretation. 6. Delany, Samuel R.--Criticism and interpretation. I. Title.

PS374.S35D38 2006
813'.0876209355--dc22   2006027408

ISBN10: 0-415-97901-3 (hbk)
ISBN10: 0-415-80289-X (pbk)

ISBN13: 978-0-415-97901-6 (hbk)
ISBN13: 978-0-415-80289-5 (pbk)

Visit the Taylor & Francis Web site at
http://www.taylorandfrancis.com

and the Routledge Web site at
http://www.routledge-ny.com

In memory of my mother, Marilyn DeGraw

Contents

Acknowledgments

First, I would like to thank Dr. Robert Shelton for his continual encouragement, insight, and patience. Without him, I would not have finished this project. In addition, Dr. Katherine Fishburn has been instrumental to the theoretical development of my ideas. Finally, I must acknowledge the support of my family. In particular, my father and mother always encouraged my educational endeavors and have helped me with my graduate studies in too many ways to name. My father was a cheerful proofreader for the present manuscript as well. Likewise, my husband has always believed in me and, since the birth of our two children, has been a wonderful 'babysitter.' Thank you all for your help—I certainly needed it.

Chapter One
Burroughs

IN THE BEGINNING

The genre of science fiction is widely considered to have started with Mary Shelley's *Frankenstein*, published in Great Britain in 1818. However, as Robert Scholes and Eric Rabkin note in a brief history of science fiction, "When Mary Shelley wrote *Frankenstein*, science fiction had neither a name or any recognition as a separate form of literature [and t]his situation lasted for a century" (7). Such generic ambiguity and critical retrospection mark the field of science fiction studies. In a more comprehensive history of science fiction, Edward James highlights the sharp rise in English language texts dealing with the future from the 1850s onward. He states that "[t]hroughout the [19th] century, most of the respected (male) writers of fiction in the United States had dabbled in what we could call science fiction" (*Science* 33)[1]. However, "[s]f was first named, and first became a genre, in the science fiction magazines published in the United States before the Second World War" (E. James, *Science* 66). In such a literary context, early writers of science fiction were not consciously writing within the genre. In fact, many wrote with other genres in mind. For example, when Edgar Rice Burroughs began his writing career in the 1910s, he wrote adventure fiction for all-fiction magazines. We simply classify many of his texts as science fiction from a contemporary critical vantage point. ERB merits special attention from Edward James because he is "probably the most influential of the writers who began in the pulps" (*Science* 45). Given the lack of generic formation before the first decades of the twentieth century, it is not surprising that "[m]any of the important names in the early science fiction magazines had already written science fiction for several years in the general fiction pulps" (ibid). The science fiction texts were simply published alongside other popular adventure tales—the westerns of Zane Grey, the African adventures of H. Rider Haggard, and the northern stories of Jack London, for example.[2]

In the United States, the combination of a *"fin de siecle"* feeling (E. James, *Science* 31), an increase in literacy, and a growing interest in "science and technology" led first to the inclusion of science fiction in cheap, all-fiction pulp magazines and then the increasing specialization of these magazines up through the 1930s (Scholes and Rabkin 35). In his book, *The Creation of Tomorrow: Fifty Years of Magazine Science Fiction*, Paul Carter chronicles the rise of the pulps and their association with science fiction. Carter begins the first chapter with Hugo Gernsback because he founded and edited *Amazing Stories*, "the first periodical in the world devoted solely to science fiction" (4). In addition, as the editor of several pulp magazines in the 1920s and 1930s, Gernsback had a formative effect on the evolution of the genre. As Edward James asserts, "The creation of specialist science fiction magazines was a recognition of the existence of a genre, and once that genre was named, in the late 1920s—first as 'scientifiction,' and then as 'science fiction'—we get our first attempts at definitions. It is no coincidence that the first definitions came with the coiner of those names, Hugo Gernsback" (*Science* 52). Both Carter and James emphasize Gernsback's scientific positivism and the tremendous influence of the "Gernsback-Sloane-Tremaine-Campbell [editorial] guidelines" on science fiction (Carter 18). Education of the public, progress, and extrapolation were all key components of the editors' focus on science. However, despite this scientific emphasis and attempts to define the genre accordingly, science fiction has always had a dual nature in which the fictional format is equally important as the science. Gernsback, for example, suggested that the ideal science fiction text would be one quarter science and three quarters romance (E. James, *Science* 52). In this context, Carter notes that some science fiction writers "were simply impatient at the necessity for interrupting their storylines to get the science straightened out. They were, after all, writing for cash for magazines published as men's-adventure pulps in which fast action was the *sine quo non*" (19). Edgar Rice Burroughs was one such writer. He serves as a representative early science fiction writer in his incredible output and the multi-generic aspect of his work. Due to the generic ambiguity of early science fiction—its lack of theoretical definition and roots in other literary genres—Burroughs combined adventure fiction, romance, and science fiction, often in one text. In fact, despite giving Burroughs a prominent place in their histories of the science fiction field, both Carter and James oppose ERB to Gernsback's scientific focus. Edward James asserts that "[t]here was little or no pretence at scientific correctness in Burroughs" (*Science* 45–6), and he follows the lead of Brian Aldiss, another science fiction historian, in labeling Burroughs' work as escapist and thought-stifling (*Trillion* 164–5).

While the debate over the definition and generic boundaries of science fiction continues to this day, [3] a strong uniformity of perspective existed in other key areas of the early science fiction field. First, a single, highly individualistic action hero took center stage in the majority of the texts due to the literary roots of American science fiction in adventure fiction. This heroic protagonist was almost always male and of Anglo descent. The protagonist's textual dominance, heroic nature, and representative status all combined to convey the normalcy and universalism of the Anglo male perspective. The hero represented not only his country and/or race, but also ideal manhood and the entire human race (in opposition to aliens). [4] Many times the protagonist also narrated the story, obscuring even the possibility of competing perspectives. Within western culture, explorers and adventurers were historically white males. However, the gender and racial/national origin of the protagonist stemmed from that of the authors, editors, and readers of early science fiction as well. In effect, a triangle of racial and gender similarity existed, composed of the protagonist, the authors and editors, and the audience.

The science fiction authors and editors are the second element in this Anglo male triangle. Female authors were the exception in the science fiction field up through the 1960s due to the general sexism existing in patriarchal western culture, the professional fields, and the publishing industry. More specifically, the strong exclusion of women from the sciences and the overwhelmingly male audience of adventure fiction and science fiction promoted male authorship. Paul Carter notes that, prior to 1940, author C. L. Moore "stood virtually by herself" in the science fiction field (180). As most writers promote their own values and beliefs, and these are usually grounded in their personal identity and experiences, the uniformity of perspective between the male authors of science fiction and their protagonists should not be surprising. John Taliaferro, for example, calls Burroughs' protagonists "his fictional alter-egos" (22) and explores the connections between Burroughs' pride in his "Anglo-Saxon lineage" and the similar background of his protagonists (19). Taliaferro also links the personal beliefs of Burroughs to the larger cultural context of early twentieth-century America: "All of his plots [. . .] boil down to survival of the fittest [. . .]. Burroughs, like so many of his contemporaries, believed in a hierarchy of race and class" (19). Like their readers, the science fiction authors were heavily influenced by the Anglo-centric, patriarchal society in which they lived. Not only did they cater to the masculine ideals of their young, male audience, but also the authors held similar ideals due to the shared culture. In addition, the large and continuous output required of authors by the pulp magazines hindered the creation of less stereotypical characters. Few authors had the time or motivation to move beyond generic formulas or to question accepted social norms. Furthermore, some science fiction editors actively promoted an Anglo male protagonist. For example, Isaac Asimov describes the influential editor of *Astounding* magazine, John Campbell, as "tak[ing] for granted, somehow, the stereotype of the Nordic white as the true representative of Man the Explorer, Man the Darer, Man the Victor" (qtd. in Carter 77). The close gender and racial correlation between the science fiction triangle of editors and authors, protagonists, and readers fostered the universality of the Anglo male perspective.

As they tried to sell their material, science fiction authors and editors catered to an overwhelmingly young, male audience. In the chapter Paul Carter devotes to the "Feminine Mystique in Science Fiction," he acquiesces with Joanna Russ' characterization of the typical science fiction reader as an adolescent boy, at least in the early years (Carter 173). Even as Carter points out the general aging of science fiction readers by the end of the 1940s, he maintains the over-all masculine make-up of the audience (ibid). Edward James explicitly, and somewhat condescendingly, links Edgar Rice Burroughs with a young, masculine audience:

> he was published in Britain as a writer of stories for boys; tales of inter-
> planetary derring-do were suitable for boys and Americans, but not for
> British adults. And, it is fair to say, those intrigued by Burroughs's brand
> of romance tend to be captured young: few young males can resist rid-
> ing in their imagination on a six-legged thoat across Barsoom's dry sea-
> beds [. . .] alongside John Carter. (*Science* 46)

John Carter, the protagonist of Burroughs' Mars series, was not a "boy," since only adult males could completely fulfill the multiple functions of a hero—including great physical strength in adventure fiction. Yet, the young men reading such texts clearly identified themselves with the hero. The authors and editors of science fiction texts knew this identification and vicarious participation would be limited by a heroine.

Furthermore, one day these young male readers would grow into men and positions of adventure and power would be open to them. While interplanetary exploration was not feasible in the early decades of the twentieth century, the young men could realistically envision themselves as adventurers, explorers, and national envoys. In her book *Primate Visions: Gender, Race, and Nature in the World of Modern Science*, Donna Haraway titles the first chapter "Teddy Bear Patriarchy" because Teddy Roosevelt was a real-life icon of turn-of-the-century western man. Haraway explores the connections between "Nature, Youth, Manhood, [and] the State" in the Roosevelt Memorial atrium of the African Hall, located in the American Museum of Natural History, and she highlights the close association of young males of this time period with powerful and world-renowned men like Roosevelt (27). The former president's rough and dangerous adventures, including safaris to Africa and explorations of the Amazon, served as an ultimate, but real-life example of manhood. After reading one of the many accounts of Roosevelt's life, the adventures of John Carter would not seem so farfetched to young science fiction fans.[5] In fact, Haraway draws such a fictional parallel in her text by prefacing the chapter on Roosevelt with a quote from Burroughs. Both Brian Street and Edward James connect juvenile males, adventure fiction, and imperialism in their discussion of turn-of-the-century British literature as well. Within this context, young male readers not only identified with the Anglo male protagonist, but also sought to emulate him in the real world. Thus, the authors created protagonists with the readers' ideals in mind and, conversely, the readers utilized the protagonists as role models. With such a close association between the audience and the protagonists, early science fiction readers normally did not question the primacy of the Anglo male perspective.

In addition, the dominance of this Anglo male perspective combined with an emphasis on science and technology to restrict the speculative element of early American science fiction. Since inventions and technical gadgets were the primary focus of early speculation, more abstract concepts like identity, gender, or race often were neglected. Paul Carter, for example, sets up the first installment of Edgar Rice Burroughs' Mars series as the progenitor of a long line of stereotypical science fiction. From the Old West hero, John Carter, to the Western American setting of Mars, to the Indians disguised as Martians, "[t]his Western Mars [. . .] was to reappear again and again in pulp science fiction" (62). According to Paul Carter, "this Western Mars," and its Anglo-American male perspective, dominated the large subgenre of Martian science fiction up through the first half of the twentieth century. It was not until 1970 that John Campbell wrote a eulogy for Burroughs' Mars, entitled "Goodbye to Barsoom" (Carter 69). Furthermore, this tendency to superficially and stereotypically transform Earth and terrestrial culture from the Anglo male perspective extended across the solar system: "Mars as nineteenth-century frontier America and Venus as nineteenth-century frontier Africa had a mythic appeal that pushed aside all demands of scientific exactitude" (Carter 65). Mercury and Jupiter were exoticized as "Asian port cities" as well (Carter 68). Paul Carter's summary of the "general archaizing and Westernizing of the space frontier" foregrounds the stereotypical tendencies and multi-generic roots of early science fiction, as well as its lack of scientific focus (72). It also emphasizes the importance of the Other to early science fiction.

Paul Carter begins the second section of his chapter, "Under the Moons of Mars: The Interplanetary Pastoral," with a quote from Leslie Fiedler which grounds the Anglo-American male perspective in the Other of American "Indians" (66). Although clearly not the main focus in early science fiction, such Other(s) were essential for the formation of the Anglo male perspective. The heroism of the Anglo male protagonist required a negative type against which to be gauged, and the tension between the protagonist and the Other(s) provided the textual action or conflict. For example, females served as secondary characters for romantic purposes and sexual titillation. In addition, the women provided both a foil and a motivation for the characteristics culturally ascribed to males: courage, power, and action. Characters of ethnic, racial, or national backgrounds other than Anglo-American or Anglo-European usually functioned as villains or stereotyped representatives of an exotic locale. Finally, aliens were mostly a thinly disguised substitute for any of these multiple Others. In her book *Aliens and Others: Science Fiction, Feminism, and Post-modernism*, Jenny Wolmark links all three of these character groups and discusses how "the alien has been used to represent Otherness" in science fiction texts (28). Including an Other, however, always creates the potential for subversion of the primary viewpoint. To forestall such a possibility, the science fiction authors subordinated, caricaturized, and/or vilified the Other(s). For example, in his discussion of the exceptional science fiction writing of Stanley G. Weinbaum in the early 1930s, Paul Carter asserts that, "[u]ntil Weinbaum's time, the reader's choice in extraterrestrial life-forms was usually between human beings (some of whom were very, very good) and monsters (most of which were very, very bad)" (73). Weinbaum merits attention from Carter, despite his extremely short career, because he created an alien character who "has an intellect at least as good as the hero's own" and, as a result, broke "clean away from both the Burroughs and the Wells stereotypes of life on Mars" (ibid).

Throughout American history, dominant Anglo-American male identity has been constructed in contrast to the multiple Others of Native Americans, African-Americans, women, Asians, and Euro-Americans of other national origins.[6] However, when science fiction was emerging in the United States at the beginning of the twentieth century, a new Other was developing—a massive influx of eastern and southern European immigrants in what became known as the New Immigration. The same technological and scientific changes which inspired science fiction combined with this New Immigration to fuel racialism and the increasing popularity of the eugenics movement. In *Bordering on the Body: The Racial Matrix of Modern Fiction and Culture*, Laura Doyle provides a useful summary of the eugenics movement in the United States at the beginning of the twentieth century. Overtly combining science and politics, eugenics connected scientific theories with social reform: [7] "Eugenics held that 'racial degeneration' in Western nations threatened what the contemporary political writer Benjamin Kidd called 'the struggle of the Western races for the larger inheritance of the future.' According to eugenicists, only racially responsible reproduction could reverse this trend and ensure success in the global economic struggle" (Doyle 11). As a result, outspoken anti-immigration advocates formed the Immigration Restriction League in 1894. "IRL leaders believed there was a racial foundation to American nationality, that heredity was more powerful than environment, and that the new immigrants were racially inferior" (*American*). Acting on these beliefs, the anti-immigration leaders wrote articles and books with titles like Edward Ross' "American Blood and Immigrant Blood" (1913) and Madison Grant's *The Passing of the Great Race* (1916). Politically, their efforts culminated in the passing of the Immigration Act of 1924, which imposed stringent quotas on southern and eastern European countries. The legislation heavily restricted the immigration of national and ethnic groups like Italians, Poles, and Jews, while encouraging immigration from western European countries. It also formalized the complete exclusion of Asians initiated earlier with the Chinese Exclusion Act of 1882. At the same time, the Indian Citizenship Act of 1924 forced Native Americans to assimilate completely to Anglo-American ideals, like private land ownership, or lose their tribal territory completely. These simultaneous, multiple examples of American racialism and nativism reveal the increasing pressure being applied to the Anglo-American male position at the turn-of-the-century. Threatened, the Anglo-American men asserted their normalcy, universality, and superiority through the discourses of science and race.

The dual aspect of science reflects the paradoxical position of Anglo men. The need to prove their normalcy and universality called for a uniform standard and overt scientific objectivity. On the other hand, the need to assert their superiority led to the underlying subjectivity of their scientific practice and discourse. In *Primate Visions*, Donna Haraway begins with the historically dominant association of science with fact and literature with fiction (3–4). From this position, "the natural sciences seem to be crafts for distinguishing between fact and fiction" (4). In most early science fiction, the viewpoint of the protagonist is allied with Western science. Therefore, it seems completely reliable, without bias, and the unquestioned norm. This emphasis on objectivity combined with the scientific positivism of most early science fiction paradoxically to both support and erase the dominance of the Anglo male perspective. As Haraway chronicles in *Primate Visions*, the history of western science tells a story of progress which entails the ever-increasing suppression of its own fictional nature (4).

Within the rapidly developing sciences of biology and anthropology, for example, race became a scientifically constructed term with overtly objective and authoritative connotations. Natural and social scientists tied both race and ethnicity to the physical body, and biology served as an anchor for individual and collective identity. It was widely believed that behavior, intelligence, and even morals had their foundations in ethnicity or race.[8] For instance, Madison Grant, head of the New York Zoological Society and trustee of the Museum of Natural History, claimed that,

> New York is becoming a *cloaca gentium* which will produce many amazing racial hybrids and some ethnic horrors that will be beyond the powers of future anthropologists to unravel. One thing is certain: in any such mixture, the surviving traits will be determined by competition between the lowest and most primitive elements and the specialized traits of Nordic man; his stature, his light colored eyes, his fair skin and light colored hair, his straight nose and his splendid fighting and moral qualities, will have little part in the resultant mixture. ("New")

Prescott F. Hall placed this "Nordic man" within the "Teutonic" or "Baltic race, [. . .] which has always been distinguished for energy, initiative, and self-reliance" (297). In contrast, the New Immigration consisted of "entirely different races—of Alpine, Mediterranean, Asiatic, and African stocks. These races have an entirely different mental make-up from the Baltic race" (ibid). Edward Ross, future president of the American Sociological Association, collectively defined the new immigrants as "the lowest and most primitive elements" of humanity, including the "Caliban type": "from ten to twenty per cent are hirsute, lowbrowed, big-faced persons of obviously low mentality."[9] He classified the new immigrants as atavistic ancestors of prehistoric humans: "clearly they belong in skins, in wattled huts at the close of the Great Ice Age." Furthermore, Ross described the new immigrant "soul [as] burn[ing] with the dull, smoky flame of the pine-knot struck to the soil." Such racial essentialism firmly linked culture and biology. Personal identity was conceived as a whole and stable entity with its roots in collective racial 'types.'

As the preceding examples vividly illustrate, the subjective aspect of this scientific discourse becomes most clear in the ranking of these 'types' within a racial hierarchy which supports the dominant Anglo male position. In her book, *The Idea of Race in Science: Great Britain 1800–1960*, Nancy Stepan discusses the replacement of the religious Great Chain of Being by a racial chain of progressive development, with primitive, darker races at the bottom and civilized, fairer races at the top. The physical components of this classification and division served as a static, essentialist base for the cultural and historical ranking. As Nancy Stepan argues, it is not coincidental that this scientific discourse, constructed by western European males, bolstered the existing hierarchy of race, culture, gender, and nationality.[10] Doyle joins Stepan and Haraway in emphasizing the subjective aspects of scientific discourse in her study of the connections between the eugenics movement and literature of the twentieth century. Discussing both American and British texts, Doyle asserts that "the contemporaneous development, on the one hand, of eugenics and, on the other hand, of the Harlem Renaissance and modernism—with their common focus on racialized mother figures—emerges as no mere coincidence" (9). The scientific focus and exotic locales of science fiction made this popular genre susceptible to these racial theories as well. As a result, the racial triangle of science fiction was connected to and supported by a pervasive current of racialist discourse. Ostensibly objective yet fundamentally subjective, these racial theories were commonly utilized by scientists, popular writers, and literary authors to bolster the dominant position of the Anglo-American male.[11]

EDGAR RICE BURROUGHS

At the convergence of these generic and racial elements lies Edgar Rice Burroughs. As noted earlier, even as science fiction historians downplay the scientific foundation of Burroughs' work and connect it with a juvenile audience, they give ERB a prominent place in their histories because of his tremendous popularity and literary and cultural influence. Scholes and Rabkin, for example, join Edward James in calling Burroughs "the most popular" of adventure writers (Scholes and Rabkin 11). Burroughs' latest biographer, John Taliaferro, asserts that since "the most conservative estimate [of Burroughs' total sales] is thirty million books sold during his lifetime" and his books "have been published in more than thirty languages [. . .], there can be little question that he was the most widely read American author of the first half of the twentieth century" (13–4). Much of Burroughs' popularity stems from his immensely famous and influential Tarzan series. However,

Burroughs also wrote scientific romances, including four series taking place on Mars, Venus, the moon, and within the Earth's core. In fact, his first published work was the first book of his Mars series, *A Princess of Mars*, serialized in Munsey's all-fiction pulp magazine, *All-Story*, in 1912. In addition, Burroughs wrote four westerns and a realistic melodrama entitled *The Girl From Hollywood*. Two of Burroughs' westerns, *The War Chief* and its sequel *The Apache Devil*, differ from Burroughs' other works in that he conscientiously researched them, striving for historical authenticity, and they are written primarily from a Native American point of view.[12] The two Apache westerns and *The Girl from Hollywood* reflect Burroughs' desire to be taken more seriously as a writer and to escape the "pulp ghetto" (Taliaferro 15). However, while all three novels were published, Burroughs' Tarzan and science fiction series remained the staple of his literary oeuvre. Furthermore, as Taliaferro aptly observes, "his work is not taught in schools or welcomed in the American canon" (ibid). In the age of pulps, Burroughs was king. Yet, he has only gained even qualified recognition in the science fiction field, while science fiction itself has struggled for the same type of literary respectability.[13]

Burroughs' association with popular culture and juvenile literature has hindered a serious critical discussion of his work and suppressed the significant racial component of his texts. Before the advent of popular culture as a field of study within the academic community, texts such as Burroughs' were not considered worthy of serious critical attention. Furthermore, the Anglo-American male triangle of protagonist, author, and audience combined to obscure racial issues within early science fiction texts, and often literature more broadly.[14] The widespread connection between science and objectivity has compounded the problem. Today, Tarzan has taken on a life of his own and has escaped from a connection to his original author. Whereas almost everyone in contemporary western society has heard of Tarzan, the name of Edgar Rice Burroughs is largely unknown outside literary circles. When critics and popular audiences alike are more familiar with the many multi-media spin-offs of his Tarzan series than Burroughs' books themselves, the racial foundation of his texts is lost. For example, how many viewers of Walt Disney's latest retelling of the Tarzan story realize that the original, textual Tarzan "is also the son and rightful heir of England's Lord and Lady Greystoke" and, "he flies a plane, quotes Latin, and oversees English and African estates" (Taliaferro 15)?[15] Tarzan's racial heritage was critical to Burroughs' texts. As Burroughs himself explained, "I selected an infant child of a race strongly marked by hereditary characteristics of the finer and nobler sort, and [. . .] I threw him into an environment as diametrically opposite that to which he had been born as I might well conceive" (qtd. in

Taliaferro 14). Even those who realize Burroughs created Tarzan usually do not connect him with science fiction as well. For example, the hero of Burroughs' Mars series, John Carter, is the neglected step-brother of Tarzan, the international celebrity. Finally, the science fiction community itself has come belatedly to an examination of the issue of race. As late as 2003, for example, science fiction historian De Witt Douglas Kilgore claims that, "[i]n the study of popular science and science fiction, [. . .] despite its ubiquitous influence, race is virtually an undiscovered country" (9).[16] Completely ignored by the literary establishment during his career, Burroughs has only gained limited critical attention in the later half of the twentieth century by science fiction historians and, more recently, by scholars interested in post- colonial studies and popular culture.

A more detailed and textual-based investigation of Burroughs reveals his interest in the scientific theories of race gaining popularity during his career. While Scholes and Rabkin correctly note that Burroughs "was a formula writer," many of his texts contain a depth and detail of racial investigation that is surprising for such a prolific and popular writer of this time period, especially within the genre of American science fiction (12). John Taliaferro admits that Burroughs did not go "beyond sketching a monkey on the title page" of the copy of Darwin's *The Descent of Man* he owned (14). However, Taliaferro insists that "[n]evertheless, he had acquired a layman's grasp of one of the burning issues of the post-Victorian era"—"the contest between heredity and environment" (ibid). As noted earlier, Burroughs investigates this issue most directly in his Tarzan character. An analysis of Burroughs' science fiction texts reveals many of the Anglo-American male biases associated with the eugenics movement in the United States as well. It is no coincidence that the same year *A Princess of Mars* was serialized, the First International Eugenics Conference was held in London (Taliaferro 227). In fact, Taliaferro chronicles how Burroughs' interest in eugenics continued to grow, even as the topic became more controversial in the scientific community (228). "At one point, he even wrote a column for the *Los Angeles Examiner* calling for the extermination of all 'moral imbeciles' and their relatives [. . . , and i]n an unpublished essay, 'I See a New Race,' Burroughs offered his own Final Solution to the world's problems" (19). As seen here, Taliaferro goes so far as to connect Burroughs' position on eugenics with that of Adolf Hitler (ibid). While Burroughs rarely explicitly utilized eugenics in his fiction, evolutionary theory appears sporadically and racial typing plays a prominent role in all of his texts.

In Burroughs' fiction, his belief in racial theories primarily took the form of stereotypical racial characterization. For instance, all of Burroughs' heroes are Anglo males. Even the hero of his relatively inclusive Apache series, Shoz-Dijiji, finally discovers he is the kidnapped son of Anglo parents. This opens the way for a romantic and sexual relationship with a white woman, and Burroughs "nimbly sidestep[s] the unspeakable eventuality of miscegenation, a well-exercised Burroughs taboo" (Taliaferro 224). Furthermore, Shoz-Dijiji, inexplicably refrains from some traditional aspects of Apache culture, such as scalping, before he learns of his biological ancestry.[17] A biological member of the Anglo race, Shoz-Dijiji represents a legitimate racial type according to scientific theories of the time period. Therefore, he cannot betray his civilized white blood, no matter his cultural environment. As Taliaferro succinctly observes, "[b]lood [. . .] always tells, an axiom that Burroughs stresses in nearly all of his stories" (15). Conversely, Burroughs often negatively characterizes members of differing races. "[I]n the Tarzan stories," for example, "blacks are generally superstitious and Arabs rapacious" (Taliaferro 19). True to his adventure story roots, Burroughs utilizes racial Others as foils for his Anglo heroes. Taliaferro also notes that, "[o]n Mars, the races descend from a Tree of Life and, like fruit, are color-coded red, green, yellow, and black" (ibid). The "color-coded" Martian races Taliaferro lists here are literally aliens, in contrast to Burroughs' Anglo, terrestrial hero. Although Burroughs does create a white Martian race, they remain relatively hidden and secretive. A Martian creation myth of a Tree of Life reveals Burroughs' interest in evolutionary theory as well.

The negative connotations of racial theory and its fictional utilization are often well deserved. Yet, when Taliaferro associates Burroughs with Adolph Hitler and a "radical fringe" of science, an exceptional area of his writing is eclipsed (19). In addition to the stereotypical and hierarchical aspects of racial theory, Burroughs utilized the speculative potential of science fiction to question and revise accepted notions of race. First, during Burroughs' early career eugenics was widely popular. It had connotations of objectivity and authority because of its scientific associations, and many considered it an important tool in progressive social reform. While certainly biased, prejudiced, and often scientifically inaccurate, Burroughs should not be judged by post-Holocaust standards. As Taliaferro himself admits, "[e]ven as he was stressing Tarzan's and John Carter's superior bloodlines, [Burroughs] honored the Algeresque notion of the common man pulling himself up by the bootstraps"(19). It is this side of Burroughs, the more democratic and egalitarian side, that surfaced in his science fiction and not the Tarzan stories.

Because the science fiction genre emphasizes invention, exploration, and speculation, authors can utilize the genre to question traditional boundaries, social conventions, and hierarchies. As mentioned earlier, the speculative element of early American science fiction usually took the form of technical inventions and exotic extraterrestrial settings. Burroughs' more extensive, detailed, and sometimes egalitarian investigation of race in the Mars series was not the norm in early science fiction. A racial analysis of Burroughs' science fiction texts, while often illustrating the societal and scientific biases of the time period, also reveals some sites of more open and truly imaginative racial exploration. In an extraterrestrial setting, largely free from Earth history and cultural norms (on a narrative level), science fiction authors have more license to construct alternative realities. The convergence of new, science fiction elements with the terrestrial concept of race could lead to a more egalitarian ethos. The fiction can combine with the science to revise even the most objectively or subjectively entrenched theories. The new context for ethnicity and race not only places it outside of Earth history, but also the larger and more inclusive galactic and/or global setting makes more narrowly national or ethnic/racial differences seem of lesser importance. In addition, race itself expands in definition: biological or ethic 'races' are joined by the more inclusive 'human race.' Within a multi-planet context, the races of Earth become united in a single human race with a common terrestrial culture. The Other is no longer terrestrial but extraterrestrial.[18] The more imaginative and expansive space offered by science fiction allows authors to create alternative relationships which challenge or undermine traditional power hierarchies. For example, whereas Tarzan can never escape the ramifications of his noble blood, John Carter can acceptably marry a red Martian princess, be the proud father of hybrid terrestrial/alien offspring, and ultimately renounce terrestrial society entirely for a life on Mars. Burroughs' characters or 'types' representing specific, scientifically-authorized racial groups remain largely essentialized, separate, and hierarchically positioned; however, some individual (exceptional) platonic, romantic, and/or sexual relationships do develop in the science fiction. These relationships cross and blur social and biological racial boundaries and, as a result, challenge the traditional hierarchies which exist in other areas of Burroughs' text(s) and the stability of racialist identity.

Burroughs' first science fiction series best illustrates these generic and racial characteristics. The first installment of the Mars series, *A Princess of Mars*, was not only Burroughs' first published work (1912), but also contains the seeds of his later writing—topically, generically, and in choice of protagonist. First, a basic topic or theme of Burroughs' fiction is the concept of progress, with its foundation in European ideology and subsequent growth in America. Both the genre(s) and the protagonist of *A Princess of Mars* are intimately linked to this progress as well. A multi-generic narrative,

A Princess of Mars begins with the (relative) realism of the western genre and then moves to an extraterrestrial setting which combines aspects of colonial literature, the scientific romance, and adventure stories. Burroughs uses the literal geographical and chronological progress of his protagonist, John Carter, as a vehicle for charting this generic movement. Carter's personal progress symbolizes the larger progress of western civilization as well—historically, culturally, and racially. As a typical Anglo-American hero, the character of John Carter foregrounds the ideological base of the concept of progress, specifically progress defined as positive, inevitable, and racially/ culturally-based. Of course, progress also entails a continual dynamic of change and movement; progress can never end. The result is the almost compulsively restless movement of the text generically and Carter physically, both of which translate to constantly changing settings as well. By the turn of the century, when Burroughs begins his writing career, there remained few areas of the globe 'unknown' to the western world. Therefore, this desire for constant movement, and the exploration and expansion it inspires, engendered the increasing popularity of extraterrestrial settings for adventure stories. Kilgore combines the concept of western progress and outer space in this desire for a new "frontier" (11). Building on "the nineteenth-century notion that conquest and empire are the logical modus operandi of any progressive civilization," the extraterrestrial focus of science fiction "represents twentieth-century American culture's attempts to deny the possibility of limits to its physical and metaphysical reach" (ibid).[19]

In *Primate Visions*, Donna Haraway more broadly discusses the restlessness of "civilized man" and its connection to both the tropics and outer space: "Space and the tropics are both utopian topical figures in western imaginations, and their opposed properties dialectically signify origins and ends for the creature whose mundane life is outside both: civilized man. Space and the tropics are 'allotopic'; i.e. they are 'elsewhere,' the place to which the traveler goes to find something dangerous and sacred" (137). While Burroughs' Tarzan series directly reflects such an investigation of the origins of man through the intersections of the tropics, primates, and "civilized man," his Mars series embodies similar interests within the larger scope of space. Paul Carter focuses exclusively on the (American) western aspects of Burroughs' Mars. However, Burroughs constructed a Martian bricolage of modern and ancient, multi-generic elements. Mars is a habitable planet with dead seas and ruins, barbarous green people, jungles, and lost civilizations. Much like the tropics of Tarzan, this Mars reflects the archaic tendencies of fantasy and some science fiction. Simultaneously, Mars supports a civilized culture of red people who possess advanced weapons, technology for atmospheric control, and mechanical travel. John Carter both fights with a sword and travels by air.[20] By combining the tropics and space in one planet and one narrative, Burroughs combines the past and the future of mankind, man's origins and his destiny. This allows Burroughs to chart the progress of humankind from beginning to end from a Euro-American perspective. Such progress entails many diverse and often intertwined elements: the social, cultural, historical, and geographic, as well as material, technological, religious, and biological. The great length of this list effectively highlights the pervasive and foundational role progress plays in western civilization.

Burrroughs' American focus in the Mars series adds a unique spin to the Western European concept of progress. While the Tarzan series deals with many of the more traditional European colonial issues, in the Mars series, Burroughs places these issues within the American colonial context of slavery and western expansion. The American West is the equivalent of the European tropics. Burroughs clearly subscribes to American exceptionalism, situating the United States as the pinnacle of western progress. In this way, Burroughs uses his protagonist to build on, and sometimes revise the western concept of progress. As Burroughs charts the development of the United States, from eastern slavery to the western frontier to the technological future of twentieth-century America, he creates a New World hero, John Carter, who far outstrips an Old World Tarzan. Burroughs begins with the American West as a third "elsewhere," an elsewhere embodying both the future of Americans in the form of manifest destiny and also the past, as the frontier or Wild West has effectively ended by the time Burroughs writes his first Mars book. He examines the specific characteristics of American progress, utilizing ethnic comparisons and hierarchies to promote American values such as individualism, the cultivation of land, and capitalism. In his choice of protagonist, Burroughs illustrates the centrality and mastery of Anglo men in the origins of humankind or man's past and also man's destiny or the future. As a prospector, adventurer, and Indian fighter, as well as a former Confederate soldier, John Carter is the epitome of the warrior hero. Yet, lest he be perceived as uncivilized or a savage, Burroughs personally attests that Carter represents the ideal gentleman. Thus, Carter confronts and conquers rather than internalizes and values the wilderness or the savage. Nature and the ethnic Other are resources for developing and/or illustrating Carter's masculinity and the frontier characteristics of physical conflict, a strong physique, courage, and individualism. While the native Other remains an anachronism, incapable of change or adaptation, John Carter embodies progress and swiftly and easily moves between environments and cultures and embraces the futuristic elements of the modern world.

The generic and geographical movement of the text to Mars entails the transformation of a racial Other into an alien Other. The Native Americans of the West become a multi-racial Martian society. On one level, an extraterrestrial Other is a welcome replacement for terrestrial othering focused on ethnicity, race, nationality, or gender. As mentioned earlier, the existence of an alien Other can foreground the unity of the human race. Yet, such a fictional transformation also suppresses the importance of race to human society. The real prejudice and oppression experienced by many groups is eclipsed, and any explicit discussion of race is effectively forestalled. Simultaneously, the guilt of oppressors is obscured and any redress of grievances becomes more difficult. In the creation of aliens, science fiction authors avoid specific details of ethnic or racial Others as well. The creation of an alien entails no research, let alone understanding or empathy for an oppressed group of people. In fact, due to the fictional license of the imaginative character, an alien Other can be either more negative or more positive than a racial Other. Burroughs, for example, represents the norm for early science fiction authors when he transforms the existing, highly negative stereotype of Native Americans, from the western segment of his Mars series, into even more terrible and alienating green Martians. On the other hand, his representation of red Martians is more favorable than that of the natives in many American and European colonial and post-colonial texts (whether Native American or Indian). In either case, however, the science fiction author can stress the fictional basis of the extraterrestrial character if anyone questions the similarity to existing terrestrial groups. With all of these underlying motivations, as well as the generic impetus of alien plausibility, it is no wonder that the portrayal of characters representing real-life racial Others was uncommon in early science fiction. While Burroughs clearly utilizes such a racial/alien transformation, he is atypical for an early science fiction author in his extensive portrayal of Native Americans and aliens based on specific racial groups. In addition, the multi-generic and geographic setting of *A Princess of Mars* explicitly draws attention to the racial/alien transformation rather than suppressing it. Burroughs directly and extensively explores race and racial theories in his texts and, in doing so, creates the potential for dialogue and change.

In *A Princess of Mars*, as Carter moves from the American West, and the historical, social, and literary limitations of Earth, Burroughs' vision expands. In addition to existing terrestrial hierarchical relations privileging Anglo men, western progress is increasingly associated with the American 'progressive' ideals of equality and diversity. In this way, Burroughs maintains the concept of American exceptionalism while undermining some aspects of western progress in the Mars context. Furthermore, the single, ethnographic viewpoint and Anglo-American bias of John Carter are challenged by the creation mythology of one of the Martian races and the history of Mars itself. Burroughs utilizes the imaginative, liberating potential of the literal unknown—the future elsewhere of outer space and its complementary literary genre of science fiction—to explore, question, and revise the cultural and racial hierarchies established in other areas of the text.

THE AMERICAN WEST

Writing in the early 20th century, Burroughs chooses to begin the Mars series within a specifically American past—the western frontier. Taking part in the turn-of-the-century "wilderness cult," Burroughs followed prominent Americans such as Theodore Roosevelt in promoting a return to frontier characteristics (Nash 141). With the frontier "moribund," "the qualities of solitude and hardship that had intimidated many pioneers were likely to be magnetically attractive to their city-dwelling grandchildren" (Nash 143). The mechanization and urbanization of western progress were considered by some to be fostering decadence and a general weakening of masculine and national virility.[21] For example, Roosevelt's "trips to the West where the virile virtues abounded were real-life pilgrimages in search of the 'race-hardening' experience of the frontier" (Dyer 169). This wilderness nostalgia, and its roots in sexual, gender, and racial insecurities, helps explain why Burroughs chose the American West and elements of the western genre for the beginning of his first published narrative. He logically started with the wilderness geographically closest, most familiar to himself and his readers, and most fundamentally and uniquely American. It is no coincidence that Zane Grey and his westerns rivaled the popularity of Burroughs at the turn of the century.

Within the context of science fiction, Burroughs reminds Americans of their virile past as a springboard to their equally virile, imperialistic future. John Carter needs a Wild West in order to demonstrate his physical abilities, his self-reliance, and his superiority in comparison to the ethnic Other of Native Americans. He cannot be a warrior hero in the geographical and social confines of a modern city; in pre-WWI, at-peace American society, violence and physical conflict were largely unacceptable modes of behavior. Nor could Carter as easily demonstrate his superior cultivation and civilized nature without the extremity of contrast offered by natural savages.[22] In addition, for Burroughs' modern (urban) reader, an exotic or unfamiliar locale would be essential for the adventure and escapism of both the main character and the reader's own vicarious participation. It is telling that Burroughs personally fits the template of the urban dweller who writes of thrilling adventures and manhood-developing hardships on the frontier.[23] Burroughs did have some personal contact with the American West: as a youth he visited his older brothers on their cattle ranch in Idaho, and he served in the Seventh Cavalry at Fort Grant in the Arizona Territory for 10 months. However, he had no contact with Indians beyond those in the U.S. military, he saw no actual combat, and his wilderness forays were of short duration.[24] The American West was an elsewhere for Burroughs, as it was for his main character, John Carter, and his readers.[25] Furthermore, like Roosevelt, Burroughs does not promote a Romantic or spiritual oneness with nature or the concept of the noble savage. The primitive does not have any intrinsic value in and of itself; the wilderness and savages are resources for the construction of a superior white, western manhood. The comparisons between civilized and savage or primitive people this process entails illustrate the general rightness, the historical actuality, and the inevitability of western, American progress.

Frederick Jackson Turner had heralded the end of the frontier in his highly influential essay, "The Significance of the Frontier in American History." He first read his essay at the Chicago World's Columbian Exposition in July of 1893, an exposition that Burroughs actually attended as a youth growing up in Chicago. The expo was organized as "a celebration of the remarkable progress the United States had made since Columbus's arrival four hundred years earlier. [. . . T]hey built a neoclassical 'White City' along the shores of Lake Michigan, which they packed with a vast array of marvelous displays of American know-how" (Taliaferro 34–5). Although there is no record of the specific exhibits or events Burroughs attended, the expo as a whole illustrates a complex nexus of themes running through Burroughs' later writing. First, the expo portrayed the future of western man culminating in dominant white American society, as the White City reflects, and its technological/scientific progress. Also, the urban location of the expo promoted the development of large, cultured urban centers like Chicago. Since progress can only be measured by the opposite, however, the expo also embodied man's past. A more positive past took the form of the neoclassical revival. Within this context, America is the heir of ancient Greek civilization, represented as the root of western civilization. Conversely, exhibits of various primitive cultures represented a more negative past: "America brashly announced its arrival at the summit of the human pyramid [; . . . i]n the Anthropological Building, [. . .] displays of ethnic costumes and handicrafts from around the world served as quaint counterpoint to the brilliant American inventions of the surrounding White City" (Taliaferro 35). This cultural 'progress' was supported by scientific exhibits as well. "Science spoke even louder than trinkets in the Anthropological hall, and thousands of tourists, curious to see where they ranked on the scale of human progress, lined up to have their heads measured—'anthropometry,' it was called—by a team of anthropologists" (ibid). Within this 'progressive' cultural and scientific context, Turner's essay on the end of the American frontier becomes another example of the superiority of Anglo people and culture, as well as the inevitability of their succession of all other people. Primitive, native, generally darker-skinned cultures and people were the first to face elimination or subjugation. In the 'natural' and 'universal' evolution of people and cultures such a model of progress entails, Native Americans become anachronisms who are destroyed or assimilated and the (western) frontier ends as Anglo, particularly American, civilization expands and develops (Turner 11).

This larger cultural picture and its progressive, western values are symbolized on a smaller scale in the characters of the Mars series. John Carter represents the civilized white American male whose identity is simultaneously based on the rough frontier and comparison to culturally, historically, and biologically primitive natives—Native Americans and Africans. Turner's history of the American frontier fleshes out the picture of Carter as a frontiersman—that unique American who combines the characteristics of both the civilized European and the savage Native American:

> the frontier is the outer edge of the wave—the meeting point between savagery and civilization. (3)

> The frontier is the line of most rapid and effective Americanization. The wilderness masters the colonist. It finds him a European in dress, industries, tools, modes of travel, and thought. [. . .] It strips off the garments of civilization and arrays him in the hunting shirt and the moccasin [. . . H]e shouts the war cry and takes the scalp in orthodox Indian fashion.[26]

> In short, at the frontier the environment is at first too strong for the man. He must accept the conditions which it furnishes, or perish [. . .]. Little by little he transforms the wilderness, but the outcome is not the old Europe. [. . . H]ere is a new product that is American. (4)

Turner emphasizes the changes that take place as the European comes into direct and sustained contact with the "wilderness" and its native occupants. However, like Burroughs, he rejects total assimilation, or in European ideology, reversion to the primitive. First, the strenuous, perilous, and unfamiliar conditions of the American wilderness and the savage behavior of the Indians justify an eye-for-an-eye, savage physical response from the civilized Europeans. If European settlers occasionally lapsed from their civilized natures and were guilty of Indian massacres, it could be justified by the pressures of the environment and the savagery of their opponents—all external factors. Furthermore, the most important element in the process of making an American is the "transformation" of the wilderness. Through confrontation with and civilization of the primitive, Europeans became Americans—a "new product" superior to the old European type.

Foreshadowing Theodore Roosevelt and the Wilderness Cult, Washington Irving touted the benefits of American frontier life in 1835. "Several weeks of camping convinced him that nothing could be more beneficial to young men than the 'wild wood life . . . of a magnificent wilderness'" because it encouraged the positive American values of independence, masculinity, and bodily strength (Nash 73). Irving wrote, "we send our youth abroad to grow luxurious and effeminate in Europe; it appears to me, that a previous tour on the prairies would be more likely to produce that manliness, simplicity, and self-dependence most in unison with our political institutions'" (ibid). Physical confrontation with the primitive environment and native occupants was believed to foster the ideals of hard work, self-reliance, virility, and physical conquest. This connection between individualism and masculinity in American ideology is not a coincidence. European males, women, slaves, poor white men, children and Native Americans were perceived as dependent, physically weaker, or lazy; they were not capable of achieving true individualism or self-reliance, and therefore, were not included in American democracy. Conversely, ideal American men must be self-reliant and individualistic; men were associated with the frontier; and white, property-owning American men were the only persons worthy of full access to the democratic system and the rights it entailed. Turner argues that the frontier inspired the fundamental American values of individualism and democracy: "the frontier is productive of individualism [. . .]. The tendency is antisocial. It produces antipathy to control. [. . .] The frontier individualism has from the beginning promoted democracy" (30).

As the ideal American hero, John Carter embodies all of these positive characteristics. As a frontiersman, John Carter is a thoroughly civilized man who confronts and conquers savage environments and native people. The influence of the primitive on the Euro-American male is not (normally or ideally) the creation of an amalgamation—a semi-civilized human. Rather, the essential civilized nature of a European acquires uniquely American, positive characteristics through exposure to the primitive. In a complex intersection of sexual, gender, racial, and national hierarchies, particularly after the wilderness and the American savages have been largely subdued or destroyed, we see the primitive, the natural becoming positive influences in the creation of a unique and superior (white) American male type. John Carter represents on an individual level what the Chicago World's Columbian Exposition represented on a collective level—America and Americans are the next step in the geographic, cultural, racial, political, and historical progress of western civilization.

The fundamental and pervasive nature of the biases and hierarchies involved in the creation of Anglo-American manhood is most apparent when investigating a highly influential and positively constructed concept like individualism. Burroughs follows Irving and Turner in associating individualism with the American West; however, John Carter's individualism also springs from the American South. Before his foray into the American West, Carter grew up in the antebellum South and was known as a "typical southern gentleman of the highest type" (*Princess* v). Within this context, the hierarchical, slave-based individualism of the plantation 'aristocracy' plays an equal role in Carter's character as the democratic individualism of the frontier.[27] Hence, Carter's individualism is connected with a more civilized society and one in which the racial othering is, paradoxically, more obscured. As a fictional narrator and character within the text, Burroughs asserts that "our slaves fairly worshipped the ground [Carter] trod" (ibid). Burroughs' uncritical affirmation of slavery here, particularly the constructed complicity of the African-American slaves in their own oppression, coincides with his personal connection to the southern, slave-owing class. Using the first-person and signing his own name to the Foreword, Burroughs places himself with the story: "My first recollection of Captain Carter is of the few months he spent at my father's home in Virginia, just prior to the opening of the civil war" (ibid). This allows Burroughs to emphasize a branch of his family tree of which he was excessively proud: he "preferred to stress those relatives of Mary Evaline Zieger Burroughs [his mother] who had settled in Virginia in the eighteenth century, including John Coleman, after whom Burroughs named his second son" (Taliaferro 27). He felt that "he was the direct descendant of the fighting cavaliers of the Old Dominion, and in several of his novels he attributes the gallantry and valor of his heroes expressly to their Virginia lineage" (ibid).

John Carter fits this template perfectly, even down to his part in the Civil War—a captain in the Confederate Army.[28] By placing Carter within the context of the antebellum South, Burroughs intends to emphasize

Carter's highly civilized nature and his superiority as a civilized, white male in comparison to the less privileged members of hierarchical southern society (slaves, blacks, women, poor whites, etc.). As a character in the text, Burroughs would embody similar characteristics through his connection to John Carter. Likewise, the authorial Burroughs would occupy an elevated position in turn-of-the-century, New Immigration American society.

A more critical reader questions this highly positive perspective on Carter and the relationship between his position in society and his personal attributes. The American individualism and democracy of the frontier are different from that of the antebellum South. Furthermore, both the antebellum South and the frontier are based on ethnic and racial othering and power hierarchies. Whereas Burroughs and Turner participate in and even promote these in their writing, many (particularly current) readers note the discrepancy between the American ideals of individualism and democracy and their historical basis in racism, sexism, and ethnocentrism. Contemporary critic Kristin Herzog, for example, argues that "The frontier [. . .] more than any other influence, made the American novel more individualistic and more male-centered than English fiction of the nineteenth century. [. . .] The violence and vigor of the frontier world and the lack of a native cultural tradition fostered the American Adam's disregard for persons different from himself" (xvii-xviii). In a similar manner, British author D.H. Lawrence undermines the "blood brother theme" (56), "democracy," and the "nucleus of a new society" (59) offered in James Fenimore Cooper's Leatherstocking novels. A 19th-century precursor of John Carter, the protagonist of the Leatherstocking series, Natty Bumppo, embodies the frontiersman—the essentially civilized white man who is also "hard, isolate, stoic, and a killer" (68). Like John Carter, Bumppo is a "man who turns his back on white society. A man who keeps his moral integrity hard and intact [. . .], who lives by death, by killing, but who is pure white" (69). Cooper, Turner, and Burroughs promote the frontier-stimulated, American values of individualism and democracy, but by associating these values exclusively with (male) whites, they illustrate the hierarchical basis of these values in America. In addition, Turner and Burroughs (in terms of the West and the South) gloss over the oppression, conflict, violence, and death, particularly of the ethnic or racial other, that occurs when such discrepancies exist. Burroughs' brief mention of the Civil War and Turner's "series of Indian wars" (9) and his metaphor of the frontier as "a military training school" (15) remind the reader of the cost involved in the creation of white, male heroes.

This combination of hierarchies and biases that underlies purported American ideals is illustrated in the self-reliance of the American hero as well. In a brief synopsis of the American literary tradition of the American Adam and its "white" and "male-centered[ness]," Kristin Herzog asserts that "egalitarianism in America casts the individual in a lonely role without heritage or tradition. The American Adam has to achieve everything he does or becomes" (xvi). Unlike his European counterpart, the "American folk hero has 'no parents, no past, no patrimony, no siblings, no family, no life cycle [. . .]. He seldom dies'" (ibid).[29] In *A Princess of Mars*, Carter begins the narrative by denying his past before the age of thirty, insisting that he does not age normally, and admitting he has died several times: "I am a very old man; how old I do not know. [. . .] I cannot tell because I have never aged as other men do, nor do I remember my childhood. So far as I can recollect I have always been a man, a man of about thirty. [. . .] I do not know why I should fear death, I who have died twice and am still alive" (*Princess* 11). Carter does later marry and have a child, continuing the "life cycle," because Burroughs included an element of the romance genre in the series as well. However, this focus on individualism and self-reliance, as well as the indestructible or immortal nature of the American hero, coincides with Donna Haraway's argument that white travelers to elsewheres are usually portrayed as lone, intrepid individuals. They courageously enter an unknown space (like the tropics, outer space, or the American West) without the direct assistance of others. As representatives of civilized, western (white) culture, they are insistently portrayed as "alone" despite their interaction with ethnic or racial Others (Haraway 154). Thus, Carter begins his story cut off from white, western civilization—his family, his native South and the eastern United States, and even his mining partner—as he fights for survival against Native American Others. Even as Carter builds relationships with the Martians over time, he remains the sole representative of Earth and always is set apart—physically, culturally, and nationally.

Logically, Carter should be defined as the Other in the American western context and the alien in the Martian context, since he is within a society different from his own. However, within western ideology, from the Anglo male perspective (author, publisher, protagonist, and historically audience as well), Carter is the unquestioned normative hero. Haraway highlights this contradictory repression of historically-specific racial, gender, and cultural markers in an attempt to collapse white, western man with "universal man" (i.e. all humans) (186). On one level (precisely because he is an egalitarian American), John Carter is a universal hero with universal cultural values. On the other hand, Burroughs goes out of his way in the Foreword to give us some historical and biographical background which clearly situates Carter as a white, cultured southern American. As Haraway notes, the implicit or indirect racial, gender, and cultural markers are essential for the construction of ethnic, racial, and national hierarchies (153). John Carter is a universal hero precisely because he is a white southern gentleman and former Captain in the Confederate Army.

Closely examining the representation of Native Americans and Carter's relationship to this first ethnic Other reveals the importance of othering to the construction of Anglo male identity and the material progress so fundamental to western, particularly American ideology. According to Haraway, Carter would be searching for "something dangerous and sacred" in his travels; he finds both in the same ethnic Other—Native Americans (137). Carter finds "danger" in the threat of hostile Indians, who kill his partner and chase him to an abandoned and mysterious cave. Here he escapes from the "danger" through the "sacred": as the "savage face[s]" peered into the cave, "[e]ach face was the picture of awe and fear"; as a "low moaning sound issued from the recesses of the cave," the Indians departed so hastily that one of them was accidentally pushed from the steep trail to his death (*Princess* 17–8). Playing on the convention(s) of first contact between Europeans and natives, Burroughs sets up this scene as if the Native Americans were deathly in "awe and fear" of Carter himself, reacting as if he were a god or of supernatural origin (ibid). Certainly such a response from the natives would reflect the Europeans' construction of their own superior, rational identity and the inferior, gullible, superstitious nature of primitives. Burroughs' representation of the superstitious nature of Native American people reflects the larger Euro-American conception of both women and ethnic or racial Others: "From earliest times until today, women have been described, like the nonwhite races, as more passive, less logical; more imaginative, less technically inclined; more emotional, less incisive; and more religious, less scientifically oriented" (Herzog xi-xii). On this mysterious note, Burroughs leaves the American West and turns to Mars. Using the American West as a framing device maintains the illusion of Carter's god-like nature and heightens the narrative suspense as well, for we leave Carter's body in the cave until the very end of the text.

We do not find out the true reason for the Native Americans' fears until the last chapter of *A Princess of Mars*: the darkness of the cave hid "the dead and mummified remains of a little old woman with long black hair, and the thing [she] leaned over was a small charcoal burner upon which rested a round copper vessel containing a small quantity of greenish powder" (158). Furthermore, "[b]ehind her, depending from the roof upon rawhide thongs, and stretching entirely across the cave, was a row of human skeletons. From the thong which held them stretched another to the dead hand of the little old woman [. . .]. It was a most grotesque and horrid tableau" (ibid). It was not Carter, then, who prompted the fearful response of the Native American men but a powerful, deadly, and perhaps sacred place. From Carter's Anglo-American perspective, a gravesite becomes a "grotesque and horrid tableau." Burroughs symbolizes the mystery or Otherness of the Native Americans as an old witch or shaman with magic powders, a kettle, and human skeletons. This association of Native Americans with age, immobility, decay, and death emphasizes the anachronistic quality and destiny of natives within the concept of western progress. Burroughs' choice of a (dead) woman as the symbol for Native American culture and the connection between women and "non-white races" foreground the feminization of Others also (Herzog xi). For example, Laura Doyle examines the scientific theory of paedomorphism and its "alignment of all women with the 'lower races' by suggesting that both embodied the childhood of humanity. [. . .] Certain races and the female sex represent, in this theory, 'older' evolutionary forms beyond which other 'younger' races and the male sex have evolved" (65). Thus, cultural anachronism is conjoined with and proven by a biological anachronism. This biological basis for cultural differences, or sexual and racial essentialism, served as a scientific rationale for the oppression of these groups.

Burroughs further emphasizes the feminization of the Other through a complex native matrix composed of the unknown, the sacred, the dangerous, and the "grotesque and horrid" (*Princess* 158). This matrix serves as a resource for the spiritual and physical rebirth of Euro-Americans. Having mysteriously lost his ability to move, Carter lies in the dark cave (a 'womb') until "possibly midnight" (*Princess* 18). Then, giving a "super-human effort" of the mind (and specifically not the body), Carter feels "something g[i]ve, [. . .] a momentary feeling of nausea, a sharp click as of the snapping of a steel wire," and he realizes that he has separated from his body (18–19). In a literal manifestation of the mind/body split of western culture, Carter becomes totally mind or spirit and remains disconnected from his physical body until the end of the text. Conversely, the feminine racial Other is only represented by a body, with no mind or spirit attached. As Burroughs utilizes a feminine and racially-other body for the concentration and strengthening of his male protagonist's metaphysical qualities, we see the gender and racial hierarchies attached to the western mind/body division.[30] Carter assures himself, and the reader, that he is not dead; he has been physically reborn in another body, exactly like his old one except it was "naked as at the minute of [his] birth" (19). Finally escaping from the "grotesque and horrid" womb of the cave/a Native American/woman, Carter is mysteriously teleported to the planet of Mars in a spiritual rebirth. John Carter not only shares the same initials as Jesus Christ, then; he similarly 'rises from the dead,' emerges from a dark 'tomb,' and asserts his immortality. The mind/body split and its hier-archical connotations in western society stem, in large part, from the valo-rization of the spirit and denigration of the body in Christian theology. In the Martian context, John Carter mirrors Jesus Christ in the emphasis on his difference from the people and society surrounding him as well. Carter may be alone in an alien world, but he is perfect, more powerful, a 'mes-siah' to others, and ultimately invincible.

Of course, the mind/body division experienced by Carter hints that he may only be dreaming the subsequent Mars sequences. While such a theory is plausible, it would only reinforce the power of the male intel-lect or spirit, as Carter mentally creates another whole world. In contrast to the Native American woman and her "grotesque and horrid" womb, Carter would be associated with the mental and artistic abilities of the authorial Burroughs in this case. Furthermore, Carter returns to Mars on many occasions over the course of the series. It is rare in science fiction or u/dystopian writing for a dream motif to happen more than once. In fact, some critics argue that science fiction should not utilize the dream motif at all because it undermines the rational or scientific foundation of the genre. In contrast to the European legacy of writers such as Jules Verne and H.G. Wells, Burroughs chooses racial othering to facilitate space travel, rather than modern technology and science. It is through the exoticism and appropriation of a native or ethnic Other that Bur-roughs empowers his hero. Because of the long history of ethnic othering in the United States, particularly of Native Americans by Euro-Americans, Burroughs' readers generally do not question the logic or credibility of this maneuver. One elsewhere gives birth to another elsewhere; one ethnic Other is a stepping stone to a more distant planetary racial Other.

Certainly, Carter cannot stay in the West indefinitely, even with the author's fictional ability to go back in time. Carter must move on as the West is settled and cultivated by pioneers and the Native Americans restricted to reservations and battled into 'submission.' The Other, the source of power and identity for the hero, has been destroyed—through disease, warfare, isolation, and assimilation. The western frontier may be ended, as Turner notes in the last paragraph of his essay "The Significance of the Frontier in American History," yet "[h]e would be a rash prophet who should assert that the expansive character of American life has now entirely ceased. Movement has been its dominant fact, and [. . .] American energy will continually demand a wider field for its exercise" (37).

THE AMERICAN WEST (IN)TO MARS

If the United States was the next step in the geographical and social progress of western civilization, and Euro-Americans had already fulfilled their duty to reach from coast to coast and "displace inferior races," as well as create an advanced cultural and technological society, then what was the next logical step (Dyer 60)? European colonialism had merged into American imperialism and, at the turn of the century, United States foreign policy was encompassing greater and greater physical boundaries. From the east to the west coast, from the North to the South, and from the North American Continent to Latin America and the Pacific islands, the United States was conquering physical territory and establishing a military, political, and cultural hegemony. Following American history, Burroughs moves from the South to the West and from the West to a combination of the imperial elsewheres of the tropics and outer space—merging them in his characterization of the planet of Mars. Burroughs' choice of an interplanetary rather than terrestrial setting, specifically of Mars, is not surprising in light of the following factors. First, by the turn of the century, most areas of the terrestrial world had been not only 'discovered' and explored, but also colonized by European countries. There was no room, no 'blank spaces' left for an American hero to conquer in the terrestrial present or future. Therefore, once out of the past of the American West, modern, cutting-edge, nationalistic American society called for the most ambitious movement of all—outside of the known world. "Space, the final frontier" is a well-known phrase to contemporary Americans thanks to the *Star Trek* series of the second half of the twentieth century.

The planet of Mars was a logical choice for the specific interplanetary setting, as Mars was named after the Roman god of war and John Carter represents the ideal warrior. From his 20th-century perspective, influenced by the national obsession with virility and physical activity, Burroughs could be speaking autobiographically when he has Carter reminisce: "My attention was quickly riveted by a large red star close to the distant horizon. As I gazed upon it I felt a spell of overpowering fascination—it was Mars, the god of war, and for me, the fighting man, it had always held the power of irresistible enchantment" (*Princess* 20). Furthermore, Mars had been attracting the attention of scientists and popular writers for sometime previous to Burroughs' writing of the Mars series. John Taliaferro chronicles the astronomical interest in possible Martian life starting in 1879 and connects Burroughs' fictional depiction of Mars to that of Gustavus W. Pope in 1894 and H.G. Wells in 1898 (67).

Burroughs choice of an interplanetary setting for his first science fiction series reflects his specifically American bias as well. While the United States was a colonial and imperial power, like its Old World predecessors, Americans chose to foreground their superiority over Europeans in terms of the revolutionary values of freedom and equality. In other words, they chose to ignore their own imperial attitudes and activities or interpret them in a more benevolent light than that of other European peoples. This can be seen in Burroughs' own work as he chooses a European, specifically a member of the English nobility, as his main character in the Tarzan series because it takes place in colonial Africa. On the other hand, as an egalitarian and freedom-loving American, John Carter travels alone, outside of a specifically delineated colonial or imperial context and, once on Mars, supposedly outside of terrestrial history altogether. Furthermore, in moving from the historical context of the American West to the imaginative setting of Mars, Burroughs transforms Carter's perspective as narrator from that of an interested, clearly biased frontiersman to a more detached, objective observer of alien native life. Burroughs attempts to ground the narrative and its hierarchies in more modern, scientific language and theory. The Mars series becomes science fiction not only in terms of an interplanetary setting but also in the narrative perspective and interests and the technological and cultural features of the various Martian societies. Thus, Americans are associated with the most modern, enlightened, and unbiased characteristics—socially, materially, and in literature. Like Burroughs' construction of America's frontier past, then, American ethnocentrism played a large role in Burroughs' movement from the American West to Mars. The interplanetary imperialism is a continuation of the geographical and cultural aspects of western progress, while the post-terrestrial setting elides American imperialism and foregrounds the American political values of freedom and equality, also a part of western progress. In either case, (white) Americans become the chosen people of the chosen mode of living—western progress.

Thus, while Burroughs may be moving to a locale and genre which promise freedom from the boundaries of terrestrial life, in promoting Euro-American progress, he largely retains the infrastructure of existing ethnic, racial, gender, and cultural hierarchies. As a result, Mars becomes a unique and complex mixture of all three elsewheres—the American West, the tropics, and outer space—as well as the (European) Old World. As Brian Steet notes, "It is significant that both Edgar Rice Burroughs and Conan Doyle also wrote science fiction. There is something in common between creating an alien society in remote parts of this earth and on distant planets" (21). In many ways, Burroughs' Mars becomes an exaggerated version of the American Dream—an ideal American hero/colonizer struggles but quickly rises to the very top of a foreign society because of his physical prowess, merit, and his participation in (and embodiment of) western progress. Burroughs' specifically American ethnocentrism is first revealed in the changes he makes in the existing concept of Mars as a habitable, evolutionarily older planet, as civilized or more civilized than Earth. The writings of astronomers Giovanni Schiaparelli (1879), Camille Flammarion (1892), and Percival Lowell (1885–1908) had helped to form the turn-of-the-century theory that "the present inhabitation of Mars by a race superior to ours is very possible" (Taliaferro 66). Burroughs begins with this model, but manipulates the time element involved, making the older, more advanced civilizations of Mars representative of the Old World. Therefore, the American hero allies himself with the most recent, melting pot culture/race on Mars—the red Martians, who have striking similarities to Americans and American culture—and quickly proves himself the superior of every Martian he encounters, regardless of race or culture. Burroughs' continuation of the terrestrial status quo is most evident in the analogy he creates between the American West and Native Americans and literally another world with alien life forms. He emphasizes the difference or Otherness of the native Earthlings as they are literally transformed into aliens, while John Carter remains the same. The hierarchy of races and cultures is exaggerated within the imaginative setting; as the Native Americans are transformed into insect-like Martians, Carter's superiority and "universal" or normative nature become even more pronounced. John Carter–American, Anglo/universal hero–not only conquers the New World, but the Old World (via the Mars inversion) and another entire planet.

Before turning to specific elements of Burroughs' transformation of the American West into Mars, a brief examination of his fictional revision of the existing model of Mars would be helpful. Burroughs' celebration of progress and maintenance of existing hierarchies, and the western optimism and American bias these reveal, are brought into sharp relief by comparison to an earlier fictional account of the planet of Mars which follows the Flammarion model more closely. In H.G. Wells' *The War of the Worlds* (1898), he creates Martians who embody the full and horrifying fruition of western progress. Burroughs reverses this model in order to promote western and particularly American values. Mars is utilized by both Burroughs and Wells as a means of cultural comparison and social critique, but from Wells' British, socialist perspective, Mars becomes a dystopic warning about western progress, while from Burroughs' individualistic, capitalist perspective, Mars becomes yet another frontier which proves the validity of western progress. Wells exposes the hypocrisy and unreality of Burroughs' idealistic emphasis on freedom, equality, democracy, and capitalism.

Wells' Martians are contemporaneously more intelligent, civilized, and technologically advanced than Earthlings, and it is the Martians who invade Earth for the purpose of colonization. Wells first places the Earthlings in the position of less developed life forms within an evolutionary framework:

> And we men [. . .] must be to [the Martians] at least as alien and lowly as are the monkeys and lemurs to us. The intellectual side of man already admits that life is an incessant struggle for existence, and it would seem that this too is the belief of the minds upon Mars. Their world is far gone in its cooling and this world is still crowded with life, but crowded only with what they regard as inferior animals. To carry warfare sunward is, indeed, their only escape from the destruction that, generation after generation, creeps upon them. (*War* 14–15)

Thus, the Martians are only following the 'laws of nature'; it is 'survival of the fittest,' and they are more advanced than humans in every way. The detached and objective perspective of Wells' narrator allows him to note the hypocrisy of Europeans as well. Reversing the position of Europeans within colonial ideology and power hierarchies, he vividly reminds them of their own violent subjugation of natives:

> And before we judge of them too harshly we must remember what ruthless and utter destruction our own species has wrought, not only upon animals, such as the vanished bison and the dodo, but upon its inferior races. The Tasmanians, in spite of their human likeness, were entirely swept out of existence in a war of extermination waged by European immigrants, in the space of fifty years. Are we such apostles of mercy as to complain if the Martians warred in the same spirit? (*War* 15)

This colonial reversal reveals the ruthlessness, destruction, and materialism of western imperialism and also stimulates sympathy and understanding for native people.[31] In contrast to Burroughs, Wells utilizes Darwinian theory and language to reveal the moral inferiority rather than superiority of Europeans [Americans] and the hypocrisy of their civilized behavior. Europeans, and all imperialist powers, become "nasty" "monster[s]" who inspire "disgust and dread" (23). Furthermore, while initially successful in their colonial ambitions, eventually the Martians succumb to unexpected natural forces which destroy them completely and leave the humans/natives decimated but capable of survival. This is a dire warning indeed about the possible fate of imperialist powers; perhaps they too are not invincible, 'naturally' destined to prevail because of their more developed historical, cultural, and technological evolution. Whereas Wells reveals the negative underside of colonialism and ethnic othering, Burroughs' belief in American equality, democracy, and manifest destiny allows him to overlook the same aspects in an American context.

Burroughs continues the American tradition begun when Europeans first started immigrating to North America and which reached full force with the colonial rebellion from England—the concept of America as a fresh start, as a more perfect embodiment of western ideals, and the final fruition of western culture. Hector St. Jean de Crèvecoeur, for example, described colonial America as "the most perfect society now existing in the world. Here man is free as he ought to be, nor is this pleasing equality so transitory as many others are" (44). In terms of western progress, de Crèvecoeur explained that "[h]ere individuals of all nations are melted into a new race of men, whose labours and posterity will one day cause great changes in the world. Americans are the western pilgrims who are carrying along with them that great mass of arts, sciences, vigour, and industry which began long since in the East; they will finish the great circle" (46). Burroughs continues the expansionist policy of western society, while eliding its colonial/imperialistic aspect, by having John Carter travel to Mars where he meets intellectually, culturally, physically, and technologically inferior Martians. Even though there are a few examples of more advanced Martian technology, like the flying ships, Carter's general superiority is illustrated by his position of prominence and power throughout the entire planet; every new group of people he meets eventually recognizes him as an equal or superior. In the case of the "black pirates of Barsoom," Carter reveals their superstition and religious fraud and they offer him their throne after their defeat (*Gods* 57, 189; *Warlord* 8). Without the extreme contrast of Wells' earlier dystopic, European vision of western progress, however, the utopic nature of Burroughs' American vision in the Mars series would be obscured.

Burroughs begins the analogy between the frontiers of Earth and Mars through the setting or planetary environment. Brian Street emphasizes the "unreality which pervades many descriptions of exotic land and their inhabitants" (21). Within this context, Carter's descriptions of the Arizona landscape clearly reflect the "unreality" of another world and foreshadow the similar descriptions of the Mars landscape contained on the same page: "Few western wonders are more inspiring than the beauties of an Arizona moonlit landscape [. . . ,] as though one were catching for the first time a glimpse of some dead and forgotten planet" (*Princess* 20). A few moments later Carter remarks, "I opened my eyes upon a strange and weird landscape. I knew that I was on Mars" (ibid). To reinforce the interplanetary analogy, Carter himself immediately notes the similarity between the sun in Arizona and on Mars: "It was midday, the sun was shining full upon my naked body, yet no greater than would have been true under similar conditions on an Arizona desert" (21). The common unreality of the West and Mars illustrates the othering of native cultures, their anachronistic quality, and the "alienation" of the western hero/reader/writer from native peoples and cultures (Street 21–2).

All of these elements are embodied in Roy Harvey Pearce's examination of American attitudes towards Native Americans and the importance of the concept of "savagism" to American identity. Pearce's analysis provides a more detailed, 19th century western context for John Carter, in contrast to Paul Carter's brief summary of the stereotypical western Mars Burroughs created. Pearce observes,

> For the American before 1850—a new man, as he felt, making a new world—was obsessed to know who and what he was and where he was going, to evaluate the special society in which he lived and to know its past and its future. One means to do this was to compare himself with the Indian who, as a savage, had all past and no future. The final result was an image of the Indian as man out of society and out of history. (135)

It is important to note the self-centered and imaginative use of natives by Anglo men emphasized in this passage. As fictional characters and as objects of scientific and historical study, natives or primitives are constructed by and for the needs and desires of Anglo men. In this case, like Haraway, Pearce analyzes the association of primitive people from foreign lands with the past and stagnation and Anglo men with the future and progress. The American West and Native Americans provide an early American version of the primitive, exploration, and colonialism; other terrestrial natives, like the Philippinoes during the Spanish-American War, and extraterrestrial natives provide subsequent venues for similar ideology and actions. In his book, *Wilderness and the American Mind*, Roderick Nash highlights an additional factor in the perceived unreality of "exotic lands and their inhabitants" (Street 21). Burroughs' description of the American West participates in the Euro-American ideology which criticizes Native American cultures for not properly utilizing the land; civilization involves transforming this 'empty' and 'unused' land (i.e. wilderness) into farmland and towns. As Nash summarizes, for "primitive man [. . . , s]afety, happiness, and progress all seemed dependent on rising out of a wilderness situation [. . .]. Gradually man learned how to control the land and raise crops. Clearings appeared in the forests. This reduction of the amount of wilderness defined man's achievement as he advanced toward civilization" (9).[32] Again, Native Americans are associated with the past and the primitive in terms of a lack of civilization and also in their association with American wilderness (Nash 28). The (perceived) primitive, anachronistic qualities of the Native Americans and their 'improper use' of the land and natural resources both served as justifications for western colonialism. As Native Americans were not a part of western progress, (Anglo-Americans believed that) they did not deserve their land, and their culture(s) must give way before a 'superior' mode of living—future-oriented, developmental western progress.

Pearce's insights into the connections between (white) Americans and ethnic Others foreground the importance of hierarchical comparisons to the construction of Anglo manhood, as well as the development of specifically American identity, values, and concepts. First, a brief overview of John Carter's relationship to both the terrestrial and extraterrestrial natives is in order, setting up the more extended analysis of the similarities between the Native Americans and the Martian natives which follows. Once the common setting has been established, Carter meets the first Martian natives/aliens, a race of green, insect-like humanoids, who bear a striking resemblance to the Native Americans he has just encountered. In case the green skin coloring and insectile features confuse the reader, Carter himself calls the green men "warriors, for I could not disassociate these people in my mind from those other warriors who, only the day before, had been pursuing me" (*Princess* 24). In this way, Burroughs uses the green men as an imaginative vehicle for promoting fundamental values and concepts involved in the ideology of western progress: Christianity, individualism, capitalism, and evolutionary progress. By transforming the Native Americans of the American West into insect-like aliens, Burroughs emphasizes the (assumed) lower physical order, more primitive culture, and lesser intelligence of native peoples. This leaves Carter (white, southern male) as the representative of American society and its ideals.

Consequently, Carter often analyzes the Martian natives and their culture(s) as if he were Haraway's (contradictory) "universal" and superior Anglo-scientist. As he notes biological and cultural characteristics, Carter takes part in the western discourse of scientific discovery, exploration, and classification associated with colonialism, empire, and ethnic othering. The cultural bias of the observer or ethnographer is most evident in the descriptive language used in the representation of the natives. It is through Carter's interested/privileged point of view and his representation of native cultures and peoples that Burroughs indirectly reinforces dominant, Anglo, Christian, 'American' values and beliefs. Much like the creation of many imaginative u/dystopias, the multiple elsewheres of the Mars series involve a biased observer. From the home culture of the author/audience, the observer's main focus is a foreign society and its difference. Without this (direct or indirect) comparison and the hierarchy of cultural values it creates, without the ethnic or racial Other in Burroughs' texts, Anglo manhood and American identity could not be constructed. Due to the first-person narrative; the exaggerated portrayal of Carter as a hero; the construction of Carter as both a universal and a white, southern male hero; and the lack of alternative viewpoint, the text as a whole promotes the same cultural hierarchy—ethnic/racial, national, economic, gender, political—as does John Carter.

Burroughs first utilizes the American valorization of Christianity to promote western progress. Similar to earlier representation of Native Americans in the West, the Martian natives are viewed and judged through a spiritual lens. Carter's descriptions of the green men augment the negative qualities of such a native association, reveal a dominant ideology underlying native representations, and emphasize the motivation behind the construction of Others. Further developing the spiritual representation of the Native Americans, begun in the darkness and unreality of the cave scene and the Arizona landscape at night, Carter describes his first view of a large encampment of "half a thousand red warriors" and the body of his (Anglo) friend Powell "[u]nder the clear rays of the Arizona moon" (*Princess* 14). Previously Carter and Powell "were wont to ridicule the stories [they] heard of the great numbers of these vicious marauders that were supposed to haunt the trails, taking their toll in lives and torture of every white party which fell into their merciless clutches," but Carter becomes "positive" that the Apaches "wished to capture Powell alive for the fiendish pleasure of torture" (12–3). Similar to these descriptions of Native Americans, the green Martian natives are described as "devils," "huge and terrific incarnation[s] of hate, of vengeance and of death," and a "materialized nightmare" (23). In addition, "[t]he death agonies of a fellow being are, to these strange creatures [the green Martians], provocative of the wildest hilarity, while their chief form of commonest amusement is to inflict death on their prisoners of war in various ingenious and horrible ways" (29). In this way, both native groups are portrayed as embodying a spiritual darkside. They are "devils" (or witches) associated with darkness, night, the moon, nightmares, and the negative qualities of hatred, torture, revenge, and death. Within this context, natives are the antithesis of the positive qualities and symbols associated with Christianity—light, love, angels, forgiveness, compassion, life, and divine revelation.

Although Burroughs does not promote Christianity directly in his writings, his language and characterization here take part in the larger good/evil discourse stemming from the western/American valorization of Christianity and the intersection of religion with morality, nationality, race, and imperialism. In a complex web of associations, the 'pagan' spiritual beliefs and practices of native peoples are an evaluative criteria for their classification by Europeans as savages or primitives. Conversely, their characterization as savages, primitives, and/or natives includes a historical, ideological, and linguistic legacy of spiritual/moral denigration and/ or demonization. From the Puritan perspective, for example, "the natives were not merely heathens but active disciples of the devil" (Nash 36). Thus, the association of native peoples with spiritual darkness, mysticism, and superstition is a criterion for their classification as uncivilized—such a definition reflecting the comparison and hierarchical cultural values being utilized in such classification (Christianity, progress, land ownership/cultivation, etc.). Furthermore, the long tradition of primitivism and savagism in European and Anglo-American thought and practice usually entails the representation of natives as spiritually inferior, deviant, and/or anachronistic. Burroughs' Mars series is a good illustration of this cultural, linguistic, and literary legacy.

Finally, the spiritual othering of natives justifies the suppression of their culture and/or race. Within the larger historical picture, we see the immorality and pagan classification of native peoples serving as a rationale for Euro-American colonialism and imperialism. Renowned American forefather, Benjamin Franklin once wrote of Native Americans:

> Their dark-coloured bodies, half-naked, seen only by the gloomy light of the bonfire, running after and beating one another with fire-brands, accompanied by their horrid yellings, formed a scene the most resembling our ideas of hell that could be well imagined. [. . . I]f it be the design of Providence to extirpate these savages in order to make room for the cultivators of the earth, it seems not improbable that rum may be the appointed means. It has already annihilated all the tribes who formerly inhabited all the seacoast . . . (Lawrence 21)

Franklin illustrates his western, American bias as he attributes the demise of the Native Americans solely to their own immorality and divine intervention, eliding the material contact and conflict between the Native Americans and Euro-Americans. Burroughs' southern slavery, western expansion, Indian fighting, and representation of the green Martians are logical extensions of such colonial American views. Because the Apaches and the green natives are immoral—they attack innocent, out-numbered whites solely for the purpose of torture—Carter is justified in killing as many of the natives as possible.

The negative spiritual and moral representation of natives allows them to act as a foil to the hero as well. They provide an enemy or adversary to illustrate the hero's extraordinary attributes and the superiority of his race and cultural values. For example, John Carter illustrates his heroism, his goodness and morality by attempting to rescue his friend, even after it is clear that Powell is dead. Furthermore, Carter's attempt is in the face of overwhelming odds and the extraordinary viciousness and cruelty of his native opponent. Whereas the natives attack, unprovoked and for the purpose of torture only, Carter loyally rescues a friend. The American natives "mutilat[e]"; Carter saves from mutilation (*Princess* 14). The green natives attack a peaceful flying ship (43) and plan to torture and kill a defenseless young woman for entertainment (49); Carter protects and eventually frees the previously unknown prisoner. In addition, Thomas Dyer's analysis of Theodore Roosevelt and his relationship to Native Americans clarifies the paradox at the heart of the Wilderness Cult: how to promote fighting abilities, while also maintaining cultural hierarchies. As Dyer notes, "[i]f the white advance were to be heroic, and the white frontiersman were to be judged an able, virile fighter in the idealistic mold Roosevelt cast for him, then the foe must be a redoubtable warrior too" (75). One answer is to portray the natives as physically powerful, skilled in warfare, and cunning to serve as worthy adversaries, but also spiritually/morally deviant or inferior in order to justify the hero's actions as he fights, kills, and/or conquers them.

Carter, and the larger text, reflects the complex ideology of western, American superiority by acknowledging the simplistic virtues of primitive societies, but overwhelmingly critiquing such societies in so far as they deviate from the accepted cultural, i.e. universal, norms of American society and its privileging of western progress. This complex and powerfully ethnocentric viewpoint is most clearly seen in the description and evaluation of native cultures and their collectivity or communalism. Because the natives refute the individualism and property ownership valued by western culture, they are perceived as unnatural and lower in the social order. In a move similar to the internalized and obscured oppression of the slaves on Burroughs' family plantation, the green natives are most overtly censored by a Martian of another race—a red Martian princess named Dejah Thoris. Her impassioned and highly critical speech embodies the values and hierarchies of western, American progress without jeopardizing the scientific detachment of John Carter:

> must you ever go on down the ages to your final extinction but little above the plane of the dumb brutes that serve you! A people without written language, without art, without homes, without love; the victim of eons of the horrible community idea. Owning everything in common, even to your women and children, has resulted in your owning nothing in common. You hate each other as you hate all else except yourselves. (*Princess* 54)

Within western ideology, individualism and property are essential for civilization and culture—a written language and the arts, a stationary abode, the nuclear family, and romantic love. Although Thoris is a Martian, her speech is an adaptation of early colonial, Euro-American descriptions of Native Americans. According to Reverend Samuel Purchas, for example, "[t]he Indians are 'so bad people, having little of Humanitie but shape, ignorant of Civilitie, of Arts, of Religion; more brutish then the beasts they hunt, more wild and unmanly then that unmanned wild Countrey, which they range rather than inhabite; captivated also to Satans tyranny in [. . .] wicked idlenesse'" (qtd. . in Pearce 7–8).[33] This passage emphasizes the nomadic existence, the animality, and the lack of culture observed in the green natives by Thoris. Implied in the negative evaluations of both the Native Americans and the green Martians is the necessity to convert them to western, American values. They "need to be matured in rich, complex, civilized humanity. The primary means to this are private property and the division of labor, as these mark the end of human progress toward its goal of high civilization" (Pearce 85).

According to western, American ideology, a lack of individualism retards progress because communalism stifles industry, competition, and invention—the cornerstones of capitalism. Highly successful capitalist, Andrew Carnegie makes these connections clear: "Individualism, Private Property, the Law of Accumulation of Wealth, and the Law of Competition [. . . ,] these are the highest result of human experience [. . . ,] the best and most valuable of all that humanity has yet accomplished" (400). Without these values, the green natives will never progress. In fact, as Thoris emphasizes, they are actually regressing towards extinction. Carter himself notes the impact of a nomadic, communal lifestyle on the material advancement of the green natives; they are ill-suited culturally and physically for civilized environments:

> the creatures were entirely out of proportion to the desks, chairs, and other furnishings; these being of a size adapted to human beings such as I, whereas the great bulks of the Martians could scarcely have squeezed into the chairs, nor was there room beneath the desks for their long legs. Evidently, then, there were other denizens on Mars than the wild and grotesque creatures into whose hands I had fallen. (*Princess* 28)

Instead of a stationary existence in which the natives would construct permanent homes for themselves and develop urban areas (i.e. become civilized), the green men wander Mars and temporarily (and rather pathetically and laughably) occupy the cast-off and clearly ill-suited abodes of civilized, "fair-haired" humans more like John Carter (*Princess* 62). The communalism of the natives hinders their development, their cultural and material progress toward western norms and ideals. While the increased size of the green Martians may give them a physical advantage in the 'wilds,' this bodily focus fits the previously mentioned native stereotype of great strength combined with moral weakness.[34] Rather than material and cultural progression, then, terrestrial and extraterrestrial communalism promotes the negative characteristics of hatred, animality, and "extinction." In Thoris' speech this extinction is placed within the context of Social Darwinism, making it seem natural and inevitable, and this elides the conflict between terrestrial natives and the expansion of western peoples and culture. However, the direct connections to western, American progress reveal the threat of extinction for native peoples through conflict with dominant, white America and its values of individualism, property, capitalism, and progress.

In his position as explorer and scientist, Carter reinforces the negative evaluation of the green Martians and their communalism. He observes,

> [t]heir mating is a matter of community interest solely, and is directed without reference to natural selection. The council of chieftains of each community control the matter as surely as the owner of a Kentucky racing stud directs the scientific breeding of his stock for the improvement of the whole.
>
> In theory it may sound well, [. . .] but the results of ages of this unnatural practice, coupled with the community interest in the offspring

being held paramount to that of the mother, is shown in the cold, cruel creatures, and their gloomy, loveless, mirthless existence.

It is true that the green Martians are absolutely virtuous, [. . .] but better far a finer balance of human characteristics even at the expense of a slight and occasional loss of chastity. (*Princess* 67)

In this way, the natives are 'scientifically' classified as uncivilized or lower in the social and natural order because of their unnatural and animal-like cultural practices. In their rejection of both romantic love and sexual attraction, the natives foster a collective ideal which actually places them below the natural animals. Carter's emphasis on the importance of the mother mirrors Thoris' earlier speech as well; the concept of the nuclear family underlies both their definitions of "home," love, and 'proper' reproduction (*Princess* 54). Even a 'virtue' such as chastity, whose acknowledgement should illustrate the objective viewpoint of the western observer/scientist, is contorted to become another characteristic which classifies the natives as subhuman. In a lengthy explication of *The Sexual Life of Savages* (1929) by ethnographer Bronislaw Malinowski, Marianna Torgovnick emphasizes a similar combination of overt cultural bias with "substantial faith in [the scientist-observer's] authority and in the power of neutral observation" (4). Burroughs constructs Carter not just as a universal and representative white, American hero; in his position as first-person narrator, Carter becomes an explorer and scientist who observes and writes as an ethnographer. In this way, Carter moves beyond the tradition of gentlemen explorers such as Henry M. Stanley and Theodore Roosevelt.[35] His authority is not only cultural, historical, and/or political, but also scientific. The factual, impersonal, objective reputation of science reinforces the reliability of Carter's narrative position and disguises cultural bias as natural hierarchies. In addition to Carter as an ethnographic narrator, Burroughs constructs a reproductive system for the green Martians which reinforces the hierarchy of western, white, and civilized as superior to native, colored, and primitive. As insect humanoids, the green Martians lay eggs which are incubated collectively, in isolation from the adults, in large enclosures resembling reptile nests. Thus, the green Martians are literally cold-blooded insects or reptiles who are lower in the evolutionary order than mammals—animal or human. Their biological inferiority is seconded by their cultural inferiority, as they differentiate themselves from even many cold-blooded life forms by not individually (or as a nuclear family, husband-wife couple) caring for a single 'nest.'

The systematic and sustained resistance by native peoples to conversion attempts by Euro-Americans contradicted and hindered the western, American concept of progress—cultural, historical, geographic, economic, biological, etc.

Like the denigration and demonization of natives because of their resistance to Christianity and the moral and cultural norms of Euro-Americans, natives were placed within larger historical, cultural, and biological continuums which often had devastating effects. Roy Harvey Pearce explains the historical and cultural continuums of progress utilized in evaluating Native Americans and the price paid for their resistance to assimilation or 'uplifting': "The idea of history as progress made it possible fully to comprehend the culturally earlier as the morally inferior, even as an environmentalist analysis of societies made it possible to account for the contemporaneity of that which should have been part of the past. Savagism could be known only in terms of the civilization to which, by the law of nature, it had to give way" (104). In a similar manner, John Carter first evaluates the green natives in terms of their deficient cultural progress, but then he adds a biological component as well. In describing the reaction of the green natives to Thoris' civilizing speech, Carter links the natives' inferior cultural "customs" to their (presumably inferior) biological "heredity":

> that they were moved I truly believe, and if one man high among them had been strong enough to rise above custom, that moment would have marked a new and mighty era for Mars.
>
> I saw Tars Tarkas rise to speak, and on his face was such an expression as I had never seen upon the countenance of a green Martian warrior. It bespoke an inward and mighty battle with self, with heredity, with age old custom [. . .]. (*Princess* 54)

It seems there is the real potential for change, for progress, for civilization for native people. However, true to the experiences of Euro-American missionaries, this optimism quickly turns into an even more extreme and entrenched negativity as the natives resist conversion/civilization/assimilation.

When another green warrior strikes Dejah Thoris (an unarmed and peaceful woman) to the ground and places his foot upon her in a gesture of superiority and contempt, he reasserts the common, primitive, non-chivalrous cultural values of the green natives. Thus, the green men prove their resistance to change and to thinking and acting independently of one another—rejecting the western ideal of individualism and maintaining their collectivity. Furthermore, the hereditary basis for their primitive, collective behavior emphasizes their biological **inability** to progress. In contrast to John Carter's freedom from the past, individualism, and self-reliance (represented by his lack of ancestors and solitary status), the natives are fundamentally shaped by their past, by their collective ancestral group. Within western ideology, this episode proves that the natives are and always will be "historically anterior and morally inferior" to western society, as well as biologically anachronistic and stagnant (Pearce 105). Euro-American ethnocentrism and their pervasive belief in western progress prevented them from comprehending or accepting the resistance of natives to their way of life. If the elements of western progress actually meant beneficial, sustained, and natural change or development (i.e. the definition of progress), then it was incomprehensible to Euro-Americans that anyone would reject such elements. As a result, Euro-Americans used the biological components to explain the continued resistance of natives to their 'logically beneficial' changes. Rather than admit that western progress was a faulty concept, Euro-Americans constructed a biological essentialism for native races. In resisting the concept of progress, then, the natives were perceived by Euro-Americans not as simply different or neutral factors, but as vital threats to the western, American way of life; they retarded western progress as a whole. Furthermore, because native resistance was based on immutable, biological factors, the only real solution was the eradication of the race or extinction of the native groups.

In addition to the hereditary basis of the native resistance, Burroughs more directly utilizes the biological theory of progress, generally conceived as evolution, through Carter's ethnographic perspective. Placing Carter's scientific evaluations within the turn-of-the-century context of biological evolution and American immigration highlights the hierarchical and exclusionary basis of 'objective' science and the continued subjectivity of 'progressive' thought. First, Morse Peckham asserts that "evolution may be considered as a fairly straightforward metaphysical theory with a long history" that existed prior to Darwin's 1859 *Origin of the Species* (23). In fact, Peckham observes that this existing metaphysical evolution "was not so much confirmed by [Darwin's] theory of natural selection as embarrassed by it" (ibid).[36] Thus, Burroughs (Carter) actually takes part in a long tradition of misreading Darwin's work, choosing to promote metaphysical or Social Darwinism which incorporates "values into a descriptive construct" (Peckham 20).[37] In contrast to Darwin's "accident" (29), imperfect adaptation (31), and the impossibility of total human comprehension of the physical world (3), metaphysical evolution substitutes a "goal-directed process" of "simple to complex means from good to better" (Peckham 29). The distinction Peckham makes between Darwinism and Darwinisticism (Social Darwinism being a primary form of the later) highlights the hierarchical and biased nature of the Euro-American viewpoint, even when encased in scientific language and theory. Carter, for example, embodies Social Darwinism in his description of the head chieftain of the green men:

> this monster was the exaggerated personification of all the ages of cruelty, ferocity, and brutality from which he had descended. Cold, cunning,

calculating; he was, also, in marked contrast to most of his fellows, a slave to that brute passion which the waning demands for procreation upon their dying planet has almost stilled in the Martian breast.

The thought that the divine Dejah Thoris might fall into the clutches of such an abysmal atavism started the cold sweat upon me. Far better that we save friendly bullets for ourselves at the last moment, as did those brave frontier women of my lost land, who took their own lives rather than fall into the hands of the Indian braves. (*Princess* 65)

Carter's use of the term atavism appeals to the objective authority of science. However, Carter reveals his Social Darwinism in such highly negative, evaluative words as "cruelty, ferocity, and brutality." His reference to the American West and the Native American/pioneer conflict only emphasizes the biased or subjective nature of the purported objective, universal perspective of scientific discourse. The scientific concept of atavism relies on a hierarchical, value-motivated biological continuum as well—the concept of progress. Finally, as mentioned previously, Euro-Americans used the biological basis of the social behavior and cultural norms of the natives to foreground their inability to change as well.

These same issues become even more relevant in the context of the anti-immigration debate at the turn of the century. If inferior 'races' are unable to change, to assimilate, or in other words, to become good (like dominant, Anglo) Americans, then their physical presence becomes a threat to American progress through the possibility of interbreeding. American biological progress becomes a matter of protecting the 'white' race from the inferior blood of darker-skinned races. The threat of rape in Carter's passage reflects this concern. Similar to the arguments of many Anglo-American, anti-immigration advocates at the turn of the century, Burroughs privileges blood over environment. In 1912, Prescott Hall wrote, "Recent investigations in eugenics show that heredity is a much more important factor than environment as regards social conditions—in fact, that in most cases heredity is what makes the environment" (300). The context of the anti-immigration debate reveals the racist basis of such biological arguments. Hall and Burroughs utilize biology, heredity, and/or race to scientifically 'prove' the inferiority of people-of-color and the superiority of Anglo-Americans. Hall targets the "barbarians" from Africa, Asia, and the "defective and delinquent classes of Europe" (298)—those from "entirely different races—of Alpine, Mediterranean, Asiatic, and African stocks" (297). In *A Princess of Mars*, Burroughs constructs the green natives as hereditarily, biologically atavistic—anachronistic and inferior. Not only are the green natives not progressing towards civilization, they are actually 'throw-backs' to past biological and cultural types.

Within this biological context, the natives are represented as anachro-nisms who threaten civilized society, especially through interbreeding. The anti-immigration emphasis on heredity over environment and the existence of racial characteristics imply such a process for the United States. Prescott Hall quotes Professor Karl Pearson: "'You cannot change the leopard's spots, and you cannot change bad stock to good; you may dilute it, possibly spread it over a large area, spoiling good stock, but until it ceases to multiply it will not cease to be'" (Hall 300). When a green Martian threatens to rape Dejah Thoris, it is not simply the emotional and physical trauma she would experience that concerns Carter. As a representative of western progress, she symbolizes the pure and privileged blood of white, American womanhood which must be protected from contami-nation by the recessive biological characteristics of natives, of people-of-color, of non-Anglo-Americans.[38] She is the "race mother" upon whose procreative func-tion rests the entire race (Doyle 5, 27). The theory of evolution here is used to illustrate the progressive racial characteristics of the white race and the static or regressive racial characteristics of people-of-color, thereby justifying or explain-ing their extinction or destruction and the continued and expanded power of Anglo-Europeans.

The pre-existing ethnocentrism of the Euro-American observer(s) com-bines with the ideology of historical, cultural, and biological progress to pre-vent an unbiased analysis of native cultures. As cultural theorist Renato Rosaldo argues, "the detached observer's authoritative objectivity resides more in a manner of speaking than in apt characterizations of other forms of life" (109). Houston Baker likewise foregrounds the connection between the ethnogra-pher and the larger cultural and political forces of her or his home country. For Baker, ethnography is "a writing of the 'Other' out of relationship to his or her native ground and into the sexual, commercial, voyeuristic fantasies of imperial-ism" (386). Donna Haraway supports both of these critiques of ethnographic objectivity in *Primate Visions*. As mentioned earlier, she discusses the similarities between the traditionally diametrically opposed categories of 'fact' and 'fiction' (3): "Scientific practice is above all a story-telling practice in the sense of his-torically specific practices of interpretation and testimony" (4). In this way, Har-away, Rosaldo, and Baker go one step beyond Peckham as they undermine even the objective, scientific, rather than metaphysical, nature of Darwin's work. By analyzing the (always) subjective element of scientific study and the privileged viewpoint of (western, Anglo, generally male) scientists, these authors highlight the hierarchical basis of science.

Using primatology as an especially fruitful lens for examining these issues, Haraway also emphasizes the importance of the concept of progress to scientific study:

> It is a story of progress from immature sciences based on mere description and free qualitative interpretation [Carter's method] to mature science based on quantitative methods and falsifiable hypotheses, leading to a synthetic scientific reconstruction of primate reality. But these histories are stories about stories, narratives with a good ending; i.e., the facts put together, reality reconstructed scientifically. These are stories with a particular aesthetic, realism, and a particular politics, commitment to progress. (4)

Thus, the material progress is enmeshed in the progress of the mediating tools as well. Although many contemporary writers and theorists are critical and/or wary of such value-laden "narratives," traditional western observers/scientists would feel doubly justified by them, since both their methods and the material illustrate their superiority, their continued progress. In *A Princess of Mars*, the material and historical progress experienced by John Carter is reflected in the narrative progress as well; the science of outer space is reflected in the science of Carter's narrative stance and style. The idea of the progress of science–away from superstition, emotion, values, and bias and towards a greater factual 'truth'–lends authority to Carter and his text. The irony, of course, is that Haraway's observations reveal the fictional foundation of Burroughs' science. Carter's position and viewpoints as a scientist are doubly fictional—science itself is a "story" and the Mars series is science fiction.[39]

MARS

While Burroughs (re)creates a cultural and racial hierarchy in the Mars series which privileges western man, there are several key areas in which this pyramid is undermined. As discussed earlier, the imaginative setting of Mars allows Burroughs to construct a planet which reflects his personal beliefs and views. In turning to science fiction and outer space, Burroughs has a much greater creative license than in the American West or even the tropics. One area he manipulates actually contradicts the science-focus of the outer-space setting: Burroughs creates a Mars which embodies an 'ideal' synthesis of the civilized and the primitive—through the red Martians and their society. Although this setting, contradictorily, illustrates the superiority of Carter as an ideal warrior hero, it also undermines some aspects of western progress. In addition, free from earth history, Burroughs creates an egalitarian brotherhood of fighting men, composed of various Martian races. This band of Carter's personal friends embodies the American ideals of freedom and equality, outside of the hierarchical boundaries of actual American society. The red Martians also represent the ideal of the American melting pot, as they are a composite race made up of various, older 'primary' Martian races. The red race stands in marked contrast to the strict boundaries between races and the fear of interbreeding exposed in Carter's observations on the green Martians. Finally, Martian mythology reverses the evolutionary hierarchy of black/primate/stagnant/less developed to white/human/progressive/advanced. In this way, Burroughs utilizes the story-making potential of science, revealed by Haraway, to question the racial and cultural hierarchy he upholds elsewhere. The elsewhere of outer space and the genre of science fiction, then, offer the possibility of a revision of traditional power hierarchies, for a literal 'progressive' change.

The lack of a historical legacy in the Mars context allows Burroughs to create a specifically American hero who represents 'progressive' American ideals, such as equality and diversity, and whose relationships with Martian natives undermine some aspects of western progress. Hence, we have greater discrepancy and conflict between a more inclusive, egalitarian social model and traditional hierarchies in the Mars series than in Burroughs' Tarzan series or most other African narratives by European writers. Marianna Torgovnick traces a progression in Burroughs' Tarzan series from "expos[ing] the shaky basis of [existing] hierarchies" to the increasing "affirm[ation of] existing hierarchies, including the hierarchy of male over female, white over black, West over rest" (46). Because Tarzan is British aristocracy and the Tarzan series takes place in Africa, the narrative(s) participates historically and fictionally in the colonial ideals and practices of Europeans. As Tarzan matures, he cannot retain the innocence of childhood; as he comes to understand who he is and his place in the world, racial and cultural hierarchies are learned as well. Earlier European narratives of Africa also set a pattern for Burroughs to follow. From Henry M. Stanley to Rider Haggard, non-fiction and fiction authors had utilized Africa as a resource—for colonialism and imperialism, for the construction of white manhood, and for the construction of narratives.[40] In the Mars series, there is no such historical legacy. In fact, the pre-existing scientific and literary concept of Mars as a more civilized society than that of Earth meant that Burroughs actually had to modify the existing template in order to make Carter a western hero at all. In moving away from the specific historical past of the American West and the actual history of Earth completely, Burroughs reverses the progression Torgovnick analyzes in the Tarzan series.

In the Mars context, Burroughs revises the turn-of-the-century wilderness nostalgia associated with the American West and also the terrestrial tropics. Outside of the bounds of American history and society, Burroughs can create a native society which is the ideal synthesis of primitive and civilized, that of the red Martians. The Martians have developed advanced air transportation and atmospheric technology, and the red Martians are interested in scientific activities (*Princess* 53). However, even the red Martians, who represent the most developed (living) culture on Mars, exist in a medieval society, with castles, hand-to-hand combat, and an aristocracy. Furthermore, they do not have any industrial components to their society. The red Martians are not as civilized as the ancient white race of Martians whose ruins dot the Martian landscape, but their largely pre-modern society is the ideal combination of primitive and civilized elements to appeal to Carter, and to a turn-of-the-century audience as well. Within this cultural bricolage, Americans can both maintain their social privilege and physical comfort and establish a pre-industrial relation to nature, complete with an opportunity to prove their physical prowess. The red skin color of this composite group could be modeled on eastern earth cultures generally perceived by westerners as "a midway stage between the primitive and the civilized," Egypt and India in particular (Torgovnick 60). Thus, the green Martians represent the complete primitive, like the Native Americans in the American context, serving as an ignoble enemy for Carter to battle so his heroism can be continuously illustrated. The red Martians are constructed as an intermediary race/culture so that Carter can both prove his superiority as a Euro-American and take part in a romance.

This intermediary state is reflected in the climate, the clothing, and the technological advancement of the Martians. First, the atmosphere is not only habitable for humans, but the climate is semi-tropical. Therefore, the major-ity of Martians, and John Carter, regularly live in a semi- to fully nude state of (un)dress. Certainly this Martian social norm owes much to sex appeal, the fantasy genre, and western narratives about the (usually colonial or impe-rial) tropics. However, the pre-modern, pre-industrial state of the Martians (or their selective technological development) appeals to John Carter to the extent that he becomes an active member of their community, establishes a family, and pines for Mars when he involuntarily returns to Earth. Simi-lar to Burroughs' subsequent hero, Tarzan, Carter is metaphorically 'born,' completely naked and without weapons, and finds himself in a dangerous, threatening foreign society. Both protagonists have lost their technological advantage as Europeans. In becoming a member of the foreign society, they both continue their primitive state of dress and hone their physical qualities.

However, the imaginary setting, combined with the red Martian synthesis of primitive and civilized characteristics, allows Carter to more fully integrate into this foreign culture than the Native American culture of the American West or Tarzan within the colonial context of Africa. Likewise, Burroughs portrays Carter's cultural assimilation and racial interbreeding as natural and positive developments. Thus, the limited or selective technological development of the red Martians and Carter's unprecedented level of accepted cultural assimilation undermine some elements of western progress.[41]

As Brian Street notes, however, the lack of clothing is a complex factor in that it illustrates an acceptance of the cultural norms of the ethnic Other, while simultaneously proving the physical equality or superiority of the Euro-American hero. Again, like Tarzan, Carter "represents the merging of the accepted intellectual superiority of the Englishman [American] with great physical qualities" (Street 20). Furthermore, like the intermediate frontiersman of the American West, Carter's genteel background and Anglo blood ensure his position of superiority in a primitive or semi-primitive society. As a result, Carter quickly becomes the most famous warrior on all of Mars, feared by his enemies and revered by his friends. Without advanced technology or armor, armed with only a sword, Carter 'conquers' a more primitive society on its own terms; his only advantage is a more developed physical system due to the lessened Martian gravity.

Carter's warrior adventures also allow Burroughs to challenge the hierarchies established in other areas of the Martian series through the creation of a diverse brotherhood of fighting men centered around John Carter. Carter slowly accumulates friends from among all the races of Mars—green, red, black, yellow, and white—as his adventures take him to the corners of the globe. Toward the end of the second book in the Mars series, *The Gods of Mars*, Carter takes stock of his companions: "In that little party there was not one who would desert another; yet we were of different countries, different colours, different races, different religions—and one of us was of a different world" (135). These are the democratic, egalitarian ideals of American society clearly expressed by an American, narrator and author. Adventure, fighting, male bonding, and most importantly, the influence, leadership, ideals, and superiority of an Anglo-American man unite otherwise separate and often conflicting societies.[42] Returning to the concept of American exceptionalism, John Carter symbolizes the unique and highly 'progressive' cultural factors associated with American society. Like the United States itself, Carter represents tolerance, equality, and unity based on individual attributes and personal worth, rather than external factors like heredity or material prosperity. Thus, Carter embodies the complex American contradiction of hierarchy based on equality—because of American exceptionalism, Americans deserve positions of greatest power. In fact, it is the "duty" of Americans to practice colonialism and imperialism because they must bring American civilization, including freedom and democracy, to others (Roosevelt, "Nation" 245). Carter's physical prowess, fighting abilities, and 'military' leadership reflect the conflict and native resistance usually involved in instituting these egalitarian ideals through such hierarchical systems.

Burroughs' choice of a male, quasi-military group for the embodiment of American egalitarian ideals illustrates his own experiences as well. It was only in the American military that Burroughs associated with ethnic Others on a roughly equal level—blacks, Native Americans, and foreign immigrants (Taliaferro 40, 42). Thus, Burroughs experienced ethnic and racial equality through a highly hierarchical institution founded on physical force and conquest (in this case the continued submission of Native Americans in the American West).[43] The military foundation of Burroughs' American equality reveals the individual nature of this equality. For example, individual Native Americans, like the Apache scouts Burroughs met in the calvary, could prove themselves worthy Americans by disassociating themselves from their tribes and joining an official American institution like the United States military. Cultural assimilation was the key to equality and acceptance; natives, African-Americans, and immigrants were expected to embrace American individualism and reject their particular cultural, ethnic, or racial (collective) heritage. Thus, they became like John Carter in the construction of Anglo-American heroes as solitary wanderers, without pasts or homes. Likewise, individual members of various Martian races could prove themselves worthy of a close, egalitarian relationship with John Carter by disassociating themselves from their particular cultural/racial communities. In this way, Burroughs can simultaneously promote hierarchical racial theories as applied to collective groups and egalitarian ideals as applied to particularly worthy (ethnic Other) individuals. He follows Theodore Roosevelt in "feeling comfortably consistent with evolutionary ideology and the rhetoric of equipotentiality alongside Republican politics in that [Roosevelt] allowed for the progress of individuals to the level of white men even if the race as a whole remained backward" (Dyer 105).

The biological characteristics of Martian evolution pose the most devastating challenge to existing terrestrial hierarchies. A striking example of American diversity and egalitarianism is the red race of Martians. As observed earlier, the red Martians are the most civilized living race on Mars. They are also a composite race, the result of "[a]ges of close relationship and intermarrying" among the white, the "very dark, almost black, and also with the reddish yellow race" (*Princess* 62). Furthermore, it is with the "fair and beautiful daughter" of this racial mix, Dejah Thoris, that Carter falls in love, marries, and produces a further racially-mixed child (ibid). In this case, Carter not only breaks existing terrestrial racial taboos (including the miscegenation laws existing in many states during this time period), but also terrestrial/extraterrestrial racial boundaries.[44] Only the green Martians are excluded from this environmentally motivated and apparently positive racial intermixing. Within the American context, such a racial philosophy is known as the melting pot, and Native Americans were conspicuously absent from the mix.[45] Thus, Burroughs retains one race (the green Martians/Native Americans) to represent the primitive, the race most relevant to America, reputed to be inassimilable, and the one from which Euro-Americans desired the most materially. Nonetheless, the inclusive racial theory embodied in the fictional evolution of the red race stands in marked contrast to the other hierarchical, race-based tenets expressed in the narrative. I would argue that it is only within the highly imaginative space of another planet that Burroughs was willing or able to visualize the diverse, intimate community of the fighting band discussed above and the more radical, racial intermixing of the red Martians. Within the context of actual American society, as with the Native Americans/green Martians discussed earlier, Burroughs maintains racial boundaries that are discarded outside of the specifics of American society or Earth history more generally.

Other biological or racial examples foster a more egalitarian ethos as well. For example, the Martians perceive Carter himself as combining features of the different Martian races: he has the white skin of the white race but the dark hair of the black race (*Gods* 67). Furthermore, Burroughs subtly undermines the evolutionary tenets found in other areas of the narrative through the alternative perspective of a "Dator" or prince of the First Born, the black race of Mars (68). As explained to Carter, the First Born are so called because their "race is the oldest on the planet" and the emergence of all the other races was dependent on the action of the "first black man" (ibid). Although there is no other substantiation of this creation myth, created by the black race itself, Burroughs never contradicts it or offers an alternative myth by a member of another racial group. Burroughs also reverses the evolutionary hierarchy of (black) primate to (white) western man in transforming the apes of Mars into great white apes and placing the black race in a position of prominence. It is the twisted remnants of the white race, the therns, that are the most corrupt race on Mars. The ancient white race of Martians also serves as an example of strict Darwinian biological theory rather than the Spencerian theory of progressive biological and cultural evolution found in other areas of the text.[46] It is explained that the highly specialized white race, a "highly cultivated and literary race," was forced to integrate with the other races in order to survive changes in the Martian environment (*Princess* 62–3). Over the centuries "much of the high civilization and many of the arts of the fair-haired Martians had become lost" (62). All that remains is the composite red race, with its more "practical civilization"; numerous ruins which dot the Martian landscape; and the inbred, bald, and corrupt white therns (ibid). The ancient white race can serve as an example of the heights of western civilization and be used as a comparison to the primitive culture of the green Martians, as noted earlier. However, Burroughs also illustrates the fragility and vulnerability of such a specialized 'organism' in the face of larger environmental factors. He turns Spencer's theory of "'survival of the fittest'" on its head as he redefines "'the fittest'" to be the most primitive, uncivilized (green) race rather than the white, ruling elite (Hofstadter 392–9).

PROGRESS

Examining Burroughs' use of the western concept of progress reveals the multiple inspirations, contexts, and applications such a nebulous term can have. On one side, Burroughs illustrates the ethnocentrism and ethnic othering involved in western progress. On the other, some of the ideals associated with American progress, like equality, are actually realized in Burroughs' science fiction. Torgovnick traces the strangled potential of Burroughs' Tarzan series but does not attempt to explain either why Burroughs would be interested in exploring less oppressive and hierarchical relationships or why he then felt compelled to reassert the existing hierarchies. Perhaps the illogical nature of the development stymies such an investigation. The concept of western progress itself reflects the primacy of change in western culture, from bad to good, undesirable to desirable, primitive to civilized. Within this framework, Burroughs would be expected to move from more conservative to more liberal and from a promotion of dominant hierarchies to the possibility of alternative relationships. He should leave behind the prejudices of the Old World, as de Crévecoeur asserts, and take part in the new, improved American, egalitarian melting pot. Not only does Burroughs not follow this western, American blueprint of progression in his Tarzan series, but also the alternation of the writing and publication of his Mars and his Tarzan series (along with other series) reveals a continuous and pervasive inconsistency in his political, social, and racial viewpoints. The increasing emphasis on egalitarianism in the Mars series, for example, was continually undermined by the increasing social and racial rigidity of the Tarzan series. With no actual progression, either positive or negative, to follow, critics generally react in one of two ways. First, many do not address the inconsistency of Burroughs' views, usually choosing to focus on his infamous racism or solely on his popularity as an adventure writer.[47] Others, like Torgovnick and Taliaferro, more accurately note the inconsistencies but do not attempt to explain why they exist. Both of these critical responses overlook the complexity of Burroughs and his writing, leading to a one-sided characterization or a confusing, contradictory list of quotes.

Looking at the convergence of the western concept of progress with Burroughs' writing reveals some possible origins of his inconsistencies. The multifarious definitions and applications of the term itself lead to inconsistent usage. As I have tried to illustrate with various American authors from across the centuries, American ideology and society have been split, from the very beginning of European colonization, between the reality of hierarchical power relations and the ideals of individualism, democracy, freedom, and equality. Acknowledging this contradiction or paradox, Toni Morrison argues that "[t]he concept of freedom did not emerge in a vacuum. Nothing highlighted freedom—if it did not in fact create it—like slavery" (38). Burroughs continues to embody this contradictory stance in his writings of the twentieth century. As a western, American hero, John Carter is both ideal representative of egalitarian opportunity and also southern gentleman and Confederate war hero. Western progress embodies primitive/civilized hierarchies, as well as increasing diversity and egalitarianism. Furthermore, the multiple contexts, the progress of elsewheres in the Mars series—historically, spatially, and generically—changes the definition and possibilities of western progress. In the American West, egalitarianism only applies to John Carter, as a frontiersman, and western progress means the eradication of the native Indian population. On Mars, egalitarianism applies to a wider range of natives and races, and western progress means cultural and racial assimilation with the natives. Western progress involves the concept of the ever-expanding frontier; it necessarily leads from the western frontier to terrestrial imperialism to extraterrestrial imperialism and the imagined, possibly utopian space of another planet. The setting, the time period, and the genre influence the author. With the expanded possibility of outer space and science fiction, Burroughs emphasizes different elements of western progress. The single narrator/protagonist unites the elsewheres, while personally enacting these changes. John Carter's contradictions and inconsistencies, as well as the continual flux of his life, make him a more representative American than if he embodied a single, static concept of American society.

While Burroughs certainly subscribes to many of the oppressive ideologies of his time period and his personal racial, socio-economic, and gender positions, his science fiction contains the seeds of 'progressive' change. He offers an example of the liberating potential of science fiction as his viewpoint becomes more egalitarian, diverse, and inclusive when writing in the extraterrestrial space of another planet. While the science fiction field as a whole continued to avoid and suppress the issue of race throughout much of the twentieth century, an increasing number of individual science fiction authors followed in Burroughs' footsteps. They not only addressed the issue of race in their texts directly and in depth, but also many of these authors expanded the small element of potential found in Burroughs' writing to include more inclusive and radical reevaluations of existing hierarchies. Writing in the 1930s, George S. Schuyler was the next author chronologically to develop this aspect of Burroughs' work. Utilizing the science fiction genre to explore race in American society, however, Schuyler broke away from the Anglo male triangle of protagonist/audience/author reflected so strongly in Burroughs' oeuvre. Likewise, he revised Burroughs' racial essentialism. Considering the time period and the powerful exclusion of race from the science fiction genre, it is not surprising that Schuyler's contribution to the field has not been generally recognized as a result. In extreme contrast to Burroughs' popular adventure texts, the literary community consistently associates Schuyler with criticism of the Harlem Renaissance. Despite their widely differing literary reputations, however, Burroughs and Schuyler shared a little-known interest in both science fiction and racial theories, which makes a comparison of their texts a fruitful area of critical inquiry.

Chapter Two
Schuyler

CRITICISM AND CONTEXT

Prior to the discovery and republication in 1991 of George S. Schuyler's serials "The Black Internationale" and "Black Empire," his fiction was thought to be limited to the 1931 satire *Black No More*.[1] The linking of Schuyler to multiple pseudonyms revealed a large new body of popular serial fiction he wrote during the 1930s.[2] "The Black Internationale: Story of Black Genius Against the World" and its sequel "Black Empire: An Imaginative Story of a Great New Civilization in Modern Africa" are two such serials Schuyler, using the pseudonym Samuel I. Brooks, contributed to the popular black weekly the *Pittsburgh Courier* between 1936 and 1938.[3] In "A Fragmented Man: George S. Schuyler and the Claims of Race," a 1992 *New York Times* Book Review, Henry Louis Gates Jr. used these newly discovered texts as a vehicle to reexamine Schuyler and his widely-fluctuating literary reputation. Gates begins his article by quoting some of Schuyler's most controversial statements critiquing Martin Luther King Jr. and the Civil Rights Movement and Malcolm X (31). After a review of Schuyler's two science fiction serials, Gates returns to the controversy surrounding Schuyler within the African-American community and asserts that "[i]f George Schuyler's place as a major figure in black letters has not been fully acknowledged, it is in part because his conception of the intellectual's role has never fully been appreciated" (43). For Schuyler, "skepticism, independent critical thinking and iconoclasm were part and parcel of the intellectual's calling, and [. . .] 'race loyalty' depended on just these qualities of mind" (ibid). While Gates does not excuse or elide Schuyler's extremely conservative viewpoints, especially later in life, he does place Schuyler squarely in the context of "the pressures of ideological conformity among blacks" (ibid). As the subtitle of Gates' article emphasizes, Schuyler has been and continues to be treated popularly and critically largely in terms of "the claims of race," judged according to his "race loyalty," or lack thereof (43). Furthermore, Gates claims that the evaluative criteria of "race loyalty" "haunts the lives of African-American intellectuals and public figures" more broadly (ibid). Gates seems to see hope in a "new generation of black intellectuals who are more likely than their forebears to recognize in the productive clash and contest of perspectives a source of strength" (ibid).

The most recent critical analysis of Schuyler, however, does not illustrate this ideal black intellectual response envisioned by Gates. In a lengthy critical response to Gates, aptly published in an anthology entitled *Race Consciousness: African-American Studies for the New Century*, Jeffrey A. Tucker asserts "the claims of race" and criticizes Schuyler and his texts directly and solely within a political context (Gates 31). Tucker focuses on both of Schuyler's major fictional texts: the aforementioned *Black No More* (1931) and the recently discovered serials, "The Black Internationale" and "Black Empire," which were collectively entitled *Black Empire* when republished in book form in 1991. Tucker claims that, "[a]n analysis of Schuyler's career reveals how Schuyler's racial theories anticipated those of the black neocons [of the 1970s, 80s, and 90s] and illustrate the logical limits and political inadequacies of such theories" ("Can" 137). In fact, Tucker refutes Gates' characterization of Schuyler as "a fragmented man" (Gates 32), who embodied W. E. B. Du Bois' theory of a black double-consciousness, and concludes that "by portraying Schuyler only as a victim of 'race,' Gates's portrait deactivates Schuyler's agency. As 'victim,' Schuyler seems less accountable for his always provocative but frequently fallacious, insupportable, and ultimately dangerous claims" (Tucker, "Can" 140). Gates' contextual information and Tucker's response to it symbolize the larger ideological struggles played out in response to Schuyler and his texts throughout his lengthy career.

Michael Peplow provides a useful overview of the critical reaction to Schuyler and his texts prior to the rediscovery of the two *Black Empire* serials.[4] In his 1976 article "The Black 'Picaro' in Schuyler's *Black No More*," Peplow first notes the generally favorable contemporary reactions to the original 1931 publication of *Black No More*. Linked to the Harlem Renaissance, *Black No More* was praised by W. E. B. Du Bois, Alain Locke, and Arthur Davis.[5] Peplow doesn't deny that "these men and others were quick to note the satire's literary flaws" but emphasizes that "none of them challenged Schuyler's *racial* loyalties" ("Black" 7). According to Peplow, it was not until later in Schuyler's career that the so-called "'assimilationism' theory" was developed (ibid). Robert Bone fostered this view of Schuyler in his 1965 critical text *The Negro Novel in America*, and Charles Larson reinforced the negative assimilationist label in his introduction to the 1971 republication of *Black No More*. To gain an adequate understanding of the great fluctuations in Schuyler's critical valuation, a connection to the historical context is essential. The critics of the 1960s and early 1970s faulted Schuyler for not promoting a collective racial identity, specifically one grounded in the Black Pride and/or Black Power movements of that time period. By the 1960s, Schuyler also had become notorious for his extreme political conservatism, in his personal and professional life. His political and racial viewpoints were increasingly distanced from the mainstream of the African-American community. As a result of this historical context, Peplow could accurately assess in 1976 that "the critics have ignored [Schuyler] entirely or merely mentioned the historical significance of *Black No More*" ("Black" 7). Writing in the 1990s, Jeffrey A. Tucker builds on this side of the Schuyler critical debate when he bases his critical evaluation of Schuyler on the political implications of Schuyler's racial theories.

Schuyler's death in 1977 coincided with a general swing of the political pendulum towards conservatism, and a more favorable critical evaluation ensued during the late 1970s and 1980s. In 1978, for example, Ann Rayson argues on Bone's own terms that "Schuyler, certainly not a black nationalist, is anything but an assimilationist" (102). In the same issue of the *Black American Literature Forum*, John M. Reilly places *Black No More* in the context of "the minor genre of the anti-utopia" (107). Taking issue with Larson's specific definition of assimilation, Reilly qualifies the assimilationist message of *Black No More*: "Assimilation, then, can only be an ideal. This, one might say, is nit-picking, and to a degree it is, but for the purpose of indicating that the logic of this anti-utopia neither leads to specific denigration of Blacks nor advocates mediocrity and the reduplication of white life-styles and culture" (108). Focusing on the **same** text, these critics produce more negative or more positive critical interpretations, largely based on the dominant political climate existing in the United States at the time of their writing.[6] With his 1976 article, "The Black 'Picaro' in Schuyler's *Black No More*," Peplow set the stage for Rayson and Reilly and their critique of the earlier assimilationism theory. Peplow gives three reasons for his refutation: the political basis of the literary criticism, the lack of historical contextualization, and the need to "examine the novel *as satire*" (7). All three of these are vital tools for a critical re-evaluation of Schuyler's texts, especially one not based solely on politics. When Henry Louis Gates, Jr. calls for a more inclusive critical environment in the field of African-American studies, he allies himself with this side of the Schuyler critical debate.

From the predominance of the assimilationism theory to a refutation of this theory based on its own theoretical terms and the less politically dogmatic and more literary-oriented evaluation of Peplow, this gradual shift in Schuyler criticism during the last half of the 20th century logically leads to an expanded connection between Schuyler and the field of science fiction in the 21st century. Schuyler's 1931 text, *Black No More*, always could have been defined as science fiction. However, because of its racial topic and the racial identification and professional affiliations of Schuyler, the text has been consistently discussed solely in the context of African-American literature. Even after the rediscovery of his additional science fiction serials, Schuyler's primary critical context remains African-American literature. The centrality of the political debate in Schuyler criticism continues to obscure both the radical nature of Schuyler's racial vision and the connection(s) of his major works to science fiction. The critical response to Schuyler's texts clearly reveals the distinct, mutual separation of the two literary fields of African-American literature and science fiction. This separation has led several science fiction critics to ask, "How do you account for the lack of involvement by blacks in science fiction and fantasy?" (Bell 91). Even after the professional establishment of several other black authors in the science fiction genre in the second half of the 20th century, and their reference to Schuyler as a predecessor, the generic separation remains strong.[7] A discussion of Schuyler's texts and the critical response to them within a science fiction context is essential for three reasons. First, the reasons behind the artificial separation of the two genres, science fiction and African-American literature, must be addressed. Second, such a context will reveal new and fruitful areas of Schuyler criticism. Finally, placing Schuyler's texts firmly within the science fiction genre contributes to a more accurate representation of the contributions of African-American writers to the science fiction genre.[8]

The 'science' half of the science fiction literary genre is the primary reason African-Americans, by-in-large, have avoided the genre. For example, the aforementioned debate between Henry Louis Gates Jr. and Jeffrey A. Tucker not only reflects the basic conflict within Schuyler criticism, but also it represents in miniature the larger debate currently taking place in the field of African-American studies. Writers and critics like Tucker and, more famously, Houston A. Baker promote the "claims of race" in the face of increasing scientific and poststructuralist challenges to the more traditional, essentialist concepts of race existing at the turn of the 19th century (Gates 31).[9] For instance, both Tucker and Baker address the writing of Kwame Anthony Appiah and take issue with his science-based critique of W. E. B. Du Bois and Du Bois' use of race. Tucker writes that "both Appiah and Schuyler base their arguments on the emptiness of 'race' as a scientific signifier, from which Appiah concludes that 'race' is an unnecessary evil" ("Can" 147). Tucker disagrees with such a stance because "'Race' is indeed a mirage scientifically speaking, and a construct socially, culturally, politically, and ideologically; but making this claim does not elide its power to shape human lives in very real ways" (148). Tucker seeks to maintain race as a viable concept despite its current lack of scientific credibility and faults Schuyler for utilizing science in his texts to deconstruct race.

In his essay, "Caliban's Triple Play," Houston A. Baker criticizes the scientific community more directly, sharing his concerns about the ideological foundations of the scientific discipline and its history of racial inequality. He summarizes the last approximately 150 years of modern science as follows: "Biology, anthropology, and the human sciences in general all believed, in former times, that there was such a phenomenon as 'race.' Current genetic research demonstrates that there is no such thing" (384). Similar to Tucker, Baker goes on to connect science and race with negative conservative political movements. Placing the scientific, social, and political challenges to the meaningfulness of race within the context of a threatened end to programs like Affirmative Action, Baker asserts: "The scenario [Appiah and evolutionary biologists] seem to endorse reads as follows: when science apologizes and says there is no such thing, all talk of 'race' must cease. Hence 'race,' as a recently emergent, unifying, and forceful sign of difference *in the service* of the 'Other,' is held up to scientific ridicule as, ironically, 'unscientific'" (385). In other words, as science was used as a new method of supporting a hierarchy of races in the 19th and first half of the 20th century, so science is now being used to undermine racial solidarity on the part of oppressed groups. It is a scientific Catch-22, highly problematic for not only racial groups, like African-Americans, but gender/sexual groups like women and homosexuals. If critics reject an essential biological difference as scientifically fallacious and historically oppressive, upon what do individuals base their membership within a particular group?

It is Schuyler's answer to this question in his fiction and non-fiction texts that Tucker, and others, finds so disconcerting and objectionable. As Tucker accurately summarizes, *Black No More* "is designed to emphasize the scientific meaninglessness of 'race' and the arbitrariness of color consciousness" ("Can" 143). The moral of the satire is that individuals should **not** participate in groups based upon race, for the above reasons. A key aspect of Schuyler's scientific deconstructions of race is the extensive racial intermingling taking place in the United States from the beginning of its history. Even before science came along to prove it, the so-called "races" had interbred to the point of the color line being founded on absurd percentages like one/sixteenth of African blood. Schuyler's dedication for *Black No More* highlights this cultural context: "THIS BOOK IS DEDICATED TO ALL CAUCASIANS IN THE GREAT REPUBLIC WHO CAN TRACE THEIR ANCESTRY BACK TEN GENERATIONS AND CONFIDENTLY ASSERT THAT THERE ARE NO BLACK LEAVES, TWIGS, LIMBS OR BRANCHES ON THEIR FAMILY TREES." Within the text, Schuyler creates an Anglo-Saxon Association of America which undertakes a genealogical study its members hope will authenticate their pure racial origins. However, the head of the study, aptly named Dr. Buggerie, summarizes the results of the study as follows:

> "these statistics we've gathered prove that most of our social leaders, especially of Anglo-Saxon lineage, are descendants of colonial stock that came here in bondage. They associated with slaves, in many cases worked and slept with them. They intermixed with the blacks and the women were sexually exploited by their masters. [. . .] There was so much of this mixing between whites and blacks of the various classes that very early the colonies took steps to put a halt to it. They managed to prevent intermarriage but they couldn't stop intermixture." (196–7)

Dr. Buggerie goes on to assert that this process has led to the intermixture of at least "fifty million" 'white' Americans by the time of his report (197). Throughout *Black No More*, Schuyler completely revises the essentialist, biological theories of race common at the time, in both scientific and popular circles, to more accurately reflect the literal melting pot of American society.[10]

Furthermore, Schuyler utilizes the 'what-if,' or speculative technique of science fiction to transform the cultural phenomenon of skin-whitening and hair-straightening products, targeted at African-Americans, into a biological medical procedure. The superficial consumer goods are replaced by a biological process which lightens skin, straightens hair, and reconfigures facial features to replicate Caucasians. While permanent and impossible to discern, the process cannot be inherited biologically. In this way, Schuyler highlights the phenomenon of 'passing'—very light-skinned blacks living socially as whites.[11] More generally, Schuyler portrays a desire on the part of many persons of color to become lighter skinned in order to reap the social and economic benefits associated with being white in a racist society.

In contrast to personal identity based primarily on a stable, static concept of race(s), with a foundation in a collective identity, Schuyler creates personal identity based on individual choice. In *Black No More*, blacks can chose to become white. Conversely, in a highly ironic cultural backlash, many whites begin tanning to prove their natural whiteness. At the end of the text, one of the few remaining naturally black women is considered highly attractive precisely because of her rarity in the United States, and foreign black women are 'imported' by businesses in order to attract customers. The cultural basis of race becomes glaringly obvious in such a topsy-turvy environment. Once freed from biology, race becomes unstable and open to both cultural and individual variables. Racist whites would be threatened and angered by such an ambiguous and fluid theory of race, based solely on cultural norms. Conversely, Afro-centric theories and activities are undermined by Schuyler's emphasis on 'whitening the race' in the text and his portrayal of the vast majority of African-Americans actively choosing to become white. Schuyler vividly reveals his characteristic iconoclasm in the cultural concept of race permeating *Black No More*.

Tucker's objections to Schuyler exemplify this second, Afro-centric reaction to Schuyler's racial iconoclasm. While often informative and insightful, Tucker's overwhelmingly political reading of Schuyler's texts sometimes leads to key mis-readings. Furthermore, Tucker oversimplifies complex phenomena and misuses scientific terminology in his general discussion of Schuyler's literary career and, more specifically, his analysis of *Black No More*. Tucker argues that "Schuyler's career in total reveals certain patterns of his thought," and the most important of these "is Schuyler's faulty theories about the way 'race' works in modern American society" ("Can" 140). The exact nature of Schuyler's "fault" is most clearly articulated at the beginning of Tucker's article: "This logic promotes the faulty notion that awareness of and attention paid to racial difference cause racial strife and division; and it justifies itself by making claims to a rational, scientific, and supposedly nonpartisan objectivity" (137). In sum, then, Tucker objects to Schuyler's rejection of race as a logical or beneficial concept and his use of science to undermine race. Unfortunately, Tucker's first objection leads him to misconstrue the second—Schuyler's reliance on and portrayal of science in his texts.

Before turning specifically to *Black No More*, Tucker offers Schuyler's 1944 essay, "The Caucasian Problem," as the best example of these two objectionable characteristics. Tucker briefly acknowledges Schuyler's display of "wit" in the reversal of a "Negro Problem" into a "Caucasian Problem" but asserts, "much of the essay dwells on a slightly different topic: the scientific bankruptcy of 'race,' its meaninglessness as a category in the context of the natural sciences. The essay correctly states that 'race' 'began as an anthropological fiction and has become a sociological fact.' But it demonstrates no awareness of 'race' beyond this scientific bankruptcy"("Can" 141). Tucker's specific quotation from "The Caucasian Problem" seems to support his larger assertion about the scientific focus of the text. However, a closer reading of the essay reveals a very limited reliance on science as a foundation for Schuyler's argument. The only time Schuyler mentions the "natural sciences" is in the one sentence quoted by Tucker and in one earlier paragraph also mentioning anthropology (285).[12] In a 17-page essay, Schuyler utilizes the natural sciences and, more broadly, an argument specifically based on science in approximately one half of a page. The actuality of the essay's scientific usage, then, varies greatly from Tucker's portrayal of "much of the essay." Similarly, Tucker quotes a lengthy excerpt from the end of "The Caucasian Problem" as evidence of Schuyler's belief in "the power of scientific reason to combat racism" (141). However, the quotation does not make reference to science or reason, nor logic, facts, or the objectivity Tucker emphasizes elsewhere. In other words, Tucker locates a "scientific reason" in the passage which does not exist. This localized misreading quickly leads Tucker to erroneous assertions about Schuyler's general connections to science.

Tucker utilizes the perceived scientific focus in "The Caucasian Problem" as a bridge to make the larger claim that "Schuyler's overemphasis on a narrowly defined scientific ideal stemmed from his faith in scientific rationality's ability to overcome racial antagonisms" ("Can" 141). As we have seen, Tucker's claim that Schuyler believed in a "scientific ideal," let alone that he overemphasized such an ideal, lacks sufficient textual support from Schuyler's essay. However, Tucker does go on to offer one other example from Schuyler's career as evidence of his scientific idealism: "his creation in the early 1940s of the Association for Tolerance In America, an organization whose mission was 'to recondition the white masses by scientific propaganda'" (ibid). Tucker utilizes a quote from Schuyler's autobiography here, in which Schuyler actually uses the word "scientific," to further support Tucker's claims of scientific idealism. However, the actual activities associated with the Association similarly have nothing to do with science: the use of new advertisement mediums like billboards and radio to emphasize the patriotic contributions of African-Americans during the war and to combat negative social stereotypes of African-Americans. Schuyler himself apparently used "scientific" as a synonym for rational or logical. However, the term "scientific propaganda," in which science is linked with propaganda, suggests Schuyler was well aware of the ideological foundations of science even as he utilized the larger cultural connection made between science and objectivity. It may be that when Tucker uses words like "scientific rationality" and "scientific reason," he is mirroring Schuyler's own linguistic usage. If so, he should pay closer attention to the specific linguistic connotations of Schuyler's sentence. First, with "scientific" as a synonym for "reason" and "rationality," both of Tucker's phrases are redundant. Furthermore, Schuyler's association of propaganda with science undermines Tucker's premise of scientific idealism.

The key to Tucker's misreading and misrepresentation of Schuyler's scientific beliefs and textual usage lies in his political objections to Schuyler's racial views. After a summary of Schuyler's racial views, and their scientific basis, Tucker voices his primary concern—his belief that there are "serious problems with the uses to which Schuyler put his racial theory. Schuyler used the claim that 'race' is merely a socially constructed illusion to critique black race leaders as frequently as white supremacists" ("Can" 141). Tucker ends his discussion of Schuyler's general racial viewpoint with examples of two of Schuyler's most famous early critiques, that of W. E. B. Du Bois and Langston Hughes. It is symptomatic that Tucker's straightforward political analysis is adequately supported with several examples from Schuyler's texts. The first half of Tucker's thesis, then, does not involve any misrepresentation or elisions; he clearly and convincingly argues that Schuyler wished to discard the concept of race altogether and, more importantly, that Tucker believes such an attitude is "politically inadequate" (137). However, Tucker is so focused on his political objections to Schuyler that he does not provide an adequate discussion of the second half of his thesis—Schuyler's justification of his racial views through "claims to a rational, scientific, and supposedly nonpartisan objectivity" (ibid).

Tucker's misreading of Schuyler's essay and subsequent focus on Schuyler's representation of black leaders foreshadows his lengthier analysis of *Black No More*. Of the three paragraphs devoted specifically to the novel, the first two paragraphs largely summarize the text. In the third paragraph, however, Tucker discusses the satiric nature of *Black No More*. He first refutes John M. Reilly's assertion that *Black No More* is anti-utopian, a "novel that features scientific deconstructions of 'race' but places little faith in humanity's ability to use that knowledge to create a better society" ("Can" 143). As Tucker correctly notes, "satiric and utopian impulses are not mutually exclusive. A satire is by definition a humorous critique intended to change behavior or thinking" (ibid). That said, Tucker misses Reilly's larger point behind emphasizing the anti-utopian nature of the novel—the all-encompassing satiric viewpoint of the text. Schuyler critiques every aspect of society implicated in race—which is, in fact, every aspect. The pervasive nature of the novel's satire affects Tucker's reading in two ways. First, Tucker argues that science is the one element of the novel not satirized: "Schuyler's satire is not aimed at the transformative potential of science itself, but is instead tightly focused on specific white supremacist and black 'race' organizations. The novel's parodies of Du Bois and Garvey are perfect examples" (143). Similar to his reading of Schuyler's other texts, Tucker's reading of *Black No More* involves an erroneous claim about science, one which, therefore, cannot be supported with evidence from the text. For example, Tucker does not discuss the characterization of Dr. Crookman—a major character and scientist. Furthermore, Tucker specifically admits in his summary of the novel that Crookman's scientific procedure is not portrayed as an idealistic solution to the 'race problem': "However, instead of solving the nation's racial problems, Black No More, Inc., creates chaos" (142). Where, then, does Tucker locate the "transformative potential of science" he describes?

Secondly, Tucker again focuses exclusively on Schuyler's negative characterization of black race leaders. Two thirds of the sole analytic paragraph on *Black No More* deals with the characterizations of W. E. B. Du Bois and Marcus Garvey. To make his main point crystal clear, Tucker not only ends this paragraph but his entire discussion of the novel with a restatement of his primary objection to the text: "The 'racial chauvinism' that these figures represent to Schuyler, not science, is his principal target. Perhaps science cannot 'succeed where the Civil War had failed,' but according to Schuyler, that is only because of what he sees as the reprehensible insistence on 'race' by the race leaders, such as Du Bois and Garvey, that his novel sharply satirizes" (144). Tucker argues here that Schuyler targets "only" black leaders as obstacles to achieving racial equality and harmony. Such an argument elides the "white supremacist" organizations Tucker mentioned once earlier in the paragraph, and it misrepresents Schuyler's satiric treatment of science in the text. The importance of Reilly's anti-utopian, satiric emphasis resurfaces here. Reilly places his analysis directly in the context of the assimilationist debate surrounding Schuyler, and he emphasizes that "the logic of this anti-utopia neither leads to specific denigration of Blacks nor advocates mediocrity and the reduplication of white life-styles and culture" (108). In this way, Reilly specifically addresses Tucker's accusations of partiality. For example, unlike most Afro-centric readings of Schuyler, Reilly's reading focuses primarily on the equally, if not more, negative portrayal of white characters. According to Reilly, "every white person in the book is an ass; every institution created by whites is debased" (ibid). Furthermore, Reilly offers an explanation for the critics' overemphasis of the negative portrayal of black characters: "Black characters are more easily identified with actual persons than are white characters, so the Black satire hurts more. The novel, however, is not anti-Black. It is simply anti-utopian, written, as befits a conservative author, in the tradition of rationalist satire" (ibid). Reilly's inclusive, literary approach to characterization serves as a model for a more accurate and productive analysis of Schuyler's scientific usage in *Black No More*.

While Tucker accurately summarizes the thesis of *Black No More*, he oversimplifies and misrepresents Schuyler's scientific connections. Tucker glosses over key aspects of scientific history, the complex portrayal of science in Schuyler's texts, and their connection to the science fiction genre. First, Tucker utilizes Donna Haraway's theories of scientific subjectivity to indict Schuyler. Tucker claims that "Schuyler overinvests in the notion of scientific objectivity, that science is a transparent medium providing clear access to truth" ("Can" 146). In contrast, Haraway argues for the subjective, the fictional aspect of science. Scientific discourse tells stories, embodies particular points of view, and supports particular belief systems.[13] Unfortunately, Tucker's use of Haraway has several major flaws. First, as previously discussed, Schuyler's association of science with propaganda in his autobiography suggests he would fully agree with Haraway's ideological emphasis. In addition, as we will see in more detail shortly, Schuyler's actual use of science in *Black No More* supports such a reading of scientific subjectivity.

Furthermore, despite the fact that Tucker quotes Haraway to critique Schuyler, he himself falls into the objectivity trap in his discussion of science. Tucker asserts that, "'Race' is indeed a mirage scientifically speaking, and a construct socially, culturally, politically, and ideologically; but making this claim does not elide its power to shape human lives in a very real way" ("Can" 148). When Tucker separates science from the other constructed concepts of race he lists here, he is accepting the better known, factual, objective representation of science Haraway combats. According to Tucker's statement, within the context of science, race either exists or it does not. The complex and multiple definitions and uses of race within the various scientific disciplines, and the conflict often taking place between these concepts and entities, are elided here. "Scientifically speaking," race is a construct also and certainly has "power to shape human lives in very real ways." Tucker criticizes Schuyler for overemphasizing science, yet Tucker himself dismisses it too quickly. In utilizing a monolithic definition of science, Tucker also overlooks the historicizing of science Haraway's scientific theories entail. For example, in her 1989 text, *Primate Visions: Gender, Race, and Nature in the World of Modern Science*, Haraway chronicles the history of race in the American scientific community.[14] Nancy Stepan similarly investigates the evolving scientific concept of race in Britain in her book, *The Idea of Race in Science: Great Britain 1800–1960*. If Tucker's assertion that "'Race' is indeed a mirage scientifically speaking" were placed in such a historical context, the resulting translation would be: "The biological essentialism at the heart of scientific racial theories emerging and developing in the 19th century and first half of the 20th century has been gradually discredited as biologically inaccurate and culturally biased." Such a historicized statement, stressing the long process of change involved, more accurately places Schuyler's fictional works.

George H. Daniels' *Science in American Society: A Social History* provides a useful, broad historical context for Schuyler's use of science in *Black No More*. In the 1920s, 30s, and 40s, when Schuyler wrote much of his fiction, science was in the process of transforming American society—from national defense, to religious beliefs, to every American's day-to-day living. In fact, from the mid-nineteenth century to the present, the scientific discipline has grown exponentially in size, as well as cultural power and influence. According to Daniels, "[s]cience and technology by the beginning of the twentieth century had begun to permeate all of life" (290). More specifically, "[i]n the nineteenth century, despite the frequent obeisance made to science and technology, social forces in America tended to shape, or at least restrict, the development of science. In the early years of the twentieth century, the relationship became more reciprocal, and in important ways: science had a substantial influence upon American social policy" (295). This "influence" was largely possible "because the American public in the twentieth century has been marked by a childlike faith in science" (293). At this point, the connection between science and progress comes into focus. Because western ideology is based in large part on the concept of progress—cultural, technological, and political—science is generally viewed as part of a progressively better world as well. This progressive, positive concept of science is called scientism, and it accurately reflects the general view of science at the turn of the century within the scientific community and the larger American public.

A key element of scientism is the promotion of the scientific method and its application to areas of life besides science and technology: "The belief that science contributed to the intellectual progress of mankind by encouraging habits of thinking which tended to make men more rational, to make them base their thinking on facts, observations, and experiments, was generally accompanied by the assumption that the scientific method could be applied to mental and social areas of study" (Daniels 297). Sociology, psychology, ethnology, education, and conservation were just some of the fields impacted by scientism and the application of the scientific method. Furthermore, "[b]y the beginning of the twentieth century, science was firmly entrenched in dozens of government agencies and legislation based on science was becoming more common" (291). Because science was synonymous with technology to the general public, it was also "upheld as a wonder-worker that promised more of the startling innovations they had experienced during their own time" (290-91)—"telephones, telegraphs, and electric lights," for example (290). Daniels acknowledges that this pervasive and overwhelmingly positive "enthusiasm" for science was "naïve," but attests that the basic premise of the Progressives was accurate—"America in the twentieth century has become, as W J McGee observed two years before this century began, 'a nation of science'" (315).

Tucker portrays Schuyler as one such naïve believer in scientism. Indeed, Schuyler's emphasis on science and use of the science fiction genre for *Black No More* do illustrate an understanding of the twentieth century as a century of science. Furthermore, Schuyler's infamous promotion of logic and rationality parallels the importance of the scientific method to scientism. Robert A. Hill and Kent Rasmussen, for example, note Schuyler's call for more scientists among black students, rather than the prevalent teachers and preachers (Hill and Rasmussen 301–2). In his 1936 essay, "New Job Frontiers for Negro Youth," Schuyler states, "This is the age of technics and the key man is the technical scientist" (qtd. in Hill and Rasmussen 301–302). Schuyler believes such a vocational shift is necessary "not only because we are living in an age dominated by science but because the psychology of the engineer is more likely to incline to Negro integration in American life and less toward tacitly accepting and promoting segregation" (Hill and Rasmussen 302). Here Schuyler exhibits the belief, discussed above, "that science contributed to the intellectual progress of mankind by encouraging habits of thinking which tended to make men more rational" (Daniels 297). Certainly, such a belief can be labeled naïve, and the vocational shift Schuyler desired did not occur. However, the context of scientism aids our understanding of Schuyler's use of science in several ways besides Tucker's single proposition of naïve idealism.

First, Schuyler's main literary activity takes place as American society was coming to terms with the scientific developments Daniels discusses. Given the overwhelmingly positivistic climate of the United States, it is not surprising that Schuyler utilized some of the same practical and ideological arguments as the Progressives. Nancy Stepan and Sander Gilman emphasize the great difficulty of distancing one's self from the dominant ideology during this time period:

> What we are arguing is that in the era of the successful establishment of science as an epistemologically neutral and instrumentally successful form of knowledge, standing "outside of" or ignoring science was very difficult. With the triumph of "positive" science and positivist ideology, even those with the most radical intellectual and political philosophies

and programs—alternate world views—tended to exempt science from their criticisms and to posit science as the one positive form of knowledge that escaped contamination from political and personal factors. A hard-hitting critique of science, as itself a political form of knowledge reflective of power, was, relatively speaking, absent. (Stepan and Gilman 101–2)

According to Daniels, even "the most respected thinkers of the day, and the most important movements of the period, were wholly captured by the magic of 'science'" (295). In such a context, even Schuyler's limited connection between science and propaganda, or science and politics, is unusual. In addition, science was a relatively new tool for anti-racist arguments. Given the excruciatingly slow progress of equality for African-Americans in the United States, an untried technique might appear an attractive option. The rational emphasis of science and scientism coincided with Schuyler's general emphasis on logic as a tool to undermine racism as well. All of these factors help to more fully explain Schuyler's use of science without simplistically labeling it idealistic. Furthermore, even with Schuyler's more balanced view of science and its potential, he could tap the wide-spread scientism of the general American public to combat racism. Schuyler could utilize the tremendous power and influence of the scientific community as a tool to undermine race, racial essentialism, and racial categorization. As Daniels attests, "[s]uch concrete evidences of the potency of science increased the authority—both within the scientific community and without—of anyone who spoke in the name of science" (293).

A final reason for utilizing science in anti-racist arguments is precisely the negative connection between science and racism. As the multiple histories of science and race uniformly highlight, science has been used extensively to promote racist viewpoints.[15] Furthermore, as Houston Baker's synopsis highlighted, the scientific community was heatedly debating the earlier, essentialist concept of biologically distinct and hierarchical races at the time of Schuyler's major literary activity. Racial typology and the racial basis of a cultural hierarchy, from primitive to civilized, were still accepted scientific theories. The biological evolutionism of Darwin was mirrored in a theory of cultural evolutionism, or Social Darwinism. Science historians Nancy Stepan and Sander Gilman, for example, focus on the period between 1870 and 1920 not only because it was "the period of transition to modern science," but also because it was the period when "the claims of scientifically established inferiority were pressed most insistently by the mainstream scientific community" (Stepan and Gilman 72). Scientific racism, as it was called, was the accepted norm for the turn of the century (73). In her 1982 book on the history of race in Great Britain, Stepan further argues that the scientific concept of race developed hand-in-hand with the growth of western imperialism and the subjugation and enslavement of people of color around the world (*Idea*). Writing approximately forty years earlier, Schuyler noticed this same connection in "The Caucasian Problem" (1944). Schuyler asserts that the general racial categories of "'Negro' and 'Caucasian,' 'black' and 'white' are convenient propaganda devices" which "very conveniently follow the line of colonial subjugation and exploitation, with the Asiatics and Africans lumped together smugly as 'backward peoples,' 'savages,' 'barbarians,' or 'primitives': i.e., fair prey for fleecing and enslavement under the camouflage of 'civilization'" (285). Clearly, Schuyler had a critical and sophisticated understanding of the ideological underpinnings of race and the political and material uses to which race(s) could be applied. Science's increasing power in western society combined with its use as a justification for colonialism, imperialism, slavery, and racism to form a formidable hurdle to racial equality. Consequently, when some scientists began to question the established essentialist theories of race, their controversial theories became the best way to combat the scientific justification of racism, as well as racism more generally. Given Americans' positivistic belief in science in the early 20th century, the scientific community's recantation of its previous racial theories could have a powerful impact on racial ideology in the United States.

A chronological pairing of Schuyler's literary career with the scientific career of early anthropologist Franz Boas will illustrate more specifically the newness and radical nature of Schuyler's racial theories, as well as the authors' shared sense of the usefulness of science for social reform. Born in Germany in 1858, Boas pioneered the field of modern anthropology during the first half of the twentieth century.[16] After moving to the United States in 1887, Boas was appointed assistant chief of the department of anthropology at the World's Columbian Exposition in Chicago (1894). Edgar Rice Burroughs' biographer John Taliaferro describes Boas' activities in the Anthropological hall of the exposition: "thousands of tourists, curious to see where they ranked on the scale of human progress, lined up to have their heads measured—'anthropometry,' it was called—by a team of anthropologists led by Franz Boas, who would soon thrust himself into the middle of the debate over eugenics and racial determinism, a topic that Burroughs himself would be drawn into" (35). Boas and Burroughs' common attendance at the World's Columbian Exposition accurately places Boas' early career. He had already dedicated himself to the scientific study of the connection between physical and cultural characteristics in humans, and this study took place in the context of racial essentialism, racial hierarchies, and specifically the growth of eugenics as a scientific, political, and popular discourse. As his scientific studies in physical anthropology continued over the next fifty years, Boas generated scientific data challenging the prevailing theories of racial essentialism. In fact, he was "at the forefront of those who combatted the transfer of principles of biological evolution to the manifestations of man's learned behavior" (Herskovits, *Franz* 6). Boas, then, had a crucial impact on both of these fields—physical and cultural anthropology—making up the larger discipline of anthropology.

For example, during the heated debate over the ability of immigrants to assimilate successfully to American society, Boas completed a study for the Dillingham Commission on Immigration of the U.S. Congress (1907–1910). His findings, published in 1911, emphasized the role of environmental factors in contrast to the established theory of biological inheritance and distinct, static racial types (Herskovits, Foreword 9). As Boas' biographer, Melville J. Herskovits, notes, Boas' "analysis of changes in head-form of immigrants [. . .] was the best-know, and the most controversial research he conducted" because it revealed the dynamic nature of the human form (*Franz* 39).[17] Head-form was the foundation of racial identification and classification, the primary objective of physical anthropologists, as a whole, during this time period (ibid). Therefore, Boas' research challenged the prevailing theories of the physical anthropologists, as well as the biologists' "doctrine of the autonomy of genetic determinants of physical type" (ibid). Not surprising, then, Boas faced a protracted and largely unsuccessful fight to gain acceptance for his controversial findings. When no other scientist stepped forward to repeat the massive project, Boas initiated several similar studies to support his findings (Herskovits, *Franz* 42). Finally, in 1928 he published the "raw data" from his study of the immigrants so that it would be available for other scientists to analyze (40). The scientific community's reaction to Boas' Dillingham study illustrates the radical nature of dynamic and fluid theories of race during this time period and how entrenched racial essentialism was even among professional scientists.

Working to change these essentialist racial beliefs within the scientific community, as well as in the larger American public, Boas became a prolific writer and lecturer. Boas' 1911 book, *The Mind of Primitive Man*, embodies his critical racial approach. Herskovits asserts that it wasn't until this text's publication that "antiracists could refer to a single work" to support a position critical of essentialist theories of race (Foreword 6). Boas summarized his findings in *The Mind of Primitive Man* as follows: "[a] close connection between race and personality has never been established. The concept of racial type as commonly used even in scientific literature is misleading and requires a logical as well as biological definition" (9). Here Boas cautiously refutes racial determinism due to a lack of reliable scientific evidence. This racial critique may seem hesitant and partial from a contemporary perspective, but Herskovits points out that such "scientific realism and methodological caution" was characteristic of Boas (*Franz* 71). More importantly, Herskovits emphasizes the importance of Boas' text by contrasting it with the preceding scientific theories of race. Herskovits identifies two major branches: one used in the United States to justify slavery and one used on the Continent to promote the superiority of an Aryan race (Foreword 5). In this way, Herskovits joins Stepan in connecting racialist science with "the era of European expansion over the world" and emphasizes the political motivation behind the newly-emerging scientific field (ibid).[18]

Furthermore, *The Mind of Primitive Man* was published contemporaneously with the rise of the eugenics movement. Utilizing the fundamental western notion of progress, eugenicists believed human biology and heredity should be systematically manipulated in order to achieve specified social ideals. Biological evolutionism translated into social evolutionism. Prominent American biologist Charles B. Davenport, for example, believed "[s]ocial and physical evolution were one. Attempts to improve man by changing his environment were [. . .] doomed to futility" (Rosenberg 94). This biological and cultural immutability lay behind the concept of racial determinism. For instance, two of Davenport's "major research interests were the effects of race-crossing and the comparative social traits of different races. Davenport never doubted that racial traits were as immutable as the genes which produced them" (Rosenberg 95). Therefore, Davenport squared off against Boas in using "the prestige of his scientific position" to support the immigration restriction movement (ibid). More broadly, science historian Charles E. Rosenberg does not locate a general break between American scientists and the eugenics movement until "the late twenties and early thirties" (96). Laura Doyle specifically names Boas and W. E. B. Du Bois as two dissenting voices among the dominant current of "racialist and deterministic science" (238).[19] Within this context, Herskovits attests that Boas' *The Mind of Primitive Man* "foreshadowed a trend that was to change almost completely the sub-science of physical anthropology from one concerned primarily with the classification of human types into a specialized science of human biology" (Foreword 9). This broad view situates Boas on the cutting edge of the slow and contested evolution of anthropology as a modern scientific discipline.

At his death in 1942, Boas was working on a collection of his works, posthumously published as *Race and Democratic Society* in 1945. "[D]irected at lay audiences," the collection embodies Boas' primary goal of using scientific theories of race and culture to undermine world-wide racism and prejudice, especially in the context of the increasing influence of "Fascist and Nazi ideology" during the 1930s and 1940s (E. Boas). Not only was the Nazi use of science to support an extreme eugenics program increasingly criticized by the scientific community generally, but also Boas, as a Jew, had a personal connection to the issue(s).[20] As Nancy Stepan and Sander Gilman note, "[a]fter 1850, critics of scientific racism and/or sexism from within science were often themselves in one way or another members of marginal groups" (74). Within the text of *Race and Democratic Society*, then, Boas began with the subcategory of "Race," the first article of this category is entitled "Prejudice," and the very first sentence refers to the ghettoizing of American Negroes. More broadly, the second portion of Boas' title, *Democratic Society*, reflects his promotion of positive American values, as well as his address of the disjuncture between these positive values and racial issues within American society. In sum, Boas sought to promote the rights of individuals in opposition to the collective, essentialist racial theories still playing a powerful role in the world.

Boas' critical revision of the field of anthropology coincided with Schuyler's major literary activity. For example, *Black No More* was published in 1931, the *Black Empire* serials in 1937 and 1938, and "The Caucasian Problem" in 1944. This historical scientific context illustrates the relative newness and controversial nature of Schuyler's racial theories, even within the scientific community. If someone in the field, like Boas, thought public dissemination of scientific findings important up through 1942, surely Schuyler's emphasis on science for a lay audience was a logical and, perhaps, necessary step as well. The gap between the scientific community and the African-American community, even more pronounced during the era of Jim Crow segregation, further increased the relevancy of such scientific information for Schuyler's primary audience. In "The Caucasian Problem," Schuyler alludes to the relatively recent chronology of racial questioning: "[n]ot only is the superiority of one race being vigorously denied but the whole concept of race is being effectively challenged. This phenomenon dates chiefly from the First World War" (294). When Schuyler concludes "The Caucasian Problem" with the assertion that racism must be addressed or "[t]he alternative here and abroad is conflict and chaos," he places his arguments in a similar context as Boas' *Race and Democratic Society*. First the "abroad" corresponds with the highpoint of a global eugenics movement, with its connections to fascism and genocide, and the ever-increasing spread of western imperialism and the rise of the United States as a world power. Second, the "here" refers to the connection of these global trends to the specific issues of race within the United States, in particular the status of African-Americans. Schuyler's creation of The Association for Tolerance in America and its use of popular advertisement mediums corresponds with Boas' lay outreach as well (Tucker, "Can" 141).

Furthermore, *Black No More* embodies an even more extreme viewpoint on race than Boas' scientific texts. In contrast to Boas' cautious scientific skepticism, Schuyler confidently asserts the complete biological intermingling of the so-called "Negro" and "Caucasian" races in the United States and playfully theorizes about the ability to change races through an exterior physical process ("Caucasian" 285). If anything, Schuyler's social-constructionist theory of race anticipated the direction eventually taken not only by the scientific community as a whole but also the literary community. Sociologist Gunnar Myrdal supports this anticipatory view in his study of race in America:

> [Myrdal] found that he was able to call upon a long tradition of scientific work produced by African-American physicians, educators, and social scientists about their own identity, meaning, and status. Myrdal remarked upon the environmentalist emphasis found in these black scientific studies of the Negro, in contrast to the innatist tendencies of the white academy. That emphasis gave black writing, he said, a much more modern tone than white writings of the same period. (Stepan and Gilman 103)

Schuyler's constructionist viewpoint, then, coincided with the larger African-American scientific community. More specifically, Myrdal highlighted the importance of black social scientists, like W. E. B. Du Bois, to this scientific counter discourse. Myrdal "noted that from the beginning black social scientists took the stand that the American dogma of race inequality was a scientific falsehood" (Stepan and Gilman 98). Schuyler and Du Bois, in fact, shared a common interest in science and rationalism as an anti-racist tool.

Schuyler, Boas, and Du Bois all utilized scientific theories to interrogate race during this time period. Therefore, adding Du Bois to the pairing of Schuyler and Boas will reveal Tucker's political bias, as he defends Du Bois but criticizes Schuyler. First, as a social scientist, Du Bois subscribed to the same basic scientific tenets as Boas—the importance of rationality, objectivity, and the scientific method to modern science.[21] Furthermore, Du Bois and Boas are often cited as leaders of the resistance against scientific racism because their work as scientists predominantly promoted a constructionist theory of race.[22] Anthony Appiah's controversial article, criticized by Tucker, chronicles Du Bois' evolution from an essentialist to a constructionist perspective. Similarly, Nancy Stepan and Sander Gilman chart Du Bois' multiple, evolving strategies of resistance to scientific racism. These critical readings are supported by Du Bois' 1940 autobiography, *Dusk of Dawn: an Essay Toward an Autobiography of a Race Concept,* in which Du Bois compares his evolving personal views on the definition of race to those of the scientific community and American society more generally.

In *Dusk of Dawn,* Du Bois gives an overview of the racial changes from the 19th to the 20th century. According to Du Bois, race was not a self-conscious term in the 19th century; it was used "as a matter of course without explanation or definition" by Americans generally (100).[23] In addition, race referred to both "physical traits and cultural affinity" (ibid). By the turn-of-the-century, race had become a self-consciously studied term within the sciences and a biological basis was emphasized, due to Darwinist evolutionary theory (Du Bois, *Dusk* 98). For example, Du Bois' early paper, "The Conservation of Races" (1897), was his "first extended discussion of the concept of race," and he utilizes biological elements in his larger "sociohistorical" argument (Appiah 23). As Appiah notes, "what Du Bois attempts [. . .] is not the transcendence of the nineteenth-century scientific conception of race—as we shall see, he relies on it—but rather as the dialectic requires, a revaluation of the Negro race in the face of the sciences of racial inferiority" (25). According to Du Bois, the "psychic-biological" difference(s) of the Negro race simply meant it had a unique and positive contribution to make to American society (Stepan and Gilman 93). Stepan and Gilman identity this technique of resistance a "transvaluation of the terms of the dominant discourse": "[t]he significance of biological race differences was accepted, but the 'inferior' element in the hierarchy revalued and renamed" (92). Stepan and Gilman's scientific context provides an explanation for Du Bois' use of the "norms and standards of science" in a period when this meant the oxymoronic combination of objectivity and racialism found in scientific racism (84–5).[24] First, scientists had to utilize ostensibly objective language and the scientific method to be taken seriously by other scientists. In addition, "to admit that race, especially one's own, was an issue in science was to make the writer immediately less than fully 'objective' and therefore less than fully 'scientific'" (86). Finally, most scientists shared a common view of "science as a progressive, instrumental, and objective form of knowledge" (ibid). Therefore, minority scientists "were tempted simultaneously to embrace and reject the field: to embrace science's methods, concepts, and the promise it held out for discovering knowledge, and to reject, in a variety of ways, the conclusions of science as they appeared to apply negatively to themselves" (87).[25] The two prominent scientists who strenuously resisted scientific racism, Du Bois and Boas, fit this template—Du Bois as an African-American sociologist and Boas as a Jewish anthropologist.[26]

By the early decades of the 20th century, race became more a "question of comparative culture" than biology (99), and Du Bois "began to emphasize the cultural aspects of race" (Du Bois, *Dusk* 102). For example, in the same year as Boas' 1911 publications, Du Bois wrote an editorial in *The Crisis* addressing the scientific community's increasing critique of racial essentialism: "The leading scientists of the world have come forward [with . . .] a series of propositions which may be summarized as follows: 1. (*a*) It is not legitimate to argue from differences in physical characteristics to differences in mental characteristics. (*b*) The mental characteristics differentiating a particular people or race are not (1) unchangeable [. . .]" (157). Moreover, Du Bois joins Schuyler and Boas in connecting the cultural, and therefore "changeable" basis of race, to a larger educational program. Since "5. (*a*) The deepest cause of misunderstanding between peoples is perhaps the tacit assumption that the present characteristics of a people are the expression of permanent qualities,"

> [*b* . . .] anthropologists, sociologists and scientific thinkers as a class could powerfully assist the movement for a juster appreciation of peoples by persistently pointing out in their lectures and in their works the fundamental fallacy involved in taking a static instead of a dynamic, a momentary instead of a historic, a fixed instead of a comparative, point of view of peoples; (*c*) and such dynamic teaching could be conveniently introduced into schools [. . . and] also into colleges [. . .] (157)

Finally, most damning, Du Bois' 7th summary point states that, "[s]o far at least as intellectual and moral aptitudes are concerned, we ought to speak of civilizations where we now speak of races" (158). As we shall see shortly, Du Bois was not willing to apply fully this last scientific assertion. Yet, he believed that the discrepancies between these scientific claims, as a whole, and the reality of "racial philosophy" in the United States revealed a "fifty year" gap (157). In this editorial, Du Bois utilizes the progressive ideology of science and implicitly connects positive progress and a cultural concept of race.

In addition, Du Bois' editorial summary was based on a complex web of interconnections with Boas. According to Appiah, Du Bois' editorial was prompted by the work of G. Spiller, presented at the First Universal Races

Congress in London in July, 1911.[27] However, Boas also presented a paper at the Congress, attended by Du Bois.[28] Therefore, Boas is one of the "leading scientists" to whom Du Bois refers as a basis for his entire summary and one of the "anthropologists" to whom Du Bois appeals in his fifth point on lay outreach (157). Du Bois had several other connections to Boas during this time period as well. For example, Boas came to Atlanta University in 1906, at Du Bois' invitation, to "deliver the university's commencement address and take part in its annual Negro conference" (Beardsley 261). Du Bois quoted extensively from this address in *The Health and Physique of the Negro American: Report of a Social Study Made Under the Direction of Atlanta University; Together with the Proceedings of the Eleventh Conference for the Study of the Negro Problems, held at Atlanta University, on May the 29th, 1906.*[29] Furthermore, Boas delivered a paper on "The Anthropological Position of the Negro" at the 1910 conference of the National Negro committee; this paper was reprinted as "The Real Race Problem" in *The Crisis* the same year (Beardsley 262). While in this paper Boas presented "a veiled endorsement of racial intermarriage as the best long-run solution to problems of race" (262), he also tried to establish an African museum (Beardsley 259–261). These tensions in Boas' work—between biology and culture, between a negative and positive view of race, between an American and an African identity for American Negroes—mirror those found in Du Bois' work. Overall, the scientific connections between Boas and Du Bois are much stronger than those of Boas and Schuyler, illustrating the (positive) importance of science to Du Bois' concept of race.

By 1940, in *Dusk of Dawn: an Essay Toward an Autobiography of a Race Concept*, Du Bois explicitly rejects a biological basis for race: "[i]t is easy to see that scientific definition of race is impossible; it is easy to prove that physical characteristics are not so inherited as to make it possible to divide the world into races" (137). Yet, Du Bois continues to emphasize the importance of race and of a collective racial identity through the substitution of a socio-historical theory of race. Trying to formulate a historical and political connection to Africa, Du Bois writes, "the real essence of this kinship is its social heritage of slavery; the discrimination and insult; and this heritage binds together not simply the children of Africa, but extends through yellow Asia and into the South Seas. It is this unity that draws me to Africa" (117). However, as Appiah notes, Du Bois' cultural definition of race continues to rely on biology, for "[h]ow can something he shares with the whole nonwhite world bind him to only a part of it?" (Appiah 34–5). Therefore, Appiah concludes that Du Bois "never quite managed to complete" his racial argument, the "logic" of which "leads naturally to the final repudiation of race as a term of difference and to speaking instead 'of civilizations where we now speak of races'" (Appiah 35). Appiah's analysis of Du Bois highlights the key difference between Schuyler and Du Bois. It is not their general use of science or belief in rationalism or objectivity, but the degree to which they applied the scientific information and to which they emphasized culture as a substitute for biology.

Schuyler "complete[s]" the argument Du Bois does not—he "repudiat[es] race as a term of difference" and "speak[s] instead 'of civilizations'" (Appiah 35). Schuyler's "repudiation" of race is well-traversed area. However, his use of "civilizations" and racial oppression as unifying techniques in "The Caucasian Problem" (1944) is often overlooked because of the focus on his conservative political agenda as a whole. Tucker, for example, highlighted the (supposed) scientific foundations of the article and Schuyler's use of science to "throw out the concept of 'race' altogether" ("Can" 140–1). Yet, Schuyler connects, in detail, the oppression of Negroes (whether in the United States or in Africa) to that of "Asiatic colored folk, " the "Indo-African masses" of Latin America (287), and people-of-color in the Caribbean ("Caucasian" 288–9). Although his emphasis is slightly different than that of Du Bois, Schuyler's common tie of oppression mirrors that of Du Bois' "social heritage of slavery, the discrimination and insult": "the so-called Negro race is a melange representing every known variety of human being with nothing whatever in common except a common bondage and a common resentment against enforced poverty and pariahdom, and an increasing determination to rid the world of the Caucasian problem which hampers its progress and development" ("Caucasian" 286). Therefore, collective racial resistance and reform is necessary. Unlike Du Bois, Schuyler does not undermine the connection between Negroes and Asians, or any other group oppressed due to its color. He emphasizes the importance of "civilizations," rather than race, to a greater degree than Du Bois.

Yet, within the concept of "civilizations," the overarching similarity of oppression is joined also by many specific cultural differences. Therefore, Schuyler believed that the geographic, historic, and linguistic differences between the many groups composing the so-called Negro race are equally as important as their common oppression. For example, "[p]rior to the rise of present imperialist Powers on the wings of piracy and conquest" and "[b]efore the inauguration of the slave trade," blacks were perceived by Europeans as members of more specific nationalist groups (like Moors, Ethiopians, or Yorubas) and as representing particular, varied vocations like "warriors, merchants, physicians, sailors and artists" ("Caucasian" 286). Schuyler objected to the general racial category "Negro" because "it facilitates acceptance of the fiction of similarity and identity which is easily translated into a policy of treating all colored people everywhere the same way" (284). If white racism and oppression were ended, for example, nothing would connect American Negroes to Africa. American Negroes would be a part of American civilization alone. The key to Schuyler's qualified racial collectivism seems to be Diana Fuss' assertion that "we can still work with 'race' as a political category *knowing* it is a biological fiction" (91). At this point in his career, Schuyler advocates collective social reform to correct a problem of international proportions. Yet, he simultaneously emphasizes the false basis of the common oppression of people of color—race. In other words, he is forced to acknowledge and address the continued collective operation of race (in a negative sense), even as he personally advocates its dismissal.

Overall, then, while different in degree of application, Schuyler and Du Bois' use of science was substantially the same. Both before and, more significantly, after Schuyler published his full-length fictional works, *Black No More* (1931) and the *Black Empire* serials (1937–38), Du Bois presents similar scientific issues as if they are on the cutting edge of American intellectual thought. Furthermore, Du Bois places these scientific deconstructions of race in a positive light—as a useful tool to counteract racism. Du Bois' usage here is the same as Schuyler's. Therefore, Tucker and Appiah's description of Du Bois applies to Schuyler as well: "Du Bois was attempting 'a revaluation of the Negro race in the face of the sciences of racial inferiority'" (Tucker, "Can" 147). Unfortunately, Tucker does not place Schuyler into the same historically-specific scientific context as Du Bois. Tucker takes issue with Appiah's discussion of Du Bois' racial views and their connection to science, while simultaneously criticizing Schuyler for his similar use of science. Therefore, the key to Tucker's criticism must lie in the first half of his overall argument—the "faulty logic" of a negative approach to race consciousness—rather than the second half: the use of "rational, scientific, and supposedly nonpartisan objectivity" to support such an argument ("Can" 137). Once again, Tucker's emphasis on Schuyler's political views leads him to misrepresent scientific issues and connections.

Schuyler, Du Bois, and Boas all shared the sense of a 'mission' to end racism and the important role science could play in such an endeavor. Tucker admits that Schuyler's conclusion to "The Caucasian Problem" is "genuinely moving," but does not give an adequate historical and scientific context to more fully explain, and perhaps justify, Schuyler's usage of science ("Can" 141). Because Tucker places Schuyler in the political context of the 1980s and 1990s, as a predecessor to the "'new black conservatism'" of figures like Clarence Thomas, Thomas Sowell, and Shelby Steele, Tucker misses the genuine newness of the scientific questioning of race in the first half of the 20th century (136). Utilizing hindsight, Tucker judges Schuyler for a lack of race consciousness and belief in scientific rationalism in the 1930s and 1940s. It may seem naive from a contemporary perspective, but at the time, science seemed a promising new tool in the fight to end racism. Furthermore, given the intense modernization of the first half of the 20th century, many saw science as the most appropriate reform technique for an increasingly modernized and scientifically-oriented society.

Furthermore, Schuyler clearly did have a sense of race consciousness, just not the same type in which Tucker and Baker believe. For Schuyler, race consciousness had primarily negative connotations. He was 'conscious' of racism and the necessity of working to end racial prejudice and violence, for example. Tucker acknowledges that Schuyler did not lack "an awareness of white racial hatred toward black America" (140), and the lynching scene Tucker discusses from *Black No More* emphasizes this awareness ("Can"). However, Tucker believes Schuyler's arguments "ignore the role 'race' plays as a building block around which political and cultural identities are created" (147). Tucker does not directly use the words positive or beneficial in conjunction with race consciousness, but his argument relies on such an implied meaning. Post-1960s, Tucker takes such a positive interpretation largely for granted: the concept of race consciousness offers the possibility of political and personal empowerment for oppressed groups. Yet, the critical controversy over Schuyler's texts reveals the evolving and contested history of the term during the twentieth century. The Harlem Renaissance, for example, was a period of intense, generally positive race consciousness for the black artistic community. Schuyler's infamous debate with Langston Hughes, in which he questions the autonomy of black American art, symbolizes Schuyler's negative response to such a project.[30] However, this does not mean Schuyler "ignore[d] the role 'race' plays as a building black around which political and cultural identities are created," as Tucker argues ("Can" 147). In fact, Schuyler had a very sophisticated understanding of how race operates in the formation of identity. Unlike Tucker, however, he thought its influence was negative.[31] Schuyler does address race's "power to shape human lives in very real ways," as Tucker desires (Tucker, "Can" 148). In the highly caustic *Black No More*, Schuyler illustrates how a comprehensive understanding of the way race operates scientifically and socially, politically, and romantically/sexually is essential to survival and 'success' in the United States.

BLACK NO MORE

Tucker focuses on the negative portrayal of "specific white supremacist and black 'race' organizations" in *Black No More* and asserts that "Schuyler's satire is not aimed at the transformative potential of science itself" ("Can" 143). Yet, **every** character in the novel has an invested interest in race, manipulates race, and tries to utilize race for his/her own gain, including those characters associated with science. Schuyler's highly caustic wit and satiric gaze are all-encompassing in *Black No More*. Not only does this seem to stem from his individual personality and beliefs, his chosen role as "debunker," but from the nature of satire itself (Gates 31). Satire complements Schuyler's perspective perfectly. The complete absurdity of American race relations affects every American, coloring almost every situation with both ironic humor and tragedy. Contemporary science fiction writer Samuel R. Delany accurately observes this oxymoronic aspect of American culture in his discussion of the same lynching scene mentioned by Tucker: "[t]hough the term did not then exist, here the 'humor' becomes so 'black' as to take on elements of inchoate American horror" ("Racism" 384).

The protagonist of *Black No More*, Max Disher, serves as an excellent example of Schuyler's definition of race consciousness. Disher manipulates race in romantic/sexual, economic, and political contexts and lives 'happily ever after.' Whether this makes him a subversive hero, a "black Picaro" or trickster figure, or an assimilationist opportunist depends largely on the critic, as well the time period (Peplow, "Black"). First, Schuyler places Disher's decision to become white through Dr. Crookman's scientific treatment in the context of his desire for a racist white woman. The novel begins with Disher's failed advances towards Helen Givens, a Southern belle who comes North for 'polishing.' Disher's immediate decision to undergo the racial process includes a desire to meet her again under more favorable circumstances, and once white, his first action is to go South in order to find her. Disher is similar in this respect to Sam, the (formerly) white female character of Samuel Delany's *Trouble on Triton*. During the course of the novel, Sam reveals the physical reconstruction s/he underwent to become a black man in order to attract blond, white women (126).[32] The two characters of these texts manipulate race based on an understanding of culturally-influenced sexual desires. In Disher's case, he understands that the racism of his Southern belle has made him romantically taboo and that he must show a white exterior in order to become a potential mate.

Whether Disher is as conscious of the cultural basis of his own sexual desires remains ambiguous. Neither he, nor the narrator, ever directly addresses the reason(s) that Disher "swore there were three things essential to the happiness of a colored gentleman: yellow money, yellow women and yellow taxis" and had never been seen with a girlfriend who didn't look white (Schuyler, *Black No More* 3). However, a scene from Schuyler's *Black Empire* serials reveals some possible reasons behind this culturally-motivated desire. In a description of a sumptuous bedroom belonging to the notorious African-American Dr. Belsidus, Schuyler highlights the cultural connections between sexuality and race:

> Between the rear windows in a concave, softly lighted recess stood an amazingly life-like male phallic symbol made of translucent porcelain and fully six feet in height. In a similar recess between the two front windows stood a statue of three nude young women in the full bloom and vigor of life with their arms on each other's shoulders. They were obviously made of the same porcelain. One was a Caucasian, one an African and the other a Mongolian. (23)

Belsidus' artistic decorations reflect his sexual activities and preferences. He explicitly seduces his wealthy, white patients in order to support his black nationalist activities, for example. The obviousness and extremity of Belsidus' sexual decoration, and activities, suggest other implicit motivation as well. For instance, Dr. Belsidus' relationship with Martha Gaskin, a white woman, "symbolize[s] his subjugation of the white race" (240).[33] Gaskin, and the other white women, are not only wealthy, but racially forbidden or taboo. They symbolize all that is denied African-American men on account of their race. Within a specifically sexual context, Belsidus and Gaskin's relationship highlights the stereotype of the extraordinary sexual appetites and virility of black men also.[34] The single,'six-foot penis' as a counterpart to three nude women, of various 'races,' obviously refers to this racial stereotype. Here Schuyler simultaneously parodies and exploits the white, particularly male, fears of miscegenation. As an 'evil genius,' Belsidus is more self-conscious and manipulative of these sexual/racial/cultural intersections than Disher. Yet, Gaskin remains by Belsidus' side at the end of the text, similar to the 'happy ending' of Disher and Helen Givens in *Black No More*. As Hill and Rasmussen suggest, Schuyler's own inter-racial marriage might have motivated this persistent inter-racial theme (282).

As his own white alter-ego, then, Disher courts and marries the white woman who had spurned him. The fact that Helen Givens' father is the Imperial Grand Wizard of The Knights of Nordica, a modern reincarnation of the Ku Klux Klan, does not deter Disher, and the only racial problem he encounters is the threat of their child emerging too dark-skinned. Disher avoids this potential problem as well, however, as his wife reveals the recently discovered, remote black ancestry of her family. Helen, in fact, begs Disher not to leave **her** on account of this racial intermixing. The text ends with a happy snapshot of Disher, Helen, the Imperial Wizard, and his wife on the beach in France—all "as dusky as little Matthew Crookman Fisher who played in the sandpile at their feet" (Schuyler, *Black No More* 250). Black has become the culturally preferred color and racial prejudice has transformed into anti-white ideology. It is interesting to note here that despite the general racial inversion, Schuyler still places the openly interracial couple outside of the United States. This coincides with his interracial couple in *Black Empire*, Martha Gaskin and Dr. Belsidus, who finally reside together in Africa. Likewise, Edgar Rice Burroughs' earlier interracial couple, John Carter and Princess Dejah Thoris, live 'happily ever after' on Mars. These examples reveal the potential, as well as the limits, of the speculative element of science fiction. Most importantly, the speculative element of science fiction allows writers (and readers) to imagine how racial relations could become more fluid and inclusive. The geographic displacement of the interracial couples, however, highlights the strength and tenacity of racial prejudice. Schuyler's racial egalitarianism, even within an imaginative construct, was constrained by divisive racial ideologies.

Disher also reveals a sophisticated knowledge of the complex economic, social, and political mechanics of race in the United States, and he uses this knowledge to his personal benefit. Running out of money and finding "[b]eing white [. . .] was no Open Sesame of employment," Disher discerns the economic potential in the threat to Southern business of the whitening treatment (Schuyler, *Black No More* 58). Therefore, he passes himself off as a Northern anthropologist, an expert on race, and quickly rises to prominence within The Knights of Nordica. As the Grand Exalted Giraw of the racist organization, Disher benefits financially both from the dues of the white laborers and from the contributions of the white businessmen. Playing both sides of the economic fence, Disher distracts the laborers with the racial threat and simultaneously assures the businessmen that his organization is firmly against organized labor. To keep the money flowing in, he actively antagonizes the economic and racial situation in the South, sabotaging strikes and planting "Communistic tracts" to frighten the business owners (111).

In addition to the economic field, Disher manipulates the socio-political elements of American society. He allies himself overtly with the organizations of the racist whites, while covertly working to keep the whitening treatment organization, Black-No-More, in operation. As he explains the complex strategy to his friend Bunny, a "status quo" must be maintained in order to ensure their continual financial gain (Schuyler, *Black No More* 120). Disher's complex schemes culminate in politics. Asked to help the Southern Democrats win the upcoming presidential elections, Disher tells Bunny, "We'll try the old sure fire Negro problem stuff" (147). Although his party does not ultimately win the election, Disher, his family, and his friend Bunny escape to Mexico unscathed and with a large monetary cache. In marked contrast, the Democratic vice-presidential candidate is lynched by a white mob because of the revelation of his remote black ancestry. In all of these situations, Disher achieves his goals because, "[t]he most successful propagandist is one who thoroughly understands the ideology of those to be propagandized" (Fields 111).

The ending of *Black No More* has led to the "assimilationism" theory within Schuyler theory (Peplow, "Black" 7). Disher's racial maneuverings finally come to an end as he flees the country and reveals his former black identity to his family. Yet, as Disher reminisces, he "had had such a good time since being white: plenty of money, almost unlimited power, a beautiful wife, good liquor and the pick of damsels within reach" (Schuyler, *Black No More* 205–6). Furthermore, his wife stays with him despite his revelation, undergoing a type of racial transformation herself: "Helen felt a wave of relief go over her. There was no feeling of revulsion at the thought that her husband was a Negro. [. . .] To hell with the world! To hell with society! Compared to what she possessed, [. . .] all talk of race and color was damned foolishness" (214). Disher, in other words, is never 'punished' for his racial manipulations—the exploitation of racism, promotion of racial divisions, and antagonism of racial conflict. As the protagonist of the story, Disher and his generally unrepentant and unpenalized color change have inspired the "assimilationism" theory of critics like Bone and Larson (Peplow, "Black" 7). Because readers are accustomed to the valorization of the perspective of a text's protagonist, Disher has often been falsely placed in the context of traditional heroism and his viewpoint has been collapsed with that of the author. The logic of such a reading goes something like this: because Disher is the protagonist, he must be the hero of the text; since the hero, Disher, seems to adopt an assimilationist attitude, racial assimilation must be valorized by the text; and finally, because the text promotes racial assimilation, so too must its author. In fact, popular and/or pulp fiction often embodies such a traditional heroic approach. For example, in Edgar Rice Burroughs' straightforward melodrama, John Carter is simultaneously the protagonist, the narrator, and a hero, and his viewpoints correspond with those of the author.

In contrast to the assimilationism theorists, Michael Peplow and John M. Reilly offer a more complex and, therefore, more accurate representation of *Black No More* and its author. First and foremost, both Peplow and Reilly correctly place *Black No More* in the context of satire. Peplow discusses the protagonist as a black Picaro or trickster figure and argues, "we must examine the novel *as satire*, as a piece representative of a genre in which the foibles and vices of man are attacked, often harshly" ("Black" 7). Likewise, Reilly asserts, "since a character such as Max Disher is given the most effective dialogue in the novel and is shown as roguishly clever, Blacks come off somewhat better than whites in Schuyler's narrative. But perhaps that is less significant than the fact that Schuyler, for the most part, deals out his scorn evenhandedly" (108). Both critics, then, note a somewhat more favorable portrayal, over-all, of the protagonist but emphasize the generally biting nature of satire in assessing both Disher and Schuyler. The literary technique of satire opens up a critical gap between the author and the protagonist, the text as a whole, and the audience. Therefore, the relationships between each must be more carefully scrutinized for the greatest possible critical accuracy.

In contrast to a more straightforward and traditionally heroic reading of the protagonist, Peplow's reading of Disher as a black Picaro or trickster figure emphasizes his subversive nature. Instead of the overt, absolute honesty and virtue of a traditional hero, Disher "is a rogue, a 'rascal of low degree' [. . .]. He is wily, cunning, a confidence artist" (Peplow, "Black" 8). As a trickster figure, Disher "uses 'wit, guile and cunning . . . to turn a situa-tion to his own advantage'" and "'outwits by any means necessary him who is stronger and more powerful.' It is [. . .] a 'recognized survival technique in the black community'" (ibid).[35] The traditional hero is strong and power-ful, righting wrongs and always triumphing over evil in the end. John Carter, for example, single-handedly conquers an entire planet, killing lecherous bad guys and rescuing virtuous princesses with nothing more than a sword. On the other hand, the black Picaro or trickster figure uses his wit for his own gain and with the ultimate goal of survival against a stronger opponent. In an imperfect world, then, Disher is one of the most sympathetically por-trayed characters, and a reader might share his grim humor as he "laugh[s] at the white folks up his sleeve" and reveals the ignorance and absurdity at the heart of America's 'race problem' (Schuyler, *Black No More* 38).

Yet, Disher works by indirection and covert manipulation, he actively aggravates social ills, and he primarily cares for himself. Not only is Disher a representative of a black Picaro figure, then, but also he illustrates qualities of the anti-hero of modern western literature.[36] Robert Hill and Kent Rasmus-sen similarly note the importance of the trickster figure and the anti-hero to an accurate understanding of Schuyler's other main character, Dr. Belsidus, of the *Black Empire* series: "[v]iewed through the prism of black folklore and mythology, therefore, Schuyler's Belsidus is not a deranged personality. He is, rather, simultaneously a hero and an authentic anti-hero who, like the African trickster, turns weakness into strength, upsets the machinery of domination, [and] deals out retribution" (Hill and Rasmussen 288). In this context, Belsidus is a darker and more powerful version of Disher as trickster or anti-hero. In both texts, the alternative point of view offered by the trickster or anti-hero challenges the monolithic, 'universal' point of view of the traditional hero protagonist.

However, the melodramatic context of Belsidus' characterization does not open up the same critical gap between the protagonist and the author as the satiric context of *Black No More*. Satire is the perfect medium for the imperfect world, or "black anti-utopia," Schuyler portrays in *Black No More* (Reilly). In such a context, traditional heroes are impossible because racism, and even race consciousness, negatively effects every person in the United States. Disher might be the closest thing to a hero in a race conscious society, but that does not mean Schuyler holds him up as an ideal model of human behavior or as representative of a solution to racism. The more Disher reveals his knowledge and mastery of all the ways race operates in American society, the more he reveals how he has been negatively changed by just such a race consciousness. As a trickster figure, Disher is the ideal vehicle to illuminate the intricate and illogical mechanics of race in American society, while at the same time entertaining the reader with his wit and antics.

Comparing Schuyler's two science fiction protagonists, Disher and Dr. Belsidus, raises a central problem for every Schuyler critic—reconciling the assimilationist Disher and the Afro-centric Belsidus. Tucker, for example, chooses a straightforward interpretation of Disher and a satiric interpretation of Belsidus. He believes Schuyler reveals his true assimilationist views through Disher and intended *Black Empire* as a closet joke on his audience: "what Hill and Rasmussen suggest tentatively deserves confident assertion, that "the *Black Empire* may have been a cynical joke that Schuyler played on his readers" ("Can" 146). Tucker's disassociation between Schuyler and the Afro-centric perspective of Belsidus, and the Black Empire serials more generally, has merit. As Tucker notes, Schuyler's "favorite rhetorical mode" was satire (145). However, several critical disclaimers must be attached to a satiric reading of *Black Empire*. First, even if Schuyler personally did not believe in the Afro-centric perspective embodied in *Black Empire*, the text itself is melodramatic. Therefore, outside of the critical debates surrounding Schuyler as an author and person, the point is moot. Secondly, if the overtly melodramatic *Black Empire* is read as a satire, the overtly satiric *Black No More* must logically be read as a satire as well. Tucker, for example, qualifies his satiric reading of *Black No More*, explicitly omitting science and implicitly omitting the protagonist. Why would the protagonist of the melodrama be read as satiric while the protagonist of the satire is read as a traditional hero?

Finally, if the *Black Empire* serials are read satirically, Tucker's thesis of Schuyler's scientific idealism and objectivity is undermined further. If Belsidus' black nationalism is a joke, so too is his status as a scientist and doctor. Furthermore, how could Belsidus be a black nationalist when as a rational scientist he should not logically believe in race at all? Of course Belsidus, like Disher and Crookman, could be knowingly and falsely manipulating the 'black masses' for his own financial and political gain. This scenario would help explain the troubling relationship between Belsidus and Martha Gaskin, a white woman. Despite Dr. Belsidus' professions of contempt for and ill-usage of many white women[37], Martha Gaskin proves herself loyal and valuable to the black cause throughout the course of the text and is actually the last image of the entire serial, "looking odd among those Negroes" but apparently finally accepted despite her 'race' (Schuyler, *Black Empire* 258). In addition, a satiric or critical reading of Belsidus has the advantage of qualifying the violence and possible moral offense of some of his actions: his policy of killing off white women after they have served their purpose to the organization, for example, and his authorization of bio-chemical warfare for a mass killing of whites. Finally, a negative reading of Belsidus corresponds with Schuyler's satiric portrayal of scientists in *Black No More*.

In marked contrast to Tucker's assertion of idealism, scientists and science are overtly linked with capitalism, consumerism, and the hypocrisy of Afro-American race consciousness in *Black No More*. Schuyler continues his typical role as debunker in the scientific field, as well as in African-American literature. Dr. Cornelius Crookman, for instance, espouses scientific theories undermining biological essentialism, so he should be the hero of this drama according to Tucker's formula. Yet, Crookman's name signifies that he, like Disher, is selling something, is swindling someone for his own profit. Dr. Crookman's cronies, a "'Numbers' banker" and a realtor, symbolize the close ties between science and capitalism (12). The Numbers banker actually refers to their new business, "Black-No-More, Incorporated" (49) as "the best and safest graft I've ever been in" (39). In addition, the elaborate advertisement outside of the very first "Black-No-More" sanitarium embodies the commercialism and consumerism of America's capitalist society and the ties between economics, science, and race. Schuyler goes to great lengths to vividly describe "the large, electric sign hung from the roof to the second floor":

"It represented a huge arrow outlined in green with the words BLACK-NO-MORE running its full length vertically. A black face was depicted at the lower end of the arrow while at the top shone a white face to which the arrow was pointed" (32). Schuyler even describes the elaborate system of delayed lighting portraying the actual scientific process of "black face" to "white face." At this point, it becomes glaringly obvious that not only Dr. Crookman, but also science more broadly is not portrayed as the objective ideal Tucker imagines. If science is a solution to the 'Negro problem,' it is only through selling African-Americans a physical exterior which will be culturally undesirable soon after.

Schuyler's emphasis on the connection(s) between science and capitalism highlights the hypocrisy of Afro-American race consciousness as well. In the preface to *Black No More*, Schuyler refers to the invention, marketing, and distribution of Kink-No-More[38] around the turn-of-the-century. He emphasizes the increasing success of such endeavors due to "the avid search on the part of the black masses for some key to chromatic perfection," and then goes on to assert that "science is on the verge of satisfying them" (vii). "Science" then takes the form of excerpts from an interview with a Japanese doctor and an Italian engineer's letter to the NAACP in which both men claim to be able to physically change darker-skinned 'races' into lighter-skinned ones.[39] Why does Schuyler place his science fiction text within the context of these real-world elements? The Kink-No-More synopsis illustrates the desire on the part of African-Americans to physically look more like whites and links it to capitalism, profit, and technology. Schuyler is emphasizing the hypocrisy of any Negro-centered activity here. Schuyler believes not only Disher, but also almost every Negro in the United States desires to be white; they have been indoctrinated by the repeated assertions of white superiority and have internalized the cultural racial hierarchy.

Crookman is a good example of this type of racial internalization. The doctor is known as a "Race Man" (47), and he "prided himself above all on being a great lover of his race" (Schuyler, *Black No More* 46). Yet, he attempts to solve the problem of racism by eradicating the very race he supposedly values. Furthermore, Crookman "was wedded to everything black except the black woman" (47). Crookman marries a woman "able to pass for white" and has "liaisons with comely and available fraus and frauliens" while abroad, researching Black history of all things (ibid). Schuyler's sarcasm is heavy in his description of Dr. Crookman and the discrepancy between his 'race consciousness' on various issues. Schuyler reinforces his irony and satire with a similar description of Dr. Shakespeare Agamemnon Beard, a caricature of W. E. B. Du Bois: "the learned doctor wrote scholarly and biting editorials in *The Dilemma* denouncing the Caucasians whom he secretly admired and lauding the greatness of the Negroes whom he alternately pitied and despised" (89). Beard mirrors the gender relationships of Crookman and Disher as well: "[l]ike most Negro leaders, he deified the black woman but abstained from employing aught save octoroons" (ibid). All of these examples reinforce Schuyler's scientific critique of race consciousness. Not only is there no such thing as race from a scientific standpoint, but also even the most race conscious Afro-Americans covertly or subconsciously subscribe to the existing racial hierarchy privileging white physical features. The scientists' lack of scientific objectivity is the basis of Schuyler's satire here. Clearly, this negative portrayal of the doctor/scientists does not support Tucker's reading of scientific idealism.

Finally, science as a discipline is portrayed as equally variable and biased as the specific concept of race itself. Schuyler not only highlights the close connection between science and capitalism, but also science and social norms. Tucker asserts that "Schuyler's satire is not aimed at the transformative potential of science itself" ("Can" 143). However, as discussed earlier, Crookman's belief that science alone will provide an answer to racism is satirized.[40] Tucker himself admits that the text as a whole illustrates that Crookman's process is not a total or ideal solution, as the color line simply reverses at the end. In addition, it is no coincidence that Disher chooses anthropology as his new occupation after becoming white. This scientific field allows Disher to 'sell' highly biased and erroneous racial ideas to his racist white audience. Through his protagonist, Schuyler satirizes the emerging scientific field of anthropology, highlighting its common use as a political and ideological tool. Disher's impersonation of an anthropologist also highlights Schuyler's decision to divide his protagonist and his scientist into two separate characters (Disher and Dr. Crookman). Disher's outsider perspective—as a lay person and as an African-American—allows him to challenge the false objectivity and positivism of the scientific discipline. In contrast, Edgar Rice Burroughs' protagonist, John Carter, embodies an ethnographic perspective; Burroughs collapses the protagonist and the scientist into a single character. A traditional hero as scientist does not allow for the same scientific critique as Disher as a trickster figure.

Furthermore, Schuyler uses the general cultural color reversal at the end to emphasize the subjective and culturally variable basis of anthropology:

> Prof. Handen Moutthe, the eminent anthropologist (who was well known for his popular work on *The Sex Life of Left-Handed Morons among the Ainus*) announced that as a result of his long research among

the palest citizens, he was convinced they were mentally inferior and that their children should be segregated from the others in school. Professor Moutthe's findings were considered authoritative because he had spent three entire weeks of hard work assembling his data. Four state legislatures immediately began to consider bills calling for separate schools for pale children. (*Black No More* 247–8)

This brief passage contains biting satire of the research techniques and popular outreach of the scientific community, as well as the political and social influence of scientific findings (scientism). In his reversal, Schuyler draws attention to the historic use of science to justify racism and oppression. There is nothing objective or idealistic in this representation of science. In fact, Schuyler's satire here resembles an early strategy of resistance to scientific racism identified by Stepan and Gilman—"the employment of wit, irony, or parody" (82–3).

Dr. Crookman and Disher, the two most sympathetically portrayed characters in *Black No More*, manipulate scientific, social, cultural, economic and political concepts of race; they are, in fact, highly 'race conscious.' For Schuyler, however, clearly race consciousness does not have the positive connotations Tucker ascribes to it. Because of the biological falsehood of race, its legacy for African-Americans of oppression, and the melting pot ideal of American society in which Schuyler obviously believed, race can only have negative implications—biologically, politically, socially, and culturally. Any act based upon a consciousness of race is only perpetuating a falsehood and, therefore, must involve manipulation of some sort—you can either be the manipulator, like Crookman and Disher, or be the manipulated, like the African-American and white 'masses.'

Even Schuyler, in his understanding of racial operations, becomes a manipulator. Tucker quotes Schuyler's private opinion of his second fictional text: "I have been greatly amused by the public enthusiasm for 'The Black Internationale' [the first half of the *Black Empire*] which is hokum and hack work of the purest vein. I deliberately set out to crowd as much race chauvinism and sheer improbability into it as my fertile imagination could conjure. The result vindicates my low opinion of the human race" ("Can" 146). Like the inventor of Kink-No-More, Schuyler is selling a racially-implicated product to the African-American 'masses.' If they are gullible enough to buy it, if they put stock in race, than he, like Disher, is doing no more than teaching them a lesson and no less than personally profiting from their erroneous thinking. The common focus of Schuyler's satire seems to be the racial fantasies or desires of his black audience—in the first text, a desire to be white and in the second text, a desire to be black.[41] In Schuyler's ideal of a raceless world, both of these extremes of the racial spectrum are false and obstructive. He utilizes science fiction and dystopic fiction as a means of wish fulfillment, illustrating the folly of these race-based desires. When Tucker criticizes Schuyler for assuming "that 'race' just does not matter anymore," he misses the forward focus of Schuyler's beliefs, symbolized by his interest in speculative fiction ("Can" 148). Schuyler's detailed and continuous focus on race in his fiction and non-fiction alike illustrates a 'race consciousness,' even as it takes the form of an attempt to rid the world of notions of race. Schuyler does chronicle race's "power to shape human lives in very real ways" in his fictional texts, but in satirizing the effects of this power, he shows the error of acting this way (Tucker, "Can" 148).

Pairing Schuyler's works with that of a third influential author and scientist, Frantz Fanon, highlights additional aspects of Schuyler's scientific connections, as well as his "poststructuralist sensibility" (Joyce, "Black" 342).[42] Writing largely within the fields of psychiatry and cultural studies, Fanon examines the complex process of colonial identity formation in his 1952 text *Black Skin, White Masks*. While significant generic and geographic differences exist between *Black No More* and *Black Skin, White Masks*, both texts share a radical deconstruction of racial identity and a promotion of individualism. The striking similarities between Tucker's critical analysis of Schuyler's *Black No More* and Diana Fuss' critical analysis of Fanon's *Black Skin, White Masks* highlight the common threads existing between the two primary texts. First, both Tucker and Fuss focus on a summary statement near the end of two texts by the primary authors. Where Schuyler writes, "At best, 'race' is a superstition" (*Black and Conservative* 352), Fanon concludes, "The Negro is not. Any more than the white man" in his text *Black Skin, White Masks* (231). Therefore, when Tucker quotes the conclusion of Schuyler's autobiography as the epitome of his "faulty theories about the way 'race' works," he could be describing Frantz Fanon and his text as well (Tucker, "Can" 140). In addition, Fuss notes the "enigmatic" nature of Fanon's conclusion, wondering if he is "suggesting, perhaps, that there is no such thing as race?" (76). Fuss seems confused because the title of Fanon's text "allows simultaneously for an essentialist and a constructionist reading; it unhinges 'race' from skin color at the same time it reinscribes the problematic association of race with biology" (75). As we will see, Schuyler too promotes a constructionist reading of race while maintaining a connection between race and the physical body or biology. Fuss' discussion as a whole, however, promotes a constructionist reading of Fanon's text. For example, Fuss utilizes Fanon's *Black Skin, White Masks* as an introduction to "the many arbitrary significations of 'race'"

(74). As Tucker's earlier critical assessment of Schuyler applies to Fanon, so Fuss' assessment of Fanon here applies to Schuyler. Not surprisingly, then, Fuss' assertion that *Black Skin, White Masks* "provides us with something of a running commentary on the arbitrariness of the racial signifier in Western culture" (74) is strikingly similar to Tucker's summary of Schuyler's *Black No More*: "The novel is designed to emphasize the scientific meaningless of 'race' and the arbitrariness of color consciousness" ("Can" 143). In this way, Schuyler and Fanon both reflect "the poststructuralist sensibility" of much contemporary science fiction dealing with race and racial identity (Joyce, "Black" 342).

Furthermore, Fuss' larger theoretical and generic context applies to Tucker and Schuyler, as well as Fanon. First, Fuss clearly articulates the threat some readers find in the poststructuralist stance of the primary authors: "The charge, then, is clear: to deconstruct 'race' is to abdicate, negate, or destroy black identity" (77). Tucker's criticism of Schuyler is a manifestation of this critical stance. In addition, Fuss begins her chapter on poststructuralist Afro-American literary theory by articulating the broad questions which underlie Tucker's analysis of Schuyler: "Is race a matter of birth? of culture? both? neither? What, exactly, are the criteria for racial identity? *Are* there criteria for racial identity? What, we might finally ask, is 'race'?" (73–4). More important for our discussion of Schuyler and his critical reputation, Fuss places these questions at the heart of current African-American literary criticism. Asserting that "the deconstruction of 'race' and its implications for reading literature by or about Afro-American subjects has emerged as one the most controversial questions in the field of Afro-American Studies today," Fuss focuses on the "three scholars at the center of the current debates on 'race'"—Anthony Appiah, Henry Louis Gates, Jr., and Houston Baker (74). It is not surprising, then, that these three names continually arise in both Tucker's work on Schuyler and my own.

Turning specifically to the primary texts, Schuyler's *Black No More* is basically an exploration of Fanon's theme within a science/fictional format. Whereas Fanon explores the non-fiction psychological and cultural process of racial construction, Schuyler utilizes the fictional aspect of science fiction to create an actual scientific process physically embodying Fanon's abstract phenomenon. Fanon describes the process and implications involved in the metaphoric "white masks" developed by colonized blacks. With Max Disher, Schuyler takes Fanon's black man, his body and his psyche, and actualizes the psychological process which Fanon analyzes. Disher's physical transformation into his white alter-ego of Matthew Fisher mirrors the process by which the "black skin" of an Antillean gradually develops a "white mask." Fanon opens *Black Skin, White Masks* with an explanation of the divided nature of black subjectivity very similar to that denoted by W. E .B. Du Bois' term "double- consciousness." In *The Souls of Black Folks*, Du Bois writes: "It is a peculiar sensation, this double-consciousness, this sense of always looking at one's self through the eyes of others, of measuring one's soul by the tape of a world that looks on in amused contempt and pity. One ever feels his two-ness,—an American, a Negro; two souls, two thoughts, two unreconciled strivings; two warring ideals in one dark body [. . .]" (8–9).[43] Similarly, Fanon writes, "[t]he black man has two dimensions. One with his fellows, the other with the white man. A Negro behaves differently with a white man and with another Negro. That this self-division is a direct result of colonialist subjugation is beyond question" (17). Within this context, Disher's white skin represents the consciousness of white society acquired by people-of-color in order to survive in a hierarchical and oppressive society. Disher's white skin/white consciousness, then, allows him to effectively blend into the white social nexus.

Schuyler's use of science fiction literary techniques in *Black No More* allows him to paradoxically make the construction of racial identity simultaneously more distanced from the reader and more vivid. Known as "estrangement," this concept is allied in science fiction with "cognition" to form the basis of all science fiction. In *Metamorphoses of Science Fiction*, Darko Suvin utilizes Bertolt Brecht's definition of estrangement as the foundation for his expanded theory of cognitive estrangement: "A representation which estranges is one which allows us to recognize its subject, but at the same time makes it seem unfamiliar" (qtd. Suvin 6). The primary advantage to cognitive estrangement is that a phenomenon so familiar that it is usually taken for granted becomes more distinct and discernable in an unfamiliar setting. Thus, the complex, yet subtle interaction between racial construction and identity formation can become more obvious and immediate in a science fiction context. Schuyler utilizes the "novum," or speculative element of a scientific procedure for racial transformation to estrange the reader from the ubiquitous yet rarely directly-confronted machinations of race in American society (Suvin 4). The readers of Schuyler's text are practically slapped in the face with the cultural basis of race and its implications. Even for those readers familiar with the concept of double-consciousness, for example, the literal chromatic transformation of the African-American characters is jarring, if not outright shocking. Not only the biting nature of Schuyler's satire and the highly volatile issue of racial identity make *Black No More* controversial, but also the extreme vividness and forcefulness of Schuyler's ideas as viewed through the cognitive estrangement of science fiction.

Schuyler's deconstruction of race is so effective that the reader might overlook the specter of essentialism raised by Schuyler's choice of novum. In the transformation of Fanon's psychological process into a physical or biological process, Schuyler runs the risk of undermining his larger cultural argument, for he maintains the traditional connection between biology and race. Schuyler counteracts this biological connection to race in several ways. First, the biological aspects of race manipulated in the scientific process are all external features. Dr. Crookman does not reveal his scientific procedure in full detail, but he does outline the features effected—facial features, skin color, and hair color and texture. [44] Schuyler logically utilizes the physical features commonly used to categorize race. Within traditional racial essentialism, these exterior physical features reflect the interior, static racial identity of a person which corresponds to a racial collective. However, the paradox at the heart of Schuyler's racial deconstruction is that these physical characteristics are **only** exterior and do not correspond to any essential racial difference. For example, the racial transformation does not affect the genetic structure of the patients, as evidenced by the failure of the process to be passed on to offspring. This means that even the physical characteristics associated with a particular race are exterior signifiers only. There can be no 'essence' involved when a process of bleaching and what now would be called plastic surgery effect racial categorization. Crookman's procedure literalizes Fanon's "white mask," then, one which conceals a genetic code for facial features signifying a second race. The essentialist racial connection between exterior and interior, as well as biology and psychology, explodes under the pressure of such diverse plurality. Distinct, static racial types are the foundation of racial essentialism and, therefore, the concept of essentialism cannot withstand Schuyler's extreme fluidity, plurality, and ambiguity of racial construction.

Continuing in this vein, Schuyler utilizes Dr. Crookman as a vehicle for espousing racial theories which both explain why his procedure is effective and why it is largely unnecessary from a scientific standpoint. For example, Dr. Crookman asserts that even if his process didn't affect facial characteristics, like nose and lip width, the racial transformation would still be effective because "the wide difference in Caucasian and Afro-American facial characteristics that most people imagine" do not actually exist (Schuyler, *Black No More* 19). This would leave color as the sole remaining physical characteristic upon which to distinguish race. The superficial nature of traditional, physical racial signifiers means that they can be manipulated and are also unreliable indicators of racial categorization. For example, Samuel Delany writes of his family's experience with lynching, uncomfortably like the lynching scene near the end of *Black No More*, when a pregnant cousin, "[a] woman who looked white," was traveling with her much darker-skinned husband ("Racism" 385). The group of white men who lynched them obviously believed the couple's relationship to be miscegenous. Similarly, Schuyler creates a character in *Black No More*, Mr. Walter Williams, who "was known to be a Negro among his friends and acquaintances, but no one else would have suspected it" (94) due to his "pale blue eyes, wavy auburn hair," and light skin (93).[45] Schuyler goes on to connect such ambiguity of racial features to the extensive interbreeding of the so-called races in the United States: Williams' "great-grandfather, it seemed, had been a mulatto" (94). With his typical satiric wit, Schuyler describes Williams as a member of the National Social Equality League, a "militant Negro organization" (86). Yet, Schuyler calls Williams, and another member of the N.S.E.L., a "white man" based on the same physical features used by racial essentialists to categorize race. In this way, Schuyler emphasizes his belief in both the logical failings of a racial essentialism founded on exterior physical features and the absurdity of basing racial identity on such a tiny portion of an individual's ancestry. The satire of this segment rests on the discrepancy between the chimeric nature of race as traditionally defined in the U. S. and the undue significance placed upon it in this country and elsewhere.

Finally, Dr. Crookman completes his deconstruction of race by addressing the issue of language. After his thorough defense of the efficacy of the procedure, Crookman's business associate asks him, "How about that darky dialect? You can't change that" (Schuyler, *Black No More* 17). Crookman replies, "There is no such thing as Negro dialect [. . .]. There are no racial or color dialects; only sectional dialects" (17–18). As support, Crookman cites the "purest French" of the "educated Haitian" and English accent of the "Jamaican Negro" (18). These examples parallel Frantz Fanon's more complicated analysis of "The Negro and Language" in *Black Skin, White Masks*, in which he discusses the connection between language acquisition and racial categorization. Fanon notes, "In any group of young men in the Antilles, the one who expresses himself well, who has mastered the language, is inordinately feared; keep an eye on that one, he is almost white. In France one says, 'He talks like a book.' In Martinique, 'He talks like a white man'" (20–1). Elevated and sophisticated language skills, especially those reflecting the linguistic norms of the colonizer and/or academic discourse, are racial signifiers linked to the white colonizers. At this point, we have come full circle, back to the issue of black subjectivity and double-consciousness discussed earlier. The black man who masters the French language/academic discourse of the colonizer in Fanon's example reflects the larger concept of a double-consciousness Fanon describes in the text as a whole. Part of the "white masks" acquired by blacks are these linguistic characteristics.

Like the young black Antilleans, Max Disher conveys a particular racial identity due to his linguistic double-consciousness. First, utilizing his understanding of the linguistic expectations of his largely uneducated, southern white audiences, Disher/Fisher tells them exactly what they want to hear in a manner designed to impress them.[46] Disher was born in the South, and "[h]e knew what would fetch their applause and bring in their memberships and he intended to repeat it over and over" (Schuyler, *Black No More* 74). In fact, Disher's ability to imitate the racist viewpoints of his poor white audience and the discourse associated with scientists enables him to be the trickster figure Peplow discusses. Again, "[t]he most successful propagandist is one who thoroughly understands the ideology of those to be propagandized" (Fields 111). The Imperial Grand Wizard's response to Disher's anthropological 'pitch' most clearly illustrates the efficacy of his racial presentation: "He nodded his head as Matthew [Disher], now glorying in his newly-discovered eloquence made point after point, and concluded that this pale, dapper young fellow, with his ready tongue, his sincerity, his scientific training and knowledge of the situation ought to prove a valuable asset to the Knights of Nordica" (65). Disher's imitation of a racist, white scientist wins him the hand of Given's daughter Helen as well: "She had always longed for the companionship of an educated man, a scientist, a man of literary ability. Matthew to her mind embodied all of these" (109). In all of these situations, Disher utilizes his "white mask," or understanding of the norms of the white society he infiltrates, to deceive and manipulate white characters who do not have a reciprocal understanding of black society and black identity construction. The monolithic, integrated nature of white identity, as portrayed here, facilitates their deception.[47]

Schuyler largely reveals Disher's other "consciousness" through covert conversations with his friend Bunny, who has also undergone Crookman's racial procedure. Reunited post-operation in the South, Bunny immediately becomes Disher's confidant and right-hand man. Disher reveals his racial manipulations to Bunny as he does to no one else. Similarly, he confides his sticky romantic problems to Bunny; Disher worries about his wife becoming pregnant and bearing a dark-skinned child. This overtly white/covertly black set-up reflects Fanon's initial observation that a "Negro behaves differently with a white man and with another Negro" (17). Schuyler's portrayal of a covert black consciousness raises the issue of 'authentic' racial identity, like the essentialism threatened by his concretion of the psychological phenomenon of double-consciousness. During their conversation about Disher's paternal fears, for example, Bunny says, "You know, sometimes I forget who we are" (Schuyler, *Black No More* 147). Disher responds, "Well, I don't. I know I'm a darky and I'm always on the alert" (ibid). Does this statement mean that, despite the emphasis on racial construction provided by Crook-man's procedure, there exists an essential racial identity after all? That despite the flux and fluidity of racial identity described elsewhere in the text, racial identity is ultimately distinct and static?

A closer examination of the context of Disher's statement miti-gates such an essentialist reading. First, Disher's statement stems from his fears that his former identity as an African-American will be discovered if his wife gives birth to a child significantly darker-skinned than both of its parents. Such a revelation would have dire consequences for Disher, as he has intimate connections with ultra racist persons and organizations. Like the presidential and vice-presidential candidates who (unconsciously) 'pass' themselves off as white, Disher runs the risk of a loss of his career and repu-tation at the minimum and a horrible death by lynching at the maximum. In this context of always-threatening discovery and reprisals, Disher's state-ment could mean nothing more than an acknowledgement of how he would be racially categorized if his full history was known and, more importantly, the terrible consequences of such a discovery. As his immediately following statement emphasizes, his black racial identity (whether essential, authentic, or socially-imposed) means he must always be "on the alert." Along a similar line, Disher could be referring to his genetic make-up and the physical char-acteristics which he knows will be passed on to his offspring. No matter how he constructs his own identity, psychologically and physically, his offspring will initially reflect his past physical identity as a "darky."

Both of these interpretations of Disher's statement reflect the psy-chological theory of double-consciousness Schuyler sets up. Disher must maintain a specifically black consciousness in conjunction with a white con-sciousness because race still operates powerfully in American society, despite the ambiguity, fluidity, and inversions heightened by Crookman's procedure. As long as racism exists, Disher must maintain this division of his psyche in order to survive in a segregated and oppressive society. After his physical transformation, for example, Disher's double-consciousness enables him to manipulate the racial situation in the Unites States to his economic advan-tage. As discussed earlier, however, this 'success' does not make Disher an ideal hero. Rather, it illustrates how he has been negatively influenced by the racial environment of the United States. Disher maintains his physical and psychological racial dichotomies until he leaves the United States at the end of the story. The first breakdown of the dichotomies doesn't occur until

Disher's 'white family'—his wife and her parents—are exposed as multi-racial and the entire family is preparing to flee the county. At that point, he feels he can reveal his own racial background. Finally, the 'happy' snapshot of Disher and his family, equally tanned at the beach, takes place in Europe and after the general cultural inversion of racial preference in the United States.

Similarly, the point of Disher's statement about being a "darky" is not that he possesses a single, authentic black identity despite his endeavors to the contrary, but that a race-conscious society can lead to an involuntary and possibly damaging psychological division within African-Americans. First, neither racial consciousness is more 'authentic' than the other.[48] They both exist simultaneously and make an individual who he/she is, although they may exist generally in different degrees, dominate in different contexts, etc. As dichotomies, they form in relationship to each other and cannot exist without the opposite, either in the same individual or in someone else. In fact, as Chris Weedon explains in the context of feminist poststructuralism, "the individual is always the site of conflicting forms of subjectivity" (32). For example, Fuss theorizes that the same condition of fragmentation affecting women could apply to African-Americans: "It does seem plausible that, like the female subject, the Afro-American subject (who may also be female) *begins* fragmented and dispersed, begins with a 'double-consciousness,' as Du Bois would say (1903, 215)" (95). However, all "forms" or parts of a person's consciousness are not equally beneficial, and all individuals' multiple forms do not conflict equally (Weedon 32). A multiple or fragmented subjectivity may be a reality, but that does not mean it is an ideal state for all individuals. For example, from the very beginning of his analysis of the formation of a double-consciousness in black Antilleans, Fanon emphasizes its foundation in colonial oppression and racism. Fanon briefly introduces the concept of a "self-division" in black individuals and then immediately asserts, "[t]hat this self-division is a direct result of colonialist subjugation is beyond question" (17). Schuyler and Du Bois similarly place the African-American formation of a double- consciousness in the context of the racially segregated and oppressive society of the United States.

Therefore, the African-American concept of double-consciousness prefigures the contemporary, Postmodernist concept of a fragmented, multiple identity in both its multiplicity and its potential negativity. Not only race, but also gender, sexuality, religion, and nationality are possible forms or fragments of a person's identity. For example, in the contemporary age of identity politics, a gay black woman could potentially identify with at least three different groups: women, people-of-color, and/or lesbians. This example illustrates the potential difficulty of reconciling multiple forms of subjectivity, especially as the number of possible forms seems to be ever increasing in society as a whole. This difficulty, in turn, raises the question, is there a point past which this trend towards ever-smaller fragmentation, in an individual or in society more generally, should be resisted? Fuss, for example, asserts that "for both the female subject and the Afro-American subject, 'the condition of dispersal and fragmentation that Barthes valorizes (and fetishezes) is not to be achieved but to be overcome' (Miller 1986a, 109)" (95). Fuss' questioning here of a more traditional poststructuralist theory of identity formation raises two important issues. First, in suggesting that an alternate theoretical framework might be necessary for black subjectivity, Fuss joins other critics in highlighting the false universalism of current poststructuralist theories of subjectivity. Fuss ends her chapter on "Poststructuralist Afro-American Literary Theory" with a quote from cultural critic Andreas Huyssen in which he reveals the ideological underpinnings of poststructuralist theories of subjectivity in the same way Donna Haraway seeks to historicize the false universalism of the scientific community: "doesn't poststructuralism, where it simply denies the subject altogether, jettison the chance of challenging the ideology of the subject (as male, white, and middle-class) by developing alternative and different notions of subjectivity?" (Huyssen 44). Both Huyssen and Fuss join Fanon and Schuyler, then, in seeking alternatives to the normative subjectivity for their time period due to its racial bias. Fuss' analysis suggests that a more integrated consciousness might be beneficial for women and people-of-color due to the extremity of the fragmentation and conflict in their multiple forms of subjectivity.

Schuyler and Fanon utilize a similar technique to pave the way for an alternative subjectivity. In her book, *Feminist Practice and Poststructuralist Theory*, Chris Weedon explains the concept of "consciousness-raising" by which a woman learns the social foundations of her contradictory forms of subjectivity and more advantageous alternatives to the destructive forms resulting from patriarchy (33). Fanon's *Black Skin, White Masks* embodies a similar form of consciousness-raising, except in the field of race rather than gender. Similar to the Women's Liberation Movement, Fanon emphasizes the social foundations of psychological phenomena, like the development of "white masks." Fanon's critique of Alfred Adler's "psychology of the individual" is symptomatic of this social focus:

> Here the difficulties begin. In effect, Adler has created a psychology of the individual. We have just seen that the feeling of inferiority is an Antillean characteristic. It is not just this or that Antillean who embodies the neurotic formation, but all Antilleans. Antillean society

is a neurotic society, a society of "comparison." Hence we are driven from the individual back to the social structure. If there is a taint, it lies not in the "soul" of the individual but rather in that of the environment. (213)

This last sentence reveals the motivation behind Fanon's emphasis on the social—the removal of the 'problem' or neurosis from the individual. Like Schuyler, even as Fanon describes the negative aspects of a black double-consciousness, he wishes to remove the label of pathological sometimes assigned to blacks as a racial group. More importantly, Fanon places the 'problem' in the individual's social environment. This not only removes any blame or guilt from an individual, but also it opens up the potential for change. As Weedon explains,

The collective discussion of personal problems and conflicts, often previously understood as a result of personal inadequacies and neuroses, leads to a recognition that what have been experienced as personal failings are socially produced conflicts and contradictions shared by many women in similar social positions. This process of discovery can lead to a rewriting of personal experience in terms which give it social, changeable causes. (33)

Especially in the context of race, essentialism is always an issue. With an individual comes a body and the potential for essentialist theories of psychology which foreclose the possibility of change. Fanon's social emphasis, on the other hand, not only locates the cause of a racial double-consciousness in colonial oppression but also offers the possibility of social reform as a vehicle to bring about alternate theories of subjectivity.

Schuyler too practices a form of consciousness-raising. In his exploration of the cultural construction of race, he unhinges race from the biological and the individual. This performs the same function as in Fanon—it places the blame for any neuroses on the social environment rather than individual blacks, and it opens the door for change. In fact, Schuyler specifically refutes the association of pathology with African-Americans, despite his detailed description of a double-consciousness in *Black No More*: "I strongly question the view of many psychologists and sociologists that most colored people regard themselves as inferior. They simply are aware that their socio-economic position is inferior" (*Black and Conservative* 18). While the social emphasis is obvious here, this statement does not necessarily negate the psychological emphasis in *Black No More*. Schuyler is not denying double-consciousness is negative; he is emphasizing the negative aspects of all racial identity. From this perspective, whites would be 'pathological' also. Where Fanon claims "Antillean society is a neurotic society," Schuyler would claim American society is a neurotic society (213).

Furthermore, in revealing the cultural basis of an individual's formation of racial identity, Schuyler emphasizes the necessity for large-scale social reform. In his role as a satiric debunker, Schuyler refuses to create a raceless utopia. However, his use of satire and consequent creation of a racially-dystopic America illustrate the danger of racially fragmented and conflicting subjectivity.[49] Like other modern science fiction, Schuyler's *Black No More* is "a diagnosis, a warning, a call to understanding and action, and—most important—a mapping of possible alternatives" (Suvin 12). Schuyler's portrayal of the negative extremes involved in a race-conscious society points the way to the more integrated perspective promoted by Fuss. Ironically, Schuyler's refusal to actually create such an integrated consciousness, or more broadly a raceless utopia, in *Black No More* allows him to highlight the variability of race to an even greater degree. The racial inversion which takes place at the end of the text emphasizes the historical context of all racial theories and, therefore, the potential for change.[50] In historicizing race and racial identity, Schuyler makes variable what once was considered static.[51] In this, he employs the second major characteristic of science fiction—cognition. Darko Suvin distinguishes science fiction from myth in that, "SCIENCE FICTION sees the norms of any age, including emphatically its own, as unique, changeable, and therefore subject to a *cognitive* view" (7). More specifically, science fiction "sees the mythical static identity as an illusion, usually a fraud, at best only a temporary realization of potentially limitless contingencies"(ibid). Science fiction, then, is a perfect medium to question essentialist theories of race and racial identity, as well as offer alternative subjectivities. Suvin's "potentially limitless contingencies" correspond with the "alternative and different notions of subjectivity" recommended by Huyssen and Fuss (Huyssen 44). Science fiction becomes a form of consciousness-raising in this context.

While Schuyler doesn't actually propose an alternative subjectivity in *Black No More*, it is clear from his negative argument that he would not endorse either aspect of the racial double-consciousness on its own. Schuyler's denial of an authentic black identity has already been addressed, and his explicit rejection of an alternate black subjectivity is what Tucker objects to so strenuously. What some critics elide, however, is that in rejecting a specifically black identity, Schuyler also rejects the corresponding white identity. Disher, for example, maintains his white identity only so long as he profits by it. Once the cultural norms invert, Disher tans along with the rest of his family. Schuyler wishes to throw out the dichotomous racial system in its entirety.[52] Fanon too attempts to create a middle ground for himself rather than valorize either a black or white consciousness. After his lengthy exploration of the "white masks" put on by black Antilleans and the foundation of this phenomenon in colonial oppression and racism, Fanon briefly addresses the emerging Negritude movement. He asks, "What is all this talk of a black people, of a Negro nationality? I am a Frenchman. I am interested in French culture, French civilization, the French people. [. . .] What have I to do with a black empire?" (203). Fanon's words here echo Schuyler's scathing private evaluation of his science fiction series, the second part of which was actually titled "Black Empire." Fanon and Schuyler refuse to accept an "*either-or*" proposition and, unlike Tucker and Baker, reject both aspects of a racial double-consciousness—a white consciousness **and** a black consciousness (ibid).[53]

The remarkable similarities between the arguments and racial perspectives in *Black No More* and *Black Skin, White Masks* combine with Schuyler's comments elsewhere to suggest Fanon and Schuyler held a common subjective ideal. At the very end of his text, Fanon reveals the alternative subjectivity he supports: "At the conclusion of this study, I want the world to recognize, with me, the open door of every consciousness" (232). Therefore, while Fanon recognizes the need for collective social reform in order to "create the ideal conditions of existence for a human world," he valorizes a subjectivity based largely on individualism rather than a racial collective (231). *Black Skin, White Masks* ends like a personal manifesto of liberation: "In the world through which I travel, I am endlessly creating myself" (229). Such a position mirrors Schuyler's individualism, also in opposition to a collective racial identity. When Tucker quotes Schuyler's infamous ending to this autobiography, he notes the scientific basis of this rejection of race (Tucker "Can" 140–41). However, the context surrounding the quote reveals the individualism upon which it rests. The sentence preceding Tucker's quote reads, "Relegating spurious racism to limbo, in our future American we need to stress the importance of the individual of whatever color" (Schuyler, *Black and Conservative* 352). For Schuyler, individualism lies at the heart of freedom, intellectual and political, as well as other positive American values. To him, racial solidarity is based on a scientific falsehood, and so intolerable to act upon as a truth. Furthermore, in "The Caucasian Problem," Schuyler emphasizes the negative legacy of race and collective racial identities—global prejudice and oppression, including slavery, segregation, colonialism, and imperialism. In addition, however, Schuyler believes racial solidarity conflicts with individualism and other positive values he holds up as national ideals.

Schuyler's relationship with his wife, Josephine, illustrates these values and provides further reinforcement of his rejection of race and racial solidarity. In a lengthy autobiography, Schuyler does not devote much space to his wife. However, it is symptomatic of his values that of the two sentences in which he addressed the cross-racial nature of their relationship, the second full sentence reads, "She saw Negroes as I saw whites, as individuals" (*Black and Conservative* 163). Furthermore, Schuyler spends the remainder of the segment on his wife describing other specific attributes. While race is directly addressed throughout the majority of the autobiography, Schuyler consciously chooses to place the relationship with his wife largely outside of a racial context. They are explicitly not race conscious, but rather relate to one other as individuals. Similarly, Schuyler does not place his daughter in a racial context. Given Schuyler's outspoken and prolific non-fiction addressing interracial relationships, his surprising silence in his autobiography seems to signal a desire to promote an individualism which transcends a collective racial identity.

Schuyler and Fanon both acknowledge a problem with black subjectivity brought about by oppression and racism and, by exploring the way race is constructed, they hope to bring about a world in which the concept of race becomes obsolete. In other words, Schuyler and Fanon are both race conscious, but not in the same way as Tucker. Schuyler and Fanon see race consciousness as negative, something to be overcome, something standing in the way of attaining individual freedom. Both authors do display a sophisticated knowledge of the power of race "to shape human lives in very real ways" in their texts (Tucker, "Can" 148). Furthermore, that is Schuyler's and Fanon's primary theme in the texts discussed above. What nettles Tucker and confuses Fuss is the desire of both men to be free of race completely, in all its manifestations, and the authors,' perhaps idealistic, belief that the best, and only, way to bring this about is to act as if it has already occurred. Barbara Jeanne Fields' emphasis on the ideological basis of race supports this racial rejection. Making a clear distinction between race and biology, doctrine and ideology, Fields asserts:

> race is neither biology nor an idea absorbed into biology by Lamarckian inheritance. It is ideology, and ideologies do not have lives of their own. Nor can they be handed down or inherited: a doctrine can be [. . .] but not an ideology. If race lives on today, it does not live on because we have inherited it from our forebears of the seventeenth century or the eighteenth or nineteenth, but because we continue to create it today. (117)

If humans did not continually "reinvent and re-ritualize" race in their daily lives, then, it would cease to be a meaningful, powerful concept (Fields 118).[54]

There is no middle position on race for Schuyler and Fanon. The concept of race was initially founded on biology so a cultural definition of race innately reveals the falseness, the fiction of race. From a strictly rational or scientific viewpoint, then, to perpetuate race as a cultural concept is illogical and misleading.[55] Walter Benn Michaels explains the ramifications of a middle position, one which acknowledges the cultural basis of race but does not then reject race: "What it means, then, to accept the idea of racial identity as a function of 'purely social and cultural perceptions' instead of as biology is to accept the idea of racial identity as the codification of people's mistake *about* biology" (132). A scientist or person with a strictly logical, rational mind tends to see race from this viewpoint and, therefore, would be hesitant to endorse it. Fanon, for example, was a psychiatrist. Not coincidentally, Fanon joins Schuyler in mentioning scientific experiments associated with skin pigmentation and modifications of biological 'race' in *Black Skin, White Masks*, and also dismisses them as false solutions (111). While not a scientist by vocation, Schuyler was deeply interested in science and places science/scientists at the heart of his fiction. It is not that Fanon and Schuyler necessarily believed in some ideal of scientific rationalism, as Tucker suggests, but that there is a connection between their idealistic and matter-of-fact response to race and their interest in science. Believing in the fictiveness, the falseness of race, the same analytic and factual turn of mind which attracted them to science prevents them from acting upon race as if it were not constructed—perpetuating a (negative) fiction, to their minds. If race is a fiction then it can have no positive manifestations.

In addition, Schuyler's use of the science fiction genre would accentuate such a scientific viewpoint, as well as a forward focus. As Darko Suvin notes, science fiction is particularly interested in the "future-bearing elements from the empirical environment" (7). Robert Scholes and Eric S. Rabkin assert that "because of their orientation toward the future science fiction writers frequently assumed that America's major problem in [the racial] area—black/white relations—would improve or even wither away" (188). Within this context, "the matter of race [becomes] comparatively unimportant" (189). While Schuyler continues to address race directly in his texts, the "what if" or speculative element of science fiction allows Schuyler to imagine a contemporaneous world in which a scientific development radically undermines the meaningfulness of race—in theory and in practice. Schuyler, then, more accurately portrays race in his fiction than it exists in reality—the complete lack of (biological) anchoring and, therefore, the tremendous racial variability. In concretizing the cultural basis of race, he highlights the illogical workings of race in American society, as well as the extreme importance placed on race both then and now.

This contradiction between factuality and importance explains the paradox at the heart of much science fiction dealing with race. Like other contemporary science fiction writers who utilize race as a literary theme, Schuyler radically undermines race from a scientific and cultural standpoint. The paradox lies in Schuyler's continued focus on race as his primary literary topic even as he explicitly rejects it. The rational or scientific mindset rejects the biological, or biological and cultural concepts of race. Furthermore, it exhibits a forward-looking tendency which sees a future idealistically without race or one in which race is a vehicle for individual expression alone.[56] Disher's decision to become white and then later to tan reflects such an individualistic interpretation of a culturally-based concept of race. In such a context, race becomes like hairstyle or clothing fashions; although grounded in collective social norms, it is used as an expression of a person's individual personality or subjectivity. In the next chapter, we will see a similar utilization of race in Samuel R. Delany's fiction. Schuyler, however, doesn't use science—in terms of scientific rationalism and/or the futuristic focus of the scientific and science fiction communities—to optimistically eradicate racism or race. The contemporary reality of race, in fact, counteracts this futuristic tendency of the scientific and science fiction communities, and Schuyler and others are forced to continually address race. Therefore, in his writing, Schuyler embodies this complex process of give-and-take whereby a scientific viewpoint embodies both sides of racial rationalism—the factuality which rejects race and the practicality which cannot deny its continued importance within a larger society. In addition, these two sides of racial rationalism interact with the forward focus of a scientific viewpoint and the overt or latent idealism usually embodied in such a focus. In his oversimplification of Schuyler's scientific beliefs, Tucker elides these complex and contradictory impulses.

Schuyler's combination of scientific interest, individualism, and racial deconstruction suit the science fiction medium. Furthermore, *Black No More* actually embodies the two characteristics essential to the science fiction literary genre—cognition and estrangement. However, Schuyler's single categorization in the Afro-American literary genre remains solid to this day. For example, the 1999 Modern Library Edition of *Black No More* lists "Afro-Americans—Fiction" and "Human skin color—Fiction" as the only Library of Congress subject headings for the text. The literary history of Schuyler's texts, then, illustrates the very problem of racial identity and racial solidarity against which he worked so tirelessly. Schuyler's texts are categorized solely on the basis of their racial theme and Schuyler's own racial background. Similarly, the assimilationist debates over Schuyler in African-American literary circles reveal not only the political foundation of Schuyler criticism, but also its racial basis.

Conversely, a discussion of race has been, and in some cases continues to be, viewed as antithetical to the science fiction genre. A glaring indication of this distinct separation is found in the lack of an entry for "Race" in the contemporary *Encyclopedia of Science Fiction*. Even the most current edition, published in 1995, subsumes race under the entry on "Politics." In the Introduction to *Into Darkness Peering: Race and Color in the Fantastic* (1997), Elisabeth Anne Leonard reveals that her motivation behind the anthology was the lack of critical attention paid to race in the genres of "fantasy, science fiction, and horror literature" (2). The collection of critical essays "is an attempt to break that silence" (ibid). The sub-title of Philip E. Baruth's article, included in the anthology, directly addresses the elision of race in primary science fiction texts: "Why No One Mentions Race in Cyberspace." While *Into Darkness Peering* does not include an essay on Schuyler, several contemporary science fiction and fantasy authors have attempted to give credit to Schuyler's early writings in the field. Samuel R. Delany, for example, highlights Schuyler's *Black No More* and recently discovered *Black Empire* serials in his brief review of his predecessors in the field. Delany's article, "Racism and Science Fiction," appears alongside several other critical articles on race in *Dark Matter: A Century of Speculative Fiction from the African Diaspora*. Published in 2000, *Dark Matter* also includes the first piece of Schuyler's fiction to be published specifically in a science fiction (or speculative) context. An excerpt from *Black No More* and a piece of short fiction by W. E. B. Du Bois, titled "The Comet" (1920), appear with fictional works by contemporary authors such as Delany, Octavia Butler, Charles R. Saunders, and Nalo Hopkinson. The editor of *Dark Matter*, Sheree R. Thomas asserts that "[l]ike dark matter, the contributions of black writers to the science fiction genre have not been directly observed or fully explored" (xi). Therefore, "[b]y uniting the works of the early pioneers in the field with that of established and emerging new writers, [. . . Thomas hopes] the necessary groundwork for the discussion and examination of the 'unobserved' literary tradition has been laid" (xii). These two recently published anthologies reveal the trend in science fiction towards a more open, accurate, and critical representation of race.

Much work remains to be done, however. In Schuyler's case, the criticism of *Into Darkness Peering* needs to be combined with the fiction of *Dark*

Matter. Discussing Schuyler's science fiction connections results in both a more accurate portrayal of the science fiction field and a more positive critical perspective on Schuyler. First, Schuyler's novel, *Black No More*, and serials, *Black Empire*, together represent a substantial contribution to the science fiction field. When Delany qualifies his title as "the first African-American science-fiction writer," he acknowledges Schuyler's earlier work and the importance of its inclusion in larger science fiction histories for an accurate understanding of the field ("Racism" 383). Similarly, Schuyler's works represents an early example of the overt ties between science fiction and race. Schuyler begins to break down the traditional white triangle of author, protagonist, and audience, as symbolized by Edgar Rice Burroughs. In this way, Schuyler highlights the false universalism and racelessness of both the literary genre and the scientific discourse (and community) with which it is connected.

Finally, a science fiction context affords a more accurate and positive reading of Schuyler and his texts; rather than a political outcast, Schuyler becomes a generic and theoretical pioneer. From a contemporary perspective, we can see how later writers, in the science fiction field and beyond, have revised and expanded upon key elements of Schuyler's texts. In addition to the inversion of the racial triangle mentioned above, Schuyler's texts are early examples of a fragmentation of identity and a cultural construction of race. Subsequent authors have taken Du Bois' theory of double-consciousness for African-Americans and expanded it dramatically through poststructuralist and postmodern theories of subjectivity. Similarly, the contemporary critical debate over Schuyler's works reveals the controversy surrounding theories of racial construction. In his early embrace of the science fiction genre and his exploration of complex, controversial, and cutting-edge subjective theories, Schuyler serves as an intermediary stage for later racial developments within the science fiction community.

Chapter Three

Delany

DELANY'S DIFFERENCE(S)

In his 1999 essay "Racism and Science Fiction," Samuel R. Delany writes of his discomfiture with the oft-given title of "the first African-American science-fiction writer" (383). In order to give a more accurate portrayal of the early contributions of African-Americans to science fiction, Delany briefly highlights the "proto-science fiction" writers M.P. Shiel and Martin Delany and the early alternate histories of Sutton E. Griggs and Edward Johnson (383–4). Delany also includes a lengthier review of George S. Schuyler's twentieth-century texts (384–6). This short literary history reveals Delany's desire to reform the science fiction community and its relationship to race; it is a first, small step towards increasing the inclusiveness of the science fiction field. While Delany acknowledges the generally liberal atmosphere of the science fiction community, he speaks of his experiences during his 40-year career in order to highlight how race and racism operate even within this liberal environment (386). He ends with specific suggestions to "combat racism in science fiction" (396): "That means actively encouraging the attendance of nonwhite readers and writers at conventions [. . . ,] actively presenting nonwhite writers with a forum to discuss precisely these problems [. . . , and] encouraging dialogue among, and encouraging intermixing with, the many sorts of writers who make up the science fiction community. It means supporting those traditions" (397). Delany's racial history, narratives, and call for action intermingle in his article, published in a 2000 anthology, *Dark Matter: a Century of Speculative Fiction from the African Diaspora*. Here Delany's fiction joins that of Schuyler and W. E. B. Du Bois, complementing the historical revision Delany sketches in his essay. Likewise, the non-fiction section of *Dark Matter* is a written "forum" for non-white writers to discuss the "problems" associated with race in the science fiction community (Delany,

"Racism" 397). More broadly, one goal of such an anthology must be to expand the "non-white readers" of science fiction and, of course, publishing these texts encourages non-white writers of science fiction as well, especially the younger and/or relatively unknown authors. In the introduction, editor Sherre R. Thomas writes, "[i]t is my sincere hope that *Dark Matter* will help shed light on the science fiction genre, that it will correct the misperception that black writers are recent to the field, and that it will encourage more talented writers to enter the genre" (xi). *Dark Matter*, then, in many ways embodies the corrective spirit Delany discusses in "Racism and Science Fiction." The 2000 publication date is an auspicious sign of a more inclusive century of science fiction to come. Yet, Delany baldly titles his essay "Racism and Science Fiction" with good reason. Whether past, present, or future, the "racism" of science fiction must be addressed in order for the science fiction community to truly come-of-age and realize its full potential.

Delany's fictional and non-fictional inclusion in *Dark Matter* illustrates his foundational, pivotal, and still central role in the science fiction community, particularly in its relationship to race. First, Delany entered the science fiction field and worked for 9 years as the sole publishing African-American writer of science fiction ("Racism" 386). From 1962 to 1971, he published nine full-length fictional texts, several of which won Nebula Awards.[1] During the1970's, Delany expanded the field of his writing to include non-fiction.[2] To date he has published seven volumes of criticism and two autobiographical texts.[3] In addition, no less than five full-length critical texts have been written about Delany and his oeuvre.[4] In *Samuel R. Delany* (1984), Seth McEvoy summarizes Delany's career as follows: "Delany went from being a middle-class black youth in Harlem to become one of the top ten best selling science fiction writers by the age of 40" (11). Finally, Delany has been a teacher, writer-in-residence, speaker, and guest-of-honor, etc. at too many campuses, conferences, and conventions to name.[5] Yet, even as Delany is a prominent member of the science fiction community, the steady divide between the African-American literary genre and the science fiction field has prevented his reciprocal acknowledgement in "the mainstream forums of Black Studies" (Freedman 160).[6] In other words, his popular and critical position is Schuyler's inverse. Therefore, Delany's literary career provides an excellent heuristic tool for investigating the relationship between science fiction and race after Schuyler's career.

Most basically, Delany promotes a form of individuality, similar to Schuyler. However, rather than rejecting race altogether as a meaningful term, Delany uses the freedom of individuality to work in a genre which has not been associated with African-Americans and is still marginalized from mainstream fiction. In "Meet Samuel R. Delany, Black Science Fiction Writer" (1979), for example, Michael W. Peplow explains the impetus behind his article: "Just over six months ago, a student in my black literature seminar asked me if there were *any* Afro-Americans who write SF (science fiction). 'I don't know,' I said, 'but I'll find out'" (115). Similarly, Jeffrey A. Tucker shares a contemporary experience which illustrates the continued division of science fiction and African-American literature. After being questioned by an uncle on the subject of his graduate work, Tucker writes, "his words indicated that for many people—black as well as white—science fiction and African-American culture are mutually exclusive" ("Racial"). Delany's career must be placed with this divisive context, with its racial expectations, in order to understand how unusual was his initial entrance and lengthy participation in the science fiction genre. In his discussion of Delany's first science fiction novel, McEvoy chronicles Delany's earlier, non-science fiction writing and his participation in a Breadloaf Writers Conference.[7] McEvoy concludes, "[o]ne would have expected such a 'young, gifted, and black' writer to go on to become a member of the 'literary' establishment" (19). During this time period, Delany would have been expected to "become a member" of a particular segment of this literary establishment as well—the African-American literary community. Once race is added to the mixture, a 'pull' towards the general realism and race consciousness of African-American literature makes Delany's ultimate choice of genre even more unusual. Likewise, the simultaneous Anglo-centrism and racial elision of science fiction often 'pushes' away people-of-color. Within this racial context, Delany's prominent career in the science fiction genre resonates with additional meaning. First, his entrance into the science fiction community in the 1960's highlights the long-time stability of the (white) racial triangle of author/protagonist/audience in the science fiction genre. On the other hand, Delany's use of science, science fictional forms and conventions, and poststructuralist theories offers a challenge to more traditional theories of African-American literature and culture. Over time, Delany's groundbreaking and influential work in the science fiction genre has opened up the field, allowing for more diverse writers and texts. He has brought science fiction several steps closer to realizing its full potential as the literature of possibility.

With his first published text, *The Jewels of Aptor* (1962), Delany continued the breakdown of the racial triangle began by Schuyler and the other writers he listed in "Racism and Science Fiction." While Schuyler introduced a black protagonist to the science fiction genre in the 1930s, his audience was primarily African-American. A racial triangle was maintained, simply changing racial affiliation. After Schuyler, the trio of Edgar Rice Burroughs,

John Carter, and Anglo male teenagers remained the overwhelming norm in the science fiction genre. It was not until Delany's emergence in the early 1960s that the authorial element of the racial triangle changed significantly within the science fiction literary community and more diverse protagonists, and other characters, became increasingly commonplace. In "Racism and Science Fiction," for example, Delany writes of his experience at the 1968 Nebula Awards Banquet. While Delany won two Nebula Awards that evening, he (along with other 'new' writers like Roger Zelazny) faced opposition to his 'experimental' or more complex writing style. Within this tense environment, Isaac Asimov told Delany in an aside, "You know, Chip, we only voted you those awards because you're Negro . . . !" (390). Delany first acknowledges the good intentions underlying Asimov's comment, but then goes on to verbalize the other meaning inherent in such a statement:

> No one here will ever look at you, read a word you write, or consider you in any situation, no matter whether the roof is falling in or the money is pouring in, without saying to him- or herself (whether in an attempt to count it or to discount it), "Negro . . ." The racial situation, permeable as it might sometimes seem (and it is, yes, highly permeable), is nevertheless your total surround. Don't you ever forget it . . . ! And I never have. (390–1)

Delany's take on race consciousness is negative here. Rather than a voluntary or personal identification and a source of pride and enrichment, race consciousness is portrayed as an involuntary, pervasive, and external evaluative tool. It is used by others to judge Delany, regardless of the contextual warrant. Not surprisingly, then, Delany's praise for the generally liberal and "permeable" environment of the science fiction community (in comparison to the mainstream literary community) emphasizes its sensitivity to overt racial labeling.[8] In his 1979 article, Michael W. Peplow wrote, "[a]fter finding so few references to color in the anthologies of science fiction, I had assumed that [Delany's] color must be a closely guarded secret" (119). Delany denied Peplow's assumption and explained instead, "The SF publishing industry 'is largely Jewish, liberal, and rooted in the tradition sometimes referred to as "30's left."' The editors have 'known their share of prejudice [. . .] and they're not anxious to be caught perpetuating it'" (Peplow 119).[9] Delany's comments here underscore his desire to be viewed as a science fiction writer first and foremost, rather than a black writer. Such an attitude highlights his published (public) texts and not his (personal) racial status.

Delany's inclusive racial attitude was essential to the success of his early career in the science fiction field. Not only did Delany face discrimination as a black writer, but also he had to struggle against the racist norms of the generic conventions. Had he challenged these norms too directly or revised them radically, at this early stage, his texts would not have been published in the science fiction genre. Robert Elliot Fox's comparison between Delany and LeRoi Jones/Amiri Baraka and Ishmael Reed is instructive here. Fox contrasts Delany with the other two writers within the African-American literary tradition because "while race is a factor in the worlds of Delany's fiction, it is not a foregrounded concern" (*Conscientious* X). Likewise, Emerson Littlefield asserts that "Delany is assuredly not a one-dimensional 'black writer,' that is to say, a writer concerned only with racial identity, revenge motives, and expressing the frustrations of the oppressed. His fiction is too humane and too rich for so simpleminded an interpretation" (238). In a complex process of give-and-take, then, Delany subtly and slowly revised elements of the traditional white, male, heroic protagonist of science fiction.

Delany utilized several strategies to walk this racial tightrope. In his first published novel, *The Jewels of Aptor* (1962), Delany begins with the traditional quest convention and a seemingly traditional hero, Geo. Yet, as Seth McEvoy notes, the reader's expectations are quickly baffled: "[t]he dramatic tension in *The Jewels of Aptor* does not follow the traditional quest form. The tension (involving the quest for the jewels) rises at first, but begins to fall at the mid-point. Geo does not really achieve the goal of getting the jewels by himself. [. . .] Nearly everything in the second half of the book is done *for* Geo; he does nothing" (15). Therefore, Geo does not embody the independence and agency or the active nature of a traditional science fiction hero. Delany also includes a diverse cast of characters in his text—male and female, multi-racial, and alien. In *The Fall of the Towers* trilogy (1963–65), for example, Delany's nominal protagonist, Jon Koshar, is an Anglo male who undergoes a fairly traditional quest though the course of the texts.[10] However, he is joined in his journey by two other characters, equally important to success: a white duchess named Petra and a dark-skinned giant named Arkor. The traditional male protagonist's monolithic heroism, then, becomes a collective, cooperative endeavor. Furthermore, in their fight against an alien villain called the Lord of the Flames, the three characters continually change worlds and assume the identities of alien life forms. In his critical study of *The Fall of the Towers*, George Edgar Slusser rightly asks, "is this a tale of one hero, two adversaries, or three races?" (18). Delany replaces the traditional white male hero altogether in *Babel-17* (1966), introducing a heroic female protagonist named Rydra Wong. In fact, when discussing his early works, Delany emphasizes more his conscious attempt to revise sexist roles and characterization for women than racial stereotypes.[11]

With his seventh and eighth novels, *The Einstein Intersection* (1967) and *Nova* (1968), however, Delany directly tackles the racial norms for science fiction protagonists. In one of the few critical texts to deal specifically with race in Delany's fiction, "The Mythologies of Race and Science in Samuel Delany's *The Einstein Intersection* and *Nova*," Emerson Littlefield argues that Delany's characterization embodies a new "Afro-American mythology which began to emerge in the literature of the twentieth century" (235).[12] Basically, the new mythology reverses the white represents good/black represents evil dichotomy of Western culture (235–6).[13] Littlefield finds such a reversal in the darker-skinned protagonist of *The Einstein Intersection*, Lobey, and Lorq von Ray, the mulatto protagonist of *Nova*. "Further, and more importantly, each of these characters is engaged in mortal combat with an oppressor who is not only inhumanly vicious but almost inhumanly white"—Kid Death and Prince Red (Littlefield 236). At this point, Delany's racial revisions stretched the protagonist past the breaking point for the "famous science fiction editor of *Analog* magazine, John W. Campbell, Jr. Campbell rejected [*Nova*, . . .] explaining that while he liked pretty much everything else about it, he didn't feel his readership would be able to relate to a black main character" ("Racism" 387). In this way, editors and publishers could use the largely young, white male readership of science fiction to justify the focus on Anglo-European characters, particularly the centrality of the Anglo male hero to science fiction texts. However, Littlefield qualifies his racial analysis of Delany's texts by claiming that "his heroes tend to represent a careful blending of racial strains: Lobey is brown-skinned and red-haired [. . .]; Lorq von Ray is a red-haired mulatto; and Rydra Wong of *Babel-17* is racially mixed" (238). Furthermore, "[i]n the plot structures of the novels themselves, [. . .] the characters seem completely unaware of any racial tension and hardly aware of any racial differences" (ibid). With these qualifications, Littlefield highlights the racially (and gender) inclusive nature of Delany's fiction and the strictness of the racial norms in the genre, since even Delany's modest revisions were rejected.

When he creates fairly race-specific characters without a race-driven plot, Delany employs a relatively common strategy in science fiction that deals with race. Robert Scholes and Eric S. Rabkin offer Robert A. Heinlein's *Starship Troopers* (1959) and Ursula Le Guin's *The Left Hand of Darkness* (1969) as other prominent examples of this technique (188–9). In both these cases, the male protagonists have dark skin, but no reference is made to their race and it plays no overt role in the story. Scholes and Rabkin describe this strategy as a "tacit attack on racial stereotyping [. . . which] has allowed science fiction to get beyond even 'liberal' attitudes, to make stereotyping itself an obsolete device and the matter of race comparatively unimportant" (189). Several factors make the science fiction authors' subtle and dismissive racial attitude possible. First, as previously mentioned, "because of their orientation toward the future science fiction writers frequently assumed that America's major problem in this area—black/white relations—would improve or even wither away" (Scholes and Rabkin 188). Also, "[t]he presence of unhuman races, aliens, and robots, certainly makes the differences between human races seem appropriately trivial" (ibid). The speculative element of science fiction, then, tends to highlight the collective human race rather than a multitude of human races, human commonality rather than difference. Campbell's rejection of *Nova* clearly illustrates the necessity of utilizing such inclusive strategies in the science fiction community. Campbell's position is clarified by an exchange between Octavia Butler and an unnamed editor at a convention. In an interview, Butler relates that

> [she] was sitting next to the editor of a magazine that no longer exists and he was also doing some science fiction stories. He said that he didn't think that blacks should be included in science fiction stories because they changed the character of the stories; that if you put in a black, all of a sudden the focus is on this person. He stated that if you were going to write about some sort of racial problem, that would be absolutely the only reason he could see for including a black. ("Black"18)

Similar to Delany's experience at the Nebula Awards ceremony, the editor perceives a black character as representative of a racial group first and foremost, and as an artist, space adventurer, or politician second. The pervasiveness of such ideological stances underlay Schuyler's desire to be seen as an individual, rather than as a member of a racial group, as well as his denial of any pathology related to race. In suppressing this type of collective racial identification, Heinlein, Le Guin, and Delany can place a member of a historically (and generically) marginal racial group in the normative position. In other words, the authors give the black character the privileged position, which includes the ability to elide race because no negative connotations or oppression are involved.

Potential drawbacks surface with such racial subtlety, however. First, readers might miss small racial clues in the description of a character, especially if it is not part of the larger plot. The largely white audience of science fiction, combined with the generic convention of an Anglo male hero, only increases the possibility of such a misreading. Even when authors directly address a character's race within a text, an illustration on the cover can mislead readers. For example, Octavia Butler discusses the African-American ancestry of her heroine, Lilith Iyapo, on numerous occasions in the *Xenogenesis* trilogy.[14] Yet, the infamous illustration on the cover of *Dawn* (the first novel in the trilogy) shows an Anglo woman performing the exact action of the heroine within the text.[15] Furthermore, the scene chosen for the illustration has this Anglo Lilith standing, looking down (with her jumper unzipped revealingly), and peeling back a cover from the naked body of a reclining Anglo woman. This sexually-charged image was clearly chosen to appeal to the stereotypically young, white male audience of science fiction.[16] Without a careful reading of the text, however, any reader could be easily thrown off by this first impression of the book.[17] More importantly, if race is "relatively unimportant," some members of the science fiction community feel it need not be addressed at all (Scholes and Rabkin 189). Butler's editor from the convention, for example, went on to suggest that black characters could be transformed into aliens as a means of avoiding the whole "racial problem" ("Black" 18). For this reason, Edward James questions Scholes and Rabkins' overall positive interpretation of the manifestation of race in science fiction: a "cynic might wonder [. . .] whether the latent xenophobia of so many members of the human race—including SF writers—has not been transferred from the human to the alien" ("Yellow" 28). James joins Gary K. Wolfe in pinpointing robots and monsters as potential disguises for the Otherness of race (James, "Yellow" 28).[18] Within this context, "deciding whether the Other—an alien, a robot, an android—is actually intended as a metaphor is a crucial problem" (James, "Yellow" 39).

At this point, the "problem" is of a different nature for a (positive) race conscious reader. When racial discourse is so disguised that it is a matter of conjecture whether race is the intended topic, the question becomes moot for readers who value collective racial identity. The general elision of a black perspective and the normative white perspective of most science fiction, both embodied in the traditional Anglo male hero, would repel race conscious blacks, for example. As fantasy writer Charles R. Saunders noted in a 1984 interview, "until recently there wasn't much in science fiction and fantasy for black readers to identity with" (Bell 91). More specifically, Saunders explains that up to the late 1970s "science fiction was still in the process of freeing itself from the grasp of its so-called Golden Age in the 1930s–1950s, when hard science was a king whose court was closed to blacks. And fantasy was still frozen in an amber of Celtic and Arthurian themes" ("Why" 399). Similarly, when asked "[w]hy is science fiction a literary form that black and female writers have not sufficiently explored?," Octavia Butler responded that "part of the reason [. . .] is that science fiction began as a boy's genre. So it was white, it was adolescent and it involved a particular kind of adolescent best described as a nerd. So this did not make it popular with blacks or adults or women for quite a long time" ("Black" 16). Furthermore, since most science fiction authors spring from science fiction readers, a negative cycle is perpetuated.[19] In addition to the racial characterization in and racist image of science fiction, several other factors combined to repel many black readers from the genre.

The common interplanetary setting of science fiction extends or severs the connection to Earth and, therefore, race as it has historically functioned. The alternate history sub-genre of science fiction sometimes breaks the connection to terrestrial concepts of race as well. Basically the function of science fiction as a 'literature of possibility,' whether through space or time ruptures, can result in a complete disavowal of race and usually necessitates a modification of race at minimum. In Delany's *The Ballad of Beta-2* (1965), for example, a multi-racial and ethnic group of humans evolves, over centuries spent in outer space, into a culturally and physically regressive 'race'—the Star Folk. In contrast, Delany's *Dhalgren* (1974) takes place in an alternate present, in an American city, and maintains linguistic and cultural connections to historical human races.[20] For some Anglo writers, like Edgar Rice Burroughs, only in breaking the connection to Earth and terrestrial history can more egalitarian relationships be envisioned. However, for many people-of-color this disassociation denies a basic element of their subjectivity and elides the lived reality of their day-to-day life. In addition, a (racial) history of collective oppression, survival, and victories disappears entirely or is submerged within a larger terrestrial history.[21] While the privilege of Anglo (especially male) writers allows them to ignore race, members of oppressed groups usually feel they cannot or should not attempt to deny the importance of race as a vital factor, as the virulent criticism of Schuyler reveals. Furthermore, within the (common and false) universalism of the Anglo male perspective in science fiction, the cultural specificity of particular racial groups would not be recognized. This general elision and/or modification of race in science fiction combines to create a radical deconstruction of race. For writers interested in a collective racial identity, these generic deconstructions are only compounded by the scientific, poststructuralist, and postmodern theories gaining precedence in the second half of the twentieth century.

The field of African-American studies offers an excellent site to explore these racial tensions and ideological conflicts. In a synopsis of the poststructuralist debate within African-American Studies during the 1980s, Diana

Fuss describes a "mainstream of contemporary Afro-American criticism" (85), "concerned with preserving the 'authentic' nature of the Afro-American text. All are wary that a preoccupation with language will de-nature black literature and culture, detach the text from its cultural roots. All attempt, in other words, to hold fast to the bedrock of essentialism" (86).[22] Fuss highlights the particularly strong resistance of female black critics to "renounc[ing] essentialist critical positions and humanist literary practices" (94–5). Within this context, Fuss discusses the controversy surrounding three contemporary male critics who utilize poststructuralist theory in the field of African-American studies: Anthony Appiah, Henry Louis Gates, Jr., and Houston A. Baker, Jr. Henry Louis Gates, Jr., in particular, has born the brunt of the critical heat due to his "interest in the sign 'black' and its discursive production in literary texts" (Fuss 85). Even Baker has attacked Gates for his editorial acceptance of "subtle and searching modes of 'reading'" in the anthology *"Race," Writing, and Difference* (Baker 383). According to Baker,

> what Gates intends by "reading" is a transcendent academic (rationalist?) discourse which escapes pitfalls of error and anachronism not through its devotion to the "vernacular" but rather through its allegiance to putatively achievable and supposedly empirical "scientific" models. In a sense (but not a cruel one), I am suggesting that Gates remains a prisoner to the Enlightenment dualism that he debunks at the outset of his introduction. (ibid)

Fuss, however, corrects Baker's oversimplification of Gates' linguistic position here, reasserting Gates' promotion of **both** the vernacular and theoretical/academic discourse (89). Further, Fuss notes the similar auditory essentialism of Baker and Gates in their emphasis on the black vernacular, as well as the scanty use of the vernacular in their own writings:

> What we see in the work of both Gates and Baker is a romanticization of the vernacular. As their detractors are quick to point out, each of these critics speaks *about* the black vernacular but rarely can they be said to speak *in* it [. . .]. A powerful *dream* of the vernacular motivates the work of these two Afro-Americanists, perhaps because, for the professionalized literary critic, the vernacular has already become irrevocably lost. [. . .] It is in the quest to recover, reinscribe, and revalorize the black vernacular that essentialism inheres in the work of two otherwise anti-essentialist theorists. The key to blackness is not visual but *auditory* [. . .]. (90)

In a field founded on a collective racial identity, then, even 'liberal' critics promote a form of racial essentialism. The need to justify racial identity is so strong that these critics "hallucinate" an authentic racial past that can be recovered (Fuss 90).

In a footnote within his chapter on Delany, Carl Freedman briefly acknowledges Delany's neglect by the African-American literary community and attributes it to the pervasive marginalization of the science fiction genre (160). However, within the critical context sketched above, a multitude of other factors surface. In addition to the generic conventions already mentioned, Delany's general use of language does not meet the prescribed requirements for African-American literature or criticism. Furthermore, Delany's reliance on scientific, poststructuralist, and postmodern theories conflicts with the general promotion in the African-American literary community of a collective racial ideal. The heated level of the debate within the community highlights the extent to which such theories threaten a genre or field founded on a collective racial identity, like African-American literature or Black Studies. This racial repulsion is only strengthened by Delany's own individuality and his desire to be seen as a writer of science fiction first and foremost and a black writer secondarily.

THE ALTERNATIVES

Delany's autobiography, *The Motion of Light in Water: Sex and Science Fiction Writing in the East Village, 1957–1965*, chronicles his early life and his entrance into the science fiction community. The years covered follow Delany from approximately the age of 15 to 23. During this relatively short time period, Delany wrote and published a substantial portion of his oeuvre, including *The Jewels of Aptor* (1962), *The Fall of the Towers* trilogy (1963–65), *The Ballad of Beta-2* (1965), *Babel-17* (1966), and *The Einstein Intersection* (1967). *The Motion of Light in Water* gives us a historical, social, and personal context for these texts. For example, Delany explains the connection between *The Fall of the Towers* trilogy and the Vietnam conflict and the emerging Women's Movement. This historical background is necessary because of the "cognitive estrangement" of Delany's science fiction. Although Delany later examines the turbulent period of the 1960s in great detail and with little speculative distance in *Dhalgren* (1974), he utilizes the estrangement techniques of time and space to discuss contemporary issues in his early works. For example, *The Ballad of Beta-2* addresses both science and race through the novum of galactic anthropology. However, its chronological and spatial distance obscures its connection to the Civil Rights and Black

Power Movements of the 1950s and 60s. This is one reason that *The Ballad of Beta-2* garners little attention within the science fiction community. Slusser, for example, ignores the text completely in his critical evaluation of Delany's early career. McEvoy very briefly discusses the text, but asserts that "*The Ballad of Beta-2* must count among Delany's minor work" and that "[i]ts significance here is chiefly as a good example of how important texts are to Delany's entire output" (46). However, in addition to this linguistic focus, *The Ballad of Beta-2* illustrates Delany's melding of the racial analysis of African-American literature and the cognitive estrangement of science fiction. As a result, his texts must be placed within the literary contexts of both fields to reveal fully the texts' revisionist nature and Delany's underlying individuality. Specifically comparing *The Ballad of Beta-2* with representative texts from science fiction and African-American literature will illustrate Delany's difference(s) more concretely.

Robert A. Heinlein's oeuvre offers a fruitful site of comparison for Delany's early works. First, Heinlein is a productive, critically acclaimed, and popular science fiction author. He also represents the older, more traditional generation of science fiction writers, whose works Delany, Zelazny, and others were trying to revise during the 1960s. In this context, Heinlein provides a specific example of Delany's revisionist attitude. Delany frequently uses Heinlein's works as representative examples for his science fiction theory and criticism, and he validates Heinlein's use of race in *Starship Troopers* (1959). However, Delany also revises Heinlein's protagonists and engages in an ideological dialogue with his texts.[23] In his introduction to Heinlein's *Glory Road* (1963), Delany summarizes his paradoxical and influential relationship with Heinlein through a comparison: "Marx's favorite novelist was Balzac—who was an avowed Royalist. And Heinlein is one of mine" (Delany, Introduction xii). Heinlein, "as much as any writer while [Delany] was growing up, taught [him] to argue with the accepted version" (ibid). In a 1990 *Callaloo* interview, Delany explains his revisionist, but not "revolutionary," attitude towards science fiction: "What I am doing in almost all my books is the genre equivalent of 'gender bending.' That's how all genres expand, progress, survive. It's a paradox that when the results look *most* revolutionary, that's when the writer is *most* attending to the tradition" (*Silent* 226). Furthermore, Delany claims that any attempt to portray him as

somehow fighting *against* the genre from which [he] draw[s] all [his] sustenance, inspiration, and strength is doomed to the same sorts of mystification that we are all too familiar with: the argument that sees every successful black as one who has successfully fought—or fought down—the socially detrimental factors that make *all* blacks into muggers, thieves, drug addicts, prostitutes, and sociopaths. (226–27)

This specific racial context or comparison, unusual in Delany's criticism as a whole, paradoxically emphasizes Delany's individuality. Critics who emphasize an adversarial or "revolutionary" position within the genre imply an exceptional or 'abnormal' position as well. Therefore, Delany's strenuous resistance to such a reading reveals a desire to be taken on the merits of his thematically conservative or traditional science fiction and not his 'exceptional' or marginal race within the science fiction community (*Silent* 225).[24] He places himself squarely and fixedly within the traditions of the science fiction genre and in specific contrast to more "radical writers in SF terms" (227). Likewise, Delany stresses thematic and/or linguistic connections between his works and that of other science fiction writers over (authorial) racial similarities.

Comparing Delany's 1965 text, *The Ballad of Beta-2*, with Heinlein's 1964 text, *Farnham's Freehold*, overtly supports Delany's claims of generic conventionality. Although Heinlein utilizes a time discontinuum in *Farnham's Freehold*, he openly focuses on white/black race relations. As we shall see, such a topic is closer to African-American literary texts during this time period than other science fiction texts.[25] However, *Farnham's Freehold* also highlights the racial stereotyping Delany helped to revise within the science fiction genre. The positive white isolationism depicted *in Farnham's Freehold* contrasts with the racial hybridity promoted by Delany in *The Ballad of Beta-2*. According to the dust jacket, *Farnham's Freehold* is "Science Fiction's Most Controversial Novel." Writing in 1979, Delany asserts that "*Farnham's Freehold* has sustained an almost constant attack" since its publication in 1964 (Introduction xi). The controversy around the novel springs from both its unusually direct and detailed focus on race and Heinlein's conservative politics. As Delany notes, "[o]ur argument is never with the truth value of Heinlein's syllogism[but] with the premises: Since P, Q, R are *not* the situation of the present world, why constantly pick fictional situations, bolstered by science fictional distortions, to justify behavior that is patently *in*appropriate for the real world?" (Introduction xii). In his discussion of race, Heinlein overtly reveals the Anglo-centrism underlying the genre. Delany writes that "Heinlein's novels have inspired a small bibliography of novel-length responses" and that these texts "give some indication of how relevant Heinlein's arguments continue to appear, even to those who disagree with them" (Introduction vii). While Delany does not specifically list his own "novel-length responses" to Heinlein's texts, *The Ballad of Beta-2* can be placed within this context, as well as Delany's later novel *Trouble on Triton* (1976).[26] *The Ballad of Beta-2* may be thematically more traditional than *Farnham's Freehold*, then, but it also embodies an ideological revision of Heinlein's text.

Similar to its neglected position with science fiction, *The Ballad of Beta-2* is 'unknown' within the African-American literary community. Ideologically, it stands in marked contrast with other speculative fiction by African-Americans writers during the time period as well. Sam Greenlee, Warren Miller, and William Melvin Kelley, for example, all wrote alternate history texts highlighting the collective racial ideology of the Civil Rights Movement and the Black Power Movement. Like Schuyler's texts, these novels from the 1950s and 1960s remain solidly in the field of African-American literature. Specifically comparing Delany's *The Ballad of Beta-2* (1965) with William Melvin Kelley's *A Different Drummer* (1959) helps to answer why two texts of speculative fiction dealing with racial issues, and written by African-Americans during roughly the same time period, have had such different generic and critical histories. While Delany is rarely mentioned within the African-American literary community, Kelly's text surfaces again and again in critical texts valorizing a collective racial identity. The racial hybridity of *The Ballad of Beta-2*, then, simultaneously revises the Anglo-centrism of the science fiction genre and challenges the collective racial ideal underlying African-American literature. In this way, Delany builds on the racial and literary convictions of George S. Schuyler. Delany also shares Schuyler's scientific emphases. Delany's more positive portrayal of anthropology, in his fiction and criticism, and his linguistic theory of science fiction, founded on "technological discourse," would make his texts even more controversial than Schuyler's within the African-American literary community (Delany, *Trouble* 286). Finally, Delany's extensive utilization of poststructural and postmodern theories simultaneously challenges the essentialist bias of African-American literary critics and the narrative, 'pulp' tradition of the science fiction genre. His explorations of the fragmented and unstable nature of postmodern subjectivity, in particular, revise key character conventions in both genres.

Beginning with a specific examination of texts in the science fiction field, Heinlein's earlier text, *Starship Troopers*, reveals the subtle use of race more typical in science fiction dealing with race, mentioned earlier, and his later text, *Farnham's Freehold*, embodies the overt discussion of race more typical of African-American literature. In "Appendix A: From the *Triton* Journal: Work Notes and Omitted Pages," Delany tells the now well-known story of the powerful, positive effect Robert Heinlein's *Starship Troopers* (1959) had on him as a young reader: "[w]hat remains with me, nearly ten years after my first reading of the book, is the knowledge that I have experienced a world in which the *placement* of the information about the narrator's face is *proof* that in such a world the 'race problem,' at least, has dissolved" (*Trouble* 287). Delany discusses *Starship Troopers* as an example of the unique possibilities of the science fiction genre. According to Delany, "[t]he hugely increased repertoire of sentences science fiction has to draw on (thanks to this relation between the 'science' and the 'fiction') leaves the structure of the fictional field of s-f notably different from the fictional field of those texts which, by eschewing technological discourse in general, sacrifice this increased range of nontechnological sentences" (*Trouble* 286). Therefore, Heinlein's gloss on race resonates with new meaning **because** of the science fiction context. Within this science fiction "*textus*," as Delany calls it, Heinlein can position race in an imaginative social environment impossible within the generic parameters of realistic fiction (287). In Scholes and Rabkin's chapter on race in *Science Fiction: History, Science, Vision*, "Sex and Race in Science Fiction," they retell Delany's story about *Starship Troopers* as an example of the generally progressive racial attitude of the science fiction community (188). Scholes and Rabkin acknowledge, however, that the transfer of "xenophobia" to an alien race of "Bugs" makes this general elision of human races possible (ibid).

There has been some critical controversy about the reliability of Delany's assertion that the protagonist of *Starship Troopers* is "black" (*Trouble* 287). Edward James, for example, notes that he has "been unable to find this passage in my copy [. . . ;] the hero is Johnny Rico, apparently Puerto Rican in origin but clearly from a rich and privileged family" ("Yellow" 47). As I mentioned earlier, this type of racial elision, while intended to show racial 'progress,' can backfire in its very subtlety.[27] The textual signs point to a person-of-color: a protagonist from Buenos Aires named Juan (his mother calls him the diminutive form of Juan—Juanito), whose father's name is Emilio Rico, and whose female interest is named Carmencita Ibanez (with thick black hair) (88,175). The issue, I believe, is how much color, not is there any color? In labeling Juan "black," Delany follows the 'one-drop' rule of American racial ideology, the collective racial ideology promoted during the 1960s, and his personal racial background as a reader of the text. Certainly there is textual support for Delany's racial interpretation. The 1997 movie adaptation of Heinlein's book, on the other hand, is similar to the cover of Butler's *Dawn*, as it highlights the ideological pressure and racial norms which quickly and easily subvert the (subtle) racial specificity of the original text. Juan "Johnnie" Rico becomes a blue-eyed, blond-haired actor named none other than Casper Van Dien.[28] Immediately following the movie's release, this racial inversion was a hot topic on science fiction listservs—apparently many other readers picked up on the textual clues and identified Rico as a person of color as well. Yet, Paul Verhoeven, the director of the film, could easily justify his casting because race is not a significant factor in this futuristic terrestrial society. Therefore, reverting back to the traditional white male hero follows the letter, if not the spirit, of such racial elisions.

In *Farnham's Freehold* (1964), Heinlein utilizes a more direct strategy to discuss race. Not only does the text include a major African-American character, Joseph, but also his race and that of the protagonist Hugh Farnham are key elements of the plot. Edward James sees *Farnham's Freehold* as offering a "more complex" message than Heinlein's earlier text *Double Star* (1956) because "it depicts a future (into which Hugh Farnham and his household have been involuntarily thrown) ruled by vicious slave-owning African blacks. But Heinlein's point is that an evil system is not the result of race, but of circumstance" ("Yellow" 36). Presumably, then, Heinlein's underlying theme remains constant—that race should not be important. These related points can be discerned in the character of Joe or Joseph, an African-American student who also works as a servant in the Farnham household. Mistreated by Farnham's racist son Duke before the atomic war which transports them to the future, Joseph proves himself a worthier man than Duke and eventually becomes romantically attached to Farnham's daughter in the future. Within the racial reversal of the futuristic society, however, Joseph becomes one of the Chosen (the colored elite), and Duke, Hugh, and the rest of the Anglo Farnham family become slaves. This racial reversal of historical American slavery makes variable what once was considered static. Slavery is not dependent on racial essentialism within this context; any person or group potentially could be enslaved or be an oppressor. When Farnham questions the morality of Joseph's decision to accept the futuristic slavery, Joseph responds, "Have you ever made a bus trip through Alabama. As a 'nigger'?" (*Farnham's* 269). Joseph sees that "[t]he shoe is on the other foot, that's all—and high time" (267). In this way, Heinlein effectively illustrates the immorality of racist ideology and social structures for a **white** audience. Indeed, when the shoe is on the other foot, the repercussions of racism become much clearer, sharper, and personal. Gary Westfahl notes that *Farnham's Freehold* would be offensive to a black reader due to its use of racist stereotypes (83–4).[29] However, a racist white reader would be incensed as well—by the extremity and vividness of Heinlein's reversal. Duke's highly racist reactions to the slavery, before his "temper[ing]," model such a response (*Farnham's* 269). Likewise, the racial inversion reveals the power, privilege, and normative position of whiteness in western society, attributes normally hidden for white readers by the very privilege attached to their racial classification.

The racial inversion also highlights the illogical, extreme, and (therefore) absurd nature of racist ideology. For example, Farnham's 'owner,' Ponse, utilizes an inverted form of the white ethnographic gaze described by Haraway and Pratt and embodied in Burroughs' John Carter. Ponse describes the free whites who hide in the wilderness as "[s]avages. Poor creatures who have never been rescued by civilization. It's hard to save them, Hugh. [. . .] They're crafty as wolves [. . .] and they are very destructive of game. Of course we could smoke them out any number of ways. But that would kill the game, can't have that" (228). The intended paternalism of Ponse's discourse quickly deteriorates under the valuation of animals over humans. In this way, Farnham's owner exhibits the hunting interests of white males in colonial India and Africa. Heinlein links such racial paternalism to the antebellum South as well. Farnham's owner tries to justify his slavery because Farnham is physically better off than when he was in the wilderness: "'Then you know how much your condition has improved. Don't you sleep in a better bed now? Aren't you eating better? [. . .] When we picked you up, you were half starved and infested with vermin. You were barely staying alive with the hardest sort of work [. . .]. Isn't all that true?'" (229). Farnham does agree, but he continues to insist, "'I prefer freedom'" (ibid). It is here that a more pessimistic reading of the text can begin. When Heinlein inverts the racial hierarchy, the white protagonist becomes the sympathetic hero and the historically oppressed groups—the Hindus, Africans, and African-Americans—become the collective villains.

In *Farnham's Freehold*, Heinlein continues the earlier science fiction (and his own) tradition of a single, white, highly individualistic male protagonist. While critics agree that Heinlein places Farnham within this normative heroic context, they disagree whether Farnham is a success or a failure and whether Heinlein intentionally created him as such. Philip E. Smith II, for example, sees a "happy ending" which validates Farnham and the values he represents (164).[30] Alexei Panshin, on the other hand, argues that Farnham reveals no agency and that that text is "almost a study in the varieties of impotence" (109). In "The Racism of American Science Fiction," Gary Westfahl summarizes these two critical positions in order to counter with a more critical authorial model. Westfahl believes the text has been traditionally misread because critics have too easily and quickly collapsed the author with the protagonist, similar to Schuyler's critical evaluations within the African-American community. Without Schuyler's satiric signposts, Westfahl argues, critics have missed Heinlein's indictment of his own racism, through the more extreme racism embodied in his protagonist: "I believe that Heinlein was aware of the racism he was projecting; that *Farnham's*

Freehold in particular was crafted as a scathing self-criticism of the racism in Heinlein and people like him; and that, after achieving this insight, Heinlein still found it impossible to change himself, and hence impossible to change Farnham" (Westfahl 72). According to Westfahl, Heinlein accomplishes this "scathing self-criticism" by undermining the heroic status of the protagonist. Westfahl argues that "Farnham fails at everything he attempts to do until the end, when he achieves only the smallest victory. Surely, if Heinlein had wished to make Farnham an heroic figure, he would have provided him with a genuine achievement or two" (73). Westfahl surveys the "major events" of the text in order to prove this inadequacy (ibid).

However, several 'failures' Westfahl lists have alternate functions in the plot. First, the 'faulty' fall-out shelter Farnham builds is a vehicle for the time travel Westfahl subsequently mentions (Westfahl 73). Likewise, the rising radiation within the shelter heightens the tensions and suspense of the plot and gives Farnham and Barbara Wells an excuse (we're going to die anyway) to reveal their attraction to one another. Westfahl also mentions the death of Farnham's daughter Karen: in the future, "Farnham set out to build his own little society; but the illusion of his competence is shattered when Karen dies in childbirth under his supervision" (ibid). Here Westfahl overlooks at least two additional reasons Karen must die. First, she is pregnant out of wedlock (conception occurred before the war), and second, she has an interracial relationship when she becomes romantically attached to Joseph after the war. In breaking these sexual and romantic taboos, Karen incurs the extreme societal punishment of death. Heinlein does not overtly judge Karen within the text, however. Having Farnham condone Karen's pregnancy and her relationship with Joseph, in direct contrast to the disapproval of her mother, allows Heinlein to overtly preach liberalism and racial tolerance.[31] Yet, having Karen already impregnated and then die in childbirth prevents the consummation of her relationship with Joseph. In other words, Karen serves as a romantic interest for the interracial relationship Heinlein sets up, but a specific description of that relationship and/or a sexual component would be too controversial—for Heinlein, the science fiction community, and/or society as a whole. Westfahl notes Joseph's excessive modesty, to the point of appearing "asexual," and attributes it to Heinlein's desire to "counter the stereotype of the male African as sexual predator" (82). Other comments made by Farnham throughout the text confirm such an interpretation. However, Joseph's overt celibacy also suppresses the issue of sexuality.

Contrasting Karen and Joseph's relationship with that of Farnham and Barbara illustrates more fully the impact of race on Heinlein's portrayal of sexuality in the text. Barbara and Farnham have an overt sexual encounter while Farnham's wife slumbers nearby, complete with "'Barbara, Barbara!'/ 'Hugh darling! I love you. Oh!'/'I love you, Barbara.'/'Yes. Yes! Oh, please! *Now!*/'*Right now!*'" (*Farnham's* 38). Barbara becomes pregnant from this encounter, and the couple later have healthy twins. While enslaved for a period of time, as Westfahl notes, eventually the couple and their children do, in fact, escape and the text ends with the family happily ensconced in their post-holocaust Freehold (taking place in a future free from the Chosen). Conversely, Karen only speaks to Barbara and Farnham about Joseph's possibilities as a suitor, and she denies any sexual attraction between them (she even claims to prefer her father as a sexual partner) (117–18). We finally hear of their relationship only as Karen goes into labor (and then dies); she tells her father, "'Something to tell you. I asked Joe to marry me. Last week. And he accepted'" (136). In the text, there is no direct dialogue between Karen and Joseph about their relationship or physical contact described. Through these multiple elements of plot, characterization, and indirect dialogue, Heinlein creates a chaste, suppressed interracial romance. In this, he follows the old example of Burroughs' John Carter and Dejah Thoris. Even the conservative Burroughs envisioned offspring for his couple, however.[32] When Karen and her baby die, the possibility of a familial and/or biological interracialism is effectively forestalled in Heinlein's text. On the other hand, the sexualized, fertile, and healthy Hugh and Barbara have already begun their roles as a new Anglo Adam and Eve, destined to repopulate the New World. As Westfahl admits, Farnham purposely isolates himself and his family from African-Americans and other races in their Freehold: "[f]ar from taking any steps to overcome racial divisions, Farnham seems intent on maintaining them" (80).[33] Finally, many parallels exist between Barbara and Karen. They are young, Anglo, female students who become pregnant out of wedlock and who are transported into the future with the same group of people. The fact that Barbara prospers in this situation and Karen dies reinforces the importance of race to the equation. The key difference between the two women is their 'destined' male partner, and the key difference Heinlein portrays between the two men is their race.

Therefore, if Heinlein's intention was to undermine the position of the protagonist, to make Farnham appear foolish, inadequate, and unacceptably racist, then the critique is too subtle and the ending too ambiguous. For example, in contrast to the "mythic" individualism of the new Farnham family, Delany ends *Trouble on Triton* with the original white male protagonist completely alone, psychotic, and transformed into a woman (Franklin 154). While there is some ambiguity about the protagonist's exact mental state, there is no question that Delany has created an "anti-hero" (Fox, "Politics"

49).[34] Perhaps Westfahl's identification of the author with the protagonist, which he initially denies but then reestablishes, explains this contradiction between authorial intention and final textual product. Rather than a "scathing self-criticism," *Farnham's Freehold* reflects the racial tensions, conflicts, and, finally, defensive strategies of Heinlein, an Anglo male writer focusing on race within a modern context. Heinlein is not incapable of "self-criticism," but this project is sabotaged by the very racism supposedly being critiqued, as well as the primacy of his own experiences and position in society (73). In fact, Heinlein does not "know exactly what he is doing," as Westfahl confidently asserts (82). For example, the relationship between Karen and Joseph promotes racial equality in theory, but in application, the textual description is truncated and subverted. Such racial equality lives a very brief and sickly half-life in the interim future but, according to Heinlein's characters, would not be pursued within historical American society and does not exist in either of the potential futures Heinlein envisions. Heinlein is unwilling to fully envision the ramifications of racial egalitarianism—unwilling, not unable. When Westfahl writes that Heinlein "found it *impossible* to change himself, and hence *impossible* to change Farnham" (my emphasis), his language reveals a defensive strategy as well (72). If the project of racial understanding and unification Westfahl suggests for Farnham and Heinlein is "impossible," why does he bother critiquing Heinlein, or the science fiction community more generally? According to Westfahl, this inability to change also applies to the larger science fiction community: "Heinlein explains why American science fiction often projects racism, and why its well-meaning writers cannot overcome their own racist attitudes" (ibid). This vocabulary of "cannot" does not bode well for a more inclusive and egalitarian racial future for science fiction.

Finally, Farnham's positive characterization rests, in large part, upon a vivid moral contrast with a racial Other. Unlike Delany's alien Other in *The Ballad of Beta-2*, Heinlein creates a human Other embodying the negative traits of both white slaveholders and (black) primitive cannibals. How can Farnham not appear a hero when he is the only person resisting the futuristic black leadership which practices both white slavery and cannibalism? He may not be very successful, as Westfahl suggests, but his position seems the only morally acceptable one presented. While the text reflects a complex and sometimes ambiguous view of racism and race relations, the well-meaning white protagonist opposed to the gratuitous, unadulterated moral degradation of the black-dominated society reveals an underlying racial hierarchy which is not critiqued within the text. Westfahl believes this futuristic society represents the "racist fears of an uneducated version" of Heinlein, namely

Farnham (79). According to Westfahl, Farnham "is explicitly identified as a less educated and less worldly version of Heinlein" (ibid). Yet, Farnham is a "junior enlisted man" and then a commissioned officer in the Navy, and, as Westfahl himself notes, Heinlein graduated from the Naval Academy (90). In addition, Heinlein is (in)famous for his glorification of the armed forces. For example, the armed forces are portrayed as racially inclusive and egalitarian in *Starship Troopers*.[35] Likewise, Farnham relates an experience abroad, in which he saw blacks in positions of power over whites: "[he] recalled an area of Pernambuco he had seen while in the Navy, a place where rich plantation owners, dignified, polished, educated in France, were black, while their servants and field hands—giggling, shuffling, shiftless knuckleheads 'obviously' incapable of better things—were mostly white men" (*Farnham's* 296). This contemporary experience is reinforced by Farnham's historical knowledge. Referring back to the Roman Empire, Farnham concludes, "any 'white man' of European ancestry was certain to have a dash of Negro blood" (297). Farnham even acknowledges his own "statistically certain drop of black blood" (ibid). Given all the other biographical similarities between Heinlein and Farnham that Westfahl relates, and the theory of self-criticism, I do not think there is sufficient textual support for a categorical educational or experiential distinction between them.

Furthermore, Westfahl argues that "[f]rom an even broader perspective, we can interpret events in the novel not as serious predictions, but as the predictable, though absurd, fantasies of an ignorant person like Farnham—to argue that the entire story is like a game being played inside Farnham's head" (78). At this point, the distinction between author and character breaks down again. In trying to expand the distance between Heinlein's authorial point of view and that of Farnham and the text as a whole, Westfahl ends up conflating the author and protagonist in a different way than the other critics. In Westfahl's interpretation, Farnham occupies an authorial position; Heinlein might not agree with everything Farnham says, but that is because the story springs from the protagonist and not the author. There are several problems with such an interpretation. First, in calling this futuristic society a "fantasy" and a "game," Westfahl contradicts the realism, stability, and gravity of the text itself. Within the historical parameters of the story, this society actually exists. In addition, Heinlein does not undermine this illusion of reality and/or in any way connect this society to Farnham's psychology. A first-person, unreliable narrator would have been an obvious choice if that were Heinlein's intention. Finally, if Farnham plays a game, it is a deadly serious one with grave repercussions for himself and his family. Heinlein could have used overt satire, as Schuyler did in *Black No More*, if he had wanted to

undermine the serious tone of the text. There is no black humor or carica-
tures in *Farnham's Freehold*, for example. Instead, the degradation and peril
of Farnham's situation reflects the terrible realities of American slavery, and
Heinlein's explicit textual parallels invite such a comparison. Rather than a
fantasy or a game, Heinlein creates an inverted image of American slavery.[36]
Within this context, Farnham's failed escape attempt reveals the historical
reality of the black slave—the need for travel passes, the difference in skin
color, the difficulty in communicating with other slaves undetected, tracking
dogs, etc. Farnham does not escape, on his first attempt, because these significant hurdles prevented him; Heinlein is trying to be historically accurate
and realistic.

In addition, Heinlein needed a vehicle to return Farnham and Barbara
to the past. Simply escaping from his slavery, but remaining in the future,
would not allow Farnham to go back in time, learn from his mistakes, and
begin Farnham Family: Part Two. In this way, Heinlein closes off the possibility, the threat of this racially inverted future, while paving the way for
the new, improved Anglo family. In fact, the opportunity of time travel
acts as a moral test for the original Farnham family group. Joseph, Duke,
and Farnham's former wife all choose to remain in the future because they
have been corrupted. Farnham and Barbara, on the other hand, pass the
test when they choose possible death, but freedom, over racial servitude.
Heinlein reinforces this positive portrayal by having Farnham and Barbara continue to make racially egalitarian statements after gaining their
freedom (*Farnham's* 323–4). These statements highlight the sincerity and
depth of their racial liberalism, in marked contrast to the indictment of
the futuristic black society's cannibalism. Furthermore, Farnham does not
have to assert himself, to reach out in a mission of racial understanding and
harmony because Heinlein changes the past as well. Farnham and Barbara
note the small changes they encounter when they return, and Farnham
happily asserts, "It could be importantly different. If the future can change
the past, or whatever, maybe the past can change the future, too. Maybe
the United States won't be wholly destroyed. Maybe neither side will be
so suicidal as to use plague bombs. Maybe—Hell, maybe Ponse [the black
slaveowner] will never get a chance to have teenage girls for dinner!" (331).
By changing the past, then, Heinlein accomplishes several objectives simultaneously. First, it is another tool (like the bomb shelter) to bring Farnham and family through the war alive. Second, it spares Farnham from an
aggressive campaign of racial reform; he can isolate his family without a
guilty conscience. Lastly, it implies that such a racially-inverted future will
not be a reality the second time around.

The basic flaw in Westfahl's argument about this futuristic society is that it does not really matter if it **were** based on Farnham's "absurd" fears rather than Heinlein's (78). Like the melodrama of Schuyler's *Black Empire*, the text stands on its own merits, and the author's attitude towards the text is a moot point, only of interest for authorial characterization. Furthermore, Heinlein valorizes such fears in imagining such a society and giving it realistic textual life. People-of-color do take over the world, enslaving, drugging, castrating, breeding, and, most outrageously, eating whites. This "shocking revelation of Black cannibalism" came in the last installment of the text's original serialization (Franklin 158–9). Bruce Franklin connects Heinlein's "spectacular popular success" with his "extraordinary ability to project the fantasies of his audience" (156). With *Farnham's Freehold*, Heinlein chooses the "most deep-seated racist nightmare of American culture"; "Just as the one nation that has ever used nuclear weapons has recurring fantasies about nuclear weapons being used upon it, the nation most notorious for enslaving and oppressing Black people has recurring fantasies about being enslaved and oppressed by Blacks" (Franklin 157).[37] Joseph, for example, illustrates the larger concept reflected in the black-dominated futuristic society—that given the opportunity, blacks would oppress and enslave others also. He asks Farnham, "'do you expect me to weep? The shoe is one the other foot, that's all—and high time [. . .] do you think I would swap back, even if I could? For *Duke*? Not for anybody, I'm no hypocrite. I was a servant, now you are one. What are you beefing about?'" (*Farnham's* 269). Within the context of slavery, such race reversals propose people-of-color possess a similar desire and ability to enslave whites (as did whites to blacks).[38] Not only is this not grounded in any historical fact, it implies there is nothing exceptional about American slavery or European colonialism. As a result, any lingering white guilt or responsibility is appeased. When Edward James finds Heinlein's simple racial reversal an anti-racist argument, because "Heinlein's point is that an evil system is not the result of race, but of circumstance," he overlooks the historical specificity (as does Heinlein) which has not made it possible for Anglo-Americans to be enslaved by African-Americans, nor revealed any collective desire to do so on the part of African-Americans ("Yellow" 36). As Delany notes, only within the speculative parameters of science fiction can such an "evil system" (James 36) be created (Delany, Introduction xii). Heinlein's supposed 'color blindness,' or switching of racial groups without regard for historical or cultural differences, is what Baker and Tucker oppose; it is a false egalitarianism because it elides white privilege and black oppression—past and present.

In contrast to Heinlein's portrayal of vindictive and power-hungry blacks, contemporary Caribbean author Jamaica Kincaid and science fiction author Ray Bradbury emphasize an increased tolerance, understanding, and compassion. In Kincaid's *Annie John* (1983), for example, her young protagonist ponders Caribbean history thus:

> we, the descendants of the slaves, knew quite well what had really happened [during colonization], and I was sure that if the tables had been turned we would have acted quite differently; I was sure that if our ancestors had gone from Africa to Europe and come upon the people living there, they would have taken a proper interest in the Europeans on first seeing them, and said, "How nice," and then gone home to tell their friends about it. (76)

Kincaid's focus on a historical, black perspective leads to a positive portrayal. In "The Other Foot" (1951), Ray Bradbury also gives African-Americans a similar choice as Joseph. After the mass migration of African-Americans to Mars, the rest of Earth is largely destroyed by an atomic third world war. When representatives from Earth come to Mars seeking help, the "shoe is on the other foot" (Heinlein 269). Heinlein's subsequent mirroring of Bradbury's language (Joseph's speech and Bradbury's title) implies an intentional reference to and, more importantly, revision of Bradbury's earlier text. Writing during the 1950s, Bradbury creates a positive version of the Civil Rights Movement. After a brief period when some blacks think about lynching and segregation, the Martian blacks collectively decide to forgive past wrongs and to allow the Earthlings to come to Mars. As Bradbury's main character learns, "'Now everything's even. We can start all over again, on the same level'" ("Other" 91). Ellen Bishop ties the dissolution of racial revenge to the changed location in space. Like Delany in *The Ballad of Beta-2*, Bradbury accelerates both time and space: "Bradbury shows us (former) African Americans who are able to see the complex relation of self and other vested in racial differences that the white man had for so long denied, because they are able to occupy another territory (a psychological time-space that come to be literally represented as Mars) from which a different view is possible" (Bishop 92).

Placed within the historical context of the1950s and 1960's, *Farnham's Freehold* also enters a debate about black independence movements.[39] Heinlein's highly negative portrayal of such a black-governed state condones resistance to these civil and foreign movements. The basic message of the Chosen's government, and Joseph's collaboration with it, is that blacks will turn on whites, taking advantage of any weakness. Furthermore, isn't the atomic war a "circumstance" which enables the "evil system" of white slavery to come into existence (James, "Yellow" 36)? The racial equality of "circumstance," then, means that not only would African-Americans have enslaved whites, but that they might in the future if present societal trends continue. While such a "nightmare [. . .] dates back in literary expression at least to *Cannibals All!* or *Slaves Without Masters*, George Fitzhugh's 1857 pro-slavery tract," Heinlein uses it for the first time in his work in *Farnham's Freehold* (Franklin 157). Bruce Franklin theorizes that Heinlein wrote *Farnham's Freehold* in reaction to "very specific events in the 1960s": the 1963 March on Washington; the Mississippi Freedom Summer; and, most importantly, "the urban revolts of 1964, 1965, 1966, 1967, climaxing in April 1968, during the week following the murder of Martin Luther King, with massive uprisings in 125 U.S. cities" (158).[40] In contrast to Bradbury's 1951 text, then, "[i]t took little prescience to realize in mid-1964 that the days of the non-violent Civil Rights movement were numbered" (ibid). When Delany shares Isaac Asimov's racial comment at the 1968 Nebula awards ceremony, he suggests that times of high "anxiety" and conflict bring racist discourse and ideology to the social surface ("Racism" 390–91). This is the case with Heinlein's *Farnham's Freehold*.[41] In this way, Heinlein's text follows the example of Schuyler's *Black Empire* serial. Writing during the socially and politically unstable 1930s, Schuyler advances the black militancy with which he believes his black audience sympathizes. Similarly, Heinlein's intention might have been to analyze and criticize white racism (look what will happen if we continue to ignore racial injustice and oppression in the U.S.), but in doing so, he created a horrifying vision of black leadership and morality which actually supports white racism, bolsters the moral image of his protagonist, and undermines historical black independence movements. With the focus on the white protagonist and white identity, as Westfahl himself acknowledges, perhaps it is not that surprising that the text as a whole is white-biased. It is not until Delany specifically takes on this subjective and ideological challenge in *Trouble on Triton* that Heinlein's 'failure' is shown to be author specific and not inevitable.[42]

Heinlein's racial reversal of historical American slavery, oppression, and resistance places his text in dialogue with other speculative texts written during the 1950s and 1960s. His detailed and relatively direct discussion of contemporary racial events links him not only with Bradbury's short stories, but also the alternate history novels of the African-American literary community. For example, Sam Greenlee, Warren Miller, and William Melvin Kelley all wrote texts examining the oppression, segregation, and collective resistance of African Americans. Therefore, these authors compare favorably with Kincaid rather than Heinlein in their emphasis upon the historical oppression of African-Americans. Greenlee, Miller, and Kelley posit separate but equal, race-based societies as the most radical alternative to the contemporaneous situation. Miller explores the formation of a separate political state in Harlem for African-Americans in *The Seige of Harlem* (1964). In *The Spook Who Sat by the Door* (1969), Greenlee chronicles the establishment of a black revolutionary underground in the United States. Finally, Kelley's *A Different Drummer* (1959) follows the story line of Ray Bradbury's short story, "Way in the Middle of the Air" (1950)–the mass exodus of blacks from the South. Like Schuyler's oeuvre, these texts remain solidly in the field of African-American literature and criticism. For example, *The Spook Who Sat by the Door*, was republished in 1990 as part of the "African American Life" series. Similarly, Kelley's text has been paired with Schuyler's *Black No More* by critics of African-American literature, and recently *A Different Drummer* has surfaced in the poststructuralist debate due to Kelley's use of the Caliban figure. *A Different Drummer's* critical popularity within the African-American literary community and neglect by the science fiction community stem from Kelley's portrayal of individual and collective racial identity. The historically-specific racial focus of all of the above texts, however, stands in marked contrast to the racial elision and estrangement of the science fiction genre as a whole. Bradbury and Heinlein are the exceptions in this area rather than the rule. Therefore, in its direct racial focus, *Farnham's Freehold* is closer to these African-American literary texts than Delany's science fiction. Even in his early, terrestrial texts, Delany transforms, distances, and suppresses the historical racial elements,[43] hence his claim that "thematically" he is an "extremely conservative" writer (*Silent* 225). However, Delany's inclusive, integrationist racial philosophy underlies his more radical use of science fiction's cognitive estrangement. *The Ballad of Beta-2*, discussed shortly, illustrates Delany's detached and integrationist approach to race within this volatile time period.

Due to its popularity and theme, Kelley's *A Different Drummer* is an ideal representative text from African-American literature to compare specifically to Delany's *The Ballad of Beta-2*. In his 1970 introduction to Schuyler's *Black No More*, Charles R. Larson utilized *A Different Drummer* as a measuring stick for Schuyler's text. Larson asserts that, at the end of *Black No More*,

> one is reminded that at least one black American novelist, treating a similar theme, took advantage of all the things Schuyler ignored in *Black No More*. The novel is William Melvin Kelley's *A Different*

Drummer (1962) which also ponders the importance of the black American's "racial culture," satirically presenting a story similar to *Black No More*: the reduction of the black population in a part of the United States. (12)

Given all these textual similarities, it is surprising that Larson does not explain what "all the things Schuyler ignored" might be. Apparently he felt the differences between the two texts were so obvious that an explanation was superfluous. Within this context, I surmise that the key difference between the two texts, to which Larson refers, is their portrayal of racial identity; in contrast to Schuyler, Kelley valorizes collective racial identity and action. John M. Reilly also praises *A Different Drummer*, in contrast to *Black No More*, but on aesthetic grounds rather than "racial culture." In "The Black Anti-Utopia" (1978), Reilly claims that "[o]f the two writers, Schuyler and Kelley, the latter is certainly the artist. Still, I believe it is useful to pair the two, as I have done here. If my description of anti-utopia has validity, then these two novels indicate the presence of the genre in Afro-American writing" (109). Reilly's context of African-American literature highlights the continued division of the two genres of African-American literature and science fiction. Over thirty years after the publication of Schuyler's text, an alternate history text by an African-American is still not considered science fiction. It is telling that Reilly must stretch to formulate a genre of two texts, rather than acknowledge the strong connections to the science fiction genre. Considering these two works within the context of science fiction reveals their relationship to Delany's texts as well.[44] Delany's negative attitude towards an emerging sub-genre of African-American science fiction will be discussed in more detail later; however, it springs from such generic divisions and obfuscation.[45] Finally, the African-American literary context affords a converse critical evaluation of Schuyler and Kelley's texts for both Larson and Reilly: whereas a science fictional context leads to a more positive evaluation of Schuyler's text, the opposite is true of Kelley's text. Comparing Kelley's essentialist portrayal of race to the poststructuralism of Delany and other contemporary science fiction writers illustrates the difficulty of avoiding negative racial stereotypes within an essentialist framework, even with the author's best intentions of more egalitarian and liberal politics.

These multiple, interrelated issues of racial identity, critical reception, and generic placement underlie Houston A. Baker, Jr.'s 1986 article "Caliban's Triple Play." Baker briefly mentions Kelley's text because of its character Tucker Caliban, and Baker connects Kelley's use of Caliban with that of George Lamming and James Baldwin. According to Baker, "Caliban's Triple

Play" is "the three-personed god of 'natural' meanings, morphophonemics, and, most important, metamorphoses" (393). Within the Shakespearean context, Baker explains this more specifically as a return to a "pre-Prosperian" island, "revising or deforming the contraries of Western civilization in order to return to a 'natural' signification. Such a world would witness Caliban not as student of 'culture as a foreign language' [. . .], but rather as an instructor in a first voice, resonant with 'a thousand twangling instruments' *in* nature" (392). In addition, Baker believes that African-American critics must become like Caliban: "[t]he Afro-American spokesperson who would perform a deformation of mastery shares the task of Sycorax's son insofar as he or she must transform an obscene situation, a tripled metastatus, into a signal self/cultural expression" (ibid). Baker's emphasis on triples reveals his intention to "escape, or explode, [the] simplistic duality" of Western culture (389).[46] However, Baker maintains these dualities in his continuation of the Prospero/Caliban trope, including the connection of Caliban with nature. First, Baker connects Caliban with animals in his discussion of the phaneric display of gorillas (390). Then, he explores Caliban's knowledge of the forms and language of nature (392). The colonized, then, maintain their 'natural' place in western dualities. Baker's emphasis on an original and natural state for people-of-color raises the issue of essentialism as well. In attempting to give Caliban a voice, a specific vernacular sound, Baker essentializes languages, as Fuss has noted. This essentialism goes beyond language, however. Underlying Baker's poststructuralist language and theory is a form of biological essentialism.

Baker's description of critics of African-American or black literature reveals this essentialism most clearly. In Fuss' discussion of Baker and Gates, she directly addresses the role of a critic's race in Gates' theories of African-American literature. She points out that, against essentialist notions of race, Gates makes a disjunction between "black critic" and "critic of black literature" (Gates; qtd. in Fuss 85). While Fuss does not directly address Baker's increasing essentialism, her note that Baker's "own affinity lies, even now, with the Black Aestheticians" points in this direction (87). In contrast to Gates, Baker seems very concerned in "Caliban's Triple Play" to link the author with the text in a display of 'authentic' racial identity:

> If we fail to hear long choruses of Caliban's triple playing in the issue
> [*Critical Inquiry*; *"Race," Writing, and Difference*], still the collection
> creates an occasion for several signifying **black** academics—those who
> have already journeyed back to the *vale* and asked their **mommas and
> daddies** what did they do to be so very black and to sound such funky

blues—to sound racial poetry in the courts of the civilized. Such soundings, I believe, augur new world arrangements, because the answers
given by the mommas asked (and the black daddies, too) is, 'You's **different**, son, and the future.' *("Race," Writing, and Difference* 395; my
emphasizes added)

Baker's references to the family reinforce the racial connection begun with
"black academics." As José David Saldívar notes in *The Dialectics of Our
America: Genealogy, Cultural Critique, and Literary History*, "[t]he Caliban-
istic self that Baker describes does not exist in empty space but in an organic
human collective—in what he calls the family. For this reason, the Calibanic
self that he lays bare is not alienated from itself; it is in his own folk" (148).
Baker's emphasis on family and kinship recalls Werner Soller's theory of
descent, in contrast to consent. Within this context, a (knowledgeable and
legitimate) critic or author of black literature must be black. Furthermore, to
be racially authentic, a black author should use the vernacular.[47]

Kelley's use of the Caliban trope mirrors that of Baker in several ways.
First, a main character of *A Different Drummer*, Tucker Caliban, embodies
key elements of Baker's Calibanic self. Like Shakespeare's Caliban, Tucker
Caliban is in a position of servitude, in this case to a Southern white family.
Like Baker's Caliban, Tucker Caliban revolts against this racial oppression. He
mysteriously decides to leave his home, destroying his house and possessions
and salting the soil so that no one else can farm the land. Several explanations
are put forward for Caliban's unusual behavior by various characters, but no
definitive reason is ever given—by the narrator or by Caliban himself. In
the void left by Caliban's silence, the points of view of the other characters
shape Caliban's characterization. The first explanation for Caliban's
departure is given by Mr. Harper, a venerable old (white) man from Sutton.
According to Harper, Caliban's revolt is a long-delayed manifestation of the
African "blood" of his initial slave ancestor (Kelley 15). Kelley uses racial
essentialism positively in Harper's story of the African, emphasizing the great
physical and mental strength, charisma, resistance, and courage of Caliban's
ancestor. As a result, Kelley supports Baker's familial connections and the
importance of descent. Similarly, Caliban's white employer, David Willson,
ponders Caliban's actions in a diary: "He HAS freed himself; this had been
very important to him. But somehow, he has freed me too. [. . .] Who
would have thought such a humble, primitive act could teach something to
a so-called educated man like myself?" (151). Willson's portrayal of Caliban
as "humble, primitive," and uneducated constructs a natural man. These
cultural racial characteristics build on the biological racial essentialism of

Harper's story of descent. In this way, Kelley's text illustrates the negative potential of Baker's naturalistic racial theories, which are too closely linked to older, biological constructions of race built on the idea of racial essentialism.[48] Despite being the titular protagonist, Caliban is effectively silenced by this naturalist characterization, and contrary to Baker's promotion of Caliban's indigenous sound, the white characters continue to tell Caliban's story for him. A Caliban entails a Prospero.

A Different Drummer does include a diverse number of character viewpoints,[49] but they are all white. The older man, Mr. Harper, a young white boy named Mr. Leland, David Willson, Dymphna Willson, Dewey Willson III, and Camille Willson each have a separate chapter devoted to their story, their point of view. Mostly first-person, some of these narratives are more focused on their connection to Tucker Caliban than others. Thus, Kelley spreads out the 'Prosperian' perspective over a group of people. However, David Willson most directly represents Prospero. Willson's narrative conveys the unhappiness and impotence of an "educated [white] man" who eventually finds 'salvation' though the instinctual agency of his employee, Caliban (Kelley 151). Furthermore, while there are other major African-American characters besides Tucker—his African ancestor, his wife Bethrah, and Reverend Bradshaw, for example—their stories are also told through that of the white characters. Kelley considerably stretches the narrative perspective of his white characters in order to include these black characters indirectly. For example, Dymphna Willson's first-person narrative includes lengthy direct quotation of conversations with Bethrah, as well as conversations Bethrah and Caliban have outside of Dymphna's presence (see the next paragraph for one such quotation). In this combination of white narratives and black silences, Kelley may be realizing Baker's claim that the sound of Caliban is "incomprehensible" to whites: "It is, of course, the latter—the [guerilla's] 'hoots' of assurance that remain incomprehensible to intruders—that produce a notion (in the intruder's mind and vocabulary) of 'deformity.' An 'alien' *sound* gives birth to notions of the indigenous—say, Africans or Afro-Americans—as *deformed*" (390). However, the white characters sympathetically portray Caliban in Kelley's text, and Kelley portrays these characters sympathetically as well. Thus, Kelley does not suggest that these multiple white viewpoints are unreliable, and their various interpretations of Caliban and his actions build upon one another, rather than conflict. In fact, Kelley follows Bradbury's lead, in "Way in the Middle of the Air," in largely focusing on the reactions of whites to the exodus of the African-Americans. From this viewpoint, the motivation of the African-Americans is elided and, again, the sound of Caliban is silenced. Like Heinlein, Kelley focuses on the white point of view (sympathetic as it may be), and the black point of view remains the effectively silenced Other as a result.

Finally, Kelley implies that the white point of view is basically accurate through the corroborating dialogue of the other black characters. For example, Caliban's wife Bethrah, an educated black woman, initially does not understand his actions and viewpoints either. At one point she explains Caliban's decision to leave the employment of the Willson family to Dymphna Willson (the narrator of this particular chapter) as follows:

> I don't really know, but maybe those of us who go to school, Dewey, myself, not so much your mother, I guess your father, maybe we lost something Tucker has. It may be we lost a faith in ourselves. When we have to do something, we don't just do it, we THINK about doing it; we think about all the people who say certain things shouldn't be done. And when we're through thinking about it, we end up not doing it at all. But Tucker, he just knows what he has to do. He doesn't think about it; he just knows. And he wants to go now and I'm going too. [. . .] I think maybe, if I do whatever he tells me to do, and don't think about it, well, for a while, I'll be following him and something inside him, but I think maybe some day I'll be following something inside me that I don't even know about yet. He'll teach me to listen to it. (Kelley 114)

Even to his African-American wife, then, Caliban is following some kind of instinct, which she hopes to develop also. Presumably the rest of the African-Americans in the state follow Caliban in his exodus for similar reasons. Therefore, the text as a whole portrays Caliban as a 'natural' man, without consciousness, who simply acts and does not think. Bethrah's comments, and the subsequent actions of the collective racial group, suggest that all African-Americans need to return to this less educated and instinctual natural state.

In addition, Kelley contrasts Caliban's actions with collective racial groups like the National Society for Colored Affairs, a fictional version of the NAACP. A chapter officer tells Caliban that the Society works to improve education and "is fighting your battles in the courts" (Kelley 111). Caliban replies, "'Ain't none of my battles being fought in no courts. I'm fighting all my battles myself. [. . .] And ain't no piece of cardboard making no difference in how it turns out'" (ibid). Kelley seems to be promoting a form of grass roots, individual action on the part of 'the folk.' This interpretation is strengthened by the negative portrayal of Reverend Bradshaw as a cynical parasite on the black community. An educated man, like David Willson, Bradshaw can do nothing but marvel that Caliban motivates a collective black rebellion, something Bradshaw has never been able to do. At the end of the text, Bradshaw is the one African-American who does not leave and, therefore, he is lynched by the angry, racist whites. Kelley constructs Caliban's revolt as an example of positive racial liberation for all African-Americans, as well as for the white descendents of slave owners, like David Willson. Kelley's solution to 'the race problem,' then, is to have both blacks and white forget what they have learned and to follow their basic human instincts instead. However, these 'instincts' prompt a massive separation of the two races in the South. Is Kelley constructing an essentialist basis for racial separatism or does the historical legacy of racism in the South simply necessitate a departure, a new social beginning for African-Americans (similar to Bishop's reading of Bradbury)? Tucker Caliban's approval for young Mister Leland's social education in racial egalitarianism supports the latter interpretation. In this case, the Caliban trope encourages a racial essentialism at odds with the competing message of social construction and variability.

Reilly believes *A Different Drummer* "relates to anti-utopia in that his characters' crucial behavior defies rational explanation" (109). Here Reilly highlights the dichotomies of rational versus instinctual or natural, as do Kelley and Baker. Kelley and Baker go further, however, in valorizing the natural over the rational, the civilized, the educated. In connecting this dichotomy only to genre (anti-utopia), Reilly overlooks the racial ramifications of privileging the natural over the civilized. When Kelley and Baker promote a natural, essential state for blacks, they reinforce racial stereotypes and the western dichotomies upon which these stereotypes are built. Utilizing the Caliban/ Prospero trope, Kelley and Baker argue within the existing parameters of these social and ideological constructions. Ironically, Baker levels this very charge at Henry Louis Gates, Jr. (383) and the anthology *"Race," Writing, and Difference* more broadly. Baker perceives a "firm inscription of the duality suggested by the venerable Western trope of Prospero and Caliban—figures portrayed in terms of self-and-other, the West and the Rest of Us, the rationalist and the debunker, the colonizer and the indigenous people" (389). At the end of his essay, Baker returns to a reconciliation of these dualities through the Caliban figure: "Caliban's triple play consists in what I described earlier as *supraliteracy*; it is a maroon or guerrilla action carried out *within* linguistic territories of the erstwhile masters, bringing forth *sounds* that have been taken for crude hooting, but which are, in reality, racial poetry" (394). Baker believes he has avoided promoting one side of the duality over the other, as well as a divided position—"[t]he colonial subject's borderlining, his or her heroic and literate stance between two worlds" (389).[50] However, the naturalist and essentialist foundations of Baker's Calibanic theory, of

self and literature, continually subvert his larger project of reconciliation. If
Baker truly seeks to "explode" these dualities, he should forsake the Caliban
and Prospero trope altogether and look elsewhere for alternative theoretical
and literary models (389). Delany would be the first to suggest science fiction as a good place to start.

According to Delany, science fiction creates a *"textus"* through the
interplay between "more conventional sentences" and the "new sentences
available to s-f" (*Trouble* 287). This textus "allows whole panoplies of data
to be generated at syntagmatically startling points" (ibid). As mentioned
earlier, Delany offers *Starship Troopers* and Heinlein's gloss on race as one
such "startling point." More generally, Delany argues that "the science-fic-
tional-enterprise is richer than the enterprise of mundane fiction. It is richer
through its extended repertoire of sentences, its consequent greater range of
possible incident, and through its more varied field of rhetorical and syntag-
matic organization" (ibid). Thus, Delany specifically describes the much-her-
alded 'possibility' of the science fiction genre. Delany does not claim all, or
even the majority, of science fiction texts fully realize this potential, but "on
repeated exposure *to* the best works" (288), the "apparent 'simple-minded-
ness' of science fiction" (287) "falls[s] away—by the same process in which
the best works charge the *textus*—the web of possibilities—with contour"
(288). Furthermore, this "web of possibilities" includes "tropes of great origi-
nality" for Baker to discover (288).[51] The expanded potential of science fiction, however, is rather like a revolution in that it is difficult to stop at a
certain prescribed point. From Baker's perspective, science fiction poses a
distinct threat to the sanctity of racial identity. The textus which allows for
new tropes also invites new concepts of identity and race. In addition, half
of the science/fiction textus is based on science: "[s]cience fiction *is* science
fiction because various bits of technological discourse (real, speculative, or
pseudo)—that is to say the 'science'—are used to redeem various other sentences from the merely metaphorical, or even the meaningless, for denotative description/presentation of incident" (Delany, *Trouble* 284–5). Baker's
resistance to rationalism, objectivity, and science poses a significant hurdle to
an acceptance of this fundamental aspect of science fiction. Therefore, if *A
Different Drummer* illustrates many aspects of Baker's racial theory, Delany's
The Ballad of Beta-2 offers a challenge.

In the *Ballad of Beta-2*, Delany depicts the scientific transformation of
ordinary sentences into literal events. In his first interplanetary text, Delany
follows the adventures of a student of galactic anthropology, Joneny Horatio
T'waboga, as he tries to decipher "The Ballad of Beta-2," a folk ballad from
the Star Folk. Joneny's professor insists that he complete a "historical analysis

of that ballad—from primary sources," but Joneny believes both the Star Folk, a group of humans who traveled across space for 12 generations, and their ballad are a waste of his time (*Ballad* 9). Joneny argues that the Star Folk are "just a dead end, with no significance at all. They were a very minor transition factor that was eliminated from the cosmic equation even before its purpose was achieved" (6). Likewise, the collection of ballads from the Star Folk does not include "a single metaphor or simile that could possibly be called original or even indigenous to life on the Star Ships. There's nothing but semi-mythical folk tales couched in terms of sand and sea and cities and nations [. . . ,] complete fantasies with no relation to the people living and dying on the ships" (8). Delany uses Joneny's dismissive and derogatory interpretation here as a vehicle for the plot, as an examination of the unique linguistic constructs of science fiction, and as an example of a common attitude towards science fiction. In addition, Joneny mirrors the enthnographic point of view of Burroughs' John Carter. However, the "cosmic" focus of galactic anthropology illustrates Delany's lesser interest in individual human races (Delany, *Ballad* 6). As the plot unfolds, Joneny realizes how wrong his initial assumptions were. He, and everyone else besides the few remaining Star Folk, made the mistake of overlooking the scientific context which transforms the fantastic language of the ballad into a historical chronicle of the events experienced by the Star Folk on their journey.

Within this context, the plot becomes a detective story, through which Joneny connects the linguistic and historical 'clues' conveyed by the ballad. For example, the first stanza of the ballad reads, "*Then came one to the City,/Over sand with her bright hair wild,/With her eyes coal black and her feet sole sore,/And under her arms a green-eyed child*" (*Ballad* 10). Joneny learns that, within the social and linguistic contexts of the Star Folk, "the City" is one of their star ships, Beta-2, and the woman is a specific captain of one of those star ships, Leela RT-857. In Captain Leela's Log Book, Joneny reads of her journey to one of the other starships, under attack by an unknown force, and her return to Beta-2 in her shuttle boat. Thus, the "bright hair" is the shuttle's exhaust, "her eyes coal black" represents the lack of visual contact with the shuttle, and the "sand" is a meson field in outer space. Likewise, Joneny eventually realizes that the "green-eyed child" is an alien/human hybrid who has been his companion during his time on the Star Folks' ships. Captain Leela returned to Beta-2 with this child "under her arms," or impregnated by an alien entity. Joneny eventually pieces together an entire alternate historical text through a combination of linguistic discoveries. First, he learns that the Star Folk heavily utilized euphemisms, in their ballads and also in their day-to-day discourse. The new physical and social environment (outer space and their space ships) led to changes in their language as well. The lack of gravity, for instance, made legs practically interchangeable with arms so that all four appendages eventually became known as arms.[52] Similarly, the Star Folks' "Market" was a place to genetically engineer children, not buy fruits and vegetables. Without direct contact with Earth, the new generations adapted their language to suit their only known environment.

Through the ballad, and its misunderstanding, Delany reveals the importance of a science fictional context. As noted earlier, in the "science" part of science fiction, the "various bits of technological discourse (real, speculative, or pseudo) [. . .] are used to redeem various other sentences from the merely metaphorical, or even the meaningless, for denotative description/presentation of incident" (Delany, *Trouble* 284–5). Therefore, the Star Folks' euphemisms initially act as "meaningless" metaphors. Without the "technological discourse" of interplanetary travel, they are "complete fantasies," "cotton-candy effusions" (*Ballad* 8). Joneny represents the reader of realistic fiction who expects hair and eyes to refer to the human body and not a small space ship. He places the ballad within his cultural textus rather than that of the Star Folk, with its extended possibilities. As his professor points out, the Star Folk are worthy of study because no one else has done what they have—lived and traveled through outer space for an extended period of time (8–9). Therefore, Joneny cannot say that they did not discover anything new. Once Joneny places himself in the physical environment of the Star Folk, "[i]mpossibilities fluttered in his mind like moths" (54). Joneny's first instinct is to deny what he sees, rejecting the impossible. However, "[t]he same thing which made him collect impossibly cumbersome books in a world of recording crystals made him look closely at all the impossibilities around him now" (ibid). As he does, he is given another semantic clue—the name of his companion, "The Destroyer's Children" (55). Delany specifically places Joneny's misunderstanding of this name within the context of linguistics: "Joneny, as has been pointed out, was not semantically alert enough to catch all he had been told by that statement" (56). Once Joneny realizes that the Star Folks' language is "for denotative description/presentation of incident" (284–5), Joneny experiences a "syntagmatically starling point" of his own: he realizes his companion's true identity, along with his full capabilities (*Trouble* 287). The Destroyer's Children is not one person, but a group of identical boys. The original "green-eyed child" has cloned himself (123). Furthermore, they share a common alien father, called The Destroyer by the Star Folk because it was he who destroyed several of their star ships. At this point, Joneny reaches the status of an experienced science fiction reader, one who knows the unique linguistic characteristics of the textus and, therefore, gains an accurate and meaningful understanding of the ballad (*Trouble* 285).

By remaining open to the (im)possibilities and learning the linguistic conventions of the science fiction textus, Joneny earns a reward. He discovers the extraordinary potential of The Destroyer's Children for communication purposes. Not only can they withstand the physical environment of outer space without protection, but also they "exist a little outside of time" and can read minds (Delany, *Ballad* 123). Their mind-reading abilities mirror that of Rydra Wong in *Babel-17* and Arkor and the other giants in *The Fall of the Towers* trilogy. The prevalence of this characteristic in Delany's fiction reveals both the great importance he attaches to language and how his perspective on essentialism differs from that of Baker. In opposition to a single natural language rooted in a human race, Delany creates characters who change the known universe through their polyglot abilities. Overcoming linguistic, cultural, national, and/or racial barriers is the priority and not maintaining them, as with Baker, Kelley, and Heinlein. The first alien/human child (Joneny's companion) can clone himself at will also. Furthermore, they have access to their father—an alien being of tremendous physical power who also shares the mind-reading and time-manipulating abilities of his offspring. Therefore, The Destroyer's Children can act as translators for humans—throughout space and time. In this way, they expand beyond even the galactic (spatial) scope of *The Fall of the Towers* and *Babel-17*.

As a student of galactic anthropology, Joneny is understandably excited by his discovery. He will return to his university with the next step in human evolution at his side. Compared to humans, the Destroyer's Children are a superior race, mentally and physically; they fulfill The Destroyer's promise to Captain Leela that her descendants would "live among the stars" (Delany, *Ballad* 114). In this highly positive portrayal of The Destroyer's Children, Delany promotes collective consciousness and racial hybridity. The Destroyer's Children are "one" with each other, as well as their father, and they can communicate with any sentient being (124). This collective consciousness "explodes" the subjective duality Baker critiques, without access to a natural or essentialist state (389). In fact, the racial hybridity of The Destroyer's Children also "explodes" the concept of a static, essentialist racial identity.[53] In this way, Delany refutes the negative portrayal of a mixed (whether double or multiple) physical or cultural background. Because of their racial hybridity, The Destroyer's Children do have a fragmented subjectivity, but all of these factors only increase their beneficent power. Within the specific context of American race relations, Delany's alien/human hybrid mirrors the mixed racial position of mulattos. Thus, The Destroyer's Children belie the motif of the tragic mulatto. The unlimited fertility of The Destroyer's Children plays on the scientific fallacy of the sterility of mulattos also.[54]

Delany highlights the promise of The Destroyer's Children through a specific contrast to the remaining Star Folk. Captain Leela becomes impregnated voluntarily because she sees the increasing intolerance and rigidity of the Star Folk, physically and culturally. She fears that by the time they reach their destination, the Star Folk will have regressed so far that they will be unable to survive, let alone complete their mission of contacting alien civilizations. A human/alien hybrid race seems to be the best chance for their survival. As Joneny later relays, Captain Leela was correct. Joneny first describes the Star Folk as "a bunch of chauvinistic, degenerate morons" (6) with a "primitive-barbaric stage" of "*civilization*" (Delany, *Ballad* 7). After his arrival on one of the starships, he sees the physical degeneration of the Star Folk first hand: "through the tubes loped men—or men and women, he couldn't tell: their eyes were small and pink, probably half blind. They were bald. Their ear trumpets had grown to their skulls. Round-shouldered, with nubby, nailless fingers, they paused and groped mechanically at instrument dials and nobs" (43). In this way, Delany connects the cultural and physical regression of the Star Folk. Because they feared change, the majority of Star Folk began to ostracize and persecute the minority who believed in diversity—cultural, social, intellectual, and physical. Eventually the dominant majority used the concept of a very narrow and rigid Norm, both cultural and physical in connotation, to kill those who deviated in any way. Through executions, pogroms, and riots (in conjunction with the mass destruction caused by The Destroyer), all of the One-Eyes, the deviant minority, were killed. Thus, the social and physical isolation or 'inbreeding' of the Star Folk led to an actual devolution over time. The message is clear: those who value stasis, racial purity, and isolationism are on their way to "extinction" (7).

This message speaks to both Heinlein's *Farnham's Freehold* and Kelley's *A Different Drummer*. While both authors explore inter-racial relationships (romantic, platonic, economic, homicidal) during the course of the text, they ultimately reinforce racial divisions. In *Farnham's Freehold*, an Anglo Adam and Eve consciously separate themselves from the rest of humanity partially because of their negative experiences with blacks in the future. Kelley removes all African-Americans from the South in order to escape their past and present oppression. In these ways, both authors promote a separate-but-equal, segregationist racial policy. On the other hand, within the social and political context of the 1950s and 1960s, Delany becomes the racial integrationist. He rejects the white privilege, social conservatism, and racial isolationism of Heinlein and the dominant white majority in the United

States. However, he also rejects the Negritude and Black Power standpoint of Kelley. Furthermore, Delany's racial integration involves both social/cultural and physical elements. In *Sarah Phillips* (1984), for example, Andrea Lee reflects on the qualified integration advocated by many African-Americans (and Anglo-Americans). While actively striving for a general social integration, they reject romantic and physical integration (sexual and/or reproductive) with other racial or ethnic groups.[55] Finally, by placing the entire plot of *The Ballad of Beta-2* in the future, Delany can assume a racially mixed human population even before the human race comes in contact with alien races. Delany's fairly positive portrayal of racial integration with aliens also stands in marked contrast to the transfer of human racial xenophobia to an alien Other (Scholes and Rabkin 188).[56]

Unlike Heinlein and Kelley, Delany chooses to use the greater possibilities of science fiction, in *The Ballad of Beta-2*, to distance the story from the contemporary historical racial situation. The distance in time and space affords a metaphoric exploration of race relations, and this metaphoric distance lessens the volatility of the text's racial message. *The Ballad of Beta-2* also illustrates the common connection in science fiction between space and time disruptions (or hyper extensions) and a deconstruction or elision of racial identity. For example, the historical specificity (cultural and geographic) of African-Americans is elided in *The Ballad of Beta-2*. The science-fictional context (space and time) blunts the general racial message, then, and this estrangement combines with the deconstruction of racial identity to repel readers interested in the promotion of collective racial identities. Thus, *The Ballad of Beta-2* does not overtly challenge the generic conventions of science fiction, but it lies outside the normative parameters of African-American literature. The importance of the "technological discourse" in *The Ballad of Beta-2* also foregrounds the scientific aspect of science fiction (Delany, *Trouble* 284). For example, astronomy and astronautics, physics, engineering, and, of course, galactic anthropology (combining linguistics, cultural studies, and race) all play roles in the text. Joneny's role as a student of galactic anthropology specifically recalls Disher's impersonation of an anthropologist in Schuyler's *Black No More*. However, Delany does not satirically and cynically undermine the profession in the way Schuyler does. If Tucker criticized Schuyler for his qualified portrayal of science, rationality, and objectivity, what of Delany's straightforward promotion of the sciences?[57]

When Tucker critiqued Schuyler's "scientific rationality" in the 1990s, he was building on the anti-rationalist, anti-scientific arguments of Baker in "Caliban's Triple Play" (Tucker, "Can" 143). While Baker asserts that he "is not interested simply in taking pot shots at 'science,'" he believes that science "is simply one system in a series of 'interlocking information orders' that often subserve state power" (386). More specifically, "a black *group* initiative [is] contrary to the interests of the academically isolated whitemales [like contemporary anthropologists] who have always done whatever was necessary (fudging data in twin studies and so forth) to make science work" (ibid). In contrast, Baker highlights the "debunking" power of Mary Louise Pratt's essay, "Scratches on the Face of the Country; or, What Mr. Barrow Saw in the Land of the Bushmen," which appears in *"Race," Writing, and Difference* along with Baker's essay (Baker 387). Baker explains that Pratt's "deeply intelligent and witty awareness of the necessity to deconstruct a disastrous scientific 'objectivity' and 'informational' neutrality as covers for state power and oppression bring her essay into harmony with what [he] would call vernacular rhythms" (387). Furthermore, texts like Pratt's "will make a difference where 'difference' is concerned in the future. 'Science,' by contrast, will more than likely continue to march to stately drums" (ibid). This pessimistic, broadly negative attitude towards science comes from one of the more liberal academicians within the African-American literary community as well.

On the other hand, Delany's promotion of the sciences in *The Ballad of Beta-2* reflects a deep and abiding interest in science. A significant portion of Delany's autobiography, *The Motion of Light in Water: Sex and Science Fiction Writing in the East Village, 1957–1965*, is devoted to his multifarious and intensive scientific activities as an adolescent. Delany notes that, "[a]s a child, I was fascinated by science and math," and he attended the Bronx High School of Science (9). Delany's primary interests in science and writing, as well as music, are reflected in his vocational leanings. At various points in his life, Delany thought he would be a scientist, a musician, or a writer. Delany's choice to combine these interests in his career as a science fiction writer is explained by a story he shares about his then-wife Marilyn Hacker. When asked by an interviewer, "Why, in this age of science [. . .] do you want to be an artist?," Hacker responded: "I don't really see that much difference between them [. . .]. Both are based on fine observation of the world" (97). Delany continues, "It was a pretty clear expression of her aesthetic back then—and one I was happy to take as my own" (ibid). Hacker and Delany's conflation of art and science mirrors the later scientific analysis of Donna Haraway in which she argues for the fictive nature of science and its ability to tell stories.[58] In fact, Haraway's critical project is a realization of Delany's belief that "self-critical models are desirable things" (*Jewel-Hinged* 82); in this case, Haraway is critical of science and traditional scientific objectivity. In a critical essay entitled "Shadows," Delany expands on his view of scientific objectivity:[59]

> Somewhere, in science, especially the human ones, we have to commit
> ourself to objectivity. And, especially in the human ones, objectivity can-
> not be the same as disinterest. It must be a whole galaxy of attractions
> and repulsions, approvals and disapprovals, curiosities and disinterests,
> deployed in a context of self-critical checks and balances which, itself,
> must constantly be criticized as an abstract form capable of holding all
> these elements, and as specific elemental configurations. (*Jewel-Hinged*
> 81–2)

This critical model of objectivity complicates the simplistic, traditional
definition of objectivity. It more accurately describes the qualified scientific
rationality Schuyler portrays in *Black No More*, for example. Furthermore,
Delany goes on to explicitly highlight the utilization of anthropology as a
"self-critical model [. . .] with which to criticize our own culture" (*Jewel-
Hinged* 82). In this context, the galactic anthropology of *The Ballad of Beta-2*
(as its name suggests) is a logical combination of the self-critical models of
anthropology and science fiction.

Delany explains this self-critical purpose of the "best science fiction"
later in "Shadows" (*Jewel-Hinged* 99). While "[m]uch science fiction inad-
vertently reflects the [scientific] context's failure," "the best science fiction
explores the attack" upon this context in contemporary society (ibid).[60]
Moreover, not only the "scientific context" but also the "social context" is
"under an internal and informed onslaught" by "Women's Liberation, Gay
Activism, Radical Psychiatry, or Black Power" (ibid). Delany links the scientific failure to "integrate its specialized products in any ecologically reason-
able way" to the social failure: the scientific failure is

> painfully understandable in a world that is terrified of any social syn-
> thesis, between black and white, male and female, rich and poor, verbal
> and non-verbal, educated and un-educated, under-privileged and privi-
> leged, subject and object. Such syntheses, if they occur, will virtually
> destroy the categories and leave all the elements that now fill them radi-
> cally revalued in ways it is impossible to more than imagine until such
> destruction is well underway. (98)

The Ballad of Beta-2 is one such act of imagination. Its racial "synthesis"
destroys the "categories" of race and "radically revalue[s]" "the elements"
which they contain. As Delany breaks down these western dichotomies in his
science fiction, he takes Baker's "guerilla action" one step farther than Baker
is willing to go (394).

Finally, Delany's deconstruction of race corresponds with current scientific racial theories. The scientific focus of science fiction entails a general coordination between contemporary scientific thought and the scientific theories of the text. While fiction, a science fiction text cannot diverge too far, or in too many ways, from contemporary scientific thought and get published and/or sell well. For example, Edgar Rice Burroughs' essentialist and hierarchical concepts of race(s) coincided with turn-of-the-century scientific theories of race and the restrictionist side of the immigration debate. Conversely, later writers like Delany, Octavia Butler, and Marge Piercy would find it difficult to publish texts which overtly contradict the current scientific and poststructuralist theories which advocate a constructed concept of race. Delany's interest in science and inclusive racial views allow him to utilize such theories with little qualification.

In his full utilization of the science fiction textus, with its technological discourse and thematic conventions, Delany challenges Baker's racial boundaries for African-American literature. For example, the technological discourse of *The Ballad of Beta-2*, and Delany's other science fiction texts, conflicts with the general valorization of the vernacular in theories of African-American literature. In addition, a significant portion of Delany's generic criticism involves his linguistic theory of science fiction, in opposition to the normative thematic foundation.[61] The subtitle of Delany's first full-length critical text, *The Jewel-Hinged Jaw: Notes on the Language of Science Fiction*, highlights the early manifestation of Delany's language-based generic theory. Published in 1977, the collection consists of a number of essays previously published between 1967 and 1976. In the 1977 introduction to the collection, Delany writes, "[r]ereading the pieces, for this edition, I am pleased with a consistency in their movement toward a language model [. . . which] is, after all, their object" (12). Delany's second collection of essays, *Starboard Wine: More Notes on the Language of Science Fiction*, was published in 1984. In the critical texts of both collections, Delany not only promotes a linguistic generic theory, but in doing so, he utilizes the academic discourse Baker rejects (in theory if not always in practice).

In his alternate history novel *Dhalgren* (1974), Delany does make significant use of the vernacular. Because *Dhalgren* takes place in an alternate, contemporary United States, rather than on another planet or in the distant future, Delany includes the historical language of the underground subculture(s) he describes. This alternate history format is more similar to *Farnham's Freehold* and *A Different Drummer* than Delany's earlier novels. As McEvoy notes, "[i]f Bellona [the specific city in which the action takes place] had been on Mars, it could be dismissed as just science fiction, not relevant to today's problem. But by having it take place in middle America, and changing a few details, he can make the book relevant to today" (109–10). In fact, by using Bellona as a place name in both *Dhalgren* and an earlier novelette, "Time Considered as a Helix of Semi-Precious Stones," Delany explicitly draws attention to the terrestrial setting of *Dhalgren* due to its contrast with the extraterrestrial setting of the earlier text.[62] McEvoy connects *Dhalgren*'s greater similarity to American society to a more autobiographical authorial perspective as well:

> [i]t is in *Dhalgren* that we get closest (of his earlier works) to Delany as a person. No longer does he hide behind the predominantly heterosexual characters that have been the focus of his earlier books. Most of the characters in *Dhalgren* are gay, and the depictions of gays is drawn in a way that is seldom seen in heterosexual literature. Delany knows gay bars, and by the time the reader has read the book, the reader has a clear picture of what a gay bar looks like and how some of the interactions go on inside one.
>
> The same applies to blacks and their separate, usually unseen by whites, culture. (116–17)

McEvoy's emphasis on authorial autobiography, and its links to the specific portrayal of sexuality and race in *Dhalgren*, raises several issues related to the vernacular. Most broadly, Delany utilizes the specific, historical vernacular of these various sub-cultures because they accurately reflect the social contexts he describes. Delany's extended use of the vernacular in this more realistic or mundane text, then, highlights the (variable) cultural foundation of all languages.[63] As the title of Barbour's *Worlds Out of Words: the SF Novels of Samuel R. Delany* highlights, the new cultural context of science fiction in time and/or space calls for linguistic changes. The evolution of the Star Folk's language in *The Ballad of Beta-2* is one such example. Similarly, in *Babel-17*, learning the alien language of Babel-17 corresponds to ideological, logical, and even practical shifts in mental processes (from targeting a new adversary to locating the fastener in an unfamiliar restraint). Delany's knowledge of and interest in semantics leads him to explore such linguistic changes, and their effects, in his other texts. While the majority of science fiction writers do not pay more than lip service to such linguistic details, the (black) vernacular is still lost due to their unfamiliarity with it. As Westfahl argues in the context of Heinlein's racial texts, the normative white authorial position in science fiction does not include first-hand or detailed knowledge of black culture(s) and, therefore, of the black vernacular.

Delany's personal experiences with the black vernacular allow him to utilize it, when the social, cultural, and/or linguistic context is appropriate. McEvoy does not expand on specific characteristics of the black culture he describes; however, Delany specifically addresses the issue of the black vernacular in "Shadows."[64] Describing his early childhood in Harlem and the private elementary school he attended, Delany asserts, "[b]lack Harlem speech and white Park Avenue speech are very different things. I became aware of language as an intriguing and infinitely malleable modeling tool very early" (*Jewel-Hinged* 119). Delany continues, "I always felt myself to be living in several worlds with rather tenuous connections between them, but I never remember it causing me much anxiety. [. . .] Rather, it gave me a sense of modest (and sometimes not so modest) superiority" (119).[65] Here Delany does not support Baker's negative evaluation of a divided subjectivity.[66] Like his positive portrayal of racial hybridity and multiple consciousness in *The Ballad of Beta-2*, Delany sees the added communicative potential instead. His experiences in multiple social contexts—black and white, privileged, poor, educated, heterosexual and homosexual (etc.)—allow him to act as a translator, like The Destroyer's Children, among these multiple, largely separated, and sometimes hostile groups. The protagonist of *Dhalgren*, Kid, also circulates freely among diverse social contexts—a gay bar; a street gang; a formal dinner party; the home of a stereotypical white, middle-class family; a classroom; etc. In this context, Kid's general 'amnesia' symbolizes the amorphous nature of his subjectivity and the "freedom" this entails (McEvoy 106).[67] Baker's essentialist, monolithic concept of racial identity, on the other hand, restricts this subjective, social, and linguistic freedom. Therefore, Delany's use of the vernacular in *Dhalgren* meets Baker's linguistic qualification for African-American literature, but the text as a whole exceeds his theoretical limitations. The most obvious sign of this is Delany's racially-inclusive use of the vernacular; both black and white characters utilize what is more accurately called a street or gang vernacular.[68] *Dhalgren* is an example of Baker's "*supraliteracy,*" but he cannot see this because of his racial blinders (394).[69] Since Delany does not essentialize sound nor privilege the vernacular, he can utilize any discourse: the vernacular in portions of *Dhalgren*, the technological discourse of science fiction in many of his texts, the "subtle" academic discourse of much of his criticism, etc. (Baker 389). Delany chooses the one(s) most appropriate to the context of his writing and, if necessary, revises an existing one to suit a new (imaginative) cultural context. As we have seen, Delany learned the "infinitely malleable" nature of language at an early age.

As *Dhalgren* comes closer to fulfilling African-American literary criteria than Delany's other texts, it is no coincidence that is controversial within the science fiction community. The same historical realism which called for the vernacular, and a corresponding subtlety of the technological discourse, prompted many science fiction readers to question *Dhalgren's* status as science fiction. Writing under a pseudonym, K. Leslie Steiner, Delany refuted this criticism of the novel:

> *Dhalgren* was a science fiction novel that (What? Yes, it *is* science fiction: the hero enters over a bridge into a parallel world—see, silly!—into an alter-version of an American city where" . . . the ordinary laws of time and space," as they used to say, "no longer apply." I mean, really!) attacked the field by being a great book [. . .] in just those ways most science fiction is not even good: by density of psychological construction and depth of social insight. (Delany, *Straits* 93)

McEvoy also felt compelled to specifically address the science fictional elements of *Dhalgren* (111), even as he acknowledged its unexpected realism (109–10). In addition to its realism and great length (even for mainstream/mundane fiction), McEvoy posits the experimental quality of *Dhalgren* as a reason for its controversial reception (103–105). *Dhalgren* presents the interesting paradox in that it has had record sales for a science fiction text, but the total "response with the science fiction community—fandom and the professionals of the SFWA—has been generally negative, or at the best averaged out to a slightly disavowing neutral" (Barbour 90).[70] Presumably, then, the majority of *Dhalgren's* sales lay outside the science fiction community. As a result, *Dhalgren* serves as an example of the difficulty in merging the African-American and science fiction genres, at least in terms of rigid generic characteristics (and expectations). Perhaps this is why Delany has refused to limit his writing to a single genre—writing science fiction, fantasy (including the sub-genre of sword-and-sorcery), autobiography, criticism, autobiographical criticism, pornography, etc. In doing so, Delany has challenged his readers, but as he notes in a *Callaloo* interview, the popularity *of Dhalgren, Trouble on Triton*, and the Nevèrÿon series suggests that "[t]oo many people have already found something in them of value" to deny a receptive audience for his generically revisionist and fluid texts (*Silent* 226).[71]

Despite Delany's optimism, however, the controversy surrounding his career persists, even growing stronger over time. Delany asserts that "thematically" he is "an extremely conservative SF writer" (225), but admits "[w]hat I am doing in almost all my books is the genre equivalent of 'gender bending'" (*Silent* 226). In his early and continued exploration of linguistic and cultural theories (the 'soft' sciences), Delany flaunted both the essentialist bias of the African-American literary community and the traditional conventions of science fiction. *The Ballad of Beta-2* (1965), *Babel-17* (1966), and *The Einstein Intersection* (1967), for example, are early, fictional manifestations of Delany's interest in language and culture. Within the science fiction community, this linguistic exploration and experimentation won Delany his first Nebula awards. However, Delany's experiences at the 1968 Nebula Awards banquet illustrate the power struggles going on between the older, more traditional science fiction writers and the younger, more experimental writers. Slusser's 1977 critical text on Delany specifically centers on his representative embodiment of a "structuralist imagination" and the importance of language to structuralism (3).[72] Even with his wider critical focus, McEvoy stresses the importance of texts and writing to the vast majority of Delany's oeuvre (45–6). McEvoy theorizes that Delany's dyslexia played a role in his linguistic interests: "[t]his difficulty with texts became a concern with texts and perhaps an obsession with words, which is especially evident in Delany's remarkable *The American Shore*, a 243 page critique of a short story by Tom Disch!" (46).[73] The increasing sophistication of Delany's linguistic discussions, in his fiction and non-fiction, has raised the theoretical bar for his readers.

By the 1995 publication of *The Encyclopedia of Science Fiction*, John Clute and Peter Nicholls assert, "[t]here is no doubt that by the 1980s [Delany's] fiction (and criticism) had become less accessible, and the real debate about his career must be whether or not he gained more than he lost with his adoption of a denser style towards the later 1970s" (317). As a result, Clute and Nicholls theorize "different audiences at different points" in Delany's career: "a very wide, traditional science fiction readership up to and including *Dhalgren* [. . .] and a narrower, perhaps more intellectual, campus-based readership thereafter" (ibid). Certainly, Delany understands the linguistic and theoretical challenges he presents to his readers. In a 1988 essay titled "Neither the First Word nor the Last on Deconstruction, Structuralism, Poststructuralism, and Semiotics for SF Readers," Delany explicitly attempts to explain these difficult linguistic, literary, and cultural theories to the science fiction community (*Shorter*). Of course, an understanding of these theories would aid readers of Delany's texts (fictional and non-fiction), but Delany gives additional reasons why "science fiction readers [should] be interested in such debates" (*Shorter* 148). The third, "personal" reason is "positioned at the very interface of [the] first two":

> [Delany] would like to see a debate about our own practices of equal
> interest grow up, here, within the precincts of science fiction—a debate

> informed by the same disposition toward analytic vigilance, with the
> same willingness to historify and demystify the vast range of sediments,
> unquestioned self-evident positions, and givens under which our genre,
> its fandom, its readership struggle, along with energetic attempts to
> deconstruct those oppositions at which so much discussion of science
> fiction stalls: "technology" vs. "science," "reviewing" vs. "criticism,"
> "pro" vs. "fan," "commercial" vs. "quality," and "craft" vs. "art." (*Shorter*
> 150)

Delany's resistance to these specific science fiction dichotomies parallels Baker's
resistance to the larger dualistic nature of western culture. As we have seen,
however, Delany's reliance on structuralism, poststructuralism, and semiotics
flies in the face of mainstream African-American criticism.

    Therefore, Delany's detailed and pervasive utilization of structuralist and
poststructuralist theories not only challenges his science fiction readers, but
also combines with his scientific interests to make his texts even more objectionable than those of Gates in the field of African-American Studies. Baker's
theory of the Calibanic Self, with its natural soundings and ties to family and
kinship, implicitly criticizes Afro-American writers who do not subscribe to
these tenets (and reflect them in their work)—they are 'inauthentic,' not racialized, not 'black.'[74] As a result, most of Samuel Delany's non-fiction and much
of his fiction, without an extensive use of the (black) vernacular and with an
emphasis on technology (vs. Baker's nature), would indict Delany himself as
somehow not being true to his authentic racial self, to his racial heritage, to his
people. Certainly, Delany resists such theories of identity and literature. In an
interview, he emphasizes difference and not uniform notions of identity which
allow a person to be categorized: "Whatever identity you have, be it the identity of a black person or a gay person, of a male, of a female, is what allows you
to be put in a category [. . .]. Identity is not what makes you an individual.
Difference is what makes us individual" (Beckerman). Delany's "difference"
here is not the racialist, essential difference utilized by Baker, but more like
the Derridian "*différance*" which is constructed through contrast with others
(Freedman 148).[75] In the context of gay identity, Delany makes his stance on
the construction of identity even more clear: "For me, Gay Identity [. . .] is
an object of the context, not of the self" (*Longer* 143). There is nothing 'natural,' then, about Delany's concept of racial identity, and Baker's connections
between naturalness, nature, and race do not apply to Delany's discussion of
(various concepts of) race in science fiction.

    The threat Delany posses to literary theories that are based on race—
like the African-American literary theories of Joyce, Baker, and Gates—is

clearly seen in his postmodern view of the "black artist" and the sub-genre of African-American science fiction ("Racism 392). Delany believes that the small 'b' for black artist is "a very significant letter, an attempt to ironize and detranscendentalize the whole concept of race, to tender it provisional and contingent" (ibid). Also, with the advent of such writers as Octavia Butler in the 1970s, Steven Barnes in the 1980s, and Nalo Hopkinson in the 1990s comes the increased threat of racial/racist labeling and grouping. Today, Delany questions the relatively new category of "African-American science fiction" (395). In "Racism and Science Fiction" (1994), Delany first shares his positive experiences at Clark Atlanta University's African-American Science Fiction Conference (395). However, "[t]his aware and vital meeting to respond specifically to black youth in Atlanta is not [. . .] what usually occurs at an academic presentation in a largely white university doing an evening on African-American science fiction" (ibid). Delany asserts that "as long as racism functions *as* a system, it is still fueled by aspects of the perfectly laudable desires of interested whites to observe this thing, however dubious its reality, that exists largely by means of its having been named: African-American science fiction" (ibid). It is in this context that Delany objects to consistently being placed with Octavia Butler at conventions, conferences, and in interviews (395–6). In terms of his writing and his influence in the field, Delany believes that he has more in common with "cyberpunk writers" like William Gibson than Butler (ibid). Yet, he has appeared only once with Gibson and more than six times with Butler (396). Delany resists a label like "African-American science fiction" because it racially segregates otherwise dissimilar writers from the genre as a whole. He simultaneously promotes individual difference and inclusive intermingling because "what racism as a system does is isolate and segregate the people of one race, or group, or ethnos from another" ("Racism" 393). For Delany, then, any reform of the science fiction community would involve greater inclusiveness, but not greater compartmentalization. In this we can see Delany joining Schuyler in resisting an over-simplified categorization as an African-American writer. Such a category or label is not only inaccurate, but also restricting and separatist.

Delany insists on exploring a dazzling multiplicity of issues in his texts, reflecting the multiplicity of his interests and his subjectivity. Therefore, any critical study of his texts poses the challenge of selection and the problem of elision. In his section on Delany and his 1984 novel, *Stars in My Pocket Like Grains of Sand*, Carl Freedman acknowledges this difficulty.[76] In addition to the "politics of gender and to specifically feminist concerns," Delany pursu[es] a close examination of the politics of sexual orientation and of that entire complex of social marginalities designated in earthly terms by such rubrics as race, ethnicity, and nation. Very few novels, within science fiction or beyond it, have ever tried to do as much as Delany's magnum opus. If the personal interest [. . .] that Delany has maintained in the texts of critical theory makes his work an inevitable or at least "natural" reference point for a study like the current essay, the immense scope of his finest novel makes it an extremely difficult text with which to come to terms. (Freedman 147)

Within the present work, Delany is also an essential "reference point." Not only does Delany investigate the intersection of subjectivity with race in his science fiction, but his extensive critical writings are an invaluable resource as well. Finally, the timing of Delany's entrance into the science fiction community offers a unique vantage point from which to critique the field after Schuyler. However, Delany's autobiography, *The Motion of Light in Water*, offers a more accurate presentation of his diverse interests and the many facets of his postmodern subjectivity.

Delany's 1988 autobiography explores the personal basis for his multiple interests. Sexuality, gender, race, and vocation are ideological sites where the social "impinges" on the psychological, or the object "contour[s] and constitute[s]" the subject (*Starboard* 188).[77] Not just serving as a historical/social background for Delany's fiction, then, the autobiography embodies his multiple subjectivity and its associated freedom, contradiction, and tension. Early on Delany shares a feeling of "pivotal suspension" between the many dichotomies dividing American society:

> I was a young black man, light-skinned enough so that four out of five people who met me, of whatever race, assumed I was white. [. . .] I was a homosexual who now knew he could function heterosexually.
>
> And I was a young writer whose early attempts had already gotten him a handful of prizes, a few scholarships [. . .].
>
> So, I thought, you are neither black nor white.
>
> You are neither male nor female.
>
> And you are that most ambiguous of citizens, the writer.
>
> There was something at once very satisfying and very sad, placing myself at this pivotal suspension. It seemed, in the park at dawn, a kind of revelation—a kind of center, formed of a play of ambiguities, from which I might move in any direction. (*Motion* 52)

First, Delany's personal "satisfaction" stems from the "romantic ambiguities" of subjective positions in the "center" of these dualities and the possibility of freedom, agency, and/or individuality attached to such neutral positions (242). His "sadness" is the flip side to this neutral coin, in that Delany does not fit within the existing, dualistic categories of American society. Therefore, he is an outsider who also faces intense social pressure to conform, to make himself fit these categories at whatever personal cost.

In fact, Delany later shares his revision of this "revelation" and places a reexamination of these issues of subjectivity in the context of a mental breakdown (*Motion* 52). In the hospital he "began to see that what [he'd] taken as a play of freedom and mystical possibility had actually meant something quite different" (242). The difference includes the oppressive ideologies of race and sexuality which, especially pre-1960's, "pull you toward the most conservative position you might inhabit, however poorly you might be suited for it" (ibid). As a means of self-examination, Delany tentatively lists three labels and subjective positions which place him within the existing social categories, but not in the "most conservative position[s]": "A black man . . . ?/A gay man . . . ?/A writer . . . ?" (212). He proceeds to take each of these fragments of his subjectivity individually and use it as a lens to zoom in on the corresponding sections of his life experiences. In this way, readers (joining Delany in his voyage of discovery) learn additional information about Delany's life not previously related in the autobiography, although overlapping in time. We also follow the process of interrogation or critical analysis through which Delany matures, coming to terms with the multiple elements of his identity and learning strategies of resistance to the way these elements were (are) "hugely devalued in the social hierarchy" (ibid).

Delany's personal struggle here seems to illustrate the extreme dispersal of identity discussed by Diana Fuss. Fuss suggests: "It does seem plausible that, like the female subject, the Afro-American subject (who might also be female [and gay]) *begins* fragmented and dispersed [. . .]. If so, then for both the female subject and the Afro-American subject, 'the condition of dispersal and fragmentation that Barthes valorizes (and fetishizes) is not to be achieved but to be overcome'" (95).[78] Delany continues the process of fragmentation begun by Fuss, adding sexuality and vocation to race and gender. While Delany does not specifically address gender in this one section, elsewhere in his autobiography he spends considerable time examining emerging feminist concerns during this time period, particularly through the vehicle of his wife Marilyn Hacker. In all of his writings, Delany takes the divided racial subjectivity of Du Bois and Schuyler and fragments it much further. Even the overarching format of the autobiography reflects this fragmentation. Small segments or "arbitrary fragments" from different contexts and time periods are numbered by individual fragment and by larger sections or groups of fragments (*Motion* 300).[79] For example, Delany begins with section "1" and continues through "85," but breaks up section "8" into everything from "8.1" to "8.103" and "8.29." Brian McHale addresses this postmodern "disintegration" in his book *Constructing Postmodernism* (254):

> Postmodernism's shift of focus to ontological issues and themes has radical consequences for literary models of the self. A poetics in which the category 'world' is plural, unstable and problematic would seem to entail a model of the self which is correspondingly plural, unstable, and problematic. If the world is ontologically unstable (self-contradictory, hypothetical or fictional, infiltrated by other realities) then so perhaps am 'I.' (253–4).

McHale's theoretical pluralism here parallels Delany's autobiographical pluralism, as well as its connection to science fiction's culture-building project (multiple worlds).[80]

As both Fuss and McHale imply, a "dispersed" (Fuss 95) or "plural," "self-contradictory," and "unstable" subjectivity can be "problematic" (McHale 253–4). However, Fuss' suggestion that such fragmentation or division should be "overcome" does not mean an indiscriminate merging of the elements into a monolithic, static identity. As Delany attempts to show in this autobiography, the multiple subjective elements should be identified and explored, and their connections to the social context critically examined. They also need to be reconciled with one another as much as possible. For example, the three elements of race, sexuality, and vocation are set side-by-side and connected to other elements of his autobiography. In this way, they are 'united' in one life story and a single artistic endeavor, yet they remain distinctly recognized individually as fundamental elements of Delany's subjectivity. At the end of the three sections, Delany no longer questions, but confidently asserts: "A black man. / A gay man. / A writer" (*Motion* 242). He also implies that these multiple subjective positions serve as bridges or "a rhetoric that joins each [column]—however tenuously—to the other" (212). The "two columns" to which he refers here are the public and private dichotomy of western discourse and its embodiment in his "two accounts" of his life (212)—"one resplendent and lucid with the writings of legitimacy, the other dark and hollow with the voices of the illegitimate" (29–30).[81] While these two "columns" or "accounts [. . .] seem as if they take place on different planets," Delany "insists that the gap between them, the split, the flickering correlations between, as evanescent as light-shot water, as insubstantial as moonstruck cloud, are really all that constitute the subject: not the content, if you will, but the relationships that can be drawn out of that content, and which finally that content can be analyzed down into" (212). Delany values bridges between subjective divisions, then, and not the maintenance of discrete units. Given his inclusive and dynamic fiction, it is fitting that Delany emphasize fluid connections rather than static separations in his autobiography.

[TROUBLE ON] TRITON

As the example of Delany's autobiography highlights, the fragmentation of subjectivity relies on social context. Therefore, not only is identity or subjectivity fragmented, but the fragments are a matter of context also—a very unstable and potentially disconcerting subjective position. In opposition to an interior, static essentialism, a constructed or provisional subjectivity relies on exterior materials—the social and physical environment. Thus, subjectivity is provisional due to the tension between the fragments and the fluid social context. The object focus of science fiction provides an ideal location for exploring this social fluidity and, logically, the corresponding provisional nature of subjectivity as well. In Delany's science fiction criticism, he discusses the unique relationship between the subject and the object in science fiction. In *Trouble on Triton*, he specifically revises the ideological position of the static, essentialist protagonist of traditional science fiction.[82] Imagine John Carter traveling to the Outer Satellites, a new social context, and finding himself the outsider, the Other. Without the traditional white, male hero, the reader must look elsewhere for viable, attractive subjective alternatives. Through the gradual deconstruction of the static protagonist and corresponding shift toward the dynamic minor characters, Delany not only critiques a heroic model, but also the larger failings of traditional science fiction. The object focus of science fiction, the change in social setting, logically entails a change in subjectivity. If subjectivity is constructed through the social environment, the protagonist should not simply change the world(s) in which 'he' comes into contact, but also be changed by that world. However, this focus of attention on the object, or world setting, has historically functioned to obscure the subject altogether in science fiction.

In "Reading at Work, and Other Activities Frowned on by Authority: A Reading of Donna Haraway's 'Manifesto for Cyborgs: Science, Technology, and Socialist Feminism in the 1980s'" (1985–88), Delany places his multiple consciousness in a causal relationship with his physical context: "my eye lifts from the text and again strays, glances about, snags a moment at a horizon, a boundary that does not so much contain a self, an identity, a unity, a center and origin which gazes out and *defines* that horizon as the horizon is defined *by* it; rather that horizon suggests a plurality of possible positions within it, positions which allow a number of events to transpire" (*Longer* 117).[83] This "horizon," object, context, or world results in similar "positions" as Delany's autobiography. At the end of his reading of Haraway's essay, Delany tries "to articulate the positions from which [he] write[s], as a male, as a black male, as a gay black male, as a gay black male whose works is the writing of paraliterary fictions" (ibid). These subjective positions (or fragments) reflect particular social contexts and they lead to a specific interpretation of Haraway's text. Therefore, Delany invites the reader to interpret Haraway's text also, "restructur[ing]" his interpretation and potentially opening up additional interpretive "positions" (118). This collective or dialogic model of reading reflects Delany's "ontology of the open horizon—which relativizes discourse to rhetoric, refuses closure and the transcendence of history, places the subject back into its object-context, and privileges the active, social self over the passive sovereign self" (K. James xxxvii).

In "Aversion/Perversion/ Diversion" (1991), Delany more fully explains the constructed and provisional nature of subjectivity in the context of his "gay" position (*Longer*). Delany asserts, "[t]he point to the notion of Gay Identity is that, in terms of a transcendent reality concerned with sexuality *per se* (a Universal similarity, a shared necessary condition, a defining aspect, a generalizable and inescapable essence common to all men and women called 'gay'), I believe Gay Identity has no more existence than a single, essential, transcendental sexual difference" (*Longer* 142). This is the point at which Schuyler discards race as a meaningful concept—of positive value for African-Americans. Delany too notes the two "strategies" composing Gay Identity (similar to those of race); one used negatively for the "heterosexist oppression of gays" and the other used positively to promote "gay rights" (ibid). However, Delany goes on to offer a qualified endorsement of the second of these two strategies (particularly necessary, presumably, because of the first), "even if, at a theoretical level, [he] questions[s] the existence of that identity as having anything beyond a provisional or strategic reality" (ibid).[84] This "provisional or strategic reality" comes into play in terms of the social and historical contexts of Gay Identity. "For [Delany], Gay Identity—like the joys of Gay Pride Day, weekends on Fire Island, and the delight of tickets to the opera—is an object of the context, not of the self—which means, like the rest of the context, it requires analysis, understanding, interrogation, even sympathy, but never an easy and uncritical acceptance" (*Longer* 143).

Therefore, Ken James believes Delany's "interest in such recondite analytical practices as Marxian critique, deconstructive criticism, and discourse analysis" lies in their "exploration of the *social* constitution of the individual subject" (xxi). In addition to the social context, Delany emphasizes the importance of a historical context. For example, Delany noted in his autobiography that the terms "gay" and "black" did not exist in the early 1960s as we know them today (*Motion* 242). Because of their contextual basis, their "meanings, usage," and rhetoric change over time (ibid).

Delany argues that this "concept of ideohistory" is very common in science fiction, in contrast to mundane fiction (*Jewel-Hinged* 272–3). Along with the "convention of idiocentric omissions (or opacities)," the concept of ideohistory "allow[s] science fiction to treat ideas as signifiers—as complex structures that organize outward in time and space (they have causes, they have results)" (273). By simultaneously historicizing an idea like 'gay' or 'race' and treating it as "a *new* idea" (the ideocentric omission), then, science fiction is freed "from the stricture that has held back so much modern thought, of treating ideas as signifieds—as dense, semantic objects with essential, hidden, yet finally extractable semantic cores" (ibid). As a result, science fiction is one vehicle for the required "analysis, understanding, interrogation" of such ideas (*Longer* 143). Science fiction highlights the historical and social fluctuation of ideas because of its object-focus, its foregrounding of the contextual background (in mundane fiction) (*Starboard* 188). In "Shadows," Delany explains how science fiction writers examine this context, this exterior "world":

> Nothing we look at is ever seen without some shift and flicker—that constant flaking of vision which we take as imperfections of the eye or simply the instability of attention itself; and we ignore this illusory screen for the solid reality behind it. But the solid reality is the illusion; the shift and flicker is all there is (Where do s-f writers get their crazy ideas? From watching all there is *very* carefully.) (*Jewel-Hinged* 51–2)

Therefore, not only does the context fluctuate due to time, spatial, and social differences, but also in its very apprehension and its metaphysical nature. Through its contextual and speculative emphases, science fiction illuminates this "shift and flicker" more than the "solid reality" portrayed by mundane fiction.

In "*Dichtung und* Science Fiction," Delany discusses the difference between the object focus of science fiction and the subject focus of other literary genres (*Starboard* 188–9). According to Delany, the other "literary modes [. . .] are all characterized—now, today—by a priority of the subject, i.e., of the self, of human consciousness" (*Starboard* 188). In contrast, "as a paraliterary mode," science fiction is "concerned with the subject, certainly, but concerned with those aspects of it that are closer to the object: How is the subject excited, impinged on, contoured and constituted by the object?" (ibid). This unusual literary hierarchy raises several issues. First, the object focus of science fiction is another factor in the longevity of the traditional white male hero. Displacing subjectivity as the center of the narrative encourages a stable, static, relatively unimportant protagonist. What fluctuates instead is the context—the physical and social environment and the specific adventures the protagonist experiences. For example, John Carter's psychology, and its development, is not the focus of Burroughs' Mars series. The first text becomes a full-length novel and then an extended series through the varying settings. Thus, the object focus of science fiction maintains an essentialist theory of subjectivity through neglect. However, as Delany's science fiction criticism highlights, if an author specifically addresses subjectivity, the object-focus of science fiction encourages a more accurate portrayal. The emphasis on the social and physical context shows us how the subject is "excited, impinged on, contoured and constituted by the object"—how subjectivity is constructed, in other words. Furthermore, the contextual and the speculative elements of science fiction emphasize subjective instability, variation, and the potential for change. Delany incorporates both of these subjective trends in *Trouble on Triton*.

The protagonist of *Trouble on Triton*, Bron Helstrom, is the traditional white, male hero of science fiction. He is not significantly influenced by his environment, and his "simplexity [. . .] is in essence a form of solipsism" (Barbour 127).[85] If *Trouble on Triton* is an exception to the general science fiction rule of subjective neglect, Delany chooses to explore the very psychology which has been elided. Furthermore, Delany uses the context or object-focus of science fiction to critique this static, isolated, selfish subjectivity. The discrepancy between Bron's point of view and the context leads the reader to question Bron's reliability and begin to see his subjective type as an anachronism.[86] In this case, Delany uses the context to illustrate how an individual's subjectivity is not significantly "contoured" by a new environment (*Starboard* 188). The new environment of *Trouble on Triton* is the Outer Satellite moon of Triton, and its contrast to Bron's home planet of Mars grounds the social and subjective critique of the text. The socially and politically more conservative planets, Mars and Earth, become political allies in a war against the more radical Outer Satellites. Bron is the reader's narrative focus for this larger social context. Within a traditional science fiction narrative, therefore,

Bron would be the warrior/hero largely responsible for winning the war on behalf of the 'good guys.' However, Bron's actual wartime activities undermine this stereotype. Furthermore, Delany contrasts Bron, his subjectivity and actions, to that of other Outer Satellite residents. They represent the new subjective possibilities which Bron rejects. Unlike Kid in the terrestrial Bellona of *Dhalgren*, Bron will not take full advantage of the new freedoms offered by his altered social context.[87]

Delany's choice of a white, male protagonist in *Trouble on Triton* continues his dialogue with Robert Heinlein. In written communications to Michael W. Peplow, Delany revealed one of his inspirations for *Trouble on Triton* and, specifically, Bron Helstrom—Heinlein's 1963 *Glory Road* (Peplow, "Meet" 120). Peplow summarizes Delany's reaction to *Glory Road* as follows: Delany "liked the pure adventure aspects of the story but hated its hero—'an incredibly conservative, "normal" six-foot blond hero (190 pound ex-athletic star)'" (ibid).[88] As a result, Delany intended *Trouble on Triton* to be a "cutting, if not killing, dissection of just what I think a primarily heterosexual blue-eyed blond male is" (qtd. in Peplow 120).[89] Delany takes the same traditional, heroic, white male, science fiction protagonist as Heinlein and offers a more radical critique than *Farnham's Freehold*. In addition, Delany's "dissection" and critique of the white, heterosexual male psyche inverts the normative psychological and literary 'pathologizing' of homosexuals, women, and blacks. In fact, as Bron models this process of psychological Othering in his daily life, he reveals his own disabling limitations and psychological disorder to the reader. In this way, *Trouble on Triton* affirmatively answers the question left by *Farnham's Freehold*—can an author focus on a white male protagonist and his subjectivity without undermining the author's critical, revisionist intentions?[90]

In Bron Helstrom, Delany takes a traditional science fiction hero and fleshes out his psychology, highlighting the negative potential of such personality characteristics. First, Bron desperately desires subjective unity, to be an integrated 'whole.' He pleads with his romantic interest, the Spike, "'Help me. Take me. Make me whole'" (*Trouble* 107). Neil Easterbrook argues that Bron "fetishizes himself as a clear and distinct Cartesian subject [. . .]. Cartesian subjectivity and hierarchy appeal precisely because they are clear, certain, coherent, stable—and so by the principle of parsimony, preferable" (67).[91] What Easterbrook's accurate and inclusive description lacks is a specific articulation of the racial, gender, and sexual components of Bron's "Cartesian subjectivity" and the privilege attached to these positions.[92] The "hierarchy" Easterbrook briefly mentions entails something besides "parsimony." When he notes that "Bron wants to be 'at the center' (306) within a culture with none," Easterbrook implies what needs to be stated explicitly—the normative and privileged position of the white, heterosexual male (Bron) in western culture and the science fiction genre more specifically. Barbour is one of the few critics to foreground the importance of Bron's racial status:

> Bron Helstrom is Delany's first WASP protagonist, a member of the dominant racial and economic group in our Western world [. . .]. He is the symbolic bearer of the social attitudes associated with the Richards in *Dhalgren* and singled out for attack in Delany's 'Sex, Objects.' That he is also the first protagonist in Delany's science fiction with whom we are compelled *not to identify* assumes great importance in this context. (122)

Without this direct and detailed ideological placement, Delany's social, generic, and subjective critique is limited. Within the generic context, for example, we would not see Bron Helstrom as the distant ancestor of Edgar Rice Burroughs' John Carter or a step-brother to Heinlein's protagonist in *Glory Road*. Only such men can utilize a theory of integrated subjectivity because they are so centrally located that the 'margins' do not overlap their subjective boundaries. Furthermore, their corresponding social (economic, political, etc.) privilege supports this illusion of subjective independence. Du Bois' theory of a double-consciousness for African-Americans, Fuss' application to women of such a multiple theory of subjectivity, and Delany's autobiographical explorations of his sexuality highlight several groups who do not make use of such an integrated theory of subjectivity. When Delany places Bron within a new social context that displaces the historical centrality and privilege of the "WASP" male, he joins Fuss and Huyssen in highlighting the false universalism of this specific, limited subjective position.[93] Bron becomes simply one of many on Triton, who is only different in his continued resistance to such social and subjective egalitarianism.

In its unity and sameness, then, a monolithic subjectivity rejects the Other and reveals a fear of possible racial, gender, or sexual 'contamination.' Bron's frequent critical label of "solipsistic" (Barbour 127) or "narcissistic" (Massé 53) highlights this subjective isolation, rejection of the Other, and repetition of the same. As Michelle Massé notes, Bron desires an "acknowledgement of [his] uniqueness *and* superiority" (53). His persistent resistance to being a "type" (5) and his longing for 'the good old days' spring from these desires (Delany, *Trouble* 254). According to Bron, the past [our present] was more "simple" in its overt sexism (254). Delany implies that Bron glorifies this historical period because it would 'justify' his now marginal ideological position(s) and its related sexism, heterosexism, and racism (ibid).[94] Bron's utilization of the past as a defensive mechanism reveals his limited understanding that he is an anachronism in the heterotopic world of Triton. As an anachronism, Bron "still thinks in binaries"—man/woman, owner/owned, client/servant, and so forth" (Easterbrook 66). Bron utilizes these outdated "binaries," and their hierarchical organization in western culture, to "classify others to establish his own difference" (Massé 54). In his classification, Bron limits by definition and misrepresents by stereotype. Therefore, he represents the 'anachronistic' divisions, prejudices, and psychological defenses prevalent in contemporary western society. More specifically, Bron mimics the ethnographic gaze of the western explorer/naturalist/anthropologist. However, Delany strips the superficial objectivity and false universalism from the classification and hierarchical ranking of a Carl Akeley, Theodore Roosevelt, or a John Carter.[95] As a result, the three characters closest to Bron in the text—Lawrence, the Spike, and Sam—become "inferior types, who show moreover no consciousness of their 'lowly' status: the Spike is a woman, Sam a black, Lawrence old and gay" (Massé 56). Similarly, "Bron is the only character in the novel who frequently uses racist and sexist terms—'crazed lesbian,' 'obnoxious faggot,' 'nigger,' 'cock-sucker,' 'whore,' and 'dyke'" (55). Bron's anachronistic terminology, then, reflects his anachronistic ideology and values, and it overtly and vividly reveals the bias of his formerly normative subjective position.

Delany also critiques the psychology of the traditional science fiction protagonist through the related characteristic of stasis. Bron's monolithic, enclosed subjectivity does not change, even when subjected to the pressure of new social and/or physical environments. "In Triton's flux, Bron is a static character" (Massé 52). According to Delany's science fiction theory, of course, Bron should change; a new subject should result from a new object. Bron's exception to the rule is not an oversight, however; it is the very basis of Delany's generic critique. Not only should the object focus of science fiction lead to new subjective models, but also the traditional science fiction protagonist supposedly embodies the larger progressive characteristics of western society and the white race. Within this traditional dualistic context, western cultures and their representatives were politically, culturally, historically, and even geographically moving toward a more advanced, positive stage of development. On the other hand, people-of-color and their 'native' cultures were incapable of cultural or psychological change.[96] Therefore, Bron's psychological and cultural stasis illustrates the contradiction and hypocrisy within the (theoretically) dynamic, progressive characterization of the traditional science fiction hero. Furthermore, Bron's persistent Othering reveals the motivation behind the traditional hero's stasis—it protects him from cultural and biological contamination and ensures his triumph against the inferior, usually adversarial natives. If he assimilated (i.e. changed) socially and/or sexually (including reproduction), he could not maintain his superior position. Within this larger context of racial essentialism, Bron's subjective essentialism reflects a desire to keep the larger 'race' pure—biologically, culturally, and psychologically. Thus, individual stasis protects posterity.

Bron's interest in the 'survival of the species' connects to stasis in this way (Delany, *Trouble* 232). As Lawrence informs Bron, his chances of meeting a woman with "a mutually compatible logical perversion" (212) are approximately "one out of five thousand" (213). With these statistical odds in mind, Bron decides to become a woman, in order "to preserve the species" (232). Bron believes that only in preserving and passing on his beliefs, his anachronistic cultural norms can "mankind" survive or have any positive value (231). In an interesting twist from the alien cloning of *The Ballad of Beta-2*, Delany has Bron attempt to reproduce through sexual and psychological alteration of himself. After his alterations, Bron's counselor tells her, "[i]n one sense, though you are as real a woman as possible, in another sense you are a woman created *by* a man—specifically by the man you were" (251). This reproduction of the Self, the same, is doomed to failure in the heterotopic society of Triton, however.[97] Unlike Hugh Farnham and Barbara in Heinlein's *Farnham's Freehold*, this new Eve will not 'go forth and bear fruit.'[98]

After the fact, Bron realizes the impossible situation s/he has created. She must be passive in order to attract the type of man she used to be, but then her chances of finding 'Mr. Right' are very slim to non-existent (Delany, *Trouble* 263). Furthermore, Bron's 'feminine' passivity basically continues her passivity as a man. According to Massé, "in the main [Bron] is passive in his actions and relationships"; "he is dependent upon the responses of others to maintain his image" (57). This critical evaluation of Bron's passivity not only contradicts the agency and assertiveness of traditional Western manhood and the science fiction hero, but also brings us full circle back to Bron's request to the Spike to "make [him] whole" (Delany, *Trouble* 107). Bron's plea reveals not only his desire for a monolithic subjectivity, but also his paradoxical reliance on others for this 'independent' subjectivity. Thus, Delany utilizes Jacques Derrida's theory of linguistic "*différance*" to highlight the logical impossibility of Bron's subjective position. As Carl Freedman points out, Derrida's theory of *différance* has important ramifications for identity:

> Not only does every signifier differ from every other; it also thereby
> *defers* to every other, in the sense that the differential determination of

its own meaning is always to be found elsewhere. Accordingly, meaning—and therefore all thought and all identity—cannot be securely
achieved in any particular act of signification. On the contrary, it operates in a fitful, problematic way throughout the entirety of the signifying system. (148)

Therefore, what Bron refuses to acknowledge is the fundamental diffusion
of his theoretically monolithic, isolated identity. It is only "elsewhere," in
relationship with others that his poststructuralist subjectivity can be constructed.

As a result, Bron's sex and gender changes are not enough to extricate
her from "the hopeless tangle of confusion, trouble, and distress" she had
hoped to leave behind on Mars (Delany, *Trouble* 277). The underlying subjective stasis eventually overcomes all of Bron's defensive mechanisms, and
she projects her subjective stasis upon the objective world. *Trouble on Triton*
ends with Bron firmly believing that "dawn [. . .] would never come"
(ibid). In Appendix B, Delany has the fictional philosopher and mathemati-
cian Ashima Slade sympathetically comment on Bron's precarious subjective
position:

> Our society in the Satellites extends to its Earth and Mars emigrants,
> at the same time it extends instruction on how to conform, the materi-
> als with which to destroy themselves, both psychologically and physi-
> cally—all under the same label: Freedom. To the extent they will not
> conform to our ways, there is a subtle swing: The materials of instruc-
> tion are pulled further away and the materials of destruction are pushed
> correspondingly closer. (*Trouble* 302–3).

Bron's mental breakdown at the end of the text is one example of such
psychological "destruction." In a moment of metafictional reversal, Delany
also compares himself to Slade as follows: "for Slade the concept of *landscape*
is far more political than it was for the author [Delany] of the older work
[*Trouble on Triton*]" (302). With Slade, Delany returns to the importance of
"*landscape*" or the object/world to the construction of subjectivity. In Triton's
different "*landscape*," the positive qualities of the traditional science fiction
hero are revealed to be flaws. On Triton, heroic "male aloneness" (216)
becomes a "logical perversion" and leads to unhappiness, dynamic becomes
passive, stasis leads to infertility, independence relies on others, and finally
male becomes female (212). A traditional science fiction hero, like Bron,
would not be able to survive in the poststructuralist world of difference fully

realized in Triton. As Delany asserts, when the results look *most* revolutionary, that's when the writer is *most* attending to the tradition" (*Silent* 226).

Delany's critique of the traditional science fiction protagonist relies on the heterotopic society of Triton. First, the changed social context illustrates the concept of an "ideohistory" (Delany, *Jewel-Hinged* 273). Bron's anachronistic sexism, for example, shows how the concepts of gender and sexuality have changed over time. These changes explain why Bron is now the unhappy minority in Triton society. When Ashima Slade notes that "there is no class, race, nationality, or sex that it does not help to be only half" (*Trouble* 302), Fox declares that this "precept [. . .] reinforces the attack on an ideology of absolute categories and 'pure' identities, positing instead the need for (minimally, at least) an acceptance of dualism, of fusions rather then separations" ("Politics" 51). Therefore, Bron's repetition of the same contrasts with the multiplicity embodied in Triton's society, a multiplicity affecting sexuality, gender, race, politics, and religion. John Fekete explicitly contrasts *Trouble on Triton: An Ambiguous Heterotopia* with Ursula Le Guin's *The Dispossessed: An Ambiguous Utopia* (1975) because of this multiplicity.[99] According to Fekete, "Le Guin's interest is in the *emergence* of the liberatory *novum*, of individual initiative [. . .]; she works [. . .] toward the classical utopian aspirations of Western philosophy: *reconciliation* in the potential harmony of all. Delany, by contrast, presents the dominance of *dispersion*" (131). As we have seen, this "*dispersion*" applies to the construction of individual subjectivity, but this reflects a larger social "*dispersion*" in Delany's text as well. Triton's society simply does not have a 'center.' The extraordinary range of acceptable sexual practice on Triton illustrates this heterotopic quality. The Spike summarizes this aspect for the reader early on: "I mean, when you have forty or fifty sexes, and twice as many religions, however you arrange them, you're bound to have a place its fairly easy to have a giggle at" (*Trouble* 99). Since Triton society rests on the inviolability of the subjective, every aspect of society is tremendously expanded to meet the subjective demands of its citizens (277).

The subjective and social "*dispersion*" of *Trouble on Triton* is reflected in the major characters. First, Delany allows the other characters, representing the Other, to speak for themselves to a much greater extent than either Heinlein or Kelley. The discrepancy between their words and actions and those of Bron aides in undermining his subjective point of view. As readers continue through the text, they perceive that Bron's point of view is unreliable and that his subjectivity embodies the Other of Triton society. Within this context, the other characters serve as examples of subjective alternatives. Bron's 'friends,' those people who get close to him and who also serve as the other major characters in the text, each represent an alternative to one of Bron's subjective positions. Lawrence, for example, offers a site for exploring Bron's heterosexuality and the position of homosexuality in Triton society. Lawrence's overt and socially-accepted homosexuality contrasts with the suppression of homosexuality in Heinlein's texts (Delany, *Trouble* 287), and the underlying heterosexism of *The Dispossessed*. In "To Read *The Dispossessed*," Delany faults Le Guin for her "fictive thinness" in portraying Bedap, a homosexual man (*Jewel-Hinged* 297). For example, Le Guin resorts to "cliché" and "mystifie[s]" Bedap's homosexuality and its relationship to offspring and familial groups on the world of Annares (292-4). Delany creates the various co-ops and communes of Triton society to revise Le Guin's exclusion of homosexuals from familial groups. Furthermore, within the "systems-off" system of reproduction on Triton, Bron's great concern about the survival of the species is unusual (*Shorter* 340). Finally, Delany places sexuality within the same constructionist grid as biological sex and race. Any person on Triton can undergo a simple psychological procedure to change their sexual "fixation," from "an ordinary, bisexual, female-oriented male," for instance, to any of the other many options (*Trouble* 227–9). Both Bron and the Spike undergo such a procedure during their lifetimes.

Bron's other friend, Sam, and Bron's love interest, the Spike, bring the issues of race and gender to the fore. Sam, a black man, primarily serves as a vehicle for investigating race on Triton, but later in the text, the issue of gender surfaces in an unexpected way. A white woman, the Spike is the primarily site for exploring gender issues. In the second note of "Appendix A: From the *Triton* Journal: Work Notes and Omitted Pages," Delany writes, "Everything in a science fiction novel should be mentioned at least twice (in at least two different contexts)" (*Trouble* 282). Race and gender act as two such contexts, along with the previously-mentioned sexuality. Delany refuses to simplify his 'heterotopic' interests, either in the multiple subjective positions available to people or in the enabling social context. In this 'love story' gone awry, race serves as a prologue to the more extensive discussion of gender in the text. For example, Bron's relationship with Sam sets up his later 'failure' with the Spike. Because Sam, the Spike, and Lawrence all embody the ideological positions Bron rejects, he treats them in the same self-centered, callused manner. Conversely, they successfully function within the heterotopic, egalitarian social environment of Triton. Their relationships with Bron, despite his shortcomings, exemplify an openness to difference he lacks. In this regard and in his combination of race and gender, Sam offers a convenient single site for discussing Bron's subjective limitations. Sam also illustrates the maintenance of racial identity within the poststructuralist, postmodern world of Triton. Delany's portrayal of an individualist, constructed, provisional concept of race answers the challenge of African-American literary criticism. However, like the science fiction readers of *Trouble on Triton*, the critics might be shocked, offended, and/or challenged by his 'answer.' In fact, Delany consciously intends for his portrayal of race to be "disturbing," as his quote from Michel Foucault's *The Order of Things* emphasizes: "*Heterotopias* are disturbing, probably because they make it impossible to name this or that, because they shatter or tangle common names, because they destroy 'syntax' in advance, and not only the syntax with which we construct sentences but also that less apparent syntax which causes words and things (next to and also opposite one other) to 'hold together'" (*Trouble* 292). In *Trouble on Triton*, race cannot be easily "named" because it does not "hold together" in the essentialist, collective manner desired by many African-American literary critics.

Delany first illustrates the limits of Bron's point of view in his portrayal of Sam, a black man in his "all-male" sexually 'unspecified' co-op (*Trouble* 27). In his unhappiness and insecurity, Bron obsessively compares himself to others, always aware of and manipulating power relations and jealous of any-one who appears more 'successful,' better adjusted, etc. Therefore, Bron per-sists in applying stereotypes and limiting Sam's subjectivity through singular, narrow classifications. At first, Sam is "handsome, expansive, friendly with everyone (including Bron), even though his work kept him away eleven days out of every two weeks. All that bluster and backslapping? Just a standard, annoying type" (25). Bron even admits his "dislike" for Sam based on these positive personal characteristics (ibid). In addition, Sam's physical description and demeanor play into common, contemporary black stereotypes. First, he is happy, easy-going, and almost 'grinning': "Sam leered hugely, jovially, and blackly over the rail" at the men of the co-op (ibid). Sam's physical body is the focus of attention as well: "[h]e had a large, magnificent body which he always wore (rather pretentiously, Bron thought) naked" (ibid). The reader also sees "a broad, black hand" and "black fists on narrow, black hips" within the three short paragraphs of Sam's entrance and introduction (ibid). Buying into this stereotypical portrayal of the 'happy Negro' and his physical attri-butes, the reader might join Bron in his later "revelation" that "Sam was *not* so average. Under all that joviality, there was a rather amazing mind" (26). Similarly, when Bron concludes that Sam "was as oppressed by the system as anyone else," his friend Lawrence tells him that "'oppressed by the system' was just *not* Sam at all: Sam was *the* head of the Political Liason Department between the Outer Satellite Diplomatic Corps and Outer Satellite Intelli-gence; and had all the privileges [. . .] of both" (ibid). Sam's subjective complexity simply will not fit Bron's narrow stereotypes then. In addition, Sam's personal, social, and economic success conflicts with Bron's negative readings.

When Bron is forced beyond a one-dimensional portrayal of Sam, he changes tactics and utilizes his standard defense mechanism of projection. Placing Sam in his own position, Bron surmises, "[t]he fact that Sam chose to live in an all-male nonspecific [co-op] probably meant that, underneath the friendliness, the intelligence, the power, he was probably rotten with neurosis; behind him would be a string of shattered communal attempts and failed sexualizationships" (*Trouble* 27). Bron's final 'illusion' of Sam's hidden "neurosis" is shattered by the knowledge that he is part of a family commune also (ibid). Left with no areas of weakness to exploit, Bron again turns to projection. He confronts Sam, asking "what are you hanging out with a bunch of deadbeats, neurotics, mental retards, and nonaffectives like us for [. . .]? Does it make you feel superior? Do we remind you how *wonderful* you are?" (ibid). Bron's narcissism is so strong, he cannot conceive of personal motivations or psychological mechanisms beyond his own. Delany describes Bron's "protective reaction"[100] as follows: "what Bron usually does to justify his behaving in the selfish and hateful ways that make him such a hateful man is manufacture perfectly fanciful motivations for what everyone else is doing—motivations which if they *were* the case, would make his actions acceptable" (*Shorter* 335). Of course, Sam again contradicts Bron's projections, explaining that he comes to their co-op as a personal refuge, to escape politics for a while (*Trouble* 27). Bron is finally at an utter loss. However, rather than incorporate this new information about Sam into a larger understanding of and respect for the differences of others, Bron decides to avoid the whole issue by simply returning Sam's friendliness (28). Bron has lost this particular battle, then, but not the larger subjective war, for he has avoided moving beyond the limits of his enclosed and defensive subjectivity. As Bron progresses through the text, his avoidance, projection, and self-delusions must become more extreme in order to protect this monolithic, static subjectivity.[101]

In this implicit comparison between Sam and Bron, Delany places the white male under intense psychological scrutiny. This is an effective reversal of Schuyler's and Fanon's analyses of the black man and his troubled psychology. In Delany's text, it is a white man who feels alienated from society, who has neuroses, who cannot build healthy sexual/romantic relationships and who, ultimately, turns to physical modification in an attempt to remedy his situation. In contrast, the black man occupies the center—the social, political, and economic position of privilege and power.

Sam seems to be genuinely happy and fulfilled as well. Thus, Delany makes the black man (and the woman and the homosexual) the dynamic character and not the traditional science fiction hero/protagonist. Unlike Bron's stasis, Sam has successfully adapted to the changed physical and social environment of the moons. Sam, then, continues to serve as a gauge, a testing ground for Bron, and the reader, throughout the text. However, Delany also utilizes Sam to undermine essentialist concepts of race and to promote an individualist approach to subjectivity.

When Bron joins Sam on a political mission to Earth, he learns that Sam has undergone extensive physical modifications. Sam once was "a rather unhappy, sallow-faced, blonde, blue-eyed (and terribly myopic) waitress" (*Trouble* 126). In addition to the physical attributes of Bron's biological sex change, then, Sam gained the physical characteristics associated with the black race: darker skin, hair color, and eye color, as well as increased musculature and possibly height. Sam reveals that her physical model was "the six-foot plus Wallunda and Katanga emigrants who had absolutely infested the neighborhood" at Lux on Iapetus (ibid). Just as Bron has modified his expectations, assumptions, and stereotypes about Sam, as a black man, the rug is pulled out from under his feet again by these revelations. Bron is shocked out of his complacency, as is the reader. In Schuyler's *Black No More* the reader is always privy to the 'origins' of the characters, and we can laugh along with Disher and Schuyler at the joke played upon the ignorant (racist) whites who do not know Disher was once a Negro. In Delany's text, the reader more immediately and, perhaps, uncomfortably, faces a thorough deconstruction of racial beliefs. Delany's scene is a test, an evaluation of the extent to which humans continue to base identity on gender and race. Bron's response to Sam's revelation, our own response as readers, and the motivation behind Sam's modification all serve as 'evidence.'

Sam's physical sex and race changes invert several specific social and literary norms. First, we see another unhappy white person who turns to physical modification for help. Similar to Bron in this respect, Sam differs in the racial modification and the subsequent success of her changes. Therefore, in the context of race, Sam is more similar to Schuyler's character Max Disher. The inversion in this case is the race which is linked to personal happiness and a successful career. Sam's decision to change into the likeness of a black man brings sexual and romantic satisfaction, social acceptance, economic affluence, and political power and prestige. In this way, Delany builds on the general inversion of racial norms at the end of *Black No More*, when whites tan to make themselves look fashionably darker, and he clearly avoids an assimilationist label for his character.[102] Sam's motivation for her sex and race changes also modifies Schuyler's portrayal of inter-racial couples. Both Max Disher and Sam are attracted to white women, and their racial modifications spring from a desire to fit the romantic/sexual ideal of these women. As Sam relays, she had "a penchant for other sallow, blonde, blue-eyed waitresses, who, as far as the young and immature me could make out then, were just gaga over the six-foot-plus Wallunda and Katanga emigrants" (*Trouble* 126). Delany plays on the social taboo of sexual and romantic relationships between white women and black men, as does Schuyler. However, Delany reverses the site of the attraction, the agency in the coupling, from the black men to the white women. It is the white waitresses in Delany's example who desire the black emigrants. Furthermore, Sam's subsequent success with white women seems to affirm her earlier belief about their desire for black men. Bron meets a "blonde, blue-eyed woman [. . . who] was part of Sam's family commune," for example, and Bron herself makes a play for Sam at the end of the novel (128).

Sam's racial modification illustrates her openness to difference and change as well. Both Sam and Bron undergo a physical sex change, but Bron's change springs from a desperate need to maintain the same, to create an appropriate Eve for her anachronistic Adam. Sam's change stems from desire, and she will incorporate any difference in order to more easily fulfill that desire. In his autobiographical writings and in his fictional texts, Delany privileges desire. First, it stands on its own as a defining element of subjectivity:

> I am the sweeping tapestry of my sensory and bodily perceptions. I am their linguistic reduction and abstraction, delayed and deferred till they form a wholly different order, called my thought. I am, at the behest and prompting of all these, my memory—which forms still another order. I am the emotions that hold them together. Webbing the four, and finally, I am the flux and filigree of desire around them all. (*Longer* 150)

The strong and pervasive influence of desire also fosters contact with Others. Sam, for example, successfully manipulates the desire of the white women for a racial, national, and sexual Other. As Robert Elliot Fox asserts in the context of Delany's pornographic novel, *The Tides of Lust*, "[t]he sexual plane becomes the level on which opposites literally come together" ("Politics" 53).[103] In his autobiographical writings, Delany also describes large groups of men, from different racial and economic backgrounds, gathering to fulfill homosexual desire. In *The Motion of Light in Water*, for instance, Delany describes his multiple sexual experiences in a group of trailers; a particularly detailed narrative includes two men, one white and one black (130–1). Even in the meeting places that predominantly drew men from a particular racial or national group, a variety of racial and economic characteristics are described: "a young man, white, with dark hair, of about twenty-five, who usually wore a suitjacket—in a population largely black and Hispanic and usually in jeans and sport shirts" (*Longer* 120). Delany's more long-term relationship with Bob Folsom also fits this pattern of desire-motivated connection with economic, racial, and/or geographic Others.[104] Finally, Delany fictionally combines this more short-term sexual and long-term 'romantic' desire in the couple of Marq Dyeth and Rat Korga in his 1984 novel *Stars in My Pocket Like Grains of Sand*. Carl Freedman specifically discusses their relationship in the context of "how desire functions as cognition in the comprehension (in some sense) of difference" (161). In these varying social contexts, both fictional and non-fiction, desire promotes communication, integration, and more egalitarian relationships.

The success of Sam's modification also stems from the compatibility of her change with the larger social norms. Unlike Bron, Sam's change dramatically increases her chances of finding a satisfactory partner. These subjective and social differences converge in the idea of a heterotopia. Both Bron's and Sam's incorporation of the (sexual and/or racial) Other in their physical bodies symbolizes the already existing multiplicity of their subjective positions, a multiplicity based on a fragmentation into multiple categories—like race, sex, and gender—and also the "*range* of possibilities" within each of these larger, ideological categories (*Trouble* 50). Delany's multiple subjective positions in his autobiography, for example, reflect some of these larger categories. The full "*range* of possibilities" within each category can be seen in the further breakdown in Triton society into "forty or fifty different sexes, falling loosely into nine categories" (*Trouble* 99). Delany vividly conveys this categorical multiplicity and complexity through a visual evaluation of Bron's sexuality: "'You could be a male who is partway through one of a number of possible sex-change processes. Or you could be a female who is much further along in a number of *other* sex change operations [. . . ;] you might have begun as a woman, been changed to male, and now want to be changed to— something else [. . . ;] Or [. . .] you could be a woman in very good drag'" (*Trouble* 219). Bron, of course, rejects such multiplicity and ambiguity of sexuality and gender.

The same type of visual ambiguity applies to color, a primary characteristic of race. As a preface to the more detailed and direct account of a multiple sexuality (above), Bron discusses the 'whiteness' of the Taj Mahal with a character specifically identified as of African descent: "'The significance of "white," like the significance of any other word, is a *range* of possibilities. Like the color itself, the significance fades quite imperceptibly on one side through gray toward black, and on another through pink toward red, and so on, all the way around, toward every other color; and even toward some things that aren't colors at all'" (*Trouble* 50). White, like black or any other color, cannot be discretely named and contained. The same principle applies to a name or category like "'white'" or "black," denoting a human race. Of course, the irony of Bron's elaborate and knowledgeable, theoretical lecture lies in his racism in personal practice. While he possesses a 'logical' understanding of the heterotopic nature of subjectivity, his narcissism and need for status prevent any direct and practical application of this knowledge to his own subjectivity. Thus, even his sex and psychological changes are an ineffectual 'rebellion' because Bron cannot admit the multiplicity, dispersion, and ambiguity of his own subjectivity—before and after the changes. As a result, Bron breaks down into "*real* psychosis" at the end of the novel, alone and locked within her room (*Shorter* 338).

Within the heterotopic society of Triton, individuals can literally construct their subjectivity through physical and psychological modifications. This "mutability and freeplay" is based in the founding principle of Triton society—subjective inviolability (Freedman 159). This great political = personal freedom combines with the technological advances of Triton to afford the type of individuality Delany promotes in the Beckerman interview. In contrast to identitarianism, Delany believes "[d]ifference is what makes us individual" (Beckerman).[105] Sam is an excellent example of a heterotopic, mutable individuality and an embodiment of Tritonian subjective inviolability. Sam first illustrates her refusal to be limited to a single, essential identity through her physical changes. In changing both her sex and race, Sam mirrors an earlier exchange between Bron and the Spike. When Bron comes to pick up the Spike clothed completely in black attire and a black mask, she responds by enveloping herself from head to toe in a white costume. The Spike tells Bron, "Now [. . .] we can roam the labyrinths of honesty and deceit, searching out the illusive centers of our being by a detailed examination of the shift and glitter of our own, protean surfaces"; "Now, proofed in light and light's absence, we can begin our wonderings" (*Trouble* 98). Readers enter into a similar process of investigation, and they might question the concepts of "honesty and deceit," as Bron does, when discovering Sam's former identity. The readers too must "search out the illusive center of [Sam's] being" because "of the shift and glitter of [her] protean surface." When race and sex become like costumes, taken on and off at will, any form of essentialist identity is impossible. A costume is an apt analogy for Sam's physical changes because of their mutual grounding in a playful, individual concept of race as well. Delany joins Schuyler in emphasizing an individual rather than collective racial identity. In *Trouble on Triton*, race can take the form of personal expression.[106]

This racial individuality highlights the cultural basis of race. First, Sam's personal changes rely on larger cultural conceptions of race; she modifies her color and musculature in order to fit a particular racial image. Therefore, in keeping with the costume analogy, Sam performs the part of a black man, physically and psychologically. These complex intersections of culture, biology, and race bring up the issue of racial authenticity. While Sam 'imitates' the African immigrants physically, and perhaps psychologically as well, she biologically modifies her body and her imitation is a success. Therefore, Sam lives the daily reality of a black man. When Lawrence notes the common oppression of women, in opposition to men, he raises the possibility of authenticity being based in a shared cultural experience(s) (*Trouble* 212). Thus, even though Sam has not always been black, his subsequent cultural experiences as a black man could accurately place him within that racial category. Bron's racial othering suggests that racial prejudice still exists, although rare in the Outer Satellites. Delany qualifies an either/or racial categorization, however. While Sam becomes a black man, he cannot erase his past as a white woman. After her sex change, for example, Bron protests that she does not feel "*all* the time, every minute, a complete and whole woman" (249–50). Her counselor responds,

> "*being* a woman is also a complicated genetic interface. It means having that body of yours from birth, and growing up in the world, learning to do whatever you do—psychological counseling in my case, or metalogics in yours—with and within that body. That body has to be yours, and yours all your life. In that sense, you never will be a 'complete' woman. We can do a lot here; we can make you a woman from a given time on. We cannot make you have been a woman for all the time you were a man." (251)

Bron's dissatisfaction with her sex change stems from her obsession with singularity and wholeness. She still resists a multiple subjectivity, even if it is experientially based. In Sam's case, he is 'authentically' a black man, "from a given time on" only. However, in her acceptance of difference, her motivation of desire, and the relative lack of racial prejudice on Triton, Sam does not feel Bron's need for a single sexual or racial categorization. This "free play," in opposition to rigid, static dichotomies, is what makes Sam an attractive subjective alternative to Bron and Triton a potentially attractive social alternative to Earth (Freedman 159).

In the reality of fluctuation, Delany highlights the contextual basis of sexual or racial identity, similar to his personal definition of gay identity. This changing context has serious implications for cultural theories of race. First, it raises the possibility of a diminishment of racial prejudice and oppression over time, as on Triton. Prejudice based on the human races, as we know them today, might disappear entirely or be subverted to another group. With a common oppression, or any other cultural factor(s), as the basis for racial identity, such changes would threaten its very existence. Also, racial identity based in common oppression maintains the 'racial problem' argument and does not afford an affirmative utilization of race. Octavia Butler, for instance, objected to the overwhelmingly negative response to a proposed "anthology of science fiction by and about black people": "Most of the stories that we got [. . .] were about racism, as though that was the sum total of our lives. Especially, and I hate to say it, all the stories we got from white people were about racism because that was all they apparently thought that we dealt with" ("Black" 18). Finally, both a diminishment of oppression and a positive valuation of race highlight the variability of personal experience. Basing racial identity on common oppression, then, relies on a false totalization, a reduction of multiple, varying racial experiences into a single, normative racial identity. Within this context, all blacks who seek racial authenticity must enact the cultural characteristics related to race in their society. They must also suppress individual differences or cultural anomalies.[107]

Delany explores the viability of a purely cultural theory of race through Sam, but also offers a more traditional example of black identity through a woman of African descent named Miriamne. First, through Sam, Delany answers a challenge later articulated by Walter Benn Michaels in *Our America: Nativism, Modernism, and Pluralism* (1995):

> If race really were culture, people could change their racial identity, siblings could belong to different races, people who were as genetically unlike each other as it's possible for two humans to be could nonetheless belong to the same race. None of these things is possible in the United States today. And, were they possible, we would think not that we had finally succeeded in developing an anti-essentialist account of race but that we had given up the idea of race altogether. (133–4)

Obviously Sam does change her racial identity, and the concept of race is maintained. Furthermore, Sam's openness to racial and sexual changes reflects a larger multiplicity of identity. When Lawrence contradicts Bron's erroneous, simplistic judgments of Sam, we learn of Sam's multiple interests, relationships, and categories. Not content with a single commune, for example, Sam has multiple, diverse living arrangements. Most importantly, Sam's active, voluntary participation in the subjective and social heterotopia Delany creates results in a very different personal outcome than Bron. In contrast to Bron's social isolation and subjective failure, Sam ends the text in the midst of a busy nightclub, happily trying to "get laid" (*Trouble* 262).

While Sam represents the great and positive potential of subjective inviolability on Triton, Delany also includes a character representing a more traditional racial identity. Bron meets a woman named Miriamne who not only fits the physical description for black identity ("dark and frizzy-haired"), but also offers a contrast to the other characters in her open acknowledgement of her personal background (*Trouble* 45). When Bron asks her how she takes her coffee, for example, Miriamne responds, "Black [. . .] as my old lady [. . .—] That's what my father always used to say. [. . .] My mother was from Earth—Kenya, actually; and I've been trying to live it down ever since" (48). Miriamne's comment about "living it down" might refer to racial prejudice. Within Triton social norms, however, it more likely refers to the social taboo of mentioning personal background, especially ties to the more conservative societies on the planets. Tritonian subjective inviolability means people can construct an identity, a life any way they desire, without direct reference to prior experiences. Bron's mental response to Miriamne's comments supports this more general reading. Certainly capable of racist stereotypes and vocabulary, Bron simply thinks, "Typical u-l [unlicensed zone or person living in this area] . . . always talking about where they come from, where their families started" (ibid). Furthermore, Delany uses their dialogue to first introduce this social norm: Bron "never" talks about his own parents "in concession to a code of politeness almost universal outside the u-l that, once he had realized it existed, he'd found immensely reassuring" (49). The subjective inviolability of Triton, then, provides a space for Sam's successful changes, but it also suppresses personal history and descent. Only persons living in the zone explicitly outside of Triton laws, and social norms more generally, comfortably speak of their personal background. Thus, this social and subjective freedom is a double-edged sword. Like the terrestrial New World, Triton offers equality and unprecedented opportunities to 'make oneself,' but only if you are willing to give up the past and your previous identity and/or status within it. Bron is a negative example of someone unwilling to do this; Miriamne is a more positive example. While she is apparently less well-off financially than Bron, Miriamne is clearly the sympathetic victim of Bron's sexual jealousy and not the target of Delany's authorial criticism. Furthermore, Miriamne may live in the u-l, but she has the freedom to maintain connections to her past, including racial affiliations. In this way, Delany illustrates the possibility of primarily cultural and descent-based theories of race existing simultaneously, and without apparent conflict, in a given social context. Finally, Miriamne's emphasis on descent parallels Sam's physical alterations. Delany does not completely divorce race from the body.

Walter Benn Michaels' racial analysis also reveals the limitations or impartial nature of Delany's cultural concept of race. While mutable, race remains tied to the physical body. Like Schuyler, Delany uses modern technology to 'construct' racial identity through physical elements. Advances in scientific understanding of the body allow Delany to expand on Schuyler's 'cosmetic' changes as well. Delany also explores the complex connections between the physical body and subjectivity. In contrast to both the earlier writing of Schuyler and the later writing of Octavia Butler, Delany explores how subjective elements lead to physical changes and, conversely, how physical changes impact a person's subjectivity. Schuyler and Butler explore diverse racial bodies, but leave a static, essentialist subjectivity intact.[108]

In *Triton's* society, changes are both physical and psychological. Delany begins by explicitly acknowledging the importance of culture in a quote from Mary Douglas prefacing *Trouble on Triton*: "the social body constrains the way the physical body is perceived"—by others and by the individual. The social/cultural half of the racial debate has been largely covered already. In *Longer Views*, Delany stresses a more balanced role for the physical body:

> I am the sweeping tapestry of my sensory and bodily perceptions. I am their linguistic reduction and abstraction, delayed and deferred till they form a wholly different order, called my thought. I am, at the behest and prompting of all these, my memory—which forms still another order. I am the emotions that hold them together. Webbing the four, and finally, I am the flux and filigree of desire around them all. [. . .] Am I the sexual surge and ebb that cannot quite be covered by any of the above, but that impinge on all the others and often drown them? What of the bodily apparati in general, as they fall, pleasingly or painfully, into the net of myself? I am always an animal excess to the intellectual system that tries to construct me. I am always a conscious sensibility in excess of the animal construction that is I.

> And that is why I am another, why my identity is always other than
> I. (150)

First, "[S]ensory and bodily perceptions" begin and ground Delany's subjectivity. In addition, "desire" and this "sexual surge and ebb" seem to be
partially based in "the bodily apparati." More generally, this "animal excess"
suggests a power and autonomy beyond containment by the mind. Thus,
although we only get a very brief synopsis of the changes Sam undergoes
as a result of the physical modification, the drastic improvement in his
general situation suggests they are quite radical, with psychological, emotional, social, as well as physical effects. Similarly, after Bron's sexual modification, she changes not only in physical circumstances (literally having
corporeal changes, having to change abodes, etc.), but also psychologically.
Delany illustrates the intimate connection between a person's body and
psyche through the racial and sexual changes of Sam and Bron. In doing
so, he enters into a debate between "essentialists and constructionists" over
the importance of the body to subjectivity (Fuss 53). Fuss, for example,
discusses Adrienne Rich's "distinction [. . .] between *the* body and *my*
body [. . .] as a useful place to begin the project of reintroducing biology, the body *as matter*, back into poststructuralist materialist discourse"
(Fuss 52). Fuss joins Delany in asserting a balance between the body and
culture: we "cannot ignore the role social practices play in organizing and
imaging 'the body,' but nor can [we] overlook the role 'my body' plays in
the constitution of subjectivity" (Fuss 52).

Fox places this body/mind debate with the larger context of global
culture and the dichotomies of western civilization. Acknowledging Delany's quotation of Douglas, Fox situates Douglas' analysis specifically within
"the West" and contrasts it to "traditional societies" in which "the physical
self gives articulate expression to the social" ("Politics" 51). Katherine Fishburn similarly links such "embodiment" to African-Americans and their
narratives (xii). First, Fishburn believes that,

> the indisputable fact of their embodiment in a culture that valued the
> mind at the expense of the debased body faced these early writers with
> two interrelated narrative dilemmas. One was how to demonstrate their
> own capacity to reason without minimizing the physical horrors of
> enslavement, the accounts of which were necessary to the abolitionist
> cause. The other, which is the obverse of the first, was how to dem-
> onstrate the fact that, however imbued with reason they already were,
> African Americans still needed a fundamental change in their material

circumstances if they were ever to achieve their full human potential. (ibid)

In addition, trying "to elude the dualistic thinking that separates mind from body, by valorizing mind over body," Fishburn realized the "*importance* of the body to slaves and ex-slaves" (ibid). The African-Americans, in effect, "were not trying to write themselves into Western metaphysics as equal to whites, but were instead, more radically and daringly, rethinking metaphysics itself" (ibid). This is the mind/body, West/traditional society, white/Other dichotomy to which Fox refers and which Delany questions in his texts. As a result, Delany's complex balance between the body and subjectivity takes part in a larger African-American challenge to the western hierarchy of the mind over and in opposition to the body.[109] While Fishburn specifically refers to early African-American writers, a similar focus on the body inspires the racial essentialism of later critics of African-American literature.

BEYOND DELANY

Within science fiction, Schuyler and Butler join Delany in utilizing the body as a site of racial exploration. However, their psychic essentialism obscures the effect(s) of the body on subjectivity. In Schuyler's *Black No More*, for example, little seems to change about Disher's personality when he becomes a white man. Schuyler focuses on how the world perceives Disher and how his exterior circumstances change. Likewise, in Butler's Patternmaster series,[110] Doro 'body hops' for centuries. Originally an African male, Doro inexplicably and frequently transfers his mind/spirit from one body to another. The 'hosts' die a spiritual death, and Doro 'occupies' the male, female, young, old, African, African-American, European, and/or Anglo-American bodies. However, each body Doro possesses seems to be little more than a temporary host (perhaps because he does not occupy any for very long), and his personality surprisingly does not change. Unlike Sam's undetected (i.e. successful) racial transformation, Doro is consistently portrayed as a black man. He usually occupies black male bodies when he is physically present in the narrative, for example. While Butler frequently mentions his other female and/or Anglo bodies, these bodies are generally occupied 'off stage' or quickly discarded. Furthermore, Doro identifies himself as a black man, despite having transferred from his original body when only a teenager. Both of these factors result in the other characters perceiving him as a black man as well. They are shocked, surprised, or unsettled when he occupies a white body. For example, Doro's daughter Mary is relieved when he visits her in a black male body because when he came in a white body, "All [she] saw was this big stranger sitting on the side of [her] bed" (Butler, *Mind* 20). Likewise, Doro seduces Anyanwu, the protagonist of *Wild Seed*, by choosing a black male body he knows will please her (225–6; 233). The texts as a whole support the characters' perceptions as well. Unlike Delany's careful and accurate use of the correct pronoun, Butler always uses a masculine pronoun in reference to Doro.[111] In these ways, Butler creates a much greater disconnection between the body and the mind/soul/emotions than either Schuyler or particularly Delany. In fact, the larger plot of the Patternmaster series, with its telepathic theme, emphasizes the mind and its independence from the body.

Doro's example is supported by the other main character of *Wild Seed*, Anyanwu. Born an African woman, Anyanwu can modify her existing physical body to become every type of person that Doro can, plus take animal form. Yet, her psyche also remains remarkably stable considering these radical physical changes. As she explains to Doro, "you have not understood how completely that one body can change. I cannot leave it as you can, but I can make it over. I can make it over so completely in the image of someone else that I am no longer truly related to my parents. It makes me wonder what I am—that I can do this and still know myself, still return to my true shape" (Butler, *Wild* 194). She tells Doro that the body of a young, dark-skinned African woman is "the shape [which] flows back to [her] most easily. Others are harder to take" (13). Unlike the genetic changes of Sam or Bron, then, Anyanwu retains an original, more authentic "true shape."

When comparing Butler's Patternmaster series to Delany's *Trouble on Triton*, Butler's treatment of the body initially seems the most destructive to any concept of race. The corporeal flux is overwhelming, almost a 'small world' of bodies, and Doro and Anyanwu travel throughout the globe and live for centuries so there remains no historical or cultural similarity on which to base race either. Yet, both characters are consistently portrayed as a black man and a black woman psychically, and this psychic configuration influences their choices of physical form. There seems to be a form of psychic essentialism at work here, with racial and sexual connotations. The lack of logical explanation or scientific grounding for the changes of the two characters only reinforces this essentialism. Doro does not undergo a physical operation to 'construct' a race; he simply is. In this context, no matter how often a body is modified or completely replaced, or in which culture a person lives, he/she will always maintain the same racialized and sexualized identity. In contrast, Delany has a much more complicated, extensive (and realistic, in my opinion) view of the implications of even constructed notions of race. He explores how physically changing a 'race' (i.e., taking on the exterior features associated with a particular 'race') would impact the "intellectual system" of an individual in ways Schuyler and Butler neglect (Delany, *Longer* 150).

Contemporary science fiction writer Marge Piercy takes Butler's dissociation of race and the human body one step further. One of science fiction's most radical reinterpretations of race consciousness involves the postulation of societies in which the culturally-constructed aspects of race(s) are explicitly assumed by groups other than those historically attached to them. Piercy's *Woman on the Edge of Time* (1976), for example, describes a society which takes up the challenge Walter Benn Michaels offers at the end of *Our America: Nativism, Modernism, and Pluralism*, namely that "[i]f race really were culture, people could change their racial identity, siblings could belong to different races, people who were as genetically unlike each other as it's possible for two humans to be could nonetheless belong to the same race" (133–4). In Piercy's text, a Mexican-American woman, Connie or Consuelo, mind travels to the future and visits a society in which,

> "Decisions were made forty years back to breed a high proportion of darker-skinned people and to mix the genes well through the population. At the same time, we decided to hold on to separate cultural identities. But we broke the bond between genes and culture, broke it forever. We want there to be no chance of racism again. But we don't want the melting pot where everybody ends up with thin gruel. We want diversity, for strangeness breeds richness." (*Woman* 103–4)

In the village Connie visits most often, a black man tells her that the "'Wamponaug Indians are the source of our flavor of culture. Our past. Every village has a culture'" (96). When Connie implies that his association with this culture must be the result of poor self-esteem and a racial inferiority complex, he tells her of another nearby village: "'I have a sweet friend living in Cranberry dark as I am and her tribe is Harlem-Black. I could move there anytime. But if you go over, you won't find everybody black-skinned like her and me, any more than they're all tall or all got big feet'" (ibid). Furthermore, while generally people remain most attached to the "culture" in which they were raised, "[w]hen you grow up [. . . ,] you can fuse into another" (104). Michaels asserts that in such a situation, "we would think not that we had finally succeeded in developing an anti-essentialist account of race but that we had given up the idea of race altogether" (134). Indeed, ethnicity might be a more appropriate term for the cultural connection Connie encounters. Piercy never actually uses the word 'race' in her text (only racism). However, when Connie speaks of "black Irishmen" and "black Chinese," it is clear that notions of race are being invoked (104).

Piercy's maintenance of racial connotations serves several functions. First, the reader, like Connie, is forced to confront the situatedness of our racial concepts. If we choose to foreground the "constitutive differences—cultural specificity, group history, political position"—of races, as Tucker does, we would likely reject Piercy's reconceptualization of race consciousness because it purposely and rather randomly scrambles the cultural signifier and the physical signified ("Can" 148).[112] In fact, Piercy is creating new kinship groups to replace the old. A revision of Werner Soller's terminology becomes helpful here as we depart from natural childbirth altogether; Piercy's futuristic society operates along familial lines of 'new descent.' While consent can be a factor, the society is characterized by a general focus on descent. In addition, Piercy's 'race consciousness' becomes not only an awareness of how race has historically operated, as in Schuyler and Fanon, but also advocacy of race's positive "power to shape human lives in a very real way" (Tucker, "Can" 148). Where the other authors deconstruct (biological) race in order to work towards a (politically, socially, ideologically, and culturally) 'raceless' society or, at most, a society with an individualist concept of race, Piercy revises race in a positive, collective context.

Margaret St. Clair does something very similar in *The Dancers of Noyo* (1973), where the culture of the Pomo Indians of California is taken up by Euro-American 'hippies' and their descendents. Through a 'performance' of the Pomo Indian culture, the Euro-Americans experience an 'authentic' spiritual vision which connects them with the original Indian inhabitants of the land (and symbolizes a validation of their tie to the culture). A 'new descent' is established here also. In this sense, Piercy's and St. Clair's texts foreground a purely cultural concept of race or ethnicity, but establish a new physical tie as well. The vocabulary of village, tribe, and family associated with historical and biological concepts of race is retained. In this way, Piercy and St. Clair parallel the 'carry-over' of Butler's psychic essentialism and Schuyler and Delany's continued utilization of the body. In their widely-varying racial revisions, Piercy, St. Clair, Butler, and Delany embody Schuyler's paradoxical position of focusing on race, but in such a way that the concept is radically redefined and revalued.

The proliferation of racial issues in contemporary science fiction, and the ease with which science fiction lends itself to such discussions, counters Houston A. Baker's uneasiness about a neglect (or discarding) of race in the context of science and technology and an emphasis on its construction. Certainly, 'Race' has not been 'erased' by the quotation marks placed around it in the field of science fiction. A new group of writers focusing on race in science fiction and fantasy includes Neal Stephenson, Steven Barnes, Nalo Hopkinson, and Mike Resnick.[113] Neal Stephenson's *Snow Crash* produced quite a splash in the science fiction community in 1992. His emphasis on technology and its intersection with ethnicity compares favorably with Marge Piercy's 1991 novel, *He, She, and It*. Stephenson and Piercy use cyberspace, cyborgs, and robots to investigate the complex construction of racial subjectivity in a postmodern era.[114] In their focus on technology and computerization, both authors develop issues generally eschewed by Butler and only briefly discussed by Delany.[115]

Philip E.Baruth's critical discussion of Stephenson's *Snowcrash*, published in *Into Darkness Peering: Race and Color in the Fantastic*, raises several questions important to this new area of extrapolation. Joining other critics from the anthology, Baruth emphasizes the utopian possibilities of the fantastic/science fiction, particularly in the context of computerization. He asserts that *Snowcrash* "experiments with the notion that racism itself may have a historical half-life, and that the process of its extinction may in fact be accelerated by out-of-body interaction and the shared computer protocols that make such interaction possible" (117). However, when Baruth calls the "novel's climactic match-up" between Hiro Protagonist and Raven, both "historical victims" of color, one of "dueling identity politics" (115) and admits that, within the novel, "skin color and nationality are all but beside the point" (116), he raises but does not discuss two important issues. First, if Stephenson has "moved aside the persistent question of race to expose the more pervasive question of the world's uneven distribution of wealth," how does this impact the intersections of subjectivity, politics, and race (117)? More specifically, how might a person of color form a personal and/or political identity without race as a viable concept? As Tucker maintains, "[a]ttacks on identity politics [. . .] are attacks on the conceptual tools that raced groups, women, and sexual minorities have used to recognize and organize themselves in order to critique, to speak back to a centered subjectivity that does not need an 'identity politics' because they have not had an identity imposed upon them" (*Sense* 24). Tucker also believes that "given the value of race pride as sustenance and a shield against continuing attacks on black humanity, [he] does not see African Americans opting out of identity because of its constructed or phantasmagorical nature any time real soon" (27). Within this context, the physical world of Hiro comes into shaper focus; even if Stephenson offers the Metaverse as a more socially progressive version of reality, with racism and its consequences lessened, Hiro still physically lives in a "'U-Stor-It'" and kills racist whites (114). A second issue raised by Baruth's criticism, then, is the connections between race, class, and technology. In blithely substituting class for race in terms of the "black-and-whites" and their access to technology, both Stephenson and Baruth elide these connections. We need to consider who has access to computers and advanced technology and in what contexts? Furthermore, this issue is not just about money, but cultural values as well. For example, Henry Louis Gates, Jr. claims that even with a consistent class, race can be a powerful influence on the level of interest in the computer and the motivation to utilize it ("One").[116]

Finally, Stephenson constructs a facile, Anglo-biased image of Western imperialism. Despite his physical hardships, Hiro tells Raven, "'I understand the depths of your feelings [. . . b]ut don't you think you've had enough revenge?'" (448). When Raven refuses to forgive the historical oppression of his people, Hiro ends up killing him to 'save the world.' Within this "duel" of "identity politics," then, Hiro's great magnanimity is the first issue; unlike Tucker's general assertions above, Hiro does choose to largely "opt[. . .] out of identity" (*Sense* 27). More importantly, however, he feels compelled to kill his alter-ego. Within the historical context of racism and oppression, making the assimilated, forgiving victim battle and kill the threatening, vengeful victim offers too easy a reconciliation of past wrongs for Anglos. The perpetrators of these wrongs do not need to acknowledge, ask forgiveness for, and/or make reparations for their actions. Basically, the victims 'battle' it out—one losing his life and the other becoming a murderer—and the perpetrators reap the benefit. For this reason and the issues mentioned above, I do not think Tucker would find Stephenson's portrayal of a cyber-based subjectivity an acceptable "alternative" to contemporary identity politics (*Sense* 27).[117] Stephenson's portrayal of imperialism and its legacy is facile and the intersection of ethnicity with technology is under-developed. Nonetheless, investigation of this new area of science fiction is sorely needed. As the promotions for *Snowcrash* attest, the novel is an "apotheosis of the information age," a "future America [. . .] you'll recognize [. . .] immediately." More broadly, the global, cyber focus of cyberpunk can work to lessen the importance of particular ethnic/racial/national groups, similar to science fiction generally. Yet, unlike science fiction generally, the global focus also necessitates at least a token acknowledgment of such groups. In this tension, cyberpunk continues the contradictory stance of most earlier texts dealing with race—visibly highlighting race while simultaneously undermining its contemporary usage.

In addition to Stephenson's cyberpunk, Steven Barnes and Nalo Hopkinson illustrate a second new trend in science fiction: the incorporation of magical realism and the marketing of ethnic fiction within the science fiction genre. Barnes began his series on Aubrey Knight in 1989 with *Gorgon Child* and continued with *Firedance* in 1994. He also wrote *Blood Brothers* in 1996.[118] While Barnes utilizes high technology/science in the Knight series (genetics in particular), he primarily focuses on magic and the supernatural in *Blood Brothers*. The text is similar to Octavia Butler's *Kindred* in the focus on slavery and the moral dilemmas involved in cooperating with slave owners, as well as the use of time travel. However, in his violently supernatural approach to the theme, Barnes comes closer to horror fiction than science fiction in the text. Labeled and marketed as science fiction regardless, *Blood Brothers* is a good candidate for the speculative fiction label. While rejected by some readers/critics, speculative fiction can be a useful term.[119] In its more inclusive boundaries, it would more accurately describe some multi-generic texts and larger oeuvres. In fact, author Charles Johnson calls Barnes' 2002 book, *Lion's Blood*, "speculative fiction" in the review excerpt at the beginning of the text.[120] A similar option is the 'fantastic' generic label. Within the library cataloging system, for example, *Blood* Brothers is labeled "fantastic fiction," rather than science fiction. Likewise, a prominent science fiction, fantasy, and horror organization is collectively titled the International Association for the Fantastic in the Arts. While better than an all-inclusive science fiction label for oeuvres like Barnes,' the 'fantastic' generic label (as well as magical realism) has a drawback which the speculative fiction label does not; it lies further away from mundane fiction on a generic spectrum.[121] Going beyond the paraliterary, a speculative fiction label could also help foster connections between fiction currently labeled mundane, like Toni Morrison's *Beloved*, and (supposedly) science fiction texts like Barnes' *Blood Brothers*. Like a multi-generic labeling for Schuyler, the point of making such connections is not to try and 'legitimate' science fiction, but to be as accurate as possible in categorization and also open more doors for readers, critics, and writers. Why might not a reader of Morrison's text also appreciate Butler's, Barnes,' or Hopkinson's, or vice versa?

Yet, a reader looking at the cover of Nalo Hopkinson's *Brown Girl in the Ring* would be hard-pressed to make such a connection because she fits a similar template to Barnes. Hopkinson has written many short stories, as well as two novels—*Brown Girl in the Ring* (1998) and *Midnight Robber* (2000).[122] She utilizes little science or technology, relying instead upon magic, rituals, and supernatural characters. However, the cover of *Brown Girl in the Ring* specifically identifies the text as science fiction in three ways: the label on the spine, the explanation about Hopkinson winning the Warner Aspect search for "science fiction's voices of the future," and the endorsement by Octavia Butler. In this case, the **positive** reputation of science fiction is being utilized to garner an established audience, more specifically, the audience built up by Butler over many years and many texts. This is the type of reader 'advertisement' between paraliterary and mundane fiction that would be useful to readers searching for new reading material and writers/publishers looking for the widest possible audience for a text. In particular, these types of marketing and categorical connections could help foster connections between the African American literary community and the science fiction community.

Mike Resnick also joins Barnes and Hopkinson in the 1990s. His portrayal of a futuristic African-inspired community sparked some controversy in 1998 because he challenges the validity of racial authenticity. The fact that Barnes, Hopkinson, and Resnick all significantly utilize Africa in their texts highlights the racial inversion that has taken place in the field; the racial focus which had to be suppressed in the past, now is a primary marketing feature of this developing branch of science fiction.[123] These newer authors can emphasize ethnicity and integrate African studies and science fiction to a much greater degree than either Delany or Butler at the time of their entrance in the field. Indeed, if Hopkinson is one of "science fiction's voices of future," than such fiction should continue to grow in size and prosperity. The fact that Hopkinson's second novel, *Midnight Robber*, was "a finalist for the Hugo and Nebula awards" supports such a prediction.[124]

The increasing number of science fiction authors utilizing race/ethnicity in their texts, in turn, will promote critical growth and an expanded readership. *Into Darkness Peering: Race and Color in the Fantastic* (1997) is a promising start, but as its editor, Elisabeth Anne Leonard, asserts, "I am aware that there are still many holes, many works to be discussed [. . .]. I have [. . .] seen this anthology as an opportunity to begin a discussion rather than an attempt to have the last word, and I hope that any readers who find this volume inadequate [. . .] take it upon themselves to continue the project and expand the examination of race" (11). This was my goal in the present text, and yet I also must acknowledge the incomplete nature of my endeavors. Unfortunately, I only had time to touch upon the last two trends in science fiction—computerization and magical realism. Similarly, I would wish the time and space to go beyond the boundaries of American science fiction. The Canopus series of Doris Lessing, in particular, would be a valuable addition to the present discussion of race and subjectivity in science fiction.[125] In addition, Jeffrey A. Tucker has recently published a full-length investigation of Samuel R. Delany and his connections to African-American Studies, *A Sense of Wonder: Samuel R. Delany, Race, Identity, and Difference* (2004).[126] I hope critical texts such as these will foster more interest in the area of race and science fiction—from other critics, science fiction writers, and readers. In this way, Samuel R. Delany's revision of the traditional science fiction triangle will continue to expand and enrich the science fiction genre. More broadly, in its speculative basis and future focus, science fiction can offer a site for reflection on current racial issues and imagining new subjective possibilities and more adequate race relations. In a job interview, I was once asked, if race is not an overt and prevalent issue in science fiction, why are you interested in it? Answers that first came to mind included a revisionist history for science fiction, personal preference, and criticism which fully addressed the texts of writers dealing with race in science fiction. However, the most important reason was this imaginative space opened up by science fiction and its possible influence on American society broadly. It is this belief that unites my work and the work of the science fiction authors discussed here. It is also what will fuel a continued investigation of race, by critics, writers, and readers of science fiction. Every time a reader of science fiction has an experience similar to Delany's first reading of Heinlein's *Starship Troopers*, the trend is strengthened. Indeed, the seed of the present text was my own reading of Burroughs' Mars series. The black pirates of Barsoom afforded an equivalent experience for me, and I hope for more such experiences, for myself and others, because they make science fiction worth reading.

Appendix

1926	Schuyler's "The Negro Art Hokum" and Langston Hughes' "The Negro Artist and the Racial Mountain" published.
1931	Schuyler's *Black No More: Being an Account of the Strange and Wonderful Workings of Science in the Land of the Free, A. D. 1933–1940* published.
1936-38	Schuyler's *The Black Internationale: Story of Black Genius Against the World* serialized under the pseudonym of Samuel I. Brooks in the *Pittsburgh Courier* from Nov. 21, 1936 to July 3, 1937. *Black Empire: An Imaginative Story of a Great New Civilization in Modern Africa* also serialized under Samuel I. Brooks in the *Pittsburgh Courier* from Oct. 2, 1937 to Apr. 16, 1938.
1940	W. E. B. Du Bois' *Dusk of Dawn* published.
1944	Schuyler's "The Caucasian Problem" published in *What the Negro Wants*.
1945	Franz Boas' *Race and Democratic Society* published.
1952	Frantz Fanon's *Black Skin, White Masks* published as *Peau Noire, Masques Blancs*.
1962	Delany's *The Jewels of Aptor* published.
1965	Robert Bone's *The Negro Novel in America* published.
1966	Schuyler's autobiography, *Black and Conservative*, published.
1971	Schuyler's *Black No More* republished with Introduction by Charles Larson. Octavia Butler publishes "Crossover."
1976	Michael Peplow's article on Schuyler published in *The Crisis*.
1977	Death of Schuyler.
1978	John M. Reilly's and Ann Rayson's articles on Schuyler published in *Black American Literature Forum*.
1991	Schuyler's *The Black Internationale* and *Black Empire* serials published together as a book, *Black Empire*.
1992	Henry Louis Gates, Jr.'s article on Schuyler published.
1997	Jeffrey A. Tucker's article on Schuyler published in *Race Consciousness: African-American Studies for the New Century. Into Darkness Peering: Race and Color in the Fantastic* published.
1999	Modern Library edition of Schuyler's *Black No More* published.
2000	*Dark Matter: A Century of Speculative Fiction from the African Diaspora* published.

Notes

NOTES TO CHAPTER ONE

1. E. James joins other prominent critics of American science fiction who link more mainstream writers with the genre. In *New Worlds for Old: The Apocalyptic Imagination, Science Fiction, and American Literature*, David Ketterer not only goes back to the 19th century for the roots of American sf (singling out Edgar Allan Poe as one such author), but also he pairs mainstream texts with sf texts to explore the connections between them.
2. See Taliaferro 16.
3. See Darko Suvin's *Metamorphoses of Science Fiction* and Delany's linguistic theory of science fiction (discussed in chapter 3) for two such alternate viewpoints on the genre.
4. The dual denotation of race as (1) multiple ethnic, biological, or kin groups within humankind and also as (2) collective humanity foregrounds the constructed nature of the term and also its utilization within Self/Other dichotomies.
5. See *The Works of Theodore Roosevelt* (1925) for examples from Roosevelt's own writings: Vol. 2: *The Wilderness Hunter: An Account of the Big Game of the United States and its Chase with Horse, Hound, and Rifle* (1893); Vol. 5: *African Game Trails: An Account of the African Wanderings of an American Hunter-Naturalist* (1909); and Vol. 6: *Through the Brazilian Wilderness and Papers on Natural History* (1902).
6. Toni Morrison's *Playing in the Dark* offers a brief introduction to this phenomenon within the context of African-Americans. Brian V. Street's *The Savage in Literature* is a more extensive examination of the same phenomenon in regard to Native Americans. Also, Hector St. Jean de Crèvecoeur offers insight into early colonial America and the competition and prejudice among white settlers—English, Scottish, German, etc. (45).
7. In addition to the New Immigration, Doyle rightly emphasizes the connection between the eugenics movement and African-Americans and women.

8. The distinction often made in contemporary discourse between race and ethnicity was not generally utilized in the first half of the twentieth century. What would be considered an ethnic or culturally similar group today, such as Italians or Jews, was conceived as a physically distinct group by most scientists and society more generally.

9. Ross' negative, biological utilization of the racialized Caliban figure will be revised by Houston A. Baker, Jr. in "Caliban's Triple Play." See 130-37 in the present text for more on the Caliban trope.

10. See *The Idea of Race in Science: Great Britain 1800–1960.*

11. Prominent anthropologist Franz Boas became a strong opponent of these racial theories in the first half of the twentieth century. In collections of his work, like *Race and Democratic Society* (1945) and *Race, Language and Culture* (1940), he joined defenders of the New Immigrants like Jane Addams and Grace Abbott in foregrounding the importance of environment over heredity and the more democratic potential of cultural assimilation over racial essentialism. See the present work, 67-70, for more on Boas.

12. See Taliaferro 215 and 219.

13. Samuel R. Delany addresses the issue of Burroughs' popular fiction in "Letter to a Critic: Popular Culture, High Art, and the S-F Landscape" (1973). Similar to my own analysis, Delany acknowledges the "slapdash writing, sloppiness, and vulgarity" of Burroughs' science fiction (*Jewel-Hinged* 15). However, he goes on to assert that "[s]ome art survives in spite of [this]" (ibid). More specifically, "in some [texts], the good is so infested with [the above negative characteristics] you cannot separate it out (Edgar R., and William S., Burroughs, gnawing at the idea of civilization from their respectively fascist and radical positions)" (ibid).

14. Toni Morrison, for example, asserts that "in matters of race, silence and evasion have historically ruled literary discourse. Evasion has fostered another, substitute language in which the issues are encoded, foreclosing open debate" (9). As we shall see, the transformation of ethnic, racial, and/or sexual Others into aliens within science fiction is one such "substitute," "foreclosing [an] open debate" of race within the field.

15. Similar to Disney's *The Lion King*, the emphasis shifts to environmentalism in *Tarzan*, a current and more politically correct topic/moral than evolution and racialism.

16. For example, De Witt Douglas Kilgore can only name two "full-length studies" discussing "the political and social future of racialized beings in the genre" (9): Daniel Leonard Bernardi's *Star Trek and History: Race-ing Toward a White Future* (1998) and Michael C. Pounds' *Race in Space: The Representation of Ethnicity in* Star Trek *and* Star Trek: The Next Generation (1999). As Kilgore notes, both of these texts focus on *Star Trek* alone. Of course, Kilgore's own text, *Astrofuturism: Science, Race, and Visions of Utopia in Space*, is an attempt to remedy this situation. Kilgore does address the

works of Robert A. Heinlein and Arthur C. Clarke in detail; however, his focus as a whole is more on popular science than science fiction. In this context, he does not address Burroughs or George S. Schuyler, and Samuel Delany and Octavia Butler surface only as minor notes.

17. I refer here to Apache culture as portrayed by Burroughs.

18. Of course, as the earlier discussion of the transformation of ethnic or racial terrestrial Others into aliens makes clear, the connections between aliens and racial Others can be either, and sometimes both, positive and negative. The common practice in science fiction of suppressing racial Others by transforming them into aliens also highlights the ubiquitous attempt to avoid race in the genre.

19. Kilgore makes these claims specifically within the context of astrofuturism, a literary/scientific/popular phenomena starting after World War II. However, I believe these general claims apply to the earlier need for a new area of exploration also. Kilgore's connection to the American West supports this more general application: "[t]he idea of a space frontier serves contemporary America as the west served the nation in its past: it is the terrain onto which a manifest destiny is projected, a new frontier invalidating the 1893 closure of the western terrestrial frontier" (1). Kilgore's parallel emphasizes the dual nature of science fiction as well. In addition to "its renewal of the geographic tradition of imperialism," astrofuturism "represents an extension of the desire to escape the logic of empire and find some space beyond the reach of old powers and obsolete identities" (11).

20. Of course the archaic tendency of science fiction has continued up through contemporary texts. George Lucas' *Star Wars* trilogy offers the best known contemporary example of such a combination of hand-to-hand sword fighting and advanced mechanical travel. Lucas' focus on an individual white male hero mirrors that of Burroughs and much early sf as well.

21. See Haraway and Taliaferro.

22. Here and throughout my discussion of Burroughs, I frequently utilize the terminology of the time period and Burroughs' racial perspective. Certainly, this does not mean I subscribe to this point of view. In fact, one of the underlying motivations for this chapter, as well as my entire project on the intersection of race and science fiction, is to question such terminology and hierarchies. However, if quotation marks were placed around every questionable term, the reader would be needlessly distracted.

23. See Nash, Chap. 3: "The Romantic Wilderness," especially pages 51–2, and Lawrence, Chap. 5: "Fenimore Cooper's Leatherstocking Novels." Both Nash and Lawrence emphasize the discrepancy between the actual living conditions of 'gentlemen' writers and their occasional excursions into the wilderness or the lives of their fictional characters. Precisely because William Byrd, Washington Irving, and Cooper were not frontiersmen themselves and, therefore, held privileged and detached perspectives, they could

write more positively of the wilderness and its influence on civilized, Anglo man. Twentieth century writers follow the same pattern. Burroughs mirrored Zane Grey and other popular western writers in his largely urban background; see Taliagerro 189. In the same vein, precisely because the American wilderness and its native inhabitants were largely subdued, Burroughs could create a fictional past and a romantic hero in a wilderness setting which would appeal to a 20th-century audience.

24. See Taliaferro or Porges for biographical information on Burroughs.

25. The tropics were an elsewhere as well; Burroughs never even visited Africa. Of course, outer space was not a viable travel destination for anyone at the time.

26. As mentioned earlier, however, Burroughs resists such an extreme assimilation of the European or Anglo-American to 'savage' behavior, such as scalping, in his western narratives. Even before he learns of his white ancestry, Shoz-Dijiji instinctively knows that he should not scalp people, despite being raised within a Native American culture which valorizes scalping as an accepted and expected activity for males during combat. Of course, this 'authentic' Native American culture is a fictionalized creation of Burroughs as well.

27. See Frederick Douglass, especially his second autobiography, *My Bondage and My Freedom*, for an analysis of the autocratic, undemocratic, and therefore unAmerican institution of southern slavery. In chapter 4, for example, Douglass describes the plantation of his childhood: "In its isolation, seclusion, and self-reliant independence, Col. Lloyd's plantation resembles what the baronial domains were, during the middle ages in Europe" (64). The hierarchical basis of southern individualism is further emphasized in a later passage: "The idea of rank and station was rigidly maintained on Col. Lloyd's plantation," equally among the whites as the blacks (78).

28. When Carter first introduces himself in *A Princess of Mars*, he says "My name is John Carter; I am better known as Captain Jack Carter of Virginia. At the close of the Civil War [. . .]" (11).

29. Herzog is quoting from Daniel G. Hoffman, 78.

30. See my discussion of Delany and Fishburn for more on western metaphysics, the mind/body split, and race (176–7).

31. Of course, this is only a limited understanding and sympathy; Wells' language here clearly reveals a negative colonial and racial hierarchy.

32. What is especially interesting to note here is the ease with which Nash himself unselfconsciously utilizes the language and theory of western progress and the way in which he too collapses white, western man with "universal man" (Haraway 186). In the "Preface to the Revised Edition," Nash reveals the influence of recent (1960s) scientific work in the natural sciences on the revised edition of his book, including the quoted material. Ironically, in the remainder of his book (written earlier) in which he focuses on later,

more limited time periods, Nash much more consciously makes distinctions between various cultural ideologies and these viewpoints and his own authorial perspective.

33. Pearce quotes here from *Hakluytus Posthumus, or Purchas His Pilgrimes*, first published in 1625.

34. This bodily focus will be continued in the next paragraph on the communal nature of the green Martians' reproduction.

35. However, two of Roosevelt's autobiographical texts reveal an attempt to combine the scientific as well: Vol. 5: *African Game Trails: An Account of the African Wanderings of an American Hunter-Naturalist* (1909) and Vol. 6: *Through the Brazilian Wilderness and Papers on Natural History* (1902) (*Works*).

36. As Peckham asserts, "the grand thesis of metaphysical evolutionism—from simple to complex means from good to better, infinitely or finitely, as your metaphysical taste determines—not only received no support from the *Origin* but, if the book were properly understood and if the individual involved felt that a metaphysic should and could have scientific support, was positively demolished" (29).

37. Peckham's distinct separation between subjective "values" and objective description will be questioned shortly in my discussion of Haraway. However, Peckham's more specific point about Darwin's works is still useful. The greater scientific objectivity of Darwin's texts has been obscured and subverted towards direct and predominantly subjective ends. I believe Delany's discussion of the objective intent of scientific discourse is useful for maintaining a necessary distinction between science and fiction, while acknowledging the subjective aspects of scientific discourse and practice (see 144). It is the strict and pure, either/or dichotomy which needs to be broken down, not the larger categories themselves.

38. While Dejah Thoris symbolizes white womanhood in a terrestrial context, she is literally 'of color' as an extraterrestrial.

39. Haraway connects science and fiction in two ways. First, "the history of science appears as a narrative about the history of technical and social means to produce the facts. The facts themselves are types of stories, of testimony to experience" (4). Haraway's radical questioning of even the objectivity of "facts" reflects her more specific assertion that "[s]cientific practice and scientific theories produce and are embedded in particular kinds of stories. Any scientific statement about the world depends intimately upon language, upon metaphor. The metaphors may be mathematical or they may be culinary; in any case they structure scientific vision" (ibid).

40. See Torgovnick Chap. 1 and Street Chap. 2.

41. Burroughs' choice to begin with the American West and the western genre and not to utilize technological means for space travel illustrates his ambiguous attitude towards science fiction and technological western progress as well.

42. This positive portrayal of a quasi-military group and the beneficent effects of Anglo leadership on natives mirrors that of American imperialism and British colonialism as well. The imperial or colonial superstructure is rationalized to prevent conflict between smaller, competing native groups (ethnic, racial, religious, etc.). Of course, there is also the infamous "white man's burden," described by Rudyard Kipling (1899). Given their superior cultural attributes (with an underlying foundation of essentialist racial superiority), Europeans have a duty to share and/or institute these cultural (social, political, and economic) norms. Of course, this is where Christianity and capitalism come in with Native Americans, as discussed earlier.

43. In *Starship Troopers*, Robert Heinlein similarly portrays military institutions positively despite the contradictory values they embody. On a related note, the movie version of Heinlein's text obscures the racial component of the text in the same way the racial implications of ERB's written texts have been generally overlooked due to subsequent visual versions. See 118–120 for more on Heinlein and *Starship Troopers*.

44. The multiple, and often confusing, definitions of race are illustrated here. In referring to multiple human races as well as the human race as a whole, 'race' is a good example of the contradictory race-specific and universal connotations of many scientific terms, and the historical/scientific context which explains such contradictions (see Haraway).

45. This is not to say that no platonic, romantic, and/or sexual relationships developed between Native Americans and Anglo Americans. However, a general policy of separation was promoted, especially by Anglo-Americans (similar to the color line for African-Americans).

46. In this way, Herbert Spencer's evolutionary theories are representative of Social Darwinism, or the Darwinisticism described by Peckham.

47. Torgovnick, for example, notes the "upbeat, heroic tone of Burroughs' biographies [published in the 60s and 70s]: their brand of buoyant, macho optimism" (44–5).

NOTES TO CHAPTER TWO

1. See the appendix for a chronological listing of Schuyler's works and relevant criticism.

2. The 1991 republication of the two serials, *Black Empire*, contains a select annotated bibliography of the stories Schuyler is known to have written, under his own name and under pseudonyms, for the *Pittsburgh Courier* between 1933 and 1939. In total, Schuyler wrote over "four hundred pieces of fiction" for the *Courier* during the 1930s (Hill and Rasmussen 260).

3. "The Black Internationale" was published between November 21, 1936 and July 3, 1937. "The Black Empire" was published between October 2, 1937 and April 16, 1938 (*Black Empire* xvii).

4. Again, see the appendix for a chronological listing of Schuyler's texts and the critical responses to them.

5. In his article "Racism and Science Fiction," Samuel R. Delany expands on Du Bois' positive review of *Black No More* (Delany, "Racism" 384). Du Bois' assertion that the text was "bound to be 'abundantly misunderstood'" because it was a satire coincides with Peplow's discussion of the satiric nature of the text (qtd. in Delany, "Racism" 384)).

6. Of course, their personal viewpoints and political perspectives are another large component. My point is the strong tendency to write and publish criticism which coincides with the larger political climate.

7. First publishing in the 1960s, Samuel Delaney is still the best known of these authors. Octavia Butler joined him in the 1970s.

8. That is not to say that Schuyler and his texts should not remain situated in the African-American literary context as well. Ideally, his works will be discussed within multiple contexts. Certainly his continued focus on race in the science fiction genre invites such multiple readings.

9. The critical debate between Langston Hughes and Schuyler in the 1920s mirror this latter debate. See note 30 below.

10. A more thorough discussion of Schuyler's racial revision in *Black No More* commences on 78.

11. Schuyler uses the new lens of science to discuss a concept utilized by other African-American writers in works of fiction. For example, Nella Larsen's *Passing* was published just two years earlier, in 1929, at the tailend of the Harlem Renaissance. James Weldon Johnson's influential fictional text, *The Autobiography of an Ex-Colored Man*, was published in 1912.

12. In this one paragraph, Schuyler quotes anthropologist Ruth Benedict.

13. See Haraway's 1989 text *Primate Visions: Gender, Race, and Nature in the World of Modern Science.*

14. See my discussion of Burroughs for a more detailed discussion of Haraway's text and its ties to adventure fiction and science fiction.

15. These include Donna Haraway's *Primate Visions* and Nancy Stepan's *The Idea of Race in Science: Great Britain, 1800–1960*. Also, T.F. Gossett's *Race: The History of an Idea in America* and George Stocking's *Race, Culture, and Evolution.*

16. This sentence and the next were taken from Herskovits, *Franz Boas: The Science of Man in the Making.*

17. Herskovits was also a student of Boas,' along with Ruth Benedict and Zora Neale Hurston (Hyatt xii).

18. See the "Heritage" chapter in Walter Benn Michaels' *Our America: Nativism, Modernism, and Pluralism* for a discussion of Herskovits' scholarly connection to African-American studies in the first half of the twentieth century (123–35).

19. Nancy Stepan and Sander Gilman discuss the "rejection of scientific racism" by African-Americans and Jews in "Appropriating the Idioms of Science: The Rejection of Scientific Racism." Acknowledging that this criticism took place largely outside the scientific community and did not have a significant impact on scientific racism within the field up to the 1930s, the authors still emphasize that the work of dissenting African-Americans and Jews "created modes of representation and knowledge essential for the stereotyped themselves" (103). Stepan and Gilman highlight W. E. B. Du Bois as one such prominent dissenting voice.

20. Unfortunately, Gilman and Sander only address Boas and his resistance to scientific racism in a footnote in their article, "Appropriating the Idioms of Science: The Rejection of Scientific Racism" (74).

21. For example, in *Dusk of Dawn* Du Bois writes, "[t]he main result of my schooling had been to emphasize science and the scientific attitude" (50).

22. See Doyle, Stepan and Gilman, and Beardsley, for example.

23. Thomas F. Gossett gives a more detailed examination of race, as a self-consciously studied term, in the 18th and 19th centuries in *Race: The History of an Idea in America.*

24. See Gould.

25. According to Tucker, the black conservatives, like Schuyler, are "attracted to claims of objectivity and 'truth' because they lack a real constituency—among either blacks or whites—and need some sort of tool to help them gain credibility" ("Can" 137). Such an assessment elides the context of science and the norm of objectivity in the field. Also, Stepan and Gilman's analysis here may help explain some tensions within Schuyler overarching view of science. First, Schuyler seems sincere in his promotion of rationality and related dissemination of contemporaneous scientific findings undermining race. Yet, he simultaneously satirizes and critiques the discipline of science generally, focusing on its pervasive subjectivity and bias.

26. Stepan and Gilman only mention Boas in a footnote, but his methods, viewpoints, and works fit their criteria for resistance to scientific racism. Given Boas' prominence and influence, to which their footnote alludes, it is surprising they do not address his work and its impact on the scientific community.

27. Subsequently published in *Papers in Inter-Racial Problems Communicated to the First Universal Races Congress Held at the University of London, July 26–29, 1911,* Ginn and Company, Boston, 1911.

28. Boas presented his paper, "Instability of Human Types," in the Second Session, entitled "Conditions of Progress (General Problems)" (Spiller). Du Bois presented "The Negro Race in the United States of America" in the Sixth Session, "The Modern Conscience in Relation to Racial Questions (the Negro and the American Indian)" (Spiller).

29. See pages 18–21.

30. See Langston Hughes' "The Negro Artist and the Racial Mountain" and Schuyler's "The Negro-Art Hokum." Tucker also gives a summary of their arguments in his article on Schuyler ("Can" 142).

31. Tucker concludes his essay on Schuyler with the assertion that, "[t]he recognition of constitutive differences, not their denial, serves as a tool for black empowerment, and is in turn a key step toward America's realization of what Du Bois called the 'ideal of human brotherhood'" ("Can" 148). However, Rusty L. Monhollon's discussion of race relations in Lawrence, Kansas between 1969–1970 (also in *Race Consciousness*) emphasizes the potentially divisive effects of 'race consciousness.' As African-Americans "embraced Black Power," "[t]he results, like American race relations in general, were paradoxical. While it was empowering for blacks, it also contributed to a polarization of the entire community along racial lines" (Monhollon 258). Monhollon's position is more closely aligned with that of Schuyler; both indict white racism but, at the same time, do not see black race consciousness as a solution to America's 'race problem.' As Monhollon notes, "blacks and whites in America confront each other in a society they have constructed together and in which they share a common history, as well as similar religions, values, ideals, and cultures" (259). Monhollon and Schuyler stress these political, social, and cultural similarities and see them as the key to an egalitarian society. Schuyler's additional focus on the physical, biological and genealogical, commonality of blacks and whites only serves to further emphasize an artificial and false nature for any racial concept and the error of race consciousness for blacks as well as whites.

32. See my discussion of Delany's *Trouble on Triton* (165–173) for a more thorough discussion of Sam.

33. Hill and Rasmussen provide a brief discussion of Dr. Belsidus' relationship with Gaskin (282–3). I am indebted to them for highlighting this particular quote.

34. See Hill and Rasmussen for Schuyler's apparent endorsement of this stereotype (282).

35. In the second half of this quotation, Peplow quotes from Joyce Nower. However, he does not document this source further, either in an in-text citation or in a bibliography.

36. As we shall see, Samuel Delany's protagonist in *Trouble on Triton*, Bron Helmstrom, is also an anti-hero. However, his anti-hero characteristics are, overall, more negative. Bron is not only selfish, but also relatively cowardly and powerless. In contrast to Disher and Belsidus, Bron does not know how race operates in his society, nor does he understand how to manipulate the social norms of his culture to his advantage. As a white male, Bron does not feel a compulsion or see the necessity of learning more about these norms. Robert Elliot Fox, for example, labels Bron an "antihero," "given the extent to which he is (unwittingly) a self-antagonist" ("Politics" 49). Bron does not

overcome racial oppression, by any means necessary, but succumbs to neurosis despite his egalitarian position in Triton society. See 158–164 for more
on Bron and 167–169 for a specific comparison and contrast of Bron and
Disher.

37. Belsidus seems to manipulate the sexual aspects of a cultural concept of
race; like Ralph Ellison's invisible man, white women seem to be continually attracted to him and he, in turn, never expresses an interest in women-
of-color.

38. Kink-No-More is a historically real product.

39. The ethnicity of the doctor and engineer highlights the connections between
African-Americans and other groups oppressed due to 'race.' In practice, the
Japanese were often associated with the Chinese, the first group to be legally
excluded from the United States on the basis of race (1882). The Chinese
and Japanese joined Jews, Italians, and Eastern European immigrants more
generally to make up the so-called New Immigration (1880–1920). The
New Immigrants were categorized as racially different and inferior from earlier groups of immigrants to the New World—English, French, Dutch, and
even the Irish, for example. Of course, a common denominator between
the new immigrant groups, besides time period, was darker skin and hair
color. The anti-immigration movement culminated in the Immigration Act
of 1924, which effectively cut off immigration from these new areas, while
allowing large quotas for the countries of origin for the older immigrant
groups. See my discussion of Burroughs for more on the New Immigration
and the Immigration Restriction Movement.

40. See page 62 in reference to this sentence and the next.

41. Hill and Rasmussen make a similar point in the context of the *Black Empire*
serials (267).

42. Fuss gives a useful summary of Joyce A. Joyce's critique of what Joyce calls
"the poststructuralist sensibility" and its application to the field of African-American literature (Fuss 77). Joyce's Afro-centric critical position
was expressed in two articles in *New Literary History*: "The Black Canon:
Reconstructing Black American Literary Criticism" and "'Who the Cap
Fit': Unconsciousness and Unconscionableness in the Criticism of Houston
A. Baker, Jr. and Henry Louis Gates, Jr."

43. While Du Bois' language here does not explicitly define "American" as
'white,' the following passage clarifies his racial intention: the "American
Negro [. . .] would not Africanize America, for America has too much
to teach the world and Africa. He would not bleach his Negro soul in a
flood of white Americanism, for he knows that Negro blood has a message
for the world" (*Souls* 9).

44. Crookman summarizes the process as follows: "it is accomplished by elec-
trical nutrition and glandular control. Certain gland secretions are greatly
stimulated while others are considerably diminished" (*Black No More* 13).

45. John M. Reilly identifies Walter Williams as Walter White (107).
46. Disher also manipulates the general scientism or scientific positivism of Americans in his role as an anthropologist. Schuyler's satiric portrayal of the manipulation of scientism by a black lay person has interesting connections to Schuyler's own use of scientism in his non-fiction and potential appeal to the scientism of his audience (see 66 in the present text).
47. The white characters are deceived by both their ignorance of blacks and their related beliefs in racial stereotypes and rigid racial boundaries—they would not imagine a Negro capable of talking like a white/educated/scientist.
48. 'Authentic' does not denote positive or negative here.
49. Reilly more generally discusses *Black No More* as a dystopia, or "anti-utopia" (107) He does not specifically address multiple subjectivity as one aspect of Schuyler's negative perspective.
50. As Tucker accurately notes, "[a]ll satire is by definition a humorous critique intended to change behavior or thinking" ("Can" 143).
51. In his introduction to the 1990, Library of America edition of *The Souls of Black Folk*, John Edgar Wideman identifies this potential for change as a primary element of Du Bois' text as well:
    > The color line raises the issue of identity. Theirs. Yours. Mine. Will we blend, change, survive, or is the color line one more measure of the limits of our collective imagination, our cultural graveyard of either/or terminal distinctions: black/white, male/female, young/old, good/bad, rich/poor, spirit/flesh? It is possible to imagine ourselves other than we are, better? These are the monumental questions reverberating in *The Souls of Black Folk*, matters unresolved by the last one hundred years, which have tumbled us, bloody and confused, onto the threshold of the twenty-first century. (xiii)

    Wideman's "imagination" corresponds with the speculative element of science fiction also.
52. Hill and Rasmussen assert, "Intellectually, Schuyler held out for a distinctly non-racialist view of the world" (297). They quote from his 1937 Views & Reviews editorial column in the *Pittsburgh Courier* to support this assessment: "'Personally, I am opposed to worship of things Nordic as I am of things Negroid'" (ibid).
53. Du Bois too rejects an "either-or" proposition (Fanon 203). However, his alternative differs from that of Schuyler in that he seeks to simultaneously maintain both a black and a white consciousness: "[t]he history of the American Negro is the history of this strife,—this longing to attain self-conscious manhood, to merge his double self into a better and truer self. In this merging he wishes neither of the older selves to be lost [. . .]. He simply wishes to make it possible for a man to be both a Negro and an American" (*Souls* 9).

54. Like Schuyler, Fanon, and Appiah, Fields highlights the negative power of race.
55. This is, of course, where Appiah's critique of Du Bois comes into play. In *Dusk of Dawn*, Du Bois attempts to rationally and logically substitute a strictly cultural definition of race for the original biological foundation. As Appiah reveals, an illogical argument results.
56. See my discussion of Delany for more on the idealistic elision of race in science fiction and Delany's individualist use of race.

NOTES TO CHAPTER THREE

1. *Babel-17* (1966) and *The Einstein Intersection* (1967) won Nebula Awards. See *Samuel R. Delany: A Primary and Secondary Bibliography, 1962–1979* for a complete listing of Delany's texts during this time period (Peplow and Bravard).
2. Once again, Michael W. Peplow gives an excellent overview. In "Meet Samuel R. Delany, Black Science Fiction Writer," Peplow covers Delany's early career (pre-1979) and provides an especially good introduction for readers outside of the sf community.
3. Delany's critical texts include *The Jewel-Hinged Jaw: Notes on the Language of Science Fiction* (1977), *The American Shore: Meditations on a Tale of Science Fiction by Thomas M. Disch-Angouleme* (1978), *Starboard Wine: More Notes on the Language of Science Fiction* (1984), *Wagner/Artaud: A Play of 19th and 20th Century Critical Fictions* (1988), *The Straits of Messina* (1989), *Silent Interviews: On Language, Race, Sex, Science Fiction, and Some Comics* (1994), *Longer Views: Extended Essays* (1996), *and Shorter Views: Queer Thoughts & The Politics of the Paraliterary* (1999). His two autobiographical texts are *Heavenly Breakfast: An Essay on the Winter of Love* (1979) and *The Motion of Light in Water: Sex and Science Fiction in the East Village, 1957–65* (1988).
4. Seth McEvoy's 1984 text, *Samuel R. Delany*, follows George Edgar Slusser's 1977 *The Delany Intersection: Samuel R. Delany Considered as a Writer of Semi-Precious Words*, Douglas Barbour's 1979 *Worlds Out of Words: The SF Novels of Samuel R. Delany*, and Jane Branham Weedman's 1982 *Samuel R. Delany*. Also, Jeffrey A. Tucker's *Sense of Wonder: Samuel R. Delany, Race, Identity, and Difference* has been published since the initial writing of the present text.
5. Jay Schuster's web page on Delany provides a sampling of such public involvement (1998–2001). Schuster also lists Delany's numerous literary nominations and awards.
6. Freedman names Robert Elliot Fox's work as one exception to this "general neglect" (160). Since the publication of Freedman's book, Jeffrey A. Tucker also published *A Sense of Wonder: Samuel R. Delany, Race, Identity, and Difference* (2004). Tucker explicitly and primarily places many of Delany's texts within the context of African-American Studies. In the first chapter, he notes

Delany's recent inclusion into the African American literary "canon" (1997), but still questions "the extent to which his work has been part of recent scholarship and teaching in the field" (48–9). Shorter examples include Peplow's 1979 article in *The Crisis*, "Meet Samuel R. Delany, Black Science Fiction Writer," and the *Black American Literature Forum*'s 1984 (18.2 Summer) issue devoted to Delany, Octavia Butler, and Charles R. Saunders.

7. McEvoy discusses the many "factors" that led to Delany's first sf or fantasy novel, *The Jewels of Aptor* (19). In his autobiography, Delany similarly mentions his initial, recurrent dream or "nightmares" (the basis of *Jewels*) and his wife Marilyn Hacker's job at Ace Books (a company which published much science fiction) (*Motion* 75–6).

8. Ironically, Delany attributes the relative lack of racial prejudice in the sf community to another factor as well—the lack of black writers. He believes that once the percentage of black writers in the field reaches "thirteen, fifteen, twenty percent of the total. At that point, where the competition might be perceived as having some economic heft, chances are we will have as much racism and prejudice here as in any other field" ("Racism" 386).

9. Peplow is quoting from Delany's letter here.

10. *The Fall of the Towers* trilogy (1970) is a revised collection of three previously-published novels: *Captives of the Flame* (1963), *The Towers of Toron* (1964), and *City of a Thousand Suns* (1965). Delany offers an overview of his revisions in the "Author's Note" at the beginning of the 1970 trilogy edition.

11. See his autobiography, *The Motion of Light in Water: Sex and Science Fiction Writing in the East Village, 1957–1965*, for example. Seth McEvoy's early chapters on Delany also highlight Delany's attempts at feminist revisions in female characterization (19, 24–27, 37–41).

12. In *A Sense of Wonder: Samuel R. Delany, Race, Identity, and Difference*, Jeffrey A. Tucker also focuses on race in Delany's fiction, particularly his later fiction.

13. Of course, this is the racial and moral dichotomy Edgar Rice Burroughs utilizes in the Mars series, particularly *A Princess of Mars*.

14. The Xenogenesis trilogy is composed of *Dawn* (1987), *Adulthood Rites* (1988), and *Imago* (1989).

15. Donna Haraway also notes the cover of *Dawn* in *Primate Visions* (381).

16. Other examples include the covers of Delany's *The Fall of the Towers* trilogy and *Babel-17*, which stereotypically foreground a female character with ample cleavage revealed.

17. In a freshman English course I taught, many of the students expressed their confusion and/or admitted to misreading the text based on the strength of this first impression.

18. James explores this issue in more detail near the end of his essay ("Yellow" 39–44). See also Gary K. Wolfe, *The Known and the Unknown: The Iconography of Science Fiction*.

19. In a 1986 interview, Butler asserts, "Science fiction writers come from science fiction readers. I think that as more and more blacks begin to read science fiction, then more blacks will take up writing science fiction, and this is already happening to a certain degree" ("Black" 16).

20. See the next sub-section (115) for more on the differences between these texts and their portrayal of race.

21. Similarly, Fuss advocates maintaining the concept of race, "even though we may recognize its essentializing usages," because "to see 'Blackness' as an ethnic marker (equivalent to Germaness or Jewishness) has historically worked to homogenize black identity, to de-particularize the black subject" (92). In addition, "to substitute 'ethnicity' for 'race' would be to e-race [. . .] the rich and color-full history of 'race' in Afro-American culture" (93).

22. See 88–89 for more on Fuss. Fuss joins me in connecting Baker's scientific and poststructuralist resistance (93).

23. See the following sub-section on *Trouble on Triton* (155) for a detailed discussion of how Delany revises a Heinlein protagonist in that text.

24. As we shall see, Delany somewhat overstates his case here. His extensive and graphic depictions of sexuality and gay identity, for example, are unusual within science fiction.

25. I realize these are false divisions in terms of the texts alone. Later, I will discuss the illogical nature of this generic division. As Schuyler's texts exemplified, the deciding factors seem to be the race of the author, the author's literary affiliations, and/or the author's position on race. This stands in direct contrast to Delany's linguistic basis for science fiction.

26. Delany's Introduction to *Glory Road* was published in July 1979. It is especially interesting that Delany does not specifically refer to his own text, *Trouble on Triton* (1976), in his "bibliography of novel-length responses" to Heinlein's texts (Introduction vii) since he had previously admitted to Michael Peplow that *Trouble on Triton* was an intentional response to Heinlein's *Glory Road* (Peplow, "Meet" 120). Peplow's article, "Meet Samuel R. Delany, Black Science Fiction Writer," was published in April 1979, and his information was taken from letters written by Delany in 1978 (121). See 159–160 for more on Peplow's article and *Trouble on Triton* as a response to Heinlein's text. Also, Tucker highlights Delany's admission that *The Fall of the Towers* was a response to Heinlein's *Starship Troopers* (Tucker, *Sense* 280; Delany, *Shorter* 322).

27. James joins Fred Erisman in seeing four other Heinlein texts as "being a deliberate attempt at education in racial tolerance" (E. James 34). The first three juvenile books (1954–56) and the fourth text, *Double Star* (1956), are "powered by [the] contemporary debate about civil rights" (ibid).

28. Likewise, Denise Richardson was cast as Carmen. All the major characters, in fact, are visibly Anglo in the film.

29. See Westfahl's Note 3.

30. This quote and the following were suggested by Gary Westfahl's summary of the two texts (73).
31. Franklin discusses this technique in more detail (156–7).
32. Delany's description of the sexual activity between Captain Leela and the alien, The Destroyer, in *The Ballad of Beta-2* also highlights Heinlein's sexual suppression here.
33. Elsewhere Westfahl argues more generally that, "as Heinlein came to realize, the stance of the Self-Reliant or Society-Generating Individual is necessarily racist" (74). Franklin emphasizes Farnham's isolation within a broader context as well (154).
34. See the next sub-section on *Trouble on Triton* (155).
35. Heinlein could be distinguishing between various branches of the armed forces. Farnham, for example, is in the navy, and Johnny Rico is in the futuristic equivalent of the army. Without any overt comment on Heinlein's part within the text, however, there is no basis for such a distinction. Interestingly, Schuyler also highlights his positive experiences with the army in his autobiography, *Black and Conservative*. While far from fully egalitarian, the army offered the possibility of respect, money, and travel for African-Americans.
36. Heinlein does use games, and particularly bridge, as a trope for the text. However, his portrayal of the 'game' of bridge seems to be in line with the highly serious and 'competitive' portrayal of race relations in the text.
37. Toni Morrison explores a similar use of the "Africanist presence" by white authors, particularly American males, in *Playing in the Dark: Whiteness and the Literary Imagination* (6). As we shall see, her ideological focus is in tune with Delany's revision of Heinlein's typical white, male protagonist in *Trouble on Triton*.
38. In *The Wretched of the Earth*, Frantz Fanon asserts that "[t]he native is an oppressed person whose permanent dream is to become the persecutor" (53). See the next paragraph on Kincaid and Bradbury for a refutation of this assertion. Even granting the general applicability of Fanon's assertion, however, his "dream" falls short of actual practice/historical manifestation. Either through the restriction(s) of inequitable power relations or personal inhibitions, these "dream[s]" have not become a collective reality.
39. Herrmann Lang's *The Air Battle: a Vision of the Future* (1859) contains an early example of a fictional black-dominated society, in this case a very positive portrayal. Steven Barnes has also recently written an alternate history novel about slavery in the United States; see footnote 120 .
40. Franklin also specifically and convincingly links the Chosen with Black Muslims, especially their negative portrayal by the media during this time period (158–9).
41. Heinlein's *Sixth Column* also fits this pattern. Serialized in 1941 and published as a novel in 1946, it springs from the anti-Asian ideology

surrounding World War II (see Westfahl 71–2). It was subsequently reprinted as *The Day After Tomorrow* in 1951.

42. See the next sub-section on *Trouble on Triton* (155).

43. *The Fall of the Towers* trilogy (1963–65), for example, takes place on a futuristic Earth, like *Farnham's Freehold*. However, Delany does not reenact the same (even if inverted) racial divisions as historical Earth (American) history. Instead, he transforms Heinlein's 'black cannibals' and Burroughs' black and green (Native American) 'savages' into the most advanced, telepathic race in the society. However, the dark-skinned tribal members are morally neither better or worse than the other races composing Toron society. Furthermore, as the trio of protagonists symbolizes, each gender, race, economic class (etc.) is responsible for and included in the rehabilitation of their shared society. This more inclusive and even integrationist philosophy (as seen in The City of a Thousand Suns, for example) also finds embodiment in *The Ballad of Beta-2*.

44. Other black, male writers do not follow Schuyler's lead until the 1960s, a time of increased racial consciousness and conflict (and general social upheaval—the Women's Movement, Anti-War Movement, Sexual Revolution, etc.). Is there a connection between times of turbulent social events/ movements and a turning towards the speculative elements of sf? When more traditional mores are being questioned and undermined, perhaps new ideas are usefully formulated and envisioned within sf.

45. See the end of this section (151).

46. See Slusser's structuralist analysis of triples in Delany's *The Fall of the Towers*, especially Book One: *Captives of the Flame* or *Out of the Dead City*, as it was later renamed (23–4).

47. Baker also makes a rather vague reference to "vernacular rhythms" (387). In his implied definition of this term, the emphasis seems to be on a particular ideological or political perspective rather than language alone. It is in this context that Delany's revisionist attitude towards science fiction comes closest to meeting Baker's literary criteria.

48. On the other hand, Mike Resnick's recent stories of Kiranyaga illustrate the impossibility of trying to reconstruct a pre-Prospero Calibanic self. A medicine man of the Kikuyu people of Kenya travels to another world to establish an 'authentic' Kikuyu society. All of the pre-modern, pre-western elements of Kikuyu culture are reestablished without revision. What the narrator comes to realize (through a long process of struggle, conflict, and death) is that his 'people' do not want such a society and that he is an "anachronism" (8). Racial constructions, reconstructions of culture and identity, do have "power to shape human lives in very real ways," as Tucker asserts, but Resnick joins Schuyler and Fanon in focusing on the negative potential of these racial constructions (especially for women) (Tucker, "Can" 148).

49. Presumably this is why Reilly finds *A Different Drummer* "a more complex and well-developed, illustration of the Black anti-utopia" (108). However, while Reilly notes the "alternative viewpoints," he does not discuss the race of these characters as a factor in the story (109).

50. Baker offers Derek Walcott as an example of such a divided position. Fanon would also fit this description. In addition, Don L. Birchfield's sf story, "Lost in the Land of Ishtaboli," includes a Native American man trapped between native and modern cultural elements. Double-consciousness (or multiple) can be perceived as both positive and negative—as a gift which allows more extensive communication or as artificial, imposed, coercive, and harming the human psyche through division and conflict. The Caribbean concept of creolization or Creoleness is similar to Baker's concept of "*supraliteracy*" (394); both of these theoretical concepts attempt to unify disparate cultural and racial elements, especially with the intention of avoiding disabling dualisms. According to Jean Bernabé, Patrick Chamoiseau, and Raphaël Confiant, "[b]ecause of its constituent mosaic, Creoleness is an open specificity [. . .]. It is expressing a kaleidoscopic totality, that is to say: *the nontotalitarian consciousness of a preserved diversity*" (892). Of course, there usually are more than two elements in the Caribbean. Therefore, Creoleness cannot rely as easily on a natural or essential racial state, like Baker's Calibanic self. Samuel Selvon's epilogue to *Foreday Morning*, "Three into one can't go—East Indian, Trinidadian, West Indian," is a more specific example of this multiplicity.

51. Of course, the Caliban/Prospero trope exists in science fiction as well. Robert Shelton, for example, discusses Wells' *The Island of Doctor Moreau* (1895) in these terms (8). He builds on the idea of Prospero as "the original model of the mad scientist" put forth by Robert Plank in *The Emotional Significance of Imaginary Beings: A Study of the Interaction Between Psychopathology, Literature, and Reality in the Modern World* (1968). Brian Aldiss also briefly mentions the Dr. Moreau-Prospero connection in his chapter on Wells in both *Billion Year Spree* and *Trillion Year Spree*. In "Quarks," even Delany briefly notes the Calibanic nature of a character in *The Stars My Destination* (1957). However, in Bester's text, Caliban is caucasian and he is opposed to the positive, "Arcadian" character, "black Robin" (Delany, *Jewel-Hinged* 147). Delany's critique of Bester's book involves Robin's "eventual marriage to the only other non-caucasian in the book," not the larger Caliban trope (ibid).

52. Joneny identifies this as "[t]he spiral of decreasing semantic functionality" (Delany, *Ballad* 48).

53. Delany's racial diversity is muted, however, by the actual embodiment of the new, hybrid race. The Destroyer's Children are white males, and the cloning form of reproduction ensures this similarity perpetually.

54. Of course, the sterility theory for cross-breeds had been proven to be a biological falsehood in the mid-1800s by Charles Darwin. However, the specific sterility of mulattos continued to be a topic of discussion in the United States into the twentieth century.

55. Lee's story portrays African-American parents from the Civil Rights Era dealing with the effects of social integration on their children. When their son brings home a Jewish girlfriend, they reject her (63–4). Their son responds angrily: "You and Daddy spend all of your lives sending us to white schools and teaching us to live in a never-never land where people of all colors just get along swell, and then when the inevitable happens you start talking like a goddam Lester Maddox!" (64).

56. Delany's portrayal of aliens and alien/human integration can be fruitfully paired with Octavia Butler's Xenogenesis series.

57. This may be one reason Tucker primarily focuses on Delany's later texts in *A Sense of Wonder: Samuel R. Delany, Race, Identity, and Difference* (2004). Delany's connection to science would be weakest in these texts: the fantasy of the *Return to Nevèrÿon* series, the "'mundane'" fiction of *Atlantis*, and Delany's pornography (Tucker, *Sense* 199). Tucker also devotes a chapter to both *Dhalgren* and Delany's autobiography, *The Motion of Light in Water*. As discussed shortly, the first text is often considered marginally sf (see 197), and the second text is non-fiction. Not coincidentally, Tucker finds the above texts most illustrative of African-American literary techniques and themes. While placing Delany within the context of African-American Studies, then, Tucker largely maintains the division between the two genres of sf and African-American literature.

58. See my earlier discussion of Haraway (7–8; 63).

59. Published in Delany's collection of critical texts, *The Jewel-Hinged Jaw: Notes on the Language of Science Fiction*, "Shadows" was also published in two parts in *Foundation* (6 and 7/8). In addition, some of the text was published as part of the "Appendix A" in *Trouble on Triton*.

60. "Shadows" was published in its different manifestations (see above note) between 1974 and 1977.

61. In the introduction to *Worlds Out of Words: the Sf Novels of Samuel R. Delany*, Douglas Barbour emphasizes how unusual is Delany's linguistic basis for the genre (7–14).

62. Delany uses the Martian context again in *Trouble on Triton*.

63. Mundane is Delany's term for mainstream fiction. Mundane highlights the generic characteristics of the text rather than an ideological position (mainstream versus marginal—science fiction).

64. Given Delany's extensive writings on linguistic issues, the relatively small space devoted to the black vernacular illustrates his inclusive racial views. He refuses to limit himself linguistically, as do Baker and Gates in their

essentialism of (a specific, authentic racial) sound. Within his purely cultural linguistic context, all discourses are potentially available for his use.

65. Delany's autobiographical comments here, where he connects language with "worlds," also explain his early and sustained discussion of the cultural basis of language and its connection to the sf enterprise of 'culture building' (*Jewel-Hinged* 119).

66. This positive portrayal is an early recollection in Delany's chronological lifetime, however, as *The Ballad of Beta-2* is a text from his early career. While ultimately emphasizing connections, bridges, and communication across divisions, Delany qualifies this early idealism in both the autobiography (see 152–155 in the present text) and in later writing (see footnote 51 in the Schuyler chapter for Delany's more pessimistic quote from his Introduction to *Shade*).

67. See McEvoy for a detailed analysis of one, representative aspect of this larger textual "freedom"—the sexual (106–109).

68. Nightmare and Dragon Lady, for example.

69. By racial blinders, I mean the limitations imposed by Baker's theories of race. Not just *Dhalgren* but also Delany's other texts (fiction and non-fiction) serve as "guerilla action carried out *within* linguistic territories of the erstwhile masters" (Baker 394). However, Delany's "guerilla action" is not solely racial in emphasis and motivation, but also in terms of sexuality, gender, economics, etc. Similarly, Baker's resistance to scientific discourse prevents him from acknowledging Delany's sf texts.

70. SFWA stands for the Science Fiction Writers of America. Douglas Barbour gives a nice overview of the major critical reviews of *Dhalgren* (89–90). He also offers some reasons why *Dhalgren* might appeal to a more general audience (90). In 1984, McEvoy bases his assertion that "90% of the sales of *Dhalgren* were outside of the science fiction audience" precisely on the fact that it "sold more than 700,000 copies"—600,000 more copies than "a good-selling science fiction novel" (102). McEvoy also discusses the generally negative response to *Dhalgren* within the sf community throughout his chapter on the text.

71. The Neveryon series consists of *Tales of Nevèrÿon* (1979), *Neveryóna* (1983), *Flight from Nevèrÿon* (1985) and *Return to Nevèrÿon* (1994). In *A Sense of Wonder: Samuel R. Delany, Race, Identity, and Difference*, Jeffrey A. Tucker discusses the series in the context of African-American Studies (Chapter 3, "The Empire of Signs: Slavery, Semiotics, and Sexuality in the *Return to Nevèrÿon* Series").

72. Slusser acknowledges that the term "structuralist imagination" comes from Robert Scholes (3).

73. Beyond the great breadth and depth of Delany's linguistic interests, McEvoy suggests that Delany intentionally made *Dhalgren* difficult to understand in order to obscure the explicit and widely varying sexual content (117).

74. Tucker gives several examples of such critical responses to Delany's works (53), and asserts that "[p]erhaps the principle obstacle facing African American SF writing [. . .] is the discourse of black authenticity" (*Sense* 51).

75. Also see the next sub-section (162).

76. In the first chapter of *A Sense of Wonder*, Jeffrey A. Tucker also explains his focus on the connections between Delany's texts and the field of African-American Studies, while simultaneously acknowledging the multifarious "ways in which we identify" (54).

77. See the beginning of the next sub-section (155) for a more detailed analysis of this phenomenon in the context of science fiction.

78. Fuss quotes Nancy K. Miller here, from her 1986 article "Changing the Subject" (109). See my chapter on Schuyler (95–96) for the beginning of this argument.

79. Delany's autobiographical format would ideally suit the hypertext medium.

80. Joanna Russ' *The Female Man* (1975) is an excellent example of the connection between a plurality of worlds and a plural subjectivity.

81. After writing the two "parallel narratives, in parallel columns," he specifically addresses this division in section 8.103:

    If it *is* the split—the space between the two columns (one resplendant and lucid with the writings of legitimacy, the other dark and hollow with the voices of the illegitimate)—that constitutes the subject, it is only after the Romantic inflation of the private into the subjective that such a split can even be located. That locus, that margin, that split itself first allows, then demands the appropriation of language—now spoken, now written—in both directions, over the gap. (29–30)

82. *Trouble on Triton* (1996) was originally published as *Triton* (1976). I have chosen to use the title *Trouble on Triton* because this is the edition of the text from which I quote.

83. I am indebted to Ken James for drawing this particular quote to my attention in his introduction to Delany's *Longer Views* (xxxvii).

84. In chapter 1 of *A Sense of Wonder: Samuel R. Delany, Race, Identity, and Difference*, "Dangerous and Important Differences: Samuel R. Delany and the Politics of Identity," Jeffrey A. Tucker acknowledges that he

    do[es] not completely agree with the critiques of race and identity just described and apparently endorsed and performed by Delany—or more accurately, their deployment as critiques of social movements called "identity politics." As valuable as such critiques can be as strategies against racisms that reduce the diversity of African American communities to a single type, or against languages of authenticity that employ a similar logic, it is [his] belief that "identity" and "race" still have their uses, particularly for African Americans. (21)

    He summarizes the project of the entire book as an attempt to "navigate a path through Delany's writing between the Scylla of universalisms and disavowals of 'race' and 'identity' made without regard for their progressive and constitutive uses, and the Charybdis of a discourse of race nationalism and racial authenticity that allows the immensity of race in America to blind us to the multiplicity of being" (54).

85. The term simplexity originates in Delany's *Empire Star*.

86. See Easterbrook, 65–66.

87. Delany's 1984 novel, *Stars in My Pocket Like Grains of Sand*, revisits this contrast between more conservative and more radical societies. Once Delany has addressed, and rejected, the traditional sf hero, he can focus on one of the new subjective characters. In *Stars*, Marq Dyeth illustrates a new subjectivity, shaped by almost total freedom. Delany contrasts Marq's subjectivity and the social context which shaped it with that of a slave named Rat and his more conservative society.

88. Peplow's quotations come from the letters Delany wrote to him in preparation for the article in *The Crisis*. Some of the foregrounded quotes are specifically dated, but those in the body paragraphs are not. In an author's note at the end of the article, Peplow generally acknowledges that "the biographical information was supplied by Samuel R. Delany in letters sent to me between June 26 and August 12, 1978. The author also very kindly read my manuscript for factual errors and made several suggestions that I have incorporated" ("Meet" 121).

89. Elsewhere, Delany relates another inspiration for the text: "[a] couple of things were devilling my memory, including a recent dinner at a French restaurant not far from our flat in London, where I'd watched some people behave with what had struck me as unthinkable insensitivity to someone else at their table" (*Shorter* 319). Subsequently, he began writing a "fictive letter a woman might write to tell a truly unpleasant boyfriend it was all over"—the Spike's farewell letter to Bron near the end of *Trouble on Triton* (ibid). This biographical inspiration involves similar issues as the literary one of Heinlein's text.

90. Peplow, however, does not believe *Trouble on Triton* completely fulfills Delany's stated critical intention. Whereas Delany describes Bron as "a protagonist who is seen by the other characters as a 'thorough louse,'" Peplow asserts that "Bron, with all his obvious faults, emerges as a human being. He's too human for Delany's obstensible purpose" ("Meet" 120). Furthermore, "*Triton* is *not* the black man's revenge that some readers might expect" (ibid).

91. Easterbrook also compares Heinlein and Delany's texts. However, he focuses on Heinlein's *The Moon is a Harsh Mistress* (1966) and *Triton*. Also, he discusses the political nuances of the texts more generally and does not address the authors' textual representations of race in any detail.

92. Michelle Massé's otherwise excellent discussion of Bron lacks specific gender and racial components as well. She comes closest to acknowledging Bron's specific ideological position in her discussion of his reactions to the other characters and his need to negatively classify or label them (55, 56). In addition, she

connects Bron to Delany's earlier novels, but only in terms of Delany's self-critique of "what seems now an impossible heroism" (53).

93. See my discussion of Schuyler for more on Fuss and Huyssen.

94. Of course, Bron makes these specific comments as a woman. However, I will argue shortly that this sexual and gender change only reinforces the stability of his earlier position (as a white male).

95. See my earlier discussion of Burroughs and Haraway's third chapter of *Primate Visions*, "Teddy Bear Patriarchy: Taxidermy in the Garden of Eden, New York City, 1908–36."

96. See my discussion of Burroughs for a more detailed explanation of this dichotomy.

97. Michelle Massé also notes this repetition of the same in Bron's change, connecting it to his dependence on others as well: "he becomes his own mirror image as well as incorporating at least the appearance of the Spike and Sam before his sex [and race] change" (60).

98. The female Bron is also an interesting rendition of the biblical Eve in that she is literally formed from the male Bron/Adam's rib.

99. Bulent Somay, Easterbrook, and Tom Moylan also compare the two novels.

100. This term comes from one of the interviewers and not Delany.

101. See Delany's explanation for the importance of Bron's lying to Audrey and the ending of the novel in *Shorter Views*, 334–6.

102. Sam's physical change, from white to black, is more similar to the main character of William Hjortsberg's *Grey Matter* (1971), who "chooses to move his consciousness into a black body because of its beauty" (E. James, "Yellow" 27). As Edward James notes, however, after the initial change, "the reader loses any sense of 'race' as being special" (ibid). Clearly, this is not the case with Sam. Not only does Delany place her racial change outside of the chronology of the text, but he also uses Sam as a vehicle for discussing the complexities of a postmodern concept of race.

103. Published in 1973, *The Tides of Lust* has a variant title of *Equinox*.

104. See McEvoy for the connections between the "triple" of Folsom, Delany, and Hacker and the "triples" of *Babel-17* (55).

105. Freedman discusses Delany's negative portrayal of identitarianism and positive portrayal of "mutability and free play" in the context of the Family and the Sygn in *Stars in My Pocket Like Grains of Sand* (159).

106. This is similar to "Appiah's vision of recreationally deployed racial identities" (Tucker, *Sense* 18; Appiah and Gutmann). However, I prefer the term individualistic because it does not elide the potentially long-term, powerful effects of such identity; "recreational" only connotes fun, a hobby, relative insignificance, etc. See also Edward K. Chan's "(Vulgar) Identity Politics in Outer Space: Delany's *Triton* and the Heterotopian Narrative."

107. For example, Delany's financial status and educational experiences growing up contrasted with the collective Harlem norm; see Delany's autobiography,

The Motion of Light in Water. Tucker also addresses this issue in the context of Delany's *Atlantis: Model 1924* (*Sense* 200).

108. More on Butler shortly.

109. Of course, this hierarchy is yet another reason to discard the Caliban/Prospero trope and its traditional privileging of the mind of Prospero over the body of Caliban.

110. Butler's Patternmaster series consists of *Patternmaster* (1976), *Mind of My Mind* (1977), *Survivor* (1978), *Wild Seed* (1980), and *Clay's Ark* (1984).

111. Delany's use of pronouns is most marked in his description of Ashima Slade and his/her multiple sex changes (*Trouble* 297).

112. I should note that technically Piercy is maintaining "constitutive differences" like "group history"; however, I do not think her random reassignment of these differences to new descent groups fits the spirit of Tucker's argument.

113. Other recent fiction texts of interest include Starhawk's *The Fifth Sacred Thing* (1993) and Stanley Kim Robinson's Mars series.

114. Darryl A. Smith also investigates the intersection of race and technology in his short story about robots specifically constructed with African-American identities and physical features (published in *Dark Matter*). Of course, Smith's story raises the issue, articulated by Edward James, of robots as substitutes for (human) racial others ("Yellow").

115. That is not to say that Delany does not use computers in his texts; however, they are not the primary focus in the text. Computers are not the organizing principle of the text and/or its encompassing context (like cyberspace), and they are often more organically integrated into the text. See the human-like consciousness of PHAEDRA in *The Einstein Iintersection*, for example. Also, the 'cyborgs' of *Babel-17* have relatively minor computer implants, largely for the purposes of personal expression and the construction of a physical image. I hope to discuss this issue of computerization in more detail in a subsequent work; similarly, the following discussion of magical realism in sf only touches the surface of this issue. I simply seek to mark out some relatively new trends in sf and raise some questions I think should be addressed in future examinations of race in the field.

116. Feminist critics have made similar claims in terms of gender and its influence on computer usage and the technology/science fields more generally. See Shirley M. Tilghman "Science versus the Female Scientist" and also Part IV: "Gender and Technology" of *Literacy, Technology, and Society: Confronting the Issues.*

117. Tucker is quoting Robert Reid-Pharr here.

118. Barnes also published *Iron Shadows* in 1998 and *Charisma* in 2002. He has co-authored novels with Larry Niven as well.

119. Delany addresses his rejection of the term speculative fiction in "The Second *Science-Fiction Studies* Interview." Delany admits that he used the term for one of his texts, *Driftglass*, due to its combination of "SF *and* fantasy"

(*Shorter* 346). This inclusiveness is exactly what recommends the term even today. However, Delany believes the term has devolved since the late 1960s to mean generally "'high-class SF'" (347); this is not the context in which I have recently seen the term used, and it certainly is not the context I intend here. I do not believe that connections to mundane fiction need to be made in order to 'legitimate' sf. In addition to the positive reasons for these connections listed shortly, I agree with Tucker that such connections can "lead to fascinating interpretive possibilities" (*Sense* 39). Tucker also addresses the term speculative fiction and Delany's response to it in *Sense of Wonder* (39).

120.   *Lion's Blood* is also overtly labeled science fiction on the spine. An alternate history novel, it centers around a racially-inverted, slave-holding 'America,' like Heinlein's *Farnham's Freehold*, only in the past rather than the future. In terms of the genre and publishing issues raised here, two additional review excerpts are pertinent—one from Octavia Butler (on the back cover) and the second from Nalo Hopkinson (at the beginning); more on this type of 'advertisement' in the next body paragraph.

121.   I believe this is one reason for the consistent science fiction label for this type of magical realism/fantasy (a consistent marketing strategy for an auther is another). In terms of a generic hierarchy in the United States, science fiction holds a privileged position over fantasy; within these stereotypes, sf is seen as more 'serious' and closer to mundane/realistic fiction, i.e. 'literature' or art, than fantasy.

122.   Hopkinson also published a collection of short stories, *Skin Folk*, in 2001.

123.   Barnes' use of a 'New Africa,' ruled by an authoritarian (despotic) black man recalls Schuyler's Dr. Belsidus in "Black Empire: An Imaginative Story of a Great New Civilization in Modern Africa" (*Black Empire*).

124.   This information serves as advertisement for Hopkinson's latest book, *Skin Folk* (placed on the back cover).

125.   The Canopus series consists of 5 books, collectively titled the Canopus in Argos: Archives. *Shikasta* was published in 1979, *The Marriages Between Zones Three, Four, and Five* in 1980, *The Sirian Experiments* in 1981, *The Making of the Representative for Plant 8* in 1982, and *Documents Relating to the Sentimental Agents in the Volyen Empire* in 1983.

126.   Both Tucker's text and my own began as dissertations (1997 and 2004, respectively). This is another sign that a new group of writers/scholars is becoming interested in the field. Likewise, the interest of publishing companies in such texts bodes well for the future of critical investigations of race in the sf field.

NOTES TO THE APPENDIX

1.   Some of these publishing dates for Burroughs' texts came from Irwin Porges' *Edgar Rice Burroughs: the Man Who Created Tarzan*. See his "List of ERB's Complete Works" for additional publishing dates (787–99).

Works Cited

Aldiss, Brian. *Billion Year Spree: The True History of Science Fiction.* Garden City: Doubleday, 1973.

Aldiss, Brian, and David Wingrove. *Trillion Year Spree: The History of Science Fiction.* New York: Atheneum, 1986.

American Identity Explorer: Immigration and Migration. Comments for Prescott Hall's "Racial Effects of Immigration." CD-ROM. Michigan State University: McGraw-Hill, 1997.

Appiah, Anthony. "The Uncompleted Argument: Du Bois and the Illusion of Race." *Critical Inquiry* 12.1 (1985). Rpt. in *"Race," Writing, and Difference.* Gates, ed. 21–37.

Appiah, K. Anthony, and Amy Gutmann. *Color Conscious: The Political Morality of Race.* Princeton UP, 1996.

Appleman, Philip, ed. *Darwin: A Norton Critical Edition.* 2nd ed. New York: Norton, 1979.

Baker, Houston A., Jr. "Caliban's Triple Play." *Critical Inquiry* 13.1 (1986). Rpt. in *"Race," Writing, and Difference.* Gates, ed. 381–95.

Barbour, Douglas. *Worlds Out of Words: The SF Novels of Samuel R. Delany.* Frome, Eng.: Hunting Raven P, 1979.

Barnes, Steven. *Blood Brothers.* New York: Tor, 1996.

———. *Charisma.* New York: Tor, 2002.

———. *Firedance.* New York: Tor, 1994.

———. *Gorgon Child.* New York: Tor, 1989.

———. *Iron Shadows.* New York: Tor, 1998.

———. *Lion's Blood.* New York: Warner Books, 2002.

Baruth, Philip E. "The Excesses of Cyberpunk: Why No One Mentions Race in Cyberspace." *Into Darkness Peering: Race and Color in the Fantastic.* Ed. Elisabeth Anne Leonard. Contributions to the Study of Science Fiction and Fantasy 74. Westport: Greenwood P, 1997. 105–18.

Beardsley, Edward H. "The American Scientist as Social Activist: Franz Boas, Burt G. Wilder, and the Cause of Racial Justice, 1900–1915." *Science in*

America Since1820. Ed. Nathan Reingold. New York: Science History Publications, 1976. 249–65.

Beckerman, Jim. "Samuel Delany: 'I'm Nobody's Prototype For What's To Come.'" *The Record Online* 20 Dec. 1998. 12 July 2001 <http://www.bergenrecord.com/ special/2000/jbdelan199812205.htm>.

Bell, John. "A Charles R. Saunders Interview." *Black American Literature Forum* 18.2 (Summer 1984): 90–2.

Bernabé, Jean, Patrick Chamoiseau, and Raphaël Confiant. "In Praise of Creoleness." Trans. Mohamed B. Taleb Khyar. *Callaloo* 13 (1990): 886–909.

Bernardi, Daniel Leonard. *Star Trek and History: Race-ing Toward a White Future*. New Brunswick, New Jersey: Rutgers UP, 1998.

Bester, Alfred. *The Stars My Destination*. New York: New American Library, 1957.

Birchfield, Don. "Lost in the Land of Ishtaboli." *Earth Song, Sky Spirit: Short Stories of the Contemporary Native American Experience*. Ed. Clifford E. Trafzer. New York: Doubleday. 1993. 105–124.

Bishop, Ellen. "Race and Subjectivity in Science Fiction: Deterritorializing the Self/Other Dichotomy." *Into Darkness Peering: Race and Color in the Fantastic*. Ed. Elisabeth Anne Leonard. Contributions to the Study of Science Fiction and Fantasy 74. Westport: Greenwood P, 1997. 85–103.

Boas, Ernst. Foreword. *Race and Democratic Society*. New York: J.J. Augustin Publisher, 1945.

Boas, Franz. *Anthropology and Modern Life*. 1928. New York: W.W. Norton & Co. Publisher, 1932.

———. *The Mind of Primitive Man*. 1911. New York: The Free P, 1963.

———. *Race and Democratic Society*. New York: J.J. Augustin Publisher, 1945.

———. *Race, Language and Culture*. 1940. Chicago: U of Chicago P, 1982.

———. "The Real Race Problem." *The Crisis* 1 (Dec. 1910): 22–25. Rpt. of "The Anthropological Position of the Negro," a speech at the Second National Negro Conference in May 1910.

Bone, Robert. *The Negro Novel in America*. New Haven: Yale UP, 1965.

Bradbury, Ray. "The Other Foot." 1951. *Human and Other Beings*. Ed. Allen DeGraeff. New York: Collier Books, 1963. 79–91.

———. "Way in the Middle of the Air." 1950. *Human and Other Beings*. Ed. Allen DeGraeff. New York: Collier Books, 1963. 61–76.

Burroughs, Edgar Rice. *The Apache Devil*. Serial. *All-Story Magazine*, May-June 1928. New York: Ballantine Books, 1964.

———. *The Beasts of Tarzan*. New York: Grosset & Dunlap, 1916. Rpt. of "Tarzan Returns." Serial. *All-Story Cavalier*, May-June 1914.

———. *The Girl from Hollywood*. New York: Macaulay Company, 1923.

———. *The Gods of Mars*. Five-part serial. *All-Story Magazine*, Jan.-May 1913. New York: Ballantine Books/DelRey, 1979.

———. *A Princess of Mars*. New York: Ballantine Books/Del Rey, 1979. Rpt. of "Under the Moon of Mars" by Norman Bean. Six-part serial. *All-Story Magazine*, Feb.-July 1912.

———. *The Return of Tarzan*. Serial. *New Story*, June-Nov. 1913. New York: Grosset & Dunlap, 1915.

———. *Tarzan of the Apes*. *All-Story Magazine*, Oct. 1912. New York: Ballantine, 1963.

———. *The War Chief*. Serial. *All-Story Magazine*, Apr.-May 1927. New York: Ballantine, 1975.

———. *The Warlord of Mars*. Four-part serial. *All-Story Magazine*, Dec. 1913-Mar. 1914. New York: Ballantine Books/Del Rey, 1979.

Butler, Octavia E. *Adulthood Rites*. Xenogenesis Trilogy. New York: Warner Books. 1988.

———. "Black Women and the Science Fiction Genre: Black Scholar Interview with Octavia Butler." *The Black Scholar* (Mar./Apr. 1986): 14–18.

———. *Clay's Ark*. New York: St. Martin's P, 1984.

———. "Crossover." *Clarion: An Anthology of Speculative Fiction and Criticism from the Clarion Writers' Workshop*. Ed. Robin Scott Wilson. New York: New American Library, 1971. 140–44.

———. *Dawn: Xenogenesis*. New York: Warner Books, 1987.

———. *Imago*. Xenogenesis Trilogy. New York: Warner Books, 1989.

———. *Kindred*. 1979. Boston: Beacon P, 1988.

———. *Mind of My Mind*. 1977. New York: Warner Books, 1994.

———. *Patternmaster*. 1976. New York: Warner Books, 1995.

———. *Survivor*. 1978. New York: New American Library, 1979.

———. *Wild Seed*. Garden City, New York: Doubleday, 1980.

Carnegie, Andrew. "The Gospel of Wealth." 1900. Appleman 399–405.

Carter, Paul A. *The Creation of Tomorrow: Fifty Years of Magazine Science Fiction*. New York: Columbia UP, 1977.

Chan, Edward K. "(Vulgar) Identity Politics in Outer Space: Delany's *Triton* and the Heterotopian Narrative." *Journal of Narrative Theory* 31.2 (Summer 2001): 180–213.

Daniels, George H. *Science in American Society: A Social History*. New York: Alfred Knopf, 1971.

Darwin, Charles. *The Descent of Man*. 2nd ed. New York: Caldwell, 1874.

———. *The Origin of Species*. 1859. New York: Dutton, 1958.

de Crévecoeur, Hector St. Jean. "Letter III: What is an American?" *Primis: Making Connections*. Michigan State U: McGraw-Hill, 1992. 43–60.

Delany, Samuel R. *The American Shore: Meditations on a Tale of Science Fiction by Thomas M. Disch-Angouleme*. Elizabethtown: Dragon P, 1978.

———. *Atlantis: Model 1924. Atlantis: Three Tales*. Hanover: Wesleyan UP, 1995. 1–121.

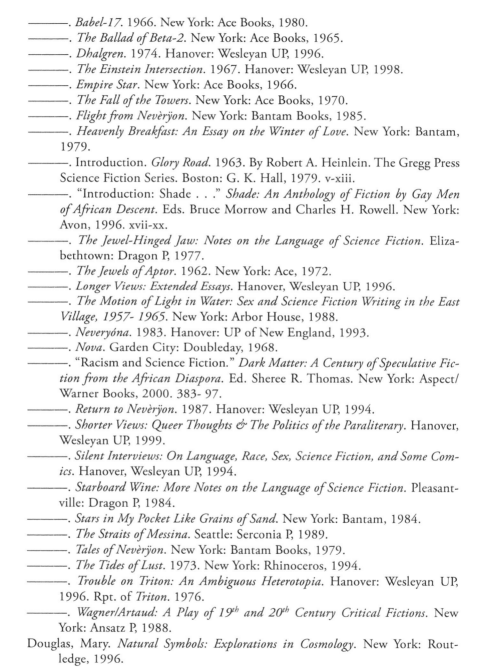

———. *Babel-17.* 1966. New York: Ace Books, 1980.

———. *The Ballad of Beta-2.* New York: Ace Books, 1965.

———. *Dhalgren.* 1974. Hanover: Wesleyan UP, 1996.

———. *The Einstein Intersection.* 1967. Hanover: Wesleyan UP, 1998.

———. *Empire Star.* New York: Ace Books, 1966.

———. *The Fall of the Towers.* New York: Ace Books, 1970.

———. *Flight from Nevèrÿon.* New York: Bantam Books, 1985.

———. *Heavenly Breakfast: An Essay on the Winter of Love.* New York: Bantam, 1979.

———. Introduction. *Glory Road.* 1963. By Robert A. Heinlein. The Gregg Press Science Fiction Series. Boston: G. K. Hall, 1979. v–xiii.

———. "Introduction: Shade . . ." *Shade: An Anthology of Fiction by Gay Men of African Descent.* Eds. Bruce Morrow and Charles H. Rowell. New York: Avon, 1996. xvii–xx.

———. *The Jewel-Hinged Jaw: Notes on the Language of Science Fiction.* Elizabethtown: Dragon P, 1977.

———. *The Jewels of Aptor.* 1962. New York: Ace, 1972.

———. *Longer Views: Extended Essays.* Hanover, Wesleyan UP, 1996.

———. *The Motion of Light in Water: Sex and Science Fiction Writing in the East Village, 1957- 1965.* New York: Arbor House, 1988.

———. *Neveryóna.* 1983. Hanover: UP of New England, 1993.

———. *Nova.* Garden City: Doubleday, 1968.

———. "Racism and Science Fiction." *Dark Matter: A Century of Speculative Fiction from the African Diaspora.* Ed. Sheree R. Thomas. New York: Aspect/ Warner Books, 2000. 383- 97.

———. *Return to Nevèrÿon.* 1987. Hanover: Wesleyan UP, 1994.

———. *Shorter Views: Queer Thoughts & The Politics of the Paraliterary.* Hanover, Wesleyan UP, 1999.

———. *Silent Interviews: On Language, Race, Sex, Science Fiction, and Some Comics.* Hanover, Wesleyan UP, 1994.

———. *Starboard Wine: More Notes on the Language of Science Fiction.* Pleasantville: Dragon P, 1984.

———. *Stars in My Pocket Like Grains of Sand.* New York: Bantam, 1984.

———. *The Straits of Messina.* Seattle: Serconia P, 1989.

———. *Tales of Nevèrÿon.* New York: Bantam Books, 1979.

———. *The Tides of Lust.* 1973. New York: Rhinoceros, 1994.

———. *Trouble on Triton: An Ambiguous Heterotopia.* Hanover: Wesleyan UP, 1996. Rpt. of *Triton.* 1976.

———. *Wagner/Artaud: A Play of 19th and 20th Century Critical Fictions.* New York: Ansatz P, 1988.

Douglas, Mary. *Natural Symbols: Explorations in Cosmology.* New York: Routledge, 1996.

Douglass, Frederick. *The Life and Writings of Frederick Douglass: Pre-Civil War Decade 1850- 1860.* Ed. Philip S. Foner. New York: International Publishers, 1950. Vol. 2 of *The Life and Writings of Frederick Douglass.* 5 vols. to date. 1950- .

———. *My Bondage and My Freedom.* 1855. New York: Dover Publications, 1969.

Doyle, Laura. *Bordering on the Body: The Racial Matrix of Modern Fiction and Culture.* New York: Oxford UP, 1994.

Du Bois, W. E. B. "The Comet." 1920. *Dark Matter: A Century of Speculative Fiction from the African Diaspora.* Ed. Sheree R. Thomas. New York: Aspect/ Warner Books, 2000. 5–18.

———. "The Conservation of Races." 1897. *W. E. B. Du Bois Speaks: Speeches and Addresses, 1890–1919.* Vol. 1. Ed. Philip S. Foner. New York: Pathfinder P, 1970. 289–309.

———. *Dusk of Dawn: An Essay Toward an Autobiography of a Race Concept.* 1940. New York: Schocken Books, 1968.

———. Editorial. *The Crisis* (Aug.1911): 157–8.

———. *The Souls of Black Folks.* 1903. New York: Vintage Books/Library of America, 1990.

———, ed. *The Health and Physique of the Negro American: Report of a Social Study Made Under the Direction of Atlanta University; Together with the Proceedings of the Eleventh Conference for the Study of the Negro Problems, Held at Atlanta University, on May the 29th, 1906.* Atlanta: Atlanta UP, 1906.

Dyer, Thomas G. *Theodore Roosevelt and the Idea of Race.* Baton Rouge: Louisiana State UP, 1980.

Easterbrook, Neil. "State, Heterotopia: The Political Imagination in Heinlein, Le Guin, and Delany." *Political Science Fiction.* Eds. Donald M. Hassler and Clyde Wilcox. Columbia: U of South Carolina, 1997. 43–75.

Ellison, Ralph. *Invisible Man.* 1947. New York: Vintage International, 1990.

The Encyclopedia of Science Fiction. Eds. John Clute and Peter Nicholls. New York: St. Martin's Griffin, 1995.

Fanon, Frantz. *Black Skin, White Masks.* Trans. Charles Lam Markmann. New York: Grove P, 1967. Rpt. of *Peau Noire, Masques Blancs.* 1952.

———. *The Wretched of the Earth.* New York: Grove P, 1963. Rpt. of *Les Damnés de la Terre.*

Fekete, John. "*The Dispossessed* and *Triton*: Act and System in Utopian Science Fiction." *Science-Fiction Studies* 6 (1979): 129–43.

Fields, Barbara Jeanne. "Slavery, Race and Ideology in the United States of America." *New Left Review* 181 (May/June 1990): 95–118.

Fishburn, Katherine. *The Problem of Embodiment in Early African American Narrative.* Contributions in Afro-American and African Studies 183. Westport: Greenwood P, 1997.

Foucault, Michel. *The Order of Things: An Archaeology of the Human Sciences*. New York: Vintage Books, 1973.

Fox, Robert Elliot. *Conscientious Sorcerers: The Black Postmodernist Fiction of LeRoi Jones/Amiri Baraka, Ishmael Reed, and Samuel R. Delany*. Contributions in Afro-American and African Studies 106. New York: Greenwood P, 1987.

———. "The Politics of Desire in Delany's *Triton* and *The Tides of Lust*." *Black American Literature Forum* 18.2 (Summer 1984): 49–56.

Franklin, Bruce. *Robert A. Heinlein: America as Science Fiction*. New York: Oxford UP, 1980.

Freedman, Carl. *Critical Theory and Science Fiction*. Hanover: Wesleyan UP, 2000.

Fuss, Diana. *Essentially Speaking: Feminism, Nature and Difference*. New York: Routledge, 1989.

Gates, Henry Louis, Jr. "A Fragmented Man: George S. Schuyler and the Claims of Race." Rev. of *Black Empire*, by George S. Schuyler. *The New York Times Book Review* 20 Sept. 1992: 31, 42–43.

———. "One Internet, Two Nations." *Patterns for College Writing*. Eds. Laurie G. Kirszner and Stephen R. Mandell. 8th ed. Boston: St. Martin's P, 2001. 599–603.

———, ed. *"Race," Writing, and Difference*. Chicago: The U of Chicago P, 1986.

Gossett, Thomas F. *Race: The History of an Idea in America*. 1963. New York: Schocken Books, 1968.

Gould, Stephen Jay. *The Mismeasure of Man*. 1981. New York: W.W. Norton & Co.,1996.

Grant, Madison. "The New Immigrants." 1916. *American Identity Explorer: Immigration and Migration*. CD-ROM. Michigan State University: McGraw-Hill, 1997.

———. *The Passing of the Great Race: or The Racial Basis of European History*. 1916. New York: Scribner's, 1921.

Greenlee, Sam. *The Spook Who Sat by the Door*. 1969. African American Life Series. Detroit: Wayne State UP, 1990.

Hall, Prescott F. "The Future of American Ideals." *Primis: Making Connections*. Michigan State U: McGraw-Hill, 1992. 297–300.

Haraway, Donna. *Primate Visions: Gender, Race, and Nature in the World of Modern Science*. New York: Routledge, 1989.

Heinlein, Robert A. *The Day After Tomorrow*. New York: New American Library, 1946. Rpt. of *Sixth Column*.

———. *Double Star*. 1956. London: Panther, 1960.

———. *Farnham's Freehold*. 1964. Riverdale: Baen, 1998.

———. *Glory Road*. The Gregg Press Science Fiction Series. Boston: G. K. Hall, 1979.

———. *The Moon is a Harsh Mistress*. New York: Putnam, 1966.

———. *Starship Troopers*. 1959. New York: Ace Books, 1987.

Herskovits, Melville J. Foreword. *The Mind of Primitive Man.* By Franz Boas. New York: The Free P, 1963. 5–12.

———. *Franz Boas: The Science of Man in the Making.* New York: Charles Scribner's Sons, 1953.

Herzog, Kristin. *Women, Ethnics, and Exotics: Images of Power in Mid-Nineteenth-Century American Fiction.* Knoxville: U of Tennessee P, 1983.

Hill, Robert A., and Kent Rasmussen. Afterword. *Black Empire.* By George S. Schuyler. Boston: Northeastern UP, 1991. 259–310.

Hjortsberg, William. *Grey Matter.* 1971. Newton Abbott, Devon: Science Fiction Book Club, 1974.

Hoffman, Daniel G. *Form and Fable in American Fiction.* New York: Oxford UP, 1961.

Hofstadter, Richard. "The Vogue of Spencer." 1955. Appleman 389–99.

Hopkinson, Nalo. *Brown Girl in the Ring.* New York: Warner Books, 1998.

———. *Midnight Robber.* New York: Warner Books, 2000.

———. *Skin Folk.* New York: Warner Books, 2001.

Hughes, Langston. 1926. "The Negro Artist and the Racial Mountain." *Primis: Making Connections.* Michigan State University: McGraw-Hill, 1998. 431–33.

Huyssen, Andreas. "Mapping the Postmodern." *New German Critique* 33 (Fall 1984): 5–52.

Hyatt, Marshall. *Franz Boas Social Activist: The Dynamics of Ethnicity.* Contributions to the Study of Anthropology 6. New York: Greenwood P, 1990.

James, Edward. *Science Fiction in the Twentieth Century.* New York: Oxford UP, 1994.

———. "Yellow, Black, Metal and Tentacled: The Race Question in American Science Fiction." *Science Fiction, Social Conflict and War.* Ed. Philip John Davies. Manchester: Manchester UP, 1990. 26–49.

James, Ken. "Extensions: An Introduction to the Longer Views of Samuel R. Delany." *Longer Views: Extended Essays.* By Samuel R. Delany. Hanover: Wesleyan UP, 1996. *xiii-xl.*

Johnson, James Weldon. *The Autobiography of an Ex-Coloured Man.* 1912. New York: Knopf, 1927.

Joyce, Joyce A. "The Black Canon: Reconstructing Black American Literary Criticism." *New Literary History* 18.2 (Winter 1987): 335–44.

———. "'Who the Cap Fit': Unconsciousness and Unconscionableness in the Criticism of Houston A. Baker, Jr. and Henry Louis Gates, Jr." *New Literary History* 18.2 (Winter 1987): 371-84.

Kelley, William Melvin. *A Different Drummer.* 1959. Garden City: Doubleday, 1969.

Ketterer, David. *New Worlds for Old: The Apocalyptic Imagination, Science Fiction, and American Literature.* New York: Anchor P/Doubleday, 1974.

Kilgore, De Witt Douglas. *Astrofuturism: Science, Race, and Visions of Utopia in Space.* Philadelphia: U of Pennsylvania P, 2003.

Kincaid, Jamaica. *Annie John*. New York: Plume, 1985.

Kipling, Rudyard. "The White Man's Burden, 1899." *Primis: Making Connections*. Michigan State U: McGraw-Hill, 1998–99. 246–7.

Lang, Herrman. *The Air Battle: a Vision of the Future*. 1859. London: Cornmarket Reprints, 1972.

Larsen, Nella. *Passing*. New York: Knopf, 1929.

Larson, Charles. R. Introduction. *Black No More*. By George S. Schuyler. New York: Collier Books, 1971. 9–15.

Lawrence, D. H. *Studies in Classic American Literature*. Hammondsworth: Penguin, 1977.

Le Guin, Ursula. *The Dispossessed*. New York: Avon, 1975.

———. *The Left Hand of Darkness*. 1969. New York: Ace Books, 1976.

Lee, Andrea. *Sarah Phillips*. 1984. The Northeastern Library of Black Literature. Boston: Northeastern UP, 1993.

Leonard, Elisabeth Anne. "Introduction: 'Into Darkness Peering'—Race and Color in the Fantastic." *Into Darkness Peering: Race and Color in the Fantastic*. Contributions to the Study of Science Fiction and Fantasy 74. Westport: Greenwood P, 1997. 1–12.

Lessing, Doris. *Documents Relating to the Sentimental Agents in the Volyen Empire*. Canopus in Argos: Archives 5. New York: Knopf, 1983.

———. *The Making of the Representative for Planet 8*. Canopus in Argos: Archives 4. New York: Knopf, 1982.

———. *The Marriages Between Zones Three, Four, and Five*. Canopus in Argos: Archives 2. New York: Knopf, 1980.

———. *Re: Colonised Planet 5, Shikasta*. Canopus in Argos: Archives 1. New York: Knopf, 1979.

———. *The Sirian Experiments*. Canopus in Argos: Archives 3. New York: Knopf, 1981.

The Lion King. Videocassette. Walt Disney Home Video. Buena Vista Home Video, 1994.

Literacy, Technology, and Society: Confronting the Issues. Eds. Gail E. Hawisher and Cynthia L. Selfe. Upper Saddle River: Prentice Hall, 1997.

Littlefield, Emerson. "The Mythologies of Race and Science in Samuel Delany's *The Einstein Intersection* and *Nova*." *Extrapolation* 23.3 (1982): 235–42.

Lucas, George, dir. and screenplay. *Star Wars*. 1977. Videocassette. Twentieth Century Fox Home Entertainment, 1995.

Malinowski, Bronislaw. *The Sexual Life of Savages in North-western Melanesia*. New York: Eugenics, 1929.

Massé, Michelle. "'All you have to do is know what you want': Individual Expectations in *Triton*." *Coordinates: Placing Science Fiction and Fantasy*. Eds. George Slusser, Eric Rabkin, and Robert Scholes. Carbondale: Southern Illinois UP, 1983. 49–64.

McEvoy, Seth. *Samuel R. Delany*. New York: Frederick Ungar Publishing, 1984.

McHale, Brian. *Constructing Postmodernism.* New York: Routledge, 1992.

Michaels, Walter Benn. *Our America: Nativism, Modernism, and Pluralism.* Durham: Duke UP, 1995.

Miller, Nancy K. "Changing the Subject: Authorship, Writing and the Reader." *Feminist Studies/Critical Studies.* Ed. Teresa de Lauretis. Bloomington: Indiana UP, 1986. 102–120.

Miller, Warren. *The Siege of Harlem.* New York: McGraw-Hill, 1964.

Monhollon, Rusty L. "Black Power, White Fear: The 'Negro Problem' in Lawrence, Kansas, 1960–1970." *Race Consciousness: African-American Studies for the New Century.* Eds. Judith Jackson Fossett and Jeffrey A. Tucker. New York: New York UP, 1997. 247–62.

Morrison, Toni. *Playing in the Dark: Whiteness and the Literary Imagination.* New York: Vintage Books, 1993.

Moylan, Tom. "Beyond Negation: The Critical Utopias of Ursula K. Le Guin and Samuel R. Delany." *Extrapolation* 21.3 (1980): 236–51.

Nash, Roderick. *Wilderness and the American Mind.* Rev. ed. New Haven: Yale UP, 1973.

Panshin, Alexei. *Heinlein in Dimension: A Critical Analysis.* Chicago: Advent, 1968.

Pearce, Roy Harvey. *Savagism and Civilization: A Study of the Indian and the American Mind.* 1953. Baltimore: Johns Hopkins P, 1967.

Peckham, Morse. "Darwinism and Darwinisticism." *Victorian Studies* 3.1 (Sept. 1959): 19–40.

Peplow, Michael W. "The Black 'Picaro' in Schuyler's *Black No More.*" *The Crisis* 83.1 (Jan. 1976): 7–10.

———. "Meet Samuel R. Delany, Black Science Fiction Writer." *The Crisis* 86.4 (Apr. 1979): 115–21.

Peplow, Michael W., and Robert S. Bravard. *Samuel R. Delany: A Primary and Secondary Bibliography, 1962–1979.* Boston: G.K. Hall, 1980.

Piercy, Marge. *He, She, and It.* 1991. New York: Fawcett Columbine, 1997.

———. *Woman on the Edge of Time.* New York: Knopf, 1976.

Plank, Robert. *The Emotional Significance of Imaginary Beings: A Study of the Interaction Between Psychopathology, Literature, and Reality in the Modern World.* Springfield: Thomas, 1968.

Porges, Irwin. *Edgar Rice Burroughs: The Man Who Created Tarzan.* Provo: Brigham Young UP, 1975.

Pounds, Michael C. *Race in Space: The Representation of Ethnicity in* Star Trek *and* Star Trek: The Next Generation. Lanham: Scarecrow P, 1999.

Pratt, Mary Louise. "Scratches on the Face of the Country; or, What Mr. Barrow Saw in the Land of the Bushmen." Gates, ed. 138–62.

Rayson, Ann. "George Schuyler: Paradox Among 'Assimilationist' Writers." *Black American Literature Forum* 12.3 (1978): 102–6.

Reid-Pharr, Robert F. *Black Gay Man.* New York UP, 2001.

Reilly, John. "The Black Anti-Utopia." *Black American Literature Forum* 12.3 (1978): 107–109.

Resnick, Mike. *Kirinyaga: A Fable of Utopia*. New York: Ballantine, 1998.

Robinson, Stanley Kim. *Blue Mars*. New York: Bantam Books, 1996.

———. *Green Mars*. New York: Bantam Books, 1995.

———. *Red Mars*. New York: Bantam Books, 1993.

Roosevelt, Theodore. "A Nation of Pioneers." 1901. *Primis: Making Connections*. Michigan State U: McGraw-Hill, 1992. 240–7.

———. *The Works of Theodore Roosevelt*. 24 vols. Ed. Hermann Hagedorn. New York: C. Scribner's Sons, 1925.

Rosaldo, Renato. "After Objectivism." *The Cultural Studies Reader*. Ed. Simon During. New York: Routledge, 1997. 104–117.

Rosenberg, Charles E. *No Other Gods: On Science and American Social Thought*. Baltimore: Johns Hopkins UP, 1976.

Ross, Edward. "American Blood and Immigrant Blood." 1913. *American Identity Explorer: Immigration and Migration*. CD-ROM. Michigan State University: McGraw-Hill, 1997.

Russ, Joanna. *The Female Man*. 1975. Boston: Beacon P, 1986.

Saldívar, José David. *The Dialectics of Our America: Geneaology, Cultural Critique, and Literary History*. 1991. Durham: Duke UP, 1995.

Saunders, Charles R. "Why Blacks Should Read (and Write) Science Fiction." *Dark Matter: A Century of Speculative Fiction from the African Diaspora*. Ed. Sheree R. Thomas. New York: Aspect/Warner Books, 2000. 398–404.

Scholes, Robert, and Eric S. Rabkin. *Science Fiction: History, Science, Vision*. New York: Oxford UP, 1977.

Schuster, Jay. "Samuel R. Delany Information." 19 Sep. 2001. 28 Apr. 2006 <http:// www.pcc.com/~jay/delany/>.

Schuyler, George S. *Black and Conservative*. New Rochelle: Arlington House, 1966.

———. *Black Empire*. Boston: Northeastern UP, 1991. Rpt. of *The Black Internationale: Story of Black Genius Against the World and Black Empire: An Imaginative Story of a Great New Civilization in Modern Africa*. Pseudonym of Samuel I. Brooks. *Pittsburgh Courier*. Nov. 21, 1936-July 3, 1937; Oct. 2, 1937-Apr. 16, 1938.

———. *Black No More: A Novel*. 1931. New York: The Modern Library, 1999.

———. *Black No More: Being an Account of the Strange and Wonderful Workings of Science in the Land of the Free, A.D. 1933–1940*. 1931. College Park: McGrath Publishing Co., 1969.

———. "The Caucasian Problem." 1944. *What the Negro Wants*. Ed. Rayford W. Logan. New York: Agathon P, 1969. 281–98.

———. "The Negro-Art Hokum." 1926. *Primis: Making Connections*. Michigan State University: McGraw-Hill, 1989. 434–5.

Selvon, Samuel. *Foreday Morning*. London: Longman, 1989.

Shelton, Robert. "Aesthetic Angels and Devolved Demons: Wells in 1895." *Utopian Studies* 2 (1989): 1–11.

Slusser, George Edgar. *The Delany Intersection: Samuel R. Delany Considered as a Writer of Semi-Precious Words.* The Milford Series: Popular Writers of Today 10. San Bernardino: Borgo P, 1977.

Smith, Darryl A. "The Pretended." *Dark Matter: A Century of Speculative Fiction from the African Diaspora.* Ed. Sheree R. Thomas. New York: Aspect/Warner Books, 2000. 356–71.

Smith, Philip E., II. "The Evolution of Politics and the Politics of Evolution: Social Darwinism in Heinlein's Fiction." *Robert A. Heinlein.* Eds. Joseph D. Olander and Martin Harry Greenberg. New York: Taplinger, 1978. 137–71.

Sollors, Werner. *Beyond Ethnicity: Consent and Descent in American Culture.* New York: Oxford UP, 1986.

Somay, Bulent. " Towards an Open-Ended Utopia." *Science-Fiction Studies* 11 (1984): 25–38.

Spiller, G., ed. *Papers on Inter-Racial Problems: Communicated to the First Universal Races Congress Held at the University of London, July 26–29,1911.* 1911. Miami: Mnemosyne Publishing Company, 1969.

St. Clair, Margaret. *The Dancers of Noyo.* New York: Ace Books, 1973.

Starhawk. *The Fifth Sacred Thing.* New York: Bantam Books, 1993.

Starship Troopers. Dir. Paul Verhoeven. TriStar Pictures and Touchstone Pictures, 1997.

Stepan, Nancy. *The Idea of Race in Science: Great Britain 1800–1960.* London: Macmillan P, 1982.

Stepan, Nancy Leys, and Sander L. Gilman. "Appropriating the Idioms of Science: The Rejection of Scientific Racism." *The Bounds of Race: Perspectives on Hegemony and Resistance.* Ed. Dominick LaCapra. Ithaca: Cornell UP, 1991.

Stephenson, Neal. *Snowcrash.* New York: Bantam Books, 1993.

Stocking, George W., Jr. *Race, Culture, and Evolution: Essays in the History of Anthropology.* New York: The Free P, 1968.

Street, Brian V. *The Savage in Literature: Representations of 'Primitive' Society in English Fiction 1858–1920.* Boston: Routledge & Kegan Paul, 1975.

Suvin, Darko. *Metamorphoses of Science Fiction: On the Poetics and History of a Literary Genre.* New Haven: Yale UP, 1979.

Taliaferro, John. *Tarzan Forever: The Life of Edgar Rice Burroughs, Creator of Tarzan.* New York: Scribner, 1999.

Tarzan. Videocassette. Walt Disney Home Video. Buena Vista Home Entertainment, 1999.

Thomas, Sheree R. "Introduction: Looking for the Invisible." *Dark Matter: A Century of Speculative Fiction from the African Diaspora.* New York: Aspect/Warner Books, 2000. ix-xiv.

Tilghman, Shirley M. "Science versus the Female Scientist." *Science and Technology Today: Readings for Writers.* Ed. Nancy R. MacKenzie. New York: St. Martin's P, 1995. 51–4.

Torgovnick, Marianna. *Gone Primitive: Savage Intellects, Modern Lives*. Chicago: U of Chicago P, 1990.

Tucker, Jeffrey A. "'Can Science Succeed Where the Civil War Failed?': George S. Schuyler and Race." *Race Consciousness: African-American Studies for the New Century*. Eds. Judith Jackson Fossett and Jeffrey A. Tucker. New York: New York UP, 1997. 136–52.

———. "Racial Realities and Amazing Alternatives: Studying the Works of Samuel R. Delany." 12 July 2001 <http://www/tcom.ohiou.edu/books/scifi/delany.htm>.

———. *A Sense of Wonder: Samuel R. Delany, Race, Identity, and Difference*. Middletown: Wesleyan UP, 2004.

Turner, Frederick Jackson. *The Frontier in American History*. 1920. New York: Holt, Rinehart and Winston, 1965.

Weedman, Jane Branham. *Samuel R. Delany*. Starmont Reader's Guide 10. Mercer's Island: Starmont House, 1982.

Weedon, Chris. *Feminist Practice and Poststructuralist Theory*. 2nd ed. Cambridge: Blackwell, 1997.

Wells, H.G. *The Island of Dr. Moreau*. 1895. New York: Berkley, 1964.

———. The War of the Worlds *and* The Time Machine. Garden City: Dolphin Books, 1961.

Westfahl, Gary. "'You Don't Know What You are Talking About': Robert A. Heinlein and the Racism of Science Fiction." *Into Darkness Peering: Race and Color in the Fantastic*. Ed. Elisabeth Anne Leonard. Contributions to the Study of Science Fiction and Fantasy 74. Westport: Greenwood P, 1997. 71–84.

Wideman, John Edgar. Introduction. *The Souls of Black Folks*. By W. E. B. Du Bois. New York: Vintage Books/Library of American, 1990.

Wolfe, Gary K. *The Known and the Unknown: The Iconography of Science Fiction*. Kent: Kent State UP, 1979.

Wolmark, Jenny. *Aliens and Others: Science Fiction, Feminism, and Postmodernism*. Iowa City: U of Iowa P, 1994.

Index